# Dead Lands

*USA TODAY* BESTSELLING AUTHOR

STACEY MARIE BROWN

All rights reserved. Published by: Twisted Fairy Publishing Inc.
Layout by Judi Fennell (www.formatting4U.com)
Cover by: Jay Aheer (www.simplydefinedart.com)
Edited by Hollie (www.hollietheeditor.com)
Edited by Mo Siren's Call Author Services (mo@thescarletsiren.com)

# ALSO BY
# STACEY MARIE BROWN

## Contemporary Romance

**How the Heart Breaks**

**Buried Alive**

**Smug Bastard**

**The Unlucky Ones**

### Blinded Love Series
Shattered Love (#1)
Broken Love (#2)
Twisted Love (#3)

### Royal Watch Series
Royal Watch (#1)
Royal Command (#2)

# Paranormal Romance

### A Winterland Tale
Descending into Madness (#1)
Ascending from Madness (#2)
Beauty in Her Madness (#3)
Beast in His Madness (#4)

### Darkness Series
Darkness of Light (#1)
Fire in the Darkness (#2)

Beast in the Darkness (An Elighan Dragen Novelette)
Dwellers of Darkness (#3)
Blood Beyond Darkness (#4)
West (#5)

## Collector Series
City in Embers (#1)
The Barrier Between (#2)
Across the Divide (#3)
From Burning Ashes (#4)

## Lightness Saga
The Crown of Light (#1)
Lightness Falling (#2)
The Fall of the King (#3)
Rise from the Embers (#4)

## Savage Lands Series
Savage Lands (#1)
Wild Lands (#2)
Dead Lands (#3)
Bad Lands (#4)
Blood Lands (#5)
Shadow Lands (#6)

## Devil In The Deep Blue Sea
Silver Tongue Devil (#1)

For those who curse me,
but still keep coming back for more...
yeah, I know how you like it!

# Chapter 1

*"There is a revolution coming, Brexley. And you are going to lead us straight into it."*

The statement echoed in my head, bouncing and smacking back into itself, tangling into one emotion.

Terror.

I struggled to breathe, my eyes darted around the room, seeing a group of mostly unknown faces. Even the one related to me was a stranger, my Uncle Mykel, who I had known only in name growing up. Father said he was a criminal and had to run off to Prague soon after I was born for safety.

Now he was the leader of the infamous rebel group in Prague— *Povstat*. Meaning "to rise up." A large growing faction fighting against both the fae and human leaders, declaring the need for real change.

"You are our trigger pin." Mykel's light brown eyes dug into me. My head jerked away from him, my chest squeezing with pain. He was so similar to my father: the way he spoke, his mannerisms, the same height, black hair and beard, similar soft brown eyes. My father, Benet, had been broader, probably from years of battle and training. He died in an uprising between fae and humans five years prior.

"The one who knows both enemies."

"Wha-what?" My voice finally found its way up my throat, my defenses mounting. Being "used" by whatever group kidnapped me seemed to be a growing theme. And I had no idea who to trust, if anyone. "What are you talking about?"

Mykel smirked, his heavy-booted feet moving in a tight back-and-forth motion. "I've been watching you for a long time now." He rubbed his beard. "Had eyes on you as much as I could. Even in Halálház."

My gaze snapped to the blue-haired demon standing feet from me.

"You were watching me?" Betrayal burned up the back of my throat, but I kept my expression clear of emotion. "Of course." I shook my head. No one did anything unless it somehow benefitted them. I thought for a moment her "friendship" had been honest, but it seemed no one in Halálház had befriended me out of kindness.

"When I learned you were there, I got word to Kek." Mykel nodded to her. "I told her to watch you but not engage. To keep her distance."

"I'm a naughty demon." Kek grinned mischievously, her fingers tugging on the end of her braid.

Mykel's lips pinched together, not responding.

"I don't understand." My head still pounded from the chloroform. I felt mentally and physically exhausted. "Why are you even with this group? You're a demon."

"You're right." She nodded, tapping her lip like she was just realizing this. "I am."

"Then why?" My frustration and crankiness skimmed over my skin. "Why the fuck do you care about this fight?"

"Because I'm fae, I shouldn't give a shit?" She lifted an eyebrow.

"*Demons* don't give a shit," I spat back.

Demons were at the top of the food chain here. Since the fall of the Otherworld wall, the Seelie, the light, and the Unseelie, the dark, ruled together in the West, forgoing the old fae ways and trying to make strides toward equality under their reign, including humans.

Many fae did not like the idea. Tired of hiding, they wanted to restore fae sovereignty above humans again, back to the time before they were forced into hiding. The East fertilized the battle between the species, like a powder keg.

Having a demon as the Unified Nations King turned the arrogance of demons throughout the world on high, thinking themselves above all. Unfortunately, they pretty much were. Only pure fairies could challenge their strength, which was why Killian was able to be lord and master of the fae in Budapest.

"We have a mix of human and fae in this cause." Mykel held up his hand, stepping between us, motioning to the large group in the room. "Half-breed and pure."

My attention darted around, taking in the different figures. All ages, colors, races, species, and sexes filled the huge windowless room. Dressed in various shades of gray and black, clean and dirty, tattered and newer, I could pick out the fae easily. Ethereal, beautiful, dynamic, and fit as hell, while the pure humans appeared a little more "worn" around the edges, with imperfections. Some were old enough to have gray hair and deep wrinkles. It was almost impossible to discern what the half-breeds really were.

Was that why they were hated the most? Jealousy on the humans' side and distrust on the fae's? With a half-breed, they couldn't tell whose side they were on or what they really were.

The more I lived away from Léopold, the more I found all of it stupid and pointless. Didn't we all want to be happy? Live peacefully?

My gaze landed on the blonde who put her boot on my throat and the guy next to her, his nose and one eye black and blue where I kicked him.

They scowled at me.

Maybe those two didn't.

Mykel's eyes darted to them and then back to me.

"I apologize for the way you were retrieved. I felt I had no other way to get you here."

"Maybe ask nicely?" I folded my arms, trying to keep my body steady, the exhaustion making me dizzy.

Mykel laughed. "And if I did, would you have come?"

No, I wouldn't have.

"Tracker and Lea said you are quite the fighter." He gestured to the pair who had attacked me back in Budapest, their glares still digging into my skin. "I warned them you might be."

"And just think." I lifted my chin. "I was hurt, alone, and had chloroform pressed to my face."

"Told you... the girl survived the Games." Kek flipped back her braid, winking at me. "She wasn't gonna go down so easy. I've seen her fight a *legend*." Her brows wiggled. "I said you needed more than the five to capture you."

3

My lids lowered on Kek. She was the reason he had a dozen people on me?

"With a normal person, five would have been enough." Mykel's head tilted in a way that reminded me of my father when he saw through my bullshit.

I glanced away, my feet shifting, my body swaying slightly.

"She'll stand here fighting you until she actually falls over." Kek waved down at me. "She's that stubborn."

"Just like her father." Mykel shook his head, breaking the scrutinizing focus on me. "You must be hungry and tired."

I was, but there was no way I could sleep right now.

Mykel must have seen it on my face because he responded. "At least come sit in my office. I think you and me, my dear niece, have a lot to catch up on."

He took my non-response as agreement, his feet stepping back.

"Tracker, Ava, Blade, Sab." He called out names, two women and two men, the ones I remembered the most from my kidnapping. "The prime minister and his consort have a meeting with some government officials in an hour. Go tail them."

The four dipped their heads, immediately heading out.

"Ava couldn't come up with a cool code name?" I watched the group leave.

"Ava is for Avalanche." Mykel peered back at me, his eyebrow curving up. "When she fights, she crushes."

"Really?" I snorted. "Didn't feel all that crushing to me."

"I told them to go easy. I didn't want you hurt," Mykel replied before he fully turned. "Follow me," he ordered, striding out of the room.

"Better follow, little lamb." Kek nodded toward him.

My attention went to her, my mixed emotions about her evident on my face.

"You'll have plenty of time to try and kick my perky demon ass later." A grin hinted on her mouth. "And I might even let you."

I could feel Kek's cheeky attitude chipping away at my anger, which annoyed me more.

My lesson was learned. Everyone wanted me for something. I was a commodity, not a person. I couldn't let my walls down again.

There was no one I could trust.

4

Following Mykel through the hallways with two guards riding my ass, my mind absorbed every detail we went by. No windows. Stone and cement walls with water pipes. Electrical wires lined the ceilings like a motorway. Fire bulbs flickered everywhere, trying to keep things bright, though the panic of being underground rubbed the base of my spine, clenching at my chest like hands. Fortunately, or unfortunately, my mind and body were too tired and loopy to really let my anxiety take over.

After living in Halálház, being underground would always trigger my panic button.

Dodging around figures through the wide hallways, I was overwhelmed by the size of the place. It had the same feel as Sarkis's base, but from what I could see, Povstat was about ten times bigger and occupied with everyday life.

The hallways were like busy roadways, and every room was filled. I saw what looked to be classrooms, offices, and training rooms, four of which we had passed so far. We went by a small cafe stand, large dining/kitchen hall, clinic, pharmacy, and food store. This place was a full underground city. Life moved through like it had been here forever, but at the same time, it felt as if at any time it could be abandoned and left. There were no signs over the shops, all the food stands were makeshift and temporary, the offices bare of anything besides tables and chairs.

Mykel stepped into an elevator, one of his guards rushing me in after him, the doors closing quickly behind the four of us. I noticed others waiting for the lift, but no one stepped on with us.

"Won't mix with the common folk?" I peered at my uncle, his face expressionless. His other guard hit the top button.

Three levels in this place.

"I was attacked by someone I thought of as a comrade in the elevator. After torturing him, we found out he was a spy. Our security changed after that." He kept his head facing front, his voice detached. "It is not about ego, but about keeping the leader of Povstat safe. Without me, this place crumbles."

I crossed my arms, staring at my boots.

"The sleeping/living quarters are the bottom level. The one we just left is called *a falu.*" *The Village.* "My office and security barracks are the top level."

5

The moment we reached the highest floor and the doors opened, it was as if someone placed a dozen bricks on my shoulders, clawing at every last bit of energy I had.

"Whoa!" Mykel and his guards grabbed me, my legs caving underneath me, bile burning up my throat. "Brexley?"

All I wanted to do was close my eyes and sleep. Each step felt like I was pouring lead into my muscles.

"I'm okay." I forced my legs to support me, my hand clutching the rail in the elevator, trying to stop the spinning in my head. "Must still be from the chloroform."

Mykel held out his arm. "Let me help you."

"No." He may have been my uncle, but I didn't know him, and I learned from the man who had been my guardian for years to never show weakness. And don't trust anyone.

"I'm fine." I cleared my throat and rolled my shoulders back. "Got a little dizzy."

I wanted to vomit. I wanted to cry. I really wanted to sleep. Instead, I lifted my chin and walked out of the elevator, trying to fight against the notion I was going to pass out.

What the hell was going on?

It was palpable, as if hundreds of mouths were latching on to me, chewing and nibbling, sucking the energy from my skin. Stubbornly I rammed against it, not willing to be fragile in front of anyone.

Mykel escorted me into his office, which was basic with a desk and three chairs. It had no cupboards or cabinets to keep files that I could see. Again, a place he could leave if found and not worry about the enemy finding anything worth the effort. I didn't doubt every secret plan or document he had was somewhere in a portable briefcase or something he could grab and run with.

"Please." Mykel motioned to the chair opposite his desk. "Have a seat." His attention went to one of his guards. "Please have Oskar bring in tea and something to eat for Brexley."

"Yes, sir."

"I'm fine." It was an automatic response. I collapsed onto the seat, my legs shaking.

Mykel ignored me, flicking his head for his guards to leave and do his bidding. Once they closed the door, he sat in his chair, gazing at me for several moments, sadness flickering in his eyes.

"You look so much like him." He shook his head. "But you have

6

your mother's eye color and her beauty." Mykel's eyes were the same warm honey-brown as my father's.

"You knew my mother?" I had my father's almond-shaped eyes from his Russian roots, but the color of my irises, the pigment of night, so dark you almost couldn't see my pupils, were hers.

"Only in a picture your father carried."

My father had one worn and blurry picture of my mother, always keeping it in his pocket next to his heart. I used to stare at it for hours, trying to see if I could find anything I had in common with her. But it was too worn and faraway to pick up any real details. I really had no clear image of what my mother looked like. My father would share only vague descriptions. It seemed she was elusive to even my father's closest friends and family.

"Well, seeing *you* was like a stab in my gut," my mouth said before I could think about it. Exhaustion did that to me.

Mykel flinched, his head dipping. "I can imagine."

Sucking in all the strength I could, I leaned forward in my seat.

"I know you didn't kidnap me because you thought after five years of my father being dead, this was a good time to start playing uncle to an orphan." I clapped my hands on my lap. "So, let's cut the bullshit and get to the real reason I'm here and how you want to use me."

"Use you?"

"Everyone has so far." I tilted my head. "I'm not going to believe you are any different. You said so earlier."

He leaned back in his chair, an amused expression in his eyes, a smile twitching under his beard. "Blunt and to the point." He dipped his head.

"We don't have the luxury in this country to be anything else."

Mykel's eyebrows danced up his forehead, his head bobbing.

"Definitely your father's daughter." He tapped his lips. "Benet always wanted to cut the bullshit, act instead of talk. It's a Kovacs trait, but I've had to learn to curb my impulses. I would not have gotten this far if I hadn't taken time to research my enemy and plan for every outcome."

That was why Andris and my father worked well together. One was the planner, the other ready to put those plans in action.

"Are you studying me then?" I challenged.

"As you are me." He laid his wrists down on the armrests. "Like you said, I didn't take you because I was ready to raise a full-grown child now."

"Why not? I'm potty trained and everything."

Mykel smirked. "Sarcasm. *Not* a Kovacs trait."

He was right. My father was kind and strong, but he didn't really have a sense of humor. He was serious and guarded most of the time. Maybe because of his job, losing my mother, or because of me, but he didn't laugh or tease a lot.

"Get to the point, Mykel."

"You may call me that only in private." He sat up with a snap. "Otherwise, I am *Kaptain*."

I understood. His name, if leaked or overheard outside the barracks, could end everything.

Just like Andris.

"After the explosion at Halálház, I lost your whereabouts. Kek was sure you survived, but it took me a while to locate you. Track you. I thought when you got back to HDF, it was over. You were home. But I should have known better. You disappeared again, but then out of the blue, you popped up on my radar at a place I wasn't expecting. It gave me hope for you."

I kept my expression blank, not wanting to give him anything until he said it first. I had no idea who I could trust inside or outside these walls.

"Sarkis's army." His fingers drummed against the metal of the chair. "Your father's best friend, who faked his own death to live with his fae lover, then became a revolutionist himself."

I sat still, saying nothing. If it came down to my "uncles," I had no doubt who I'd pick.

"Cautious." He nodded. "That's a good quality."

Silence.

"We might share the same blood, but it doesn't mean I trust you either." He sat up. "I know about your stay with the fae leader, Killian."

Heat rushed up my neck, and I had to force myself to not react in any way.

"You grew up in HDF, survived Halálház, been inside Killian's palace."

"How do any of those things help you here in Prague?"

His gaze met mine.

"If we hurt Budapest, Prague suffers as well. Our city benefits from many imports from you guys, both fae and human. Weapons, fae drugs, human trafficking."

"I doubt my knowledge will bring them down."

"Look at the big picture. Start to cut off the hand that feeds them, and you weaken their hold. Make them desperate. We chip away at their power while we work on the real plan."

"And that is?"

A knock rapped on the door, and an older man with gray hair stepped into the room with a tray.

"Tea, Kaptain?" The man set down the tray with a *chlebíčky,* an open-faced mini sandwich, a few cookies, and a teakettle.

"Thank you, Oskar." He nodded at the man, watching him leave quickly.

Mykel's hand motioned at the food. "Please eat. You need your energy."

Refusing would only hurt me. I was almost sliding out of my chair; my body was barely able to move. Picking up a cookie, I shoved it into my mouth. The treat was dry and bland compared to the ones I ate at HDF, but the sugar tasted good on my tongue. I devoured another two before I turned my attention to Mykel.

"What is the real plan?"

The door opened again, and Kek stepped in.

"Kaptain?"

"Kek, take Brexley—"

"X," I replied, taking Birdie's nickname for me. I didn't want my name being used either.

"X." Mykel dipped his head, repeating it. "Take her to the bunkers. She needs to rest. Room 418 is now vacant."

"Across from mine." Kek lifted a blue eyebrow. "What fun."

I was being dismissed.

Rising from the chair, I grabbed the sandwich, staring at my newly found uncle.

"I gather you aren't going to tell me the plan," I said.

"You haven't earned that yet. The person who attacked me in the elevator was my right-hand man. I don't have the *luxury* of trusting anyone, including my own niece. Especially because you were under Istvan's thumb for so long."

I could understand and respect that.

Heading for the door, his voice paused me just as I stepped out.

"When the time comes, you will understand your role here." He stared intently at me, flicking his chin at Kek. "Welcome to Povstat. Do not disappoint me."

9

With that, Kek shut the door, leaving me hoping the same thing about him.

The cookies and sandwich must have helped my blood sugar because as Kek and I descended into the belly of the base, I started to feel better. The weight and clawing sensation ebbed slightly, letting me breathe fully and walk on stable legs.

When we reached the bottom level, the demon exited the elevator, strolling down the corridor without a glance back.

"Come on, little lamb. Keep up," she purred. This time I could feel the power in her, the seduction and command of a demon. Imprisoned fae were blocked from their power in Halálház, so they couldn't use their "gifts" to escape or kill guards. Humans still weren't on even ground, and even without their powers, demons had full command and dominance over us.

My gut instinct was to be wary of why a demon helped me when my own human colleagues wanted to destroy me, but after a few weeks, I started to believe she did like me.

I should have trusted my gut.

"Now you are cautious of me?" Her pale navy-blue eyes peered at me from over her shoulder. The color indicated she was powerful, but not the most dominant of demons. Didn't matter if they were blue, red, yellow, or chartreuse, she was still stronger than me.

"I've always been cautious of you." I stepped out of the elevator, my tone firm. "Now I see I had a reason to be."

Her bow lips pressed together, her head swinging back. For as petite as she was, she covered ground quickly, rushing after me to keep up.

"There's the movie slash game room." She motioned her hand to a large room we passed. I could see a homemade ping-pong table and pool table, raggedy sofas, shelves full of books and board games. A sheet was attached to a far wall to be used as a screen, and an obsolete TV hung on another wall with a stack of dated movies underneath. Food, drinks, and more types of games were shelved on another wall.

Again, nothing that couldn't be left behind.

My mouth dropped as I saw a few children looking to be around five or six playing, some with games, some with building blocks, and others were coloring.

"There are kids here?" I gawked at the handful squealing and laughing as a few played tag.

"Why wouldn't there be?" Kek stopped next to me at the doorway, watching the children. "We have a lot of families here. Most of these kids were born here. The older ones are in school upstairs." She motioned to them. "Though personally, I don't get why anyone would want something so messy, annoying, and loud. Ick." She shivered. "But fighting for freedom is our life, not a weekend hobby. This is a home," she added before starting back down the hallway.

"Most of us share bathrooms. There are ten rooms to every toilet." She pointed at a community bathroom. "Some people paid to have a private one, but those are limited and only in family-size rooms. People have been on waiting lists for years, so don't even ask."

"I wasn't going to." I picked up my pace when she turned down another hallway. "How long has this place been here? How has no one found it?"

"Kaptain has been able to build this place and keep it safe for over ten years now," Kek replied, twisting us down another hallway. "He's gone to great lengths to keep it hidden with misdirection spells and protective barriers in place. This is the main base, but we also have several safe houses we move to when we're in the city, pointing Prime Minister Leon's soldiers in all the wrong directions. I think we have them looking up their ass by now. Here we are—four-eighteen." Kek stopped at a door that looked like every other one we passed. "The latrine is right at the end here." She pointed to a larger doorway about three doors down. "Little more privacy than Halálház, though I warn you, sex is even more rampant in there."

She shoved open the door to my room.

It was tiny and almost identical to the one I had at Sarkis's, with a bed, nightstand, and trunk at the end of the bed, but this one was a single, barely accommodating the basic furniture. And like before, clothing and a bathroom kit were left on the mattress for me.

"You are fortunate this one came up. People kill for singles." Kek leaned against the doorframe. "Guess there is a perk to being the Kaptain's niece."

I bit down on my lip. The last thing I wanted was to cause ripples with people because of my relation to the leader. Not that it sounded like Mykel would be giving me many.

"It's almost six-thirty. Dinner is served up in the canteen from six to eight, breakfast is also six to eight. Lunch and snacks are whatever you can grab from the carts or cafes."

11

Six-thirty? I'd lost almost a whole day since they took me. It was late afternoon/early evening when I was kidnapped in Budapest. It was almost a seven-hour journey by train or car between the two cities. I had to have been unconscious for at least twelve hours.

Was Ash freaking out? Did Warwick head back? Were they looking for me?

I wagged my head, clearing the gnawing questions burrowing into my mind.

"I think I'm good." The last thing I wanted to be was around people. I needed to sleep off the chemical still polluting my veins and reassess tomorrow.

Plopping down on the squeaky cot, I rubbed my head, feeling Kek's eyes on me.

"At Halálház... I was told to watch you." Kek tugged on her blue braid. "Not befriend you."

My eyes went up to her, not sure how to respond.

"What I told you was true. I'm not good with friendships or people in general. But you were different." Her eyes darted away. She cleared her throat, straightening, her manner shifting to the arrogant, blasé attitude I was used to. "Besides, I didn't mind watching over you at all." Her gaze ran over me, an eyebrow lifting. I didn't respond. "If you get lonely or scared in the middle of the night and want a *cuddle*, I'm right across the hallway." She winked before stepping out and shutting the door.

A snort huffed from my nose, my hand rubbing my face. The silence ticked at my nerves, carving an unsettled feeling in my chest.

Just the other morning, I woke up at Ash's, feeling safe and hopeful for the first time in a long while. This after Warwick took my body to places I couldn't even fathom without actually doing more than washing my hair. Now I was isolated and defensive, going to sleep in a different country, within the hidden walls of Povstat, where no one could find me, and my real uncle, whom I didn't know, was the leader.

So much had happened in the last twenty-four hours—hell, in the last few months—my brain struggled to keep up. Last spring, high up on HDF's roof, I would never have imagined I'd be been here.

Plunking back on the thin pillow, I felt utterly alone. I lost my home, the boy I thought I would love all my life and my best friend, everything I thought I believed in. Even Hanna was gone to me now.

Kek, Zander, Lynx (Ling), and Warwick had been spying on me because of an order. Not one had been genuine. And once again, the one who hurt me the most was the one I should have been most guarded from.

Warwick already betrayed me once, but this seemed worse—the hazy memory of seeing him with a beautiful woman and boy. The boy with the same black hair. They looked so content and happy.

*He has a son.*

A family.

Not bothering to take off my clothes or even my boots, I curled on my side, the echoes of pain reverberating in my hollow chest.

With no one around in this cold, unfamiliar room, I let myself feel the heartache and pain before my lids dropped and the darkness claimed me.

# Chapter 2

"Kovacs?" My name sounded like it was heaved through gravel, pulling at my bones, marking them with every syllable. "Kovacs!"

The anger and desperation punched through my chest, stirring desperation in my muscles to find the owner of the voice.

My mouth wouldn't move, my feet wouldn't budge, and pure blackness surrounded me. I tried to writhe against the invisible restraints.

"I'm here!" My mind screamed, but nothing made it out.

"Fucking answer me, Kovacs."

Thrashing and fighting, panic bubbled up, as the more I fought, the tighter I felt locked in place.

"Ko-vacs." My name was growing distant, like he was leaving.

"No! I'm right here!" I tried to yell. Not a sound came off my tongue.

"Brexley..." The name was more a whisper, only a thread left, my last chance.

A sob wracked my chest, my body still trying to fight. Something clamped down on my leg, snapping my attention down, horror freezing the air in my lungs.

Dozens of bony fingers wrapped around my ankles. Skeletons from every direction clamored for me, clawing and grabbing, yanking themselves from dirt graves, trying to pull me down with them.

A chilling scream tore up from my gut.

With a gasp, I bolted up, fear dancing over my shoulders and shooting down my spine. Sweat dampened my forehead and back, my chest heaving.

My gaze darted around the compact room. The fire bulb above my head allowed me to search every corner, the anxiety from the dream still coating me.

Memories quickly filed back in order, my brain registering where I was.

Povstat.

I was in Prague. Inside my Uncle Mykel's rebel base.

Taking slow breaths, I tried to calm my racing heart. Chills ebbed from the back of my neck while the feeling of the dream sat heavy in my stomach.

I glanced at a clock on the wall, which read 4:12 a.m.

Blowing out the breath I'd been holding, I fell back on my pillow. I was still tired, but my mind raced wildly, and I knew there was no way I would fall back to sleep.

I shifted with a groan, a light headache clinging to me. Ruffling through the clothes left for me, I grabbed what I needed, along with the bathroom kit, and moved to the lavatory. The showers and toilets were private, the tile and counters clean. It didn't smell like chlorine and shit like Halálház, though any bathroom with no windows or air filter system always had a heavy smell of mold coming from the walls and water trapped in pockets in the drain. I had lived most of my life with a bathroom that could rival noble palaces, but this was becoming my norm, more familiar than a fancy palace.

A few early risers were getting ready for the day, the communal bathroom still quiet. Quickly showering and dressing, I pulled my wet hair up in a ponytail and headed up to the second floor. A man was setting up a coffee cart near the elevator, and I practically mugged him for a cup.

"Seventy korunas." He held out his hand right as the coffee hit my lips. I blinked.

"What?"

"You have to pay for the coffee." His eyebrows furrowed. I couldn't tell if he was human, fae, or a mix. He was handsome, young-looking, but had creases near his eyes and a grouchy countenance.

"I-I don't have any money." The humiliation over how pampered I grew up colored my cheeks. Caden and I never had to pay for anything, from food to clothes. It was all put on Istvan's account. You never saw money being traded for products in Leopold; it was all taken care of behind the scenes, like a dirty secret. I heard many of the wealthy had racked up such high tabs they would be forever indebted to Istvan. Probably exactly what he wanted.

"You can't simply take something if you can't pay or trade for it." The man's voice went up a little higher, his glower going to where I was already sipping at the coffee. "What world have you come from, girl? Things aren't free."

"I got it." A corded arm reached over my shoulder and dropped a bill into the vendor's hand. I wrenched my head to look behind me.

A handsome guy smiled at me, making me swallow. Dressed in dark cargo pants and a T-shirt, the guy was about six foot and fit, with caramel-colored hair and bright green eyes. One eye was black and blue, as if he had recently been in a fight. Clean-shaven with a sharp jaw with a dimple in it, he reminded me of some superhero I had seen in old American movies.

"Tha-thank you." I cleared my throat, hating the shame and entitlement clinging to my skin. "I'll pay you back." I stepped back.

"It's no problem." He grinned again, showing off his perfect teeth, moving in beside me. "I'll take one too, Jan."

The guy behind the stand fixed another coffee, handing it over with a frown.

"Don't mind him." The cute guy nodded at Jan. "He's been cranky for the last forty years."

Jan snarled at him, only making the cute guy laugh. He flicked his chin in a motion for me to walk with him.

"He should have given you a break knowing who you are."

"You mean niece of the Kaptain? Nepotism precedes me, huh?"

He laughed, the sound deep and light at the same time.

"That,"—he shrugged—"and the fact you are new and could probably kick his ass in three seconds."

My brows lifted as I sipped the coffee. "And how do you know that?"

"Because." The guy stopped in the doorway of one of the training rooms, grinning down at me, his finger touching his discolored eye. "You did this."

The coffee cup paused at my mouth.

"I was on the team to retrieve you. You have a serious right hook; got me in the gut as well."

I blinked, not sure how to respond. "I'm sorry?"

"No, you're not." He chuckled like we had been friends forever. "Nor should you be. I was seriously impressed."

"Thanks." My lids lowered, still unsure how to react. I respected he held no ill will or resentment, nor strangely did I for him.

"I'm Lukas, by the way, but most call me Luk." He reached his hand out to me.

"Brexley—" I stopped myself, shifting quickly. "But call me X."

"X." He shook my hand with a playful wink. "Was actually hoping I'd run into you... I think my ego needs a rematch." He flicked his head to the mats. "You game?"

A smile curved on my mouth. It was the one place, no matter what was going on or where I was, I felt comfortable. At home.

It might be odd to some, but fighting was something I knew and could control. And a bonus, this time it wasn't to the death.

"Absolutely." I sucked down more of my caffeine, hoping it would kick in. I still wasn't feeling my best, my energy low, but I wouldn't turn down a fun warm-up match.

Following him into the room, I saw half was covered with mats. The other half held items like old car tires, metal poles, used cannonballs, and ropes turned into workout equipment. Nothing like the nice workout room back at HDF with machine arm presses, hand weights, and stationary bikes. This felt more real, true to the actual fights on the streets.

Raw and dirty.

Setting my cup on the floor next to the wall, I peeled off the black sweatshirt I was given to wear, leaving me in my sports bra, faded black cargo pants, and black boots.

"Trying to knock me off my game?" He stepped onto the mat, his eyes going down to my breasts. "Think tits will trip me up?"

"Not *my* tits." I stepped opposite him. I had never been voluptuous by any standards, but after Halálház, my figure had become nothing more than skin and bones, my thin skin showing every rib. I was slowly putting weight back on, but I was still far from being the curvy girl I saw working out on the other side of the room.

"You sure you want to do this?" I stepped back in a defensive position, both of us starting to circle and gauge each other. He remembered how I fought, but I had no memory of his moves. "Your ego is already pretty fragile. Hate to make you cry in the corner for your mommy."

He snorted. "I haven't cried for my mommy since I was eight when she walked out on my father and me and became the prime minister's whore."

Leon's young wife had died only a few years into their marriage, and all I knew was he took a lover *very* soon after. That woman was Lukas's mom? Shock stilled me with his blunt and honest revelation, my guard going down for a second.

Luk pounced on the opportunity, his fist jabbing for my stomach. Curving, I barely got out of the way, his knuckles clipping my hipbone as I twisted. Flinching from the hit, I instantly threw up my defenses, chastising myself for a stupid rookie mistake. My mind and body seemed to be groggy and slow still.

As we rounded each other, I couldn't help but ask, "That true?"

His lips pinched in a bitter smile; his silence made me believe it was.

"And you're here?" I didn't know if I was really asking a question. "On the side that wants to take Prime Minister Leon down?"

"Even more so." He swiped out for me. I dodged it, but barely. Frustration creased my forehead. I fought in Halálház when I was sleep-deprived, starved, beaten, and tortured, and still moved faster than I was this morning. My comrades at HDF used to tease I was like a ghost. I moved so fast they could barely see me.

This morning I resembled a sloth. The sensation of heaviness I felt yesterday, of being sucked of energy, still hung over me.

"The first thing I did when my dad died was join Povstat." He sidestepped my attack. "When we do take them down, I want to look in Sonya's eyes, for her to know her son was part of the group who ended them."

He lunged for me; this time, I could tell talking time was over.

Ducking, my leg swung out, kicking at his knee as I socked him in the kidney. His large body stumbled back, but he quickly leaped for me, and I tripped him. As he fell over me, I grasped his arms. Using the momentum, I flipped him over on his back with a loud thud, his breath catching. Scrambling, it only took him a moment to leap up. He crouched low and barreled into me, his arm looping around my waist, slamming my spine onto the mat. Straddling me, he pinned my arms to the mat. The guy was fit and six inches taller than me, but I had fought against a legend and killed three in the Games. How had he taken me down so easily?

18

Luk grinned smugly at me, but out of the corner of my eye I saw another figure strolling into the room, a beefcake of a man who stripped off his T-shirt. He made his way over to some bars to do pull-ups on the far wall.

Luk's attention went to him, breaking off of me. It was all I needed.

Sliding one arm up and over to the other side of my head, the move twisted his body off center. Ramming up my legs, I used every drop of caffeine pumping in my veins and swung my hips over. Luk flipped like a pancake, a huff coughing from his lungs as I leaped on top of him. I sunk my elbow into his neck, his Adam's apple bobbing underneath the sharp bone digging into his throat.

"How's that ego now?" My lips puckered with self-satisfaction.

Grabbing my hips, he tossed me over as if I weighed nothing, my ass hitting with a smack, making him howl with laughter.

"About as bruised as your tailbone."

"Asshole."

He let out another chuckle, groaning as he got up, rubbing at his side where I hit him. "Damn, you've got a mean punch."

"I wasn't raised to play with dolls." I smirked.

He reached down for me, pulling me up to my feet.

"Good way to get the blood moving in the morning," he replied, rolling his shoulders and stepping back. It was so subtle I almost missed it, but I saw his gaze dart to the guy working out, then back down. Looking over my shoulder at the ripped man, I realized it was Tracker, the one who led the group to retrieve me. The one I kicked in the face.

My attention returned to Luk, and I was expecting to see male testosterone. Maybe a hint of jealousy or rivalry between them. But the way Luk shot quick glances didn't feel like hatred.

I stared at Luk for a while, my arms folding.

"Why do I feel no pair of tits in the world would trip you up?" I looked at Tracker doing pull-ups, his back muscles flexing under his bronze skin. He was young, hot, and had a body most would want to worship. "He's really hot."

Luk snorted. "Surprised?"

"A little," I replied honestly. It was not just because of how I grew up. We knew there were gay people in Leopold. I had caught a few in compromising positions over time in HDF, soldiers and nobles, but we never talked about it there. Never bought into the gossip papers. It didn't exist. The skeletons stayed in the closet.

It was also because Lukas didn't fit the "norm" of what you thought. He was the sexy, manly superhero. Every girl's fantasy.

"Well, let's say I'm the worst of the worst. Not only am I gay, but I'm also a half-breed." Luk swiped two towels off the shelf, tossing me one as he rubbed the cloth over his neck and face. "I'm what the *pure human nationalists* call the trifecta of depravity. Gay, half-breed, and a progressive radical." He held out his arms, defensiveness in his stance.

"Then that makes you the trifecta of perfection in my book." I shrugged, patting at the sweat dripping down my chest.

"Really?" A grin grew up the side of his mouth.

"Open-minded, wants this world a better place, hot as hell, but I don't have to worry about you hitting on me." I sighed dreamily. "I think I found my perfect man. You sure you won't marry me?"

Luk let out a laugh.

"You comfortable with letting other men into the bedroom?"

"Hell yeah."

His chest shook as he moved to me, his arm wrapping around my shoulders.

"Think I finally found the perfect woman. My father can finally lay at peace in his grave."

"He didn't accept it?" I turned my face up to him. I already felt close to Luk. I had known him less than an hour, and I already felt nearer to him than people I had known all my life at HDF.

Luk shrugged, dropping his arm. "It wasn't that. I think he knew, but we never talked about it. He was human, and he understood how hard it was out there being a mixed-breed kid. He didn't want more struggles for me, you know?"

"Yeah." I nodded, understanding how cruel this world was. Though the Fae side might be prejudiced against half-breeds, they weren't when it came to sex and your preference. They were commonly known to be very open to sex with either male or female—to the disgust of closed-minded humans.

My father spoke of times when things had been changing—freedoms over who you were, loved, and married, were becoming more widely accepted. Then the barrier fell and humans tucked back into their dark corners again, becoming even more purist and uptight, which made them angrier and crueler. It was easy to judge and rip apart someone else, choosing hate over love. We were all constantly looking over our shoulders and no one could be trusted.

"Wait." I tipped my head, confusion twitching my eye. "Your father was human?" That meant his mother was fae. A lover of the *human* prime minister. The one in league with Istvan to fight *against* the fae.

"I'm confused."

"Tell me about it." Luk rubbed his nose. "Seems the purity thing only matters if you are a commoner. People know she's Seelie, old noble blood, but it's just not talked about, or when it is, it's used to show he's not prejudiced against fae. How can he be if he sleeps with one, and together they can build the bridge between the sides to peace while he's doing everything opposite?" Luk's voice sounded strangled. "Neither my mother nor Leon cares about anything but power. Not fae or human. They don't care who suffers or dies, as long as they stay in command. But people buy his bullshit, while he paints us the extremists who need to be squashed and killed when we're the ones who really want justice and rights for all."

"Damn." I blew out in surprise. By looking at Luk, you'd never know how fucked up his past and family life were. He was the straight link to the human leader of Prague, and I was the direct link to the human leader of Budapest.

Both joining the progressive side. We were a pair. Kindred spirits, in a way.

Tracker grunted loudly, dropping from the pull-up bar, our attention darting back to him. His eyes met ours for a moment, annoyance creasing his face when his gaze fell on me before he flipped back around, grabbing ropes to pummel into the ground.

"Still stings that you laid him out first." Luk leaned over to me, talking low.

I folded my arms with a *humph*. "Don't tell me... he doesn't think women are worthy challengers?"

"He's human," Luk replied, nudging me playfully, all the heavy stuff we were talking about dropping away. "We all have our faults."

"Hey." I punched his arm. "I'm human." Though the words felt strange on my tongue. A lie.

"I think he suffers from massive fae-envy. Overcompensates." Luk winked at me. "He wants to be the best out of anyone, including fae, and his ego believes himself to be."

"Too bad the role is already taken." I nudged him back.

"I don't want to sleep with you, but damn, I think I love you," he teased.

21

"So?" I lifted an eyebrow, wiggling them at Tracker.

Luk guffawed. "He's as straight as they come. He and Ava are basically fuck buddies, which doesn't mean a guy can't dream." He gave me a look, suggesting it was more than dreaming he did with Tracker's image. "Even if he is an insufferable asshole."

Yeah, I fantasize about one of those too.

"How about some breakfast?" Luk looked at his watch, tossing his towel into a basket. "The canteen just opened."

"Sounds good. I'm starving." I copied his throw into the laundry basket.

"Wait, wait." A woman's voice spun us around to see Kek strolling in the door, her blue hair loose and messy, with a steaming cup of coffee in her hand. "Did I miss you two rolling around together? All hot and sweaty and moaning... Can we rewind, please? I think you need to reenact every move. Without clothes."

Both Luk and I huffed in amusement, our eyes rolling.

"You don't even have to pretend to enjoy it. Actually, it would be hotter." She twirled her fingers, telling us to return to the mat.

"Why don't you go instead?" Luk indicated to her. "Be my guest."

"Look, I have no problem rolling around naked with her." Kek nodded to me, then scanned him up and down. "Or you... or even better, both at one time. But I don't work out. It's like pointless foreplay for demons. Plus, it's against my religion."

"You're a demon; you don't have a religion," I quipped.

"Exactly!" Kek pushed back the strands of hair in her face like they annoyed her. "Just being me is enough. Show me assholes who need to be taken down right then, I'm your girl, but I don't 'fake' fight or get sweaty unless there's a point."

"How about breakfast instead?" Lukas asked.

"How about breakfast then sex, pretty boy?" Kek padded his toned chest. "I swear I could change your mind."

"I doubt it." He pushed past her, heading for the door. "I really crave sausage for breakfast."

We barely made it ten steps before a crackle sounded from above, a voice coming from a speaker. "Attention! First Unit, report for debriefing in ops room as soon as possible. I repeat, First Unit report to ops room for debriefing." There was a slight pause. "Also report to the briefing, new member X."

A buzz of activity came from the canteen across the way, a few people jogging out, and I saw Tracker instantly respond, grabbing his items and leaving the gym area.

"That's us." Luk tapped my arm. "We've got to go."

"Me?"

"You're X, right?" Luk started to turn the opposite way, waving me on. "Come on."

"Better go, little lamb." Kek flicked her head to follow Luk. "Looks like your test day is already here."

"Test day?"

"Prove your loyalty to the cause," Kek spoke over her shoulder, heading for the canteen. "Try not to die. Hate to think I spent so much energy saving your bony ass for it to die now."

"Come on!" Luk yelled back to me, my feet moving to catch up with him, anxiety over what was going to happen tapping at the pulse in my neck.

Lukas directed me upstairs, forgoing the elevator. It was only a floor up, but the moment we pushed out onto the top floor, fatigue punched me in the gut, curving me over and rendering me breathless.

What the hell? What was going on with me? Bakos used to make us do five hundred steps twice a day. It had to be the chloroform. That stuff had wicked aftereffects. Still, I shouldn't be this tired suddenly.

"You okay?" Luk peered back at me.

"Yeah, fine." I forced a smile on my face, pushing through the heavy sensation.

"We'll get some food before we head out wherever we're going."

"Where are we going?"

"About to find out." He turned into a room, me right on his tail. It had a large table and creaky metal chairs. A screen was pulled down where a detailed map of what looked like a train station in Prague was projected.

Tracker, Ava, Blade, Sab, and two others I didn't know were already settling in around the table when we walked in.

Mykel's eyes slid to me, giving me a nod, affirming he wanted me present.

Luk and I took our seats. No one was really talking, but the room buzzed with energy and murmurs.

My uncle stepped up to the head of the table, in full Kaptain mode. A pretty but stern-looking woman on his right side handed him a file.

"We just got word from our scouts in the city there is a huge cargo shipment coming in. Someone on the inside has relayed back to us that whatever the train is carrying from Budapest is important enough for the prime minister to want his personal guards to be there."

*Train from Budapest?* A sinking sensation plunged into my stomach.

"Last time, we were too late to intercede, and the spies inside Leon's camp could not find out what the shipment was, only it was extremely valuable to him."

Dread wiggled deeper into my gut, twinging with the notion I knew exactly what was in the cargo, though the claim of my knowledge stuck in my throat. I didn't know for sure if it was the pills. I also wasn't absolutely sure I could trust Mykel. He wasn't like Andris. If he found out about them, would he want to use them as well?

"The station is going to be heavily guarded, but it is still open to civilians. While they are unloading this cargo, passengers will be getting on for the return journey."

We were lucky in this part of the world that we had a functioning rail system at all, but there were very limited trains, most working double duty for passengers and cargo.

"Blade, Sab, Lea, and Jak, I want you guys on all exits." Mykel indicated to the two I didn't know and turned to the map on the screen, the slide switching to a floorplan of the train station. "Tracker, Ava, you are going to cause a distraction on the opposite platform, while Luk and X..." He looked straight at me, and once again, I could see so much of my father in him. It was the look I got when he challenged me to not let him down. "You two will try to steal it... at the very least find out what it is."

"Steal?" I was a little stunned he wanted me on the most precarious part of the job. Not that I wasn't perfect for it. Stealing was my favorite pastime. "Me?"

"It's sink or swim here," he replied sternly. "We don't have time to coddle you. Every day, more and more people die in poverty or are killed because of who they are. The war is on our doorstep. Are you in or out?"

I glanced around the room of strangers, their gazes giving me no support. But then I felt Luk's fingers squeeze my knee, telling me he'd be right by my side. This was someone who was fighting against his own mother for what was right.

"I'm in."

Something resembling pride flickered in Mykel's eyes, his head dipping. I felt like I had passed the first half of the test.

"The train comes in at twelve-fifteen p.m. on platform six."

That meant the train would have left at 4:45 a.m. from Budapest. The exact train I used to lie in wait for, pushing the two minutes and twenty seconds I had to rob it.

"Departing in twenty minutes, with an hour drive, will land you at the train station at half-past eleven, giving you time to evaluate and scope out the guards, exits, and situation. There is also the possibility the train will change arrival platforms," Kaptain stated. "Is everyone clear about their role?"

All nodded, confirming a solid yes, acting like this was the millionth time they had done this type of mission.

"Good. All communication between you and the base will be cut off. Watch out for fae doors and the Mongrels. My inside spies are telling me they are getting bolder and more ruthless, not sticking to the nights anymore."

"Mongrels?" I asked.

"A group of cutthroat bandits who prowl the motorways and around the borders of the privileged, murdering and robbing," Mykel answered. "They have no purpose or goal except to thieve. They are loyal to no one or no side."

They sounded exactly like the Hounds in Budapest. It wasn't surprising they had their own gangs here as well. They always popped up in desperate times to take the scraps while the top was too busy fighting over power. Istvan always brushed the Hounds off as nothing but a nuisance. A small splinter in your finger, but in my experience, the sliver could fester and turn into a much bigger problem if ignored.

"Okay. Good luck, everyone." Kaptain dipped his head and strolled out, not even looking back at me, which made me feel like he believed in me more than I thought. He didn't act like my hand needed to be held.

Sink or swim.

"That's all the instruction?" In HDF, I was used to detailed, step-by-step directions.

Luk rose from the chair. "We've been doing this for a long time, and he trusts us to figure out our moves in a moment's time. So many things can change, and if you aren't able to adjust in a blink, a lot of things can go wrong. People die." He yanked on my chair, getting me out and moving. "Plus, we aren't his number one team for nothing. You're lucky—people have been waiting years to join this crew."

"Wow." I fluttered my lashes at him. "I'm so honored I get to be in the presence of Kaptain's grade-A beef." I motioned to him. The man's physique was seriously top-shelf.

He huffed out a deep laugh. "You and I are going to be good friends."

I hoped he would be right, but I was still on guard. Being friendly and flirty was one thing. Letting someone in was another.

I had learned that lesson.

A dagger stabbed at my chest every time I pictured Warwick with his family. The dream of him calling to me only hurt more. Because it was just a dream.

He was clear he wanted our connection to end, to be rid of me—now I saw why. Who would want to have a connection like we had to another woman when you were already with someone else? But why wasn't he honest with me from the beginning? Was the moment in the shower an act of pity? A way to cheat without actually cheating?

The man was a head fuck. Walling myself up against Warwick was what I had to do. If not for us, or even the woman I saw, at least for the child.

My life was here now, and whether it was a good or bad thing didn't matter. Severing my connection with Warwick was for the best.

"Get food and do whatever you need to do and meet me back here in fifteen," Luk said, running off.

My stomach was dancing around like the polka, but I knew today was going to be long and stressful. I needed energy—a lot of it—and a gallon of coffee.

The lethargic feeling shook down into my bones, and I had to clear it out.

For once, I wanted whatever unique, superhuman quality I had to show up today.

Lives depended on it.

Twenty minutes later, I was on the back of a motorcycle, holding on to my partner, the nippy morning air slicing across my face on our way to Prague. Luk had put me in a heavy jacket, and I was thankful it cut some of the chill from the crisp October day. The slight warmth of the hazy sun heated the black fabric of my clothes, melting into my skin.

When I met back up with him, everyone was in an artillery room across from the ops room. This held every type of weapon, jackets, goggles, small walkie-talkies, and other things we might need for this mission. We were strapped with guns and knives while still trying to look like everyday pedestrians heading for a train.

The egg sandwich I scarfed down must have sat wrong in my stomach because as soon as the group went down a long hallway, climbing out of the earth through a hatch, I vomited in the bushes. My head spun, my body wanting to collapse into the ground and sleep. But I shoved through, forcing my shoulders back and my feet to move forward.

"Don't worry, you're not the first." Luk handed me a cloth to wipe my mouth. "Most get sick on their first mission."

*"Go ahead and throw up. All do at some point."* Zion's voice crept back into my head, the memory of when I first was led into Halálház, the terror raging through my body. I could barely stand, my body wanting to shut down. But I didn't throw up then, so why now? Sure, I

was nervous, but I wasn't terrified. My training, the ability to compartmentalize, allowed me to do what was needed.

No, this felt like all my energy was being siphoned away, making me nauseous and dizzy.

"You gonna be okay?" Luk's concern was written over his face. They couldn't risk having someone not at their best.

"Yep." I forced a bigger smile.

"Kaptain has our transportation stored in a building over here."

I followed Luk, my head turning back as if something called for me. In the distance, only about a hundred yards away, I spotted what looked like the top of Czech baroque-style church spires.

"The barracks is under a church?" I twisted back to Luk.

"And a graveyard." He smirked with a shrug. "Guess it was pretty well known back in the day. There was already a crypt and tunnels below it where Kaptain hid out once. I guess he thought it was the perfect cover to hide a base for the army that was expanding daily."

You couldn't fault his plan. Most would not consider looking for a rebel base under sacred ground.

"Come on," Tracker yelled back at us. Luk took off jogging after him. I glanced back at the small Roman Catholic church again, a strange sensation tugging at me, tightening my throat.

"X!" Luk shouted, tugging me from my trance as I trotted after them into a gutted structure.

Jak, a demon with red eyes who was a rung above Kek, jumped into a beat-up car, which was a rarity for me to see. Lea was with him. I couldn't tell if she was fae, human, or both, but she was close to my height and built. I was tough and could look extremely unfriendly, but she seemed like she really was, and by the few annoyed glares she shot me, she wasn't thrilled I was on this mission.

The others were paired up on motorcycles, all of us hurrying away from the village where the base was located. There were tiny, mostly abandoned houses and what looked like boarded-up hotels and long-closed souvenir shops, their signs decaying and worn.

Whether it was the fresh air, my adrenaline, or throwing up the breakfast sandwich, for the first time since I arrived, the weight of exhaustion and low energy dissipated as we rode toward the capital, the cool wind lashing against my cheeks.

Growing up, I had never left Budapest, nor knew much about the Czech Republic, so I had no real understanding of where I was. So far, it reminded me very much of the area outside the busy streets in Savage Lands. Poor and abandoned. You could feel the emptiness of the villages and towns we passed. Ghosts of the past loomed, remnants of the life which once filled these streets. The buildings were now deserted and dilapidated, crying for the days that were long gone.

The ride was rough, as the main motorways were crumbling and bumpy, pushing the time past what Kaptain estimated. I knew when we started to get close to the city as houses and buildings became closer together until they were an endless string of deteriorating concrete and sagging wood. Starving people huddled around fires, and homes built out of cardboard and pieces of wood, tarps, and blankets were used to make shelters.

"Same where you live?" Luk nodded at the destitute. "Everyone starves while the leaders eat like spoiled kings, tossing away leftovers with little care."

I nodded; my mouth pinned together. Once, I had been part of that group. The overindulged elite, completely unaware of the situation outside the walls of Leopold. The only link I had beyond those walls was from Maja, my maid, hearing about her grown kids. My response? Thinking I was so great to steal crumbs from Istvan, declaring myself some kind of Robin Hood, when in reality, it was for the thrill of stealing. It disgusted me now. The entitlement, the arrogance, and the condescending ignorance I had.

"Leon has walled off the entire area from the Palladium, past the Staromak, Prague's old town square." From my studies, Staromak was where the famous and stunning Astronomical Clock was, right next to the soaring gothic towers, spires, and buttresses of the Church of Our Lady before Týn. Like Istvan, Leon kept the rich and famous safe in their snug bubble of wealth and beauty.

On the other side of the famous gothic bridge, identical to Budapest, the fae resided in the castle on the hill. I had no idea what their fae lord was like, but rumors suggested he was commonly high on fairy dust and too busy engaging in orgies to care what was happening within his own noble house, let alone give a thought about the human side.

I wondered if that was how the human leader, Leon, had carved such a hold in Prague.

Up ahead, I saw Tracker's arm make a circular motion above his head. Instantly, the bike behind him broke off from the group, turning down a road, the car going the opposite way.

"We split up from here. We can't look like we're together," Luk explained, though he didn't need to. From here on out, all communication was limited and came through an earpiece hidden under our hoods. I had never seen anything like it. Luk said it was something they stole from one of Leon's shipments from the west. It was the size of a pebble and fit into your ear. Its technology told me it came from the Unified Nations. No Eastern Bloc country I'd heard of had anything like this.

Lukas parked the bike near the entrance buzzing with people arriving and exiting the front doors. A few police were stationed at the front. They were armed with rifles, fingers on the triggers, ready to shoot without question. I pulled my hood farther over my head, nerves bouncing around as Luk and I jogged across the old motorway. A few horse carriages and motorbikes were the only traffic. My pulse thrummed against my neck, sweat gathering at the base of my spine when I felt the armed guard look at me, a huge German shepherd sitting at his side. The dog stood up, eyes on me, a bark coming up its throat.

*Fuckfuckfuck.*

"Stop," the guard ordered.

Everything inside plunged to the ground, freezing me in place. Acid built up the back of my throat as the guard moved for me.

Would they know who I was? I wouldn't put it past Istvan to have a bounty on my head, plastering my picture all over the elite papers and having his "buddies" on the lookout for his mentally unstable ward.

I could fight them. Pull out my gun and shoot them both dead in a moment. I would risk everything, not just this mission, but possibly Luk and the others. I knew I would do it if it came down to it. My mind buzzed, my body preparing for a fight. My fingers grazed the gun in my jacket as the officer stepped closer.

Fear spiked my adrenaline, yanking me away from my current space.

For a blink, I stood in Ash's comfy home. I could smell the herbs and fire, but at the same time, I was still watching the police officer dressed in his Czech uniform stomping for me, the dog lurching my way. A massive familiar physique paced in front of Ash's fireplace, a pair of aqua eyes snapping to mine. He froze in place.

Warwick.

His mouth parted slightly as if he were going to speak, but his attention went over my shoulder, his eyebrows furrowing. I knew he could see my surroundings like I could see his.

30

It was a second, and then he was gone, but seeing him was like a knife to the gut. Because every cell in my body craved him. Like my heart was given air to breathe again.

"You," the guard yelled. My heart skipped when he stepped past, snatching the arm of someone right behind me.

"What are you carrying?" The guard grabbed the small man roughly, slamming him face-first into the wall, forcing him to cry out.

"I have nothing. I swear," the man wailed, panic filling every syllable. The guard ignored him, being overly aggressive as he patted the guy down, the dog whining and barking, the guard still not noticing it was for me.

"Move," Luk hissed in my ear, gripping my bicep as he shoved me forward. Relief tangled with fear as we slipped through the doors, my lungs tripping over themselves when we were inside.

Luk cursed under his breath, letting go of my arm, but he kept up the pace, moving us deeper into the train station, purchasing our tickets so we could show proof and get on the platform. "I thought we were done for."

"Me too." I exhaled another breath, the knot in my stomach loosening a bit, though I spotted more police staggered throughout the train station, keeping guard, some with dogs.

"Is it usually this guarded?" I mumbled to Luk, trying to get my head back in the game. Trying to forget the brief moment of seeing Warwick and chastising my weakness. Heightened emotion, especially fear, seemed to link us. I needed to curb that.

His image flashed back into my head. He was wearing dark jeans and a black T-shirt, his scruff becoming a full beard, and his long tangled black hair looked like he had been running his hands through it over and over. Fuck, that man was sexy and scary as hell...

"Yes." Luk's voice brought me back to reality, clearing my mind of Warwick Farkas. Luk was the opposite of Warwick's ferociousness. They were sunshine and darkness, though both were extremely attractive. Luk was polished and handsome, while Warwick was feral and sexual, the kind which hit on every erotic and carnal fantasy you had. "Leon likes to keep everything in his control."

"I think he and Istvan would be good friends."

"Not really." Luk smirked. "Too much ego and need to be the dominant one."

Maybe that was why Istvan never brought Leon into his circle. Too much ego in one room. Though if what I expected was on the train, a

31

relationship was building, or more likely, Istvan was using this to win dominance over Leon.

*If those two got over their pride and came together...* I gulped at the thought. *They would be a force even the fae might not be able to handle.*

"Jak and Lea, in position." A woman's voice in my ear almost made me jump. Luk's eyes turned to me, and I shrugged.

"Blade and Sab in position," a male voice responded, and I figured it had to be Blade.

I liked that my uncle had an even number of women to men in the lead group, which Istvan never did. Hanna and I were the only girls in our class in HDF. Most were raised to be wives of powerful men. It seemed Kaptain played more favoritism between fae and human than between sexes. Except for Tracker, the rest of the squad was at least half fae.

"Track and Ava in position." Ava's voice crackled in my ear.

"Luk and X moving in," Luk muttered next to me, his voice echoing through my earpiece.

"Four guards just stopped in front of platform one." Tracker's voice spoke as Luk and I strolled through what used to be shopping stores to the train platform. This place used to be a hub of transportation; now only six platforms were being used. All the shops were boarded up, and only a few carts with coffee and bakery items were sprinkled around. Once a symbol of its beauty, the decaying art nouveau-style building was another thing on the endangered list.

"No guards are at platform six," the voice I now knew as Lea's muttered through the earpiece.

"Still says it's arriving on six," Blade spoke, his Polish accent thick.

"Stand by," Tracker ordered. It was clear he was the alpha of the group.

My gaze went to platform one, my mind taking in every detail around it. Next to the platform was an arched doorway leading through an old waiting room and then outside to the street. Guards paced inside the doorway.

"Can people exit there?" I flicked my chin. Luk's gaze slid casually over to where I was indicating.

"No, all exits except the main one are blocked off to civilians, so they can check everyone going in and out."

"But not for a prime minister wanting to get cargo off as fast and subtle as he can?" My eyebrows arched up.

"Attention! Train arriving for Budapest on platform six." A man's voice boomed over the station's speaker. Passengers immediately headed for that area, but something in my gut told me I was right.

"It's coming on platform one."

"But they just said—"

"I'm telling you it's coming in at platform one." I looked into Luk's eyes, the implied *trust me* expression stretched over my features.

Luk glanced over to the platform, biting down on his lip. I knew he was taking in how the train carriage could line up with the double doors, how easy it would be for them to wheel whatever they wanted off the carriage and into a waiting cart or car outside the exit.

"Trust me," I said, his eyes holding mine. I could see the struggle in him. He had no reason to trust me.

Inhaling and exhaling, he muttered into the com, "Tracker, get everyone in position for platform one."

"What? No. The announcer said six," Tracker snapped back.

"Trust me." Luk gritted his teeth. "Platform one."

"Are you sure? If you're wrong, this whole mission was for nothing," Tracker replied gruffly.

Luk's blue eyes met mine, his head dipping. "I'm sure."

Luk and I moved through the space. It was busy, but not as much as I hoped. The shield of people was better to hide among. I spotted a train coming up the track right before they split off into the six separate lanes.

My stomach twisted with nerves. *Please be right, please be right.*

The loud squealing of metal rang out as the train switched tracks. I held my breath. And then it curved, coming up track one. My heart rapped in my chest, my shoulders lowering with relief.

"Looks like you were right." Luk winked at me, lacing his fingers with mine, making us look like a couple. We strolled toward the platform, where two guards stood at the front of the track. You couldn't pass them without a ticket.

While Luk showed them our tickets, my gaze wandered down the platform, spotting guards propping open the double doors on the side, four moving through with a cart, as three train guards hopped from the train, heading for the last carriage.

It was exactly as I figured, confirming to me what was likely being smuggled in the cargo. The night I was captured and sent to Halálház, when I found the pills, the train had been heading here.

I think we were wrong about Leon and Istvan, at least about their willingness to work with each other for more power and money. It wasn't out of friendship, but out of necessity.

"How did you know the train was arriving on this platform?" The soldier blocking the path to the platform tilted his head, handing Luk back our papers.

"Attention! Track change for the train heading to Budapest. You are now on platform one. I repeat, platform one." The announcer's voice came overhead like he was trying to highlight the fact that we were already there.

"It changed on the board first," Luk replied smoothly, not even a flicker of doubt.

The two guards peered at each other, both skeptical. Everything you did in this country and mine was suspect, and the young guards were looking for a fight, even if there was none, so they could be praised by their superior.

Both Luk and I kept our chins up, confidence radiating off us, while sweat dripped down my back, panic bubbling under my skin. I heard Prague's prison tried to compete with Halálház, seeing which one could be crueler.

I couldn't go back.

I *wouldn't*.

People started to line up behind, taking the attention solely off us.

"Go ahead." The one closest to me stepped out of our way, allowing Luk and me to walk through them.

The internal relief blew from my lips, my fingers squeezing Luk's. He clenched mine back, and I could see his lids shut for a moment, then open. Reset.

Now the real challenge lay ahead.

"Look," he muttered. Men were unloading large crates from the caboose, the back part of the trains holding the cargo, placing them on carts to wheel out.

We walked slowly toward the last passenger carriage, waiting for whatever disturbance Tracker and Ava were going to pull.

"Any time," Luk said into the earpiece.

"There was a hiccup. Hold on," Tracker growled back.

"We don't have time," Luk hissed.

Right then, two guards with a dog walked toward us, my body stiffening as I watched the guard dog sniff, his eyes landing on me, making me feel like he could see right through me.

As if they could sense I was not right. Abnormal. Wrong.

"Relax. They can smell fear." Luk pulled me to him like we were a couple in love. We both had packs stuffed with sweatshirts to look like we could be going somewhere.

The huge dog yanked against its blond owner's lead, a low growl vibrating in its throat. What the hell? Did I roll in hamburger on my way here?

The sentry tried to rein him back, the dog straining to reach me. The man's beady eyes narrowed on me, twisting my stomach again.

"You," his dark-haired partner ordered, stepping up to us. The dog whined and pranced in his place. The whimper was so odd even his owner was looking at the dog with bewilderment.

"My girlfriend and I... were just getting on the train." Luk pointed, his hand drawing me toward the carriage.

"Stop," the guy ordered again, reaching for his gun.

*"Do prdele." Fuck. Holy shit*, Luk hissed under his breath in the old Czech language before putting up his hands. "Yeah, yeah, we've stopped."

"Let me see your tickets." The dark-haired one opened his palm, even though we couldn't get this far unless we had them.

Luk nodded, placing the documents in his hand, all of us knowing he'd learn nothing from the tickets except we were heading to Budapest, which was where the train was going.

"What are you going for?"

"I'm meeting her parents for the first time. We're going to get married." Luk's explanation flew off his mouth like it was truth.

Both guys still glowered at us like the reason wasn't good enough.

"Where?" the dark-haired one asked.

"North Leopold." I shot in before Luk could speak. The area north of Leopold wasn't inside the bubble, but it wasn't Savage Lands either. The area was poor, but people in Leopold worked or had businesses that kept them slightly above the poverty line. These guys would never believe we came from either the desolate or the rich side.

Their eyes dragged over us, assessing my claim. The dark-haired asshole flicked his thumb over the trigger with a smug smile, loving the dominance he had over us, especially because Luk physically stood taller than both of them. By holding a gun, they felt powerful.

Little did they know they weren't the only ones carrying weapons.

"How long?"

"A few days," I replied.

"Let me see your bags." The dark-haired one demanded, gesturing for our bags.

Shit.

"Now!" He reached for my pack, yanking it off my shoulder. The violent movement caused the dog to bark and jump, making passengers shriek around us, darting for entry onto the train. Fear shot through my nerves, the moment escalating quickly. I knew if they didn't find anything in my pack to confirm our plans, things would go south fast.

All the while, I could see the guards behind them rolling out the first load of crates. We might miss our opportunity.

The instinct to fight, to kick this asshole in the head, shook through my bones. I could put him on his back in two seconds, but all they had to do was release the dog, and I'd be in shreds.

"Step back!" The blond one screamed at us, pointing his gun at Luk, the dog's incessant piercing barks filling my veins with anxiety.

The guy with my pack snatched my bag, unzipping it.

Fuckfuckfuck.

He yanked out a sweatshirt and pair of leggings.

"This is it? Does not look like you are going for a couple of days." He sneered. "Both of you put your arms up and turn around!"

Acid burned up my throat. We were done if they patted us down, finding us both loaded with guns and knives. Or worse, if they discovered our earpieces.

The skinny dark-haired guy ripped Luk's bag off, shoving at his shoulder, to face the train.

"Don't move!"

My eyes slid to Luk, my muscles twitching with the need to fight. *What do you want to do?*

Our options were slim, and it seemed whatever we did, our mission was over.

Luk's jaw rolled, and I could tell he gathered the same thing.

"Fight," he muttered to me.

My chin dipped in response, my lungs taking in a full breath, ready to respond.

The guard's hands went straight to my breasts, his slimy palms moving down my figure. I knew the moment he felt the gun inside my jacket. The pause. I could almost hear the click in his brain that told him what he was feeling.

My muscles contracted, primed to swivel around and attack.

He opened his mouth to yell at his partner.

*Booooom!*

An explosion rocked through the train station with a deafening roar.

Our awaited diversion.

# Chapter 4

The ground vibrated under my feet, screams and cries instantly ringing out through the air, people rushing for the exit. The guards behind us darted down the platform, trying to see what happened, while officers blowing whistles and shouting ran from every direction toward the billowing smoke coming from the farthest platform from us.

My head snapped to Luk.

"We got our distraction." He shrugged, watching soldiers who were unloading the train take off toward the commotion.

"You boys and your bombs." I snorted, my mind jumping to another man who liked to blow shit up to cause chaos.

"It works." He motioned for me, heading to the caboose. "And it couldn't have come at a better time. Come on."

I couldn't argue with either of those things. We had almost been caught. A few moments ago, I thought our cover was blown and we'd be captured and thrown in prison. Now we're back on course, sneaking to the last carriage.

Bedlam reigned around us, but no one paid us any attention since most of it was far on the other side. My focus zeroed in when we came up on the final car, spotting one last crate in the cargo. They had almost gotten them all off and out of reach.

Pushing Luk aside, I leaped into the carriage, snapping into thief mode. Yanking a knife from my pant leg, I shoved it under the seam of the lid, using it as leverage to pop off the nailed down top. Only a few tries and the wood splintered, prying away from the metal stakes trying so hard to hold on.

"Shit, that was fast." Luk breathed in, his head shaking. "Done this before?"

I smirked. If he only knew.

"Watch the door," I ordered, nearly forgetting he was my superior. I could almost pretend it was Caden and me, when times were innocent and we were carelessly reckless. A lifetime ago. I was a girl who had no idea what was out in the world, what was ahead of her, and what she would live through.

Everything I thought I believed— even who I was—was wrong.

Shoving the top over, I cleared away the stuffing protecting the contents of the box, and my finger hit metal.

Guns.

Picking up the newly made rifle, I tossed it at Luk. "This is the way Istvan sends his love."

"Damn." Luk peered at it, flipping it around in his hands. "This is grade-A level here."

I had a clear idea where Istvan could get these kinds of weapons. The very country Caden's soon-to-be wife was from.

Ukraine.

"They're nice, but this is what Leon is sending in his own men to guard? Some guns?" Luk's confusion twitched his cheek. "Guns aren't worth deploying in special guards, nor were they worth us risking this mission."

My gut twisted with what I knew was underneath, my hand digging farther, reaching the bottom.

A false bottom.

"Fuck... I see Leon's guards heading back. We have to go."

My stubbornness buckled down, my hands clawing at the wood, like the drug was mocking me.

"X! Come on."

Pain shot through my nerves as I peeled back the plank, my fingers grazing the plastic bags underneath filled with tiny capsules.

I fucking knew it.

"X!" Luk grabbed my arm, yanking me with him, my finger

pinching the baggy as I tried to pull one up. The plastic caught on the side, ripping apart.

Neon blue pills spilled across the floor, tapping on the wood planks like raindrops.

"What the hell?" Luk's brows furrowed together as he stared at them rolling across the floor.

"Hey!" A man's voice yelled at us, jerking our heads to the guards running for us.

"Fuck!" Luk darted for the back door, bursting through and leaping to the tracks. "Come on!"

"Hey! Stop!" A shot went off, pinging off the roof of the carriage. Ducking, I scrambled toward the back door.

"Hurry!" Luk bellowed for me.

It was a second.

One breath.

An instinct.

My gaze darted down to the pills.

"X!"

I swiped up a few, shoving them into my pants before my boots hit the tracks, taking off after Luk.

*Bang!* A bullet whizzed by me, a whimper crawling up my throat. I flashed back to a moment—a dark night, Caden waving me on, pain exploding in my back. And then darkness. I should have died that night. I should have died a lot of nights.

Now my boots strummed along the uneven tracks. I tried to pick up my pace as the soldiers' voices and sounds of gunshots crawled up the back of my neck. The panic and terror clotted my throat when another bullet zinged by, and the sound of boots clipped behind me.

*"Kovacs!"* A body slammed into me, flattening me to the ground, heavy and warm. A bullet zinged right past where I had been. One more millisecond and my head would have exploded over these tracks.

Inhaling sharply, my eyes shot over my shoulder; aqua eyes and a smirk filled my vision.

*"You're welcome."* He winked, his mouth close to mine. I could feel his breath slipping over my lips, his solid physique and his cock pressing into me. Fuck. He felt so real. To me, there wasn't any difference, but I knew he was hours away. *"Didn't think you were the damsel-in-distress type, princess."*

"X?" Luk shot back at the guards, then grabbed at my arm,

breaking the link to Warwick, yanking me up. Both of us volleyed back bullets, dodging and weaving around a train, using it as a shield.

"You all right?" Luk's looked at me strangely.

"Yeah."

"It was just..." He shook his head. "I don't know... it was like you were tackled or something."

"Tripped."

Luk nodded, but his brows still clung together with confusion. Yells and footsteps were circling around us.

"Shit." Luk's head bobbed around, trying to pinpoint where more guards were coming from. They were surrounding us. "Little help would be nice, guys," Lukas spoke into his earpiece.

"We're working on it." Tracker's voice pinged in our ears as six guards came around the back of the train, yelling they'd found us.

"Work faster!" Luk shot back at Tracker, instantly lunging for our attackers, his fist cracking one across the nose, blood spurting into the air.

Yanking a knife from my boot, energy crackled down my spine, with the lust to fight. I charged for another guard, barreling into him so hard he flew back onto the tracks with a thud. Twisting back around, my arm swiped out, slashing another across the throat with my knife.

A third one grabbed me by the neck, yanking me back, forcing the gun in my hand to drop. The barrel of a pistol pressed into my temple. "One move and you're dead, pretty girl," the man snarled in my ear, his nose brushing up the curve of my neck. "Or maybe I will find a better use for you."

I heard and felt the growl before I even saw Warwick. Whatever cheeky smugness he had a moment ago was gone. Anger radiated off the legend; his shoulders hunched to his ears, his eyes blazing with hate. He looked every bit the brutal and vicious beast he was known to be. Too bad none of these little boys could see him. They'd all be pissing on their boots.

"Bet you'd like that, you fucking *kurva*." *Whore. Bitch.* The guy gripped my neck, yanking me back into him, wanting me to feel how hard he was as he pressed the gun deeper into my temple.

*Use your weakness against them.* Sergeant Bakos's teachings came into my head, but when three more guards moved in front of me, their weapons pointed at me, I knew my options were zilch.

By the sounds of thrashing, grunting, and swear words, I was pretty sure the police had taken Lukas as well. A dozen more guards came around the train, confirming we'd be retained. I could fight a couple of people at once, but this was far too many. And unlike my escape from HDF, none of these knew me all my life, and they weren't afraid to shoot.

I looked up and saw the Wolf towering behind the men surrounding me; Warwick's chest heaved with fury.

*"Use me."* His voice was so deep and gravelly, it took me a moment to understand.

"What?" I blinked at him.

*"Use me, Kovacs."* He stomped up to me, his shit-kickers hitting mine, his form looming over me, invisible to all others.

"Maybe before they lock you away in prison, I can get to play with you." A nasal voice scratched at my ear. I felt fingers digging into my neck, the guard pushing his pelvis into me.

*"Use my strength. You've done it before."* Warwick growled, nerves pulsating down his jaw. He looked ready to combust, while strangely, his presence centered and challenged me.

My nose flared as we stared into each other's eyes.

"What the fuck is wrong with her?" The guard facing me waved a hand over my face.

"She looks like she likes this." The third one grabbed his crotch. "You like being the submissive one, *kurva*? Finally seeing real men for once?"

Warwick scoffed. *"You're gonna be dead in about thirty seconds, fucker."*

I had no idea how to do it. Nothing about my connection with Warwick made sense, but I knew I could. It happened before. His energy stepped into mine and helped me fight Kalaraja.

*"Do it, princess,"* Warwick barked at me.

Gunshots rang through the air, yanking the guards' attention from me for a moment, turning them away.

I didn't waste any time.

Stepping to the side, my arm swung back, hitting my captor's groin. With a groan, he bent over as my elbow slammed up into his chin, knocking him onto his ass. Ripping the gun from his hand, I twisted back to the others now coming for me.

I shot.

The first three went down before the gun clicked empty. The commotion I made gave Lukas the chance to break free, battling the group around him. More and more came running for us. There was no question I was tough and could fight, but I also understood when reality outweighed my fighting skills. Between Luk and me, it was eight to one at least.

I could feel Warwick around me and I let go, allowing his energy to slip through me, spill in my veins, and seize my muscles. I was still me, but I could feel his power clawing into my bones. The rush of adrenaline coursed through me like a wild beast. Intense, terrifying, and familiar... like every molecule in me recognized his.

The officer who so easily spoke of raping me leaped back up. Warwick's shadow roared inside me with rage. Swiping up the knife I dropped and a gun from another guard, I spun, shooting. A bullet struck one dead in the eyes as my dagger sliced through the throat of the dickhead. It spurted, and he choked on his blood, his hand going to his throat, his eyes wide with terror.

"You were wrong, Farkas; he was dead in twenty seconds," I muttered, spitting on the guy as he dropped.

Shots rang out, boots stomping toward us. I went straight for them.

"X?" I heard Lukas yell for me, but as if death could not touch me, I moved through the throng of police. Shooting, kicking, punching, and stabbing with speed and power I alone could not possess.

Possessed was exactly what it felt like. Riding the highest high but so centered and clean in my movements, everyone seemed slow and clumsy. I saw every move and every pull of the trigger before it even happened.

My body glided through my attackers, ruthless and quick. I always got a rush when fighting, but this was on another plane.

I was draining Warwick's strength, ripping through it with brutality. A hunger made me want more. To take until nothing was left.

"X!"

The shrill whistle of the departing train on the track next to us screeched through the air, breaking me out of my trance, fracturing my hold on Warwick, his strength leaving my body.

My chest heaved with exertion. My body trembled as I felt my energy drain, already craving more of the high of Warwick's energy. I blinked, peering at the litter of dead bodies strewn around me. Their blood covered me and dripped off my lashes into my eyes.

Holy shit.

What had I done? They were slaughtered, and I barely had a cut. It wasn't possible. Definitely not for a human... not even fae.

My eyes drifted back to Lukas. He stood there, his eyes wide, a touch of fear in them, then his mouth opened, his finger pointing. "Behind you!"

Whirling around, I saw a guard spring for me, his gun ready to shoot. I dropped out of the way of the bullet, rolling on the ground, my legs kicking him in the groin before rising back up, my fist plunging into his throat.

With a groan, he stumbled back, falling onto the rails, the tracks trembling as the train rolled forward, its momentum picking up.

He turned his head to see it coming, but it was too late. A guttural scream plunged from the guard's throat and was cut off almost as fast and was replaced by the crunch of his skull, the sound of matter and brains crushing under the weight of the train, beheading him.

I jerked my head to the side, though I knew the image would haunt me forever.

"Come on!" A woman's voice bolted my head up to see Ava and Sab, motioning from the conductor's cabin.

They hijacked a train?

I darted for it, reaching for them to pull me up, Luk right behind me.

"Took you long enough, fuckers." Luk climbed in, spitting blood onto the floor.

Our team was stuffed in the cabin. Blade had a gun to the conductor's head, telling him to ignore the calls to return.

"They'll be waiting for you at the next stop." The conductor's voice was more confident than I would have thought.

"We won't be on then," Blade replied, keeping the gun primed on the man.

"Good." The guy dipped his head. I had a feeling he was pro-Povstat.

Peering out the open door to see if anyone was coming for us, my gaze ran over the sea of death and damage scattered over the tracks, some guards still breathing.

Lukas contributed to the body count, but most of the kill was from me. Warwick poured his strength into me and let me take it until there was nothing. I couldn't feel any connection now, as if I burned it out. A surge of fear laced through my gut, wondering if this lack of a link would be for good. Wasn't it what we wanted, though? I wanted to ignore the sick feeling in my stomach and answer yes.

Luk's gaze, still full of confusion and alarm, burned into the side of my face. He had seen it. Seen the impossible speed and skill no human, trained as the best or not, should have.

The train pulled out of the station, the whistles and yells behind us bleeding into the afternoon air. I rubbed my head, fatigue hitting me like a hammer, rushing over me, my bones aching.

"You okay?" Ava reached for me as my body stumbled back. Darkness circled my peripheral, and my head spun.

"Guys!" Ava yelled over her shoulder. Jak, Sab, and Luk rushed over. Their hands caught me as I fell to the floor.

Tired. So tired, like coming down from the biggest adrenaline high ever and crashing painfully to the earth.

"X? What's wrong?" Ava leaned over me, then peering over at Luk. "Was she shot or stabbed?"

Luk ripped open my coat, his fingers pressing down, trying to find any wound. I couldn't muster the energy to tell him I was fine.

"No." Luk shook his head. "This isn't even her blood."

My lids fluttered, everything growing dim.

The darkness didn't bleed in; it crashed like a wave and tumbled me into nothing. I couldn't fight it.

*"Kovacs!"* My name roared through the fog as I sank, making me want to reach for the voice like I could almost touch him here... but he slipped through my fingers.

The coldness of losing him was as if death had finally found me.

Chapter 5

*Chirp.*

"You know, I think you're right. She does like it."

*Chirp.*

"No, not there."

*Chirp.*

"I do not! I told you it was a big misunderstanding!"

"Oh gods... " I groaned, batting at the obstruction in my nose, my lashes fluttering open to Bitzy's huge ears and eyes. Sitting in her bag, her ears were decorated with dried flowers that seem to have been glued on. "Please tell me I'm dreaming."

"Fishy!" Opie pushed past his friend, his hands clapping excitedly.

Another groan fell from my lips. "Nope, this is real."

Opie stood there in see-through gauze wrapped around himself like a bodysuit with strategically placed dried flowers and herbs covering his bits. His beard was braided with flowers, his feet in cotton balls. Leaves and twigs circled his head in a dramatic crown, and his lips and eyes were painted glittery green.

Pushing up, my murky brain registered I was in my room at Povstat, but it took me a moment for it to click in that my two friends were also here with me.

"Wait. How are you here? How did you find me?" I rubbed my

face, heaviness sucking out my energy, making me groggy and slow. I couldn't remember anything past being on the train. How did they get me back here? How long had I been out?

"We will always find you, Master Fishy. We are your family now," Opie replied, his attention back on his outfit, twirling. "Do you like it?"

"It's very... nature-y."

"It took me the whole way here. Though seeing his face when we went through all his supplies... Wow. Didn't think he could get so red."

*Chirp! Chirp!* I swore it sounded like Bitzy giggled evilly, her two teeth showing.

"Whole way here? Who turned red?"

"But he was nothing in comparison to the other. He was one big crabby pants the whole way here. Scary with extra hot sauce."

*Chirp!* Bitzy's fingers went flying out, her forehead crinkling with annoyance.

"No, he was by far grouchier!"

*Chirp! Chirp! Chirp!*

My eyes went wide as she went off, her fingers flying about.

"You're just mad because your mushrooms were taken away." Opie placed his hands on his hips.

Mushrooms. Holy shit.

"Again, how did you get here?" I sat up straighter. If Opie and Bitzy found me...

*Chirp-chirp.* A strange smile pulled on Bitzy's face, her three-prong fingers rolling up, her arms outstretched like she was holding on to handlebars.

"We rode on a vroom-vroom." Opie picked at the flowers in his beard.

"You mean a motorcycle?" No, no way. Did he find me? We had a link, but I didn't think he could track me down to the exact spot. "How did you find me?"

"I told you, Fishy, I will always be able to find you now." He tapped his nose. "Smelled you out."

Warwick knew enough of the area I was in, and Opie could find my exact spot.

That meant...

A howl of the alarm screeched through the bunker, announcing the base was being invaded.

And I knew exactly by who.

"Fuck!" I yelled, scrambling off my bed.

"Oh yeah, we should probably warn you... he's really, really grumpy," Opie added.

*Chirp!* Bitzy waved her middle fingers in the air, bobbing her head in agreement.

I flung the door open.

"Have a good day, Fishy." I heard Opie yell after me as I charged down the hallway, racing through the labyrinth of passageways, past people stumbling out of their rooms, shouts and commotion filling the air with tension.

Reaching my uncle was my only thought before he sent out his top team to fight. Even if just one man stood on the other side, I was afraid for the seven who would be out first to fight the enemy.

"Get out of my way!" I yelled, shoving past people, taking the stairs up. I felt fatigue setting in the higher I climbed, but my determination barreled me through the door to the top floor.

Tracker, Ava, Lea, Jak, Sab, Blade, Luk, and Mykel were already in the ops room. The screen filled with images from outside the bunker as they flipped through all the cameras' angles. The squad was loading themselves with weapons as Mykel laid out a plan.

"Tracker, Ava, and Luk, you three head out the northwest exit and come around. Sab, Blade, you two take the south exit, and Jak and Lea, you go up through the church. Don't hesitate. Shoot to kill."

"No!" I stepped into the room, every head snapping to me, my heart thumping in my chest. "You don't want to do that. It's not what you think."

"I don't know what to think except every alarm has been triggered, and one of our guards is lying at the entrance, either dead or unconscious," Mykel exclaimed.

"And this all started when *you* arrived," Tracker shot at me.

Suddenly, I noticed guards come up behind. My muscles twitched as I felt them move on me, and several arms clamped down, pinning me in place.

"What are you doing?" I tried to get out of their grasp.

Mykel stared at me as Tracker stomped over to me, getting in my face.

"It's interesting that a few days after you show up, our mission goes bad, and our base that's been safe for over a decade is suddenly found." Tracker's chest puffed with hatred, accusation glaring from his eyes. "I think you are a fucking traitor and spy."

My eyes shot around the room. Everyone stared back at me with the same disgust. Luk's eyes were also filled with betrayal. Disappointment. That hurt the most. He saw me fight. He knew something wasn't right about me. But I would never betray them.

Tipping my head to look at Tracker, not one molecule of me feared him. I had taken on much greater threats than him. And, honestly, I would have accused me of the same thing.

"I get why you think that, but right now is not the time," I spoke to him while looking over at my uncle. "I do know who is attacking the base, but it's not who you think it is."

"I think we know exactly what this is," Tracker spat.

"Put her in the cell until we have dealt with this," my uncle ordered the guards. His voice was cold, his eyes already slicing away from me, like he had cut any family tie between us.

"No!" I thrashed against the three guys holding me. "You don't want to do this. I know who is out there. He will kill all of you! Send me out instead."

There was a good chance if they went out, none of them would come back. Warwick would kill whatever was in his path, thinking they were holding me prisoner. I tried to reach out for him, the link hummed between us, but I couldn't seem to break past it.

"Send you out so you can run back to your people?" Tracker barked out a laugh, cocking one of his handguns, his confidence saturating the air. The Wolf would kill him in a blink.

"Warwick is out there!" I yanked against the guards, dragging them a few feet forward.

"Warwick? You mean the legend Warwick Farkas?" Blade burst out laughing. "This girl... she's fuckin' crazy," he howled. "Next she's gonna say the Easter Bunny and St. Nicholas are out there too."

"Holy shit!" Jak yelled, pointing at the screen behind Mykel, shooting their attention there.

Everyone froze.

As if I summoned the devil, Warwick's face filled one of the screens, his expression set so coldly it was like death himself was knocking on the door.

I sucked in, feeling his rage burning through his eyes, his head tipping to the side in a taunt. There was no sound, but there didn't need to be. With one look at the camera, his threat was laid out.

*Come get me.*

"He's in the church!" Mykel ordered, breaking everyone out of their trances. "Go!"

"No!" I bellowed, watching Luk and the others dart out of the room, guns loaded, headed for their target. "Mykel, don't do this! He will kill everyone. He thinks you're keeping me prisoner."

"Take her away." He flicked his hand, and the guards dragged me out of the room. Desperate to stop what I knew was coming, the fighter Halálház created growled up my throat.

Stomping my boot on one guard's foot, I slammed my head back into his face. The crack of cartilage correlated with his scream, his frame bending over in agony.

I swung around, my fist smashing into the throat of the second guard as my elbow knocked into the gut of guard three. Free of their hold, I darted away from them, my legs sprinting out the passage, shouts ringing out behind me.

My boots hit the stone steps, which led to what looked like a crypt.

As if someone poured cement on my muscles, every movement was set in slow motion. Vomit rolled in my stomach, my feet stumbling over the steps, but I fought to get to him, to stop any senseless death.

If he saw me, he'd know I was okay.

"Warwick!" I tried to scream, but it came out garbled.

*What is wrong with me?*

I tried to cry out his name again, my hands and feet pushing me up the last few steps. I tumbled out of a faux stone grave, which disguised the entry down into the barracks. Sounds of grunts, screams, gunfire, bones crunching, and skin being hit slapped the stone walls.

"War-wick!" My voice sounded strangled while I tried to link to him, but nothing happened. The energy to reach him fizzled. My head spun like a thousand voices were murmuring in my head, all trying to reach me. Out of the side of my eye, I swore I saw things hovering around me. The pressure slashed pain across my vision, my body wanting to shut down.

*No, Brexley! Don't give up!*

It was like I had hundreds of leeches sucking every ounce of my life from me, the murmurs in my head growing more shrill. Whispers of words, hisses of syllables, but nothing I could understand, though it continued to grow louder and louder.

"Stop!" I cried, my hands going to my ears as my legs pushed me closer to the sounds of the fighting. I only made it a few more steps

49

before my body gave out, the darkness coming for me. My frame lay on the floor like roadkill, barely holding on to consciousness.

With everything I had inside, I shoved myself out of my own body.

For one blink, I stood in front of Warwick as he fought Tracker, Sab, Blade, and Ava. Not far away, Ash was fighting the others.

Warwick froze, his aqua eyes finding mine. I tried to open my mouth, but nothing came out, my finger pointing in the direction of my actual body, like some creepy ghost. And then I was back in my body, slipping away.

"Kovacs?" The ground shook with my name, the pounding of boots, the feel of arms, warmth, and... life.

Before I slid under.

When my lashes opened this time, I wasn't in my room. Instead, I lay in a bed in what looked like a clinic, tubes dripping into my arm, my head pounding.

"You're awake." A woman peered over my bed. I knew right away she was fae. She was dressed in flower scrubs, and her silky golden blonde hair pulled back in a tight bun, her eyes the color of amber.

Tree fairy.

"What's this?" I tugged at the things going into my veins.

"Keeps you hydrated." She gently tugged them out of my arm. "You are perfectly healthy, and your vitals are fine, but when they brought you in, you were in a comalike state. It was really odd. I've never seen anything like it." She shook her head. "He practically tore this place down trying to get to you. Had this base all up in a tizzy and demanded someone watch over you. It was the only way he would go quietly."

"Warwick!" I bolted up and heard the sound of metal scraping metal. My wrist was cuffed to the side. I stared at it with a chilling sense of déjà vu—the time I woke up in Killian's clinic, after being shot in the back, my wrist manacled to the infirmary bed. "Uncuff me," I sneered at her.

"Calm down." She took a step back.

"Un. Cuff. Me. Now," I seethed, my arm yanking on the metal.

*"Kovacs."* His voice growled from the doorway, my eyes darting to him. Seeing his huge muscular physique filling the entire doorway hitched the air in my lungs. I knew he wasn't really there, as I could see him chained in a cell, Ash in another one next to him, the smell of rot

and body odor filling my nostrils. He sat with his back against the wall, his arms on his knees, letting the world believe the bars could keep someone like Warwick Farkas in. He dropped his head back against the wall, his lids shutting briefly, his chest exhaling oxygen, like he could breathe fully again.

Relieved.

*"I'm coming. I'll get you out,"* I said quietly, though no one could hear me.

My voice opened his eyes again. He didn't move or respond, but his gaze burned into me. Stripping me bare. Shredding my skin, ripping through my soul. I could feel him everywhere.

Intruding.

Invading.

Consuming.

What scared me the most was I had missed it.

Him.

The realization popped me back to the clinic, cutting off the link with a hitched gasp deep in my lungs.

*No, Brex. He is not yours to miss or want.*

"Dahlia, give us a minute." Mykel's voice drew my focus to the door. Instead of Warwick, my uncle filled it. His stature was so much like my father, it made me turn away, blinking away the jolt of pain.

The healer nodded, stepping out of the room, leaving us alone.

Mykel sighed heavily, strolling around the room, his hand rubbing his graying brows.

"I don't know what to do with you, Brexley."

"I get that a lot." I fiddled with the shackle around my wrist.

"You are my niece, my brother's only child. My blood." He turned to me. "But it means nothing in the world where we live. I've seen brothers betray brothers, and mothers turn their backs on their children. Blood means shit. Loyalty and allegiance are what are important here. We are family because we all believe in the same goal. And anyone who makes me question their devotion to our cause, I can't have here. Doubt is death. You understand that?"

It really wasn't a question, but I dipped my head in acknowledgment.

"When someone doesn't tell me everything, it also makes me start wondering what else they are hiding. As the leader, I need to know everything."

My throat tightened. I felt the pills still wedged deep in my pocket, digging into my hip. My secret felt like it had a heartbeat, pounding and squirming, ready to tattle on me. Information was life in a world where no one trusted. Everything was a weapon or leverage.

"I am putting a lot on the line with you because you are the only family I have left." Mykel slid his hands in his dark cargo pants. "I don't like being in this position, but I want to believe you are on our side."

"I'm not a spy for Istvan or Leon if that's what you think." I brushed my tangled hair away from my face with my free hand. "But you know that." I tipped my head, understanding Mykel wasn't in his position for nothing. "You know I am being hunted by my own people."

He dipped his head. "What a great setup, though. Send in my niece, pretend to be after her while she burrows deep into the enemy lines." Mykel strolled over. "Trust is earned here, not given. I don't fully trust you, Brexley. And after what happened this morning and who I have in my prison, I don't see how I can."

My lips rolled together, knowing I had just one path I could take here. Give him information he'd want. A way to have him trust me. The last thing I needed was more enemies, especially from the largest rebel party in the Eastern Bloc.

"I can prove it to you." I lifted my head, my gaze meeting his. "But I need Warwick and Ash released."

"No." Mykel shook his head. "Out of the question."

"You know the rumors about Warwick Farkas?" I curved an eyebrow. "They don't even skim the surface of the truth. He could break out of the tiny prison you have him in and kill almost every person here in minutes. The only reason he hasn't *is because of me.*" The declaration felt strange on my lips, but somehow, I knew it was true. "He is keeping his word to behave... but the moment I say, he will level this place."

Mykel's lids lowered. "Is that a threat?"

"It's a fact." I shrugged.

"You don't even know where he is."

A sinister smirk hinted on my lips. While I smiled at my uncle, I stood in front of Warwick again, his eyes watching me like a cat.

*"Care to stir up a little fuss for dramatic effect, Farkas? I'm trying to make a point."*

Warwick lifted his brow, deliberately pushing up to his feet like a predator getting ready to attack. "I could probably do one better than that, princess."

"Oh shit." Ash's attention pinged from Warwick to the empty spot where Warwick looked before standing up. "Brexley's here? Are you talking to her now?"

Warwick didn't look away from me or answer, his intrusive gaze scraping my skin.

"What do you want us to do?" Warwick's voice climbed up my vertebrae, gnawing on the bone.

*"Come find me,"* I taunted Warwick with a wink before cutting the link.

Facing my uncle, I tugged on the cuff holding me to the bed. "Better agree, because in about two minutes, you are going to have a huge pissed-off fable stomping through those doors."

"What are you talking about? He is locked up." Mykel peered at me like I was nuts until he heard bellows and the ruckus coming from down the hall.

"Stop!" I heard men and women ordering. Things crashed to the floor, the alarm overhead going off, this one different from the one this morning. They probably had different alarms for various situations.

"Get. The. Fuck. Out. Of. My. Way." Each syllable ground into my bones, like he was marking me. Not even using the link, it was like I could feel him near, his presence slamming into the room before he did.

Warwick came around the corner, Ash on his heels, people leaping out of his way as he stomped in.

Mykel's mouth parted, his eyes bugging in his head.

"Tag." Warwick leaned against the doorframe, folding his arms. He winked at me. "You're it."

Mykel stood frozen for another beat before guards rushed in after the two escape artists. He looked back at me, and I smiled with a shrug.

He held up his hand to keep the guards at bay, but I could feel we were teetering on a thin line.

"You can keep us handcuffed if you want—"

"Speak for yourself, Kovacs," Warwick rumbled, his glare piercing me. "I've only let myself be handcuffed once. The night I spent with three succubi and four water fairies."

Ash's head bobbed as he leaned against the other wall. "Oh yeah... that was a good night."

I glared at both, making Ash grin.

"So, unless it's going in that direction... it's a no from me." Warwick's gaze slid to Mykel, danger billowing off his skin like

53

cologne, a threat lining his words. "But *if* she stays safe... I won't kill you."

Mykel's Adam's apple bobbed, though he tried to hide any emotion, keeping his shoulders back. It was a few beats before he flicked his chin.

"Fine." He turned to his guards. "You can go."

They hesitated but slowly ebbed out, responding to their leader's order.

Mykel twisted to me, pulling a key to my cuffs from his pocket. "I am giving you a huge amount of trust right now." He unlatched my cuff, stepping back. "Remember, your father was *my* brother. If you betray me, you betray him and all he was trying to do for you." He huffed. "And I will not hesitate to lock you up if you force my hand," he said coolly, marching out of the room, making me feel every stab digging into my heart.

Chapter 6

A few minutes later, Warwick, Ash, and I stood in Mykel's office, guards on both the outside and inside ready to shoot us if we made a wrong move, which was hilarious to me. Warwick could take down a giant with his bare hands. These boys would be dead before they got one shot off.

The Wolf himself stood on one side of me with his arms crossed, his expression hard and dangerous, his presence filling up the office more than his actual physique. Ash was on the other in the same stance as Warwick, both slightly behind me, like guard dogs.

Mykel pretended like the two men didn't intimidate him, but the way his eyes kept darting to them, especially Warwick, told me it was all an act. You couldn't not react to Warwick, either good or bad. He demanded a reaction... usually to pee your pants and run.

My uncle stood behind his desk, his fingers tapping on the top, his attention going from me to the legend behind me. "I have heard many stories of you, but I will be honest, I thought they were just that. I didn't even fully believe Kek's accounts of you in Halálház. Seems I was wrong."

"Kek's here?" Warwick's thick brow arched up, though his tone gave nothing away.

"Yeah." I glared back at him. "Seems you two have a lot in common." Both spies. Both got close to me because they were ordered to.

"You said you could prove something to me?" Mykel drew my focus back to him.

I took in a deep breath, feeling Warwick's form skimming my skin without him moving.

*"What are you doing, Kovacs?"* His phantom body strolled around me, his breath grazing my ear.

*"Telling him about the pills."*

*"No. Bad idea."*

*"Not your choice."*

*"Princess..."*

Ignoring him, I dug into my pocket, my fingers curling around the capsules. Trust had to be a two-way street, and I knew I had to prove myself first.

*"Kovacs..."* Warwick growled with warning, his shadow moving in closer to me.

Tugging out the pills, I stepped up to the desk, opening my hand. "The mission yesterday wasn't a total loss."

Neon blue pills tumbled from my palm, rolling out onto the desk. Mykel's eyes latched on to them, his forehead wrinkling with confusion.

"What are these? Drugs?" He picked one up. "If you think I give a shit about drug smuggling—"

"It's not a drug." I rolled my shoulders back. "Well, not in the way you're thinking of them."

"You got these from the train?" Mykel rolled it around in his hand, not listening to me. "Leon is sending his own men to obtain this black-market crap? That makes no sense." He pinched the bridge of his nose with his free hand. "These mean nothing to me. Useless."

"Listen to me—"

"You think this will prove anything to me? This is elementary shit." Mykel tossed it back on his desk, his brown eyes glowering at me.

"Better shut the fuck up." A deep growl vibrated the room. Warwick's body nudged mine as he stepped up. "And listen to her."

Mykel froze, feeling the fury rattle through the room. His eyes snapped to me, his mouth pinning together.

"Look closer at them." I motioned to them. I could see the color inside thrumming with energy.

Mykel eyed me but picked them up again. Taking out his glasses, he put them on, really examining the iridescent pills. His head jerked closer, and I knew he finally noticed it. They were full of life... of fae

56

essence. The magic swirled and pulsed inside the capsule. Most would overlook it. I did the first time too, but I could feel them in my pocket like a heartbeat.

"What is this?" He peered over at me.

"I don't know everything in them, but one of the main ingredients is fae essence."

"What?" He blurted, shock popping his eyes, his spine stiffening. "Fae essence? That's impossible..." His head turned to the two men behind me, searching for them to concur with him. Neither Ash nor Warwick did.

"They're the reason I ended up in Halálház, but it wasn't until I was with Killian—" Another low snarl coiled in my ear. Warwick's chest pulsed against my spine at the mention of his name, "That I found out what they really did. What's in them. What they mean. What I think Istvan is trying to do."

"Wait... Killian, the fae leader of Budapest? What does he have to do with this?" Mykel pressed his hands into the desk, demanding answers. "And what do you mean what Istvan is trying to do?"

Yeah, this got complicated.

"Long story short... I was stealing these pills from Istvan's cargo train, to piss him off really, when I got caught by fae and thrown into Halálház. Killian later found the pills in the bag I had been carrying when I was captured the first time." *Thanks to the asshole behind me.* My narrowed gaze slid to Warwick.

Now I was pretty sure why I had been traded. Not that it hurt any less; it actually hurt more to know he had a family. Whether she was his mate or only his son's mother, they had a child together, especially with how good it felt to have him next to me again. It was a calmness and thrill I had never known before.

"I discovered what they were when I was Killian's prisoner."

Warwick didn't even blink, but his other form moved into me, taking up all the air in my lungs.

*"Prisoner, my ass. Don't pretend you didn't enjoy your time there, princess."* He snarled into the back of my neck, shivers spreading over my arms. *"Seemed to me you were loving being his captive. Though you liked me watching, didn't you? Make your pussy wet?"*

I sucked in.

"Jealous?" I muttered under my breath.

*"Of Killian or that little pretend soldier boy you have downstairs*

or even Captain One-Pump back at HDF?" Warwick snorted; the feel of his fingers glided up my thigh. *"Not even a little."*

"Brexley?" My uncle's voice snapped me back to the world outside of Warwick and me. Out of the corner of my eye, I saw Ash's head shake, sensing what was going on between us.

"Sorry." I cleared my throat. "Killian started testing the pills on human subjects." With a quick decision, I pulled my part from the narrative. "They all came willingly, but I saw what they did." I shook my head, the memory of the people down in those cells forever haunting me. "It changes people."

"What do you mean *changes*?"

Picking up one of the pills I stole, I peered at it. So small, yet so devastating.

"They turn humans into mindless drones. They give humans fae-like strength. They no longer understand pain, and they are a lot harder to kill. Their minds were vacant, just waiting for orders."

Mykel's head jerked. "What do you mean *orders*?"

"The ones I saw, after a few days, mentally shut down. They would stand there like robots, but as soon as they were given an order to attack..." I swallowed, recalling how the woman clawed and scratched to get to me, almost forcing her bones through the cell bars. "They became feral, and their only thought was to kill and destroy."

I could see the doubt and fear warring inside Mykel. It was hard to believe. "I know." I shook my head with a sigh. "It sounds like a made-up story, but I promise you, it's true. I saw every stage, from beginning to end."

"End?" Mykel asked.

"Every one of them died after a week. Horrifically." I had a flash of that woman becoming an empty shell, her brains leaking out of her ears and nose.

"If this is true, you are saying General Markos is producing these and loading crates with them, sending them to Prime Minister Leon, and Lord Killian has them as well."

"Yes." I cringed. "But I don't believe Killian is our worry."

Both Ash and Warwick snorted as Mykel let out a dry laugh.

"Killian would love to end the human reign and make us nothing more than slaves." Mykel's nose wrinkled with disgust.

Everyone kept telling me that, but I couldn't bring myself to think the worst of Killian. Maybe I *was* a fool, and he had tricked me the whole time. But why? Why would he bother? If I was so beneath him, why would he try to play me? Kiss me...

"Before I left HDF, I found documents Istvan was hiding. Documents that back up the idea he has someone making these pills."

"Documents? What kind?" Mykel asked.

"Notes from some quack doctor and scientists from long ago." I tried to recall his name. "Fringe stuff about taking fae DNA and trying to create some kind of superior soldiers."

Mykel's face blanched, his jaw rolling. "Dr. Rapava?"

My stomach sank hearing the man's name and wondering how my uncle knew it. "How do you know about him?"

"I learned about his experiments from my research of a Dr. Novikov." He stared at me in awe. I remembered Dr. Novikov's name from the letter as well. Another scientist searching for ways to make humans stronger. "They stopped working together when Rapava's went to the States, where he became radicalized and unstable." He licked his lips. "Istvan is studying Rapava's work?"

"Yes," I confirmed. "Not just studying." I pointed to the pills. "He has Rapava's formula."

"These?" Mykel gestured at the blue pills, his reaction icing my veins. "These are made up from the Rapava formula? He found it?"

"Yes." I nodded.

Mykel started pacing, his hand running through his hair. "The doctor was crazy, and though some of his testing resulted in some interesting headway, almost everyone died. Also horrendously. He was known around the science community as Dr. Death. It was some of the reason Dr. Novikov parted ways with him." He pinched his nose. "Are you saying Markos is using this nutjob's theories for an actual purpose?"

"It wasn't until I came back from Halálház that I saw how obsessed Istvan was with becoming the most powerful ruler of the East and ending the fae, no matter the costs." I dipped my head. "Actually, I think he was always like that. Guess I didn't notice or care before." Because I also believed fae were soulless and should be killed. I was another mindless minion Istvan had been grooming into a soldier. Not much different from the living corpses in Killian's cells.

"Fuck," he hissed, his hand running over his dark mop, with silver sprinkled through it. "Fuck!" He started pacing behind his desk. "This is so much worse than I thought." He paused, taking a breath before he pushed a button on his phone. "Bring in the Novikov file," he spoke into the speaker.

"Yes, sir."

Only about thirty seconds later, Oskar, the man who brought his tea the day I arrived, came in carrying a file and placed it on the desk.

"Here you go, Kaptain."

"Thank you." Mykel nodded as the man left the room. "At least fifteen years ago, talk was going around about a 'fae-like nectar' that was found, which caught my notice."

*Nectar...* The word dropped into my stomach like cement.

"It was said to be the only thing left after the barrier fell, which could give humans fae-like qualities: infinite life, no diseases or sickness, harder to kill... basically turning a human to 'fae' without any consequences." Mykel shifted on his feet. Something about his demeanor told me there was more to his story. "That was when I noticed Dr. Novikov's research. He was one of them leading the charge to find it. Many of us thought he had."

"What happened to him?"

Mykel flipped the folder open, pushing it out for us to see. Both Ash and Warwick moved in, all of us peering down at the paper.

On top was an old, grainy newspaper clipping with a picture of an older man, dated over fifteen years ago. The headline stated:

### Dr. Novikov Goes Missing After He Is Said to Have Found the Nectar of The Gods.

Dr. Novikov, a well-known scientist and partner of Dr. Rapava, has disappeared in China after claims of finding the fae nectar, which is said to give humans fae qualities. This nectar is reported to make humans stronger and faster and end disease, sickness, and aging. For a long time, the idea of fae food was considered a myth, which died when the barrier between the Otherworld and Earth fell. But before his disappearance, Dr. Novikov claimed he had found the last known object to give humans eternal life, along with strength and power similar to a fae's.

The clipping was cut, leaving out the rest of the article, but it was all I needed to read. A memory slunk in—the night of Caden's engagement, when he declared he loved me.

*"They have* Sergiu *set to marry some leader's daughter in China, which is a huge blow to Father since they have some object or substance my father wants. Some special nectar."*

China. Nectar.

"Holy shit." My gaze rose until I met my uncle's. "Then Romania is after this too."

"Romania?" Mykel's eyes widened. I felt the guys stir behind me.

"What the hell are you talking about, Kovacs?" Warwick grunted.

"The man I was being forced to marry before I was put in prison was Prime Minister Lazar's son, Sergiu." I swallowed. "Because I could no longer fulfill that duty, I guess they moved on to the leader of China's daughter. Caden hinted it was a blow to Istvan because the Chinese found the possible whereabouts of some special nectar.'" I did air quotes, mimicking Caden's words.

A slow roguish smile curled Mykel's mouth. "Romania is going to be greatly disappointed with that marriage."

"What do you mean?"

"China doesn't have the nectar. All traces of it disappeared from that area when Dr. Novikov did. It was said he moved it into hiding or someone killed him and took it."

"What?" I blinked. "Where is it now? Do you know?"

"No." Mykel shook his head. "I've been searching for it ever since and have found nothing. I mean, it's vanished without a trace."

"Do you know if it even existed?" I held out my arms.

"Yes." Mykel nodded, his feet shifting again.

I peered at him suspiciously. "How do you know?"

"Because..." Mykel inhaled, tipping his head back for a moment. "I was one of those who tried to steal it from the doctor."

"What?" My mouth fell.

He cleared his throat, his eyes not meeting mine. "At one time, I became, well, *zealous* with the notion of having eternal life, strength, and power. To grow an army and fight against all the wrongs." He cleared his throat. "I won't sugarcoat it. I was one of those fiends out hunting for it. Like in the days long ago when gold was found, and people would slit each other's throats in the night to steal it. This nectar was causing at least double the level of greed. The desire to claim it turned those hunters into murderers. Fanatical and feral."

"Did you see it? You know it's real?"

"It is very real. It disappeared soon after I *saw* it." His hands curled

61

as if the nectar was once there. Been so close before it was lost. "And the night I saw it was the night it disappeared... forever. Along with Dr. Novikov."

I watched my uncle, wondering what he was keeping from me. I sensed there was *a lot* more to his story.

"I didn't even imagine Markos would be following Rapava's more manufactured method. Nothing good ever came from his experiments. This is very bad. This changes everything." He rubbed his head again. "If Markos found a way to create them and is selling them to Leon? We are so fucked." He picked up the pills, staring at them like they could give him the answers. "I need to see what else is in these."

"Why?" I folded my arms.

"This is not the time to get righteous." He tipped his head at me. "We are fighting for our lives here, and I need to know what Markos is up to, what kind of army he and Leon can create, and why the 'nectar' is being talked about again. If it is still out there, I need to find it before Markos puts his plan in action."

"No matter if it harms and kills humans?" I knew Istvan wouldn't care about the fae he had to kill to make them, but what about the humans?

"The one thing I know when it comes to war, which Markos and Leon both believe as well, is sometimes you have to sacrifice a few for the greater good."

*In science, there will be sacrifices, but it is for the greater good.* Those exact words in Dr. Rapava's notes came back to me.

I felt sick and disgusted by their way of thinking, but as a survivor of Halálház, I couldn't help but understand and agree. I knew too well the world wasn't rainbows and happiness.

Living came with a sacrifice.

A price to pay.

My head wanted to crack open with all the new information rolling in it. Questions and worries pounded against my skull like waves. And I hadn't even dealt with the biggest one yet. The beast strolling behind me. The tension between us was so sharp, it felt like a thousand cuts burrowing into my skin.

"Don't disappoint me, Brexley," Mykel said before we left, and the same brown eyes of my father pinned me.

Mykel was letting us stay, but I understood our freedom was on a very short leash. The Kaptain of Povstat had other business to deal with and excused us from his office with the warning.

With a simple nod I left, feeling the weight of his decree. Me staying in line was one thing, but keeping Warwick under control was a feat I wasn't up for.

The moment the three of us stepped out in the hallway, I whirled around on them, annoyance folding my arms.

"What are you guys doing here?"

"We came to save you." Ash tucked back his blond hair.

"I don't need to be saved."

"You're welcome, princess," Warwick growled, mimicking my stance, treading closer.

"I don't *ever* need to be rescued... by you or anyone." I matched his step, getting into his face.

"Really?" Warwick huffed, his boots knocking into mine, snapping his teeth. "That's not what it seemed when you had a hundred guards trying to kill you, and you needed *my* strength."

"I never asked for your help!" I spat back, my fists curling. "Stuff your ego back into your pants, Farkas."

"I have other ideas where I can stuff it."

"Whoa-whoa." Ash tried to push us apart, only able to move me a few steps back. "Take a breath... both of you." His gaze bounced between us. "You two are going to have to address this *obvious* sexual tension disguised as anger thing as soon as possible, but for the time being, it has to wait." Ash glanced at the guard close by, his voice lowering. "I have an idea."

"Fuck." Warwick rubbed his face. "Those never turn out good."

"Hey." Ash pointed to him. "Don't even start with me after all the shit you got me into. The number of times I should have died."

"But you didn't." Warwick shrugged.

Ash glared at him until Warwick dipped his head, his lips twisting, like *fair enough*. Ash flicked his chin, his eyes moving to the soldiers. "Let's go somewhere we can't be overheard. Follow me."

Tracking back up to the surface of the church, a weight pushed down on my bones, my head spinning, my heart pounding harder.

What the fuck was going on with me? So much had happened I hadn't even had time to contemplate why I passed out earlier. Why did I keep feeling like my energy was being siphoned?

63

Clamoring out of the faux grave, my limp legs didn't quite make the edge, and I tripped forward, my body falling toward the ground.

In a blink, Warwick whirled around, his arms grabbing me before I hit. He growled in my ear, tugging me into his chest, getting me on my feet. The feel of his solid warm frame, his heartbeat, the energy pulsed off him. It was like I could finally breathe, the weight gone.

"Is everything all right?" Ash slanted his head in worry.

"Y-yeah." I tried to pull away from Warwick, but he didn't let go. Peering up in his eyes, his brows furrowed like he was trying to sense the truth of my response or feel it.

"I'm fine." I pushed his chest, his arms dropping away. The moment his hand left me, a force plowed into me. Voices filled my head so loud I started to black out, and bile choked up my throat.

"Kovacs." Warwick grabbed for me again, taking most of my weight. "What the fuck is going on?" With his skin on mine, the darkness dissipated, and the muddled voices cleared away.

"It's nothing."

"Don't give me that bullshit. You almost blacked out... *again*." His teeth gritted, his hands gripping my biceps firmly. "I can feel you... you can't fuckin' lie to me. You passed out earlier up here."

"I-I don't know what's happening to me."

"I might." Ash's somber tone jerked both of our heads to him.

"What do you mean, you know?" Warwick grunted.

"I said *I might* know," Ash said to him, keeping his focus on me. "Keep holding on to her." He moved up to me, his green eyes full of raw sexual energy and compassion. "Look around you, Brex."

This was my second time up here, but for the first time, I fully took in the small Roman Catholic church. It had rounded doorways and gothic design, but it was not the structure that made this place unique.

"Holy shit." My jaw dropped as I inhaled sharply.

Human bones were draped everywhere. Used as macabre art, thousands and thousands of bones were strung together like garland, dripping the room like streamers. Wall art made of femurs and skulls, sconces from a pelvis, a crest of rib bones. Every inch was covered, every part of a skeleton used. Skulls were piled from floor to ceiling or made into artistic statues. The most fascinating was a ghoulish chandelier, using every bone in the body, hanging in the middle. Chilling, but at the same time morbidly beautiful. Like it wasn't just our faces or muscular torsos that made us beautiful but our framework, stripped and bare, with no costumes or facades to hide behind. The truth that we were all the same underneath it all created true beauty. Not one skull or bone showed you what race, sex, religion, social standing, or species they came from.

Fae or human. Sick or healthy. Woman or man.

We were all one here. The same.

Equal.

Joining together to create something beautiful.

"It's... it's amazing." My head craned around, taking in every inch.

Ash smirked, amused by my answer. "Not surprised."

"Why?"

"Some would find this blasphemy."

"They are wrong." I shook my head. "This is a celebration. A place where we can appreciate how alike we are instead of what makes us different. There's no prejudice here. No hate between races or species." I saw Ash's smile widen, liking my response. "I would want to be here. Celebrated and awed with my friends instead of being put in a box in the ground to rot."

"I'll keep it in mind." Warwick snorted, making me glare at him, his hands still tight around my arms.

"I read on a plaque, there are over forty thousand bones used in here. Think about how many skeletons surround you right now." Ash gave a look to Warwick. "Let her go for a moment."

Warwick's forehead wrinkled, but he did what his friend asked, his fingers leaving me.

Like an avalanche, the buzzing of voices and energy dropped me to the ground with a blinding cry. My head pounded, vomit burning my tongue; the need to sleep weighed me down.

I heard Ash mutter something, but it wasn't until Warwick's hands clamped down on me, yanking me back up, did everything sharpen, my lungs gasping for air, the weight vanishing.

"Shit... I was right," Ash muttered to himself. "And *you* shield her."

"What the fuck are you talking about?" Warwick barked at his friend.

Ash rubbed his head, lifting his chin to look at us. "It was just a theory when I saw her pass out up here last time. I didn't even think I was right."

"What do you mean?" Warwick turned to him, his hand loosening.

"Brex, what do you feel when he lets go?"

"Um..." I exhaled. "Drained. Nauseous. Tired... like all my energy is being siphoned."

Ash bobbed his head, his lips quirking with self-satisfaction, like my answer proved his theory. "This was a shot in the dark, but I'm pretty sure I'm right. And I think you just made it clearer to me." Ash nodded to Warwick.

"About what?" I asked.

"I don't know how all this works or what it means." Ash swallowed. "But don't you find it curious the girl who brought Warwick back from the dead hears voices and blacks out in a place which holds thousands of *dead* people?"

Chapter 7

Dread dropped into my gut like sticky molasses, sliding slowly down, leaving a track of panic. Heat burst over my cheeks and down my neck like I had been called out for something I thought I was hiding.

"It's not just me she's brought back to life," Warwick said low, but every syllable was like a bullet.

"What?" Ash's head snapped from Warwick to me.

"A cat." Warwick's penetrating stare burrowed into me. "And there were others, weren't there?"

Looking away from the guys, I stared at a skull, its empty eyes feeling like they were looking straight through me, seeing the truth.

"Kovacs?"

"It doesn't matter." I tried to wiggle out of Warwick's grip without success.

"It doesn't *matter*?" Ash sputtered in shock. "The fact you can bring things back from the dead is not important?"

"I've never really brought anything back from the dead. Not fully anyway."

Both men stared at me.

"Okay! Fine! Yes, Andris said I brought back a cat when I was young."

"And..." Warwick tipped his head knowingly. I swallowed,

realizing he had seen what happened with Elek in the alley when we were trying to escape Sarkis's base.

"I might have started to bring back a few others," I mumbled, peering at my boots. "But I could have totally imagined it." Mio, Rodriquez, Aron, Elek, the cat Aggie, the woman in Killian's cell... the list was getting too long to ignore.

"Think we passed that a while back." Ash's hand brushed my cheek, warm and comforting, wiping a tear away. "I told you that you would feel like both life and death."

I hadn't even known I was crying, my terror turning into tears. "Can you tell me what it means?" I sniffed, rubbing my wet cheek on my shoulder. "What I am?"

"You are nothing I can explain. You are not fae, human, or even Druid." A worry line creased Ash's forehead. "But the more I understand about you, hopefully, the more we can figure it out. I told you, Brex, you are not alone."

*"Literally."* Warwick's apparition whispered hoarsely into my ear from behind, his touch gliding up my spine, my eyes flicking up to him. Warwick, as usual, showed no emotion, but his gaze burrowed into mine. *"I'm on your ass all the time now. You can't escape me. Dependent on me, aren't you, princess?"*

My nose flared, hating how weak and scared I felt, my defenses kicking in. "Let go."

Warwick scoffed, his tone condescending. "You sure, princess?"

"Fuck you. Let me go." I yanked my arm from his grasp.

It was instant.

A blinding flood crashed on me, nausea spinning my head, forcing my lids shut. So many voices hissed together into shrill noise, the sensation of ghostly hands clawing at me, battering me against the rocks as they all tried to get to me.

I felt a hand grab my arm, but this time it didn't stop their attack. I could feel thousands of spirits crowding me, taking me away from consciousness.

Then just as fast, they disappeared.

My lungs heaved for oxygen, my lashes fluttering open to see Warwick's hand on one arm, Ash's on the other, both men staring at me like a lab experiment.

"Interesting. My touch did nothing." Ash tipped his head, his tongue sliding over his lip. "But I guess it makes sense."

"What makes sense?" Warwick's grip on me felt like energy and balance were being pumped into my veins, clearing the sickness and darkness away, stabling my legs.

"That only your touch would protect her. You are each other's shields and swords."

"Fucking hell, Ash," Warwick growled. "Stop talking in riddles with your woo-woo shit. Just say it."

"You can take each other's pain away or at least ebb it. Share it. This," he nodded to where Warwick touched me, "is the same sort of thing." Ash turned his head to me. "What is happening when he lets go?"

I swallowed, knowing again where this was going. "They attack me..." I said quietly.

"The spirits?" Ash's question wasn't one at all. We all knew.

"Yes." I gulped roughly again. "There are so many of them. I can hear them, feel them trying to reach me." I shook my head. "But this has never happened to me before. I've been around graveyards and dead people, but I've never felt them like this."

"That was what, maybe a dozen in a graveyard?" Ash snorted. "This small church has over *forty thousand* bones in one confined space, not counting the cemetery outside." His voice lowered. "I can feel their energy too. Tree fairies can feel life and death in everything. I don't think they are trying to attack you so much as they are drawn to you... moths to flames... like we all are."

A noise came from Warwick's throat, his stern gaze on Ash.

"Calm down, big man." Ash huffed with amusement at his friend, turning his focus back on me. "I don't think they mean you any harm. But so many coming at you at once can be overwhelming."

"How do I stop it?" I sputtered.

"I don't think you can stop it." Ash bit down on his lip. "You have to control and dictate the way they interact with you. Show them who's in charge."

"In charge? Dictate?" I shook my head. "What do you mean?"

"Think of them like a classroom full of disobedient school children who need a strong teacher to get them in line. To understand their boundaries."

"Why now? Why have I never heard or felt ghosts before?"

"Again, I don't have an answer to that, but I'm wondering if something awoke when you two met. I mean, this all started then, right?" Ash looked between us.

69

It did all lead back to when Warwick and I met; things started to change after that. It was solidifying the bond that tied us together— whether or not we wanted it.

"Whatever the reason, it doesn't change the fact they are drawn to you. You have to make sure they know you're the boss."

"How about I leave this place?" I motioned around with my free arm.

"You could, but I don't think it will go away. If death is attracted to you, then you need to start learning to handle it. The Eastern Bloc is one big graveyard." Ash cocked his brow to where Warwick touched me. "And I doubt you want to depend on him every time it does."

*Depend.* Ash said the key word, hitting my mind with utter clarity and determination. Fuck no, I didn't.

"What do I do?" I lifted my chin.

"You have to confront them. With his help at first." He nodded to where Warwick touched me. "In intervals until they understand you are dominant. In control."

"Him?" My eyes narrowed. "Why can't you help me?"

"Because I can't help you block them like he does. You two are connected." He took one step back. "Plus, I need to go back to Budapest."

"What?" Confusion creased my face. "Why?"

"What the fuck do you mean you're going back to Budapest?" Warwick snarled, his fingers pinching my elbows.

"Well, the reason I brought you guys up here..." Ash paused. "Before we got distracted with the issue of the dead clamoring for her. I had an idea..." Ash rubbed his chest absently. "It might not even work. But you remember how your uncle said the nectar disappeared, and no one knows where it is or what happened to it?"

"Yes," I said slowly, watching Ash closely, feeling prickles of nervousness.

"There is something that might..." His mossy green eyes met mine, a tiny grin hinting on his lip. "It might tell us."

"You mean... ?" I didn't know if terror or excitement was bubbling in my stomach.

"The fae book." Ash dipped his head, his voice lowering as he looked around, trying to see if anyone had come in on us.

"You think it would know?" Warwick shifted on his feet, turning more toward Ash, his hand firmly on me. "It would show you?"

"It knows everything. The problem is... if it is willing to share this information. I thought it might show *her*." Ash tipped his head at me. "It's worth a shot, don't you think?" Ash's whispered voice rose slightly. "If people are out searching for it again, imagine if it fell into the wrong hands. If this nectar is everything they say it is, it would be as desired as the treasures of Tuatha Dé Danann. Especially for humans. People would kill for this. Start *wars* for it."

Warwick jerked around, glowering at Ash, his head shaking.

I had heard about the four treasures of Tuatha Dé Danann—another name for the Otherworld—a sword, cauldron, spear, and stone. The treasures were treated like sacred items. Hardly ever talked about. Whispered in dark corners like scary ghost stories.

It was ancient fae folklore. Four treasures were made by high Druids for fae kings as gifts. Unfortunately, anything with so much power tended to turn people into monsters, breeding power, greed, and death. Druids separated the treasures and hid them from the fae. Queen Aneira later slaughtered almost all the Druids for their secret. Around the time of the fae war, it was rumored some pieces had been found and that Queen Aneira was actually killed by the current ruler, Queen Kennedy, a Druid, using the sword of Nuada, which still sparked hate. I guess many thought Aneira's niece, "the rightful ruler," should have been queen.

The treasures were said to have been destroyed while others thought they were hidden again, still out there to discover. Just like the nectar, the human's equivalent to the fountain of youth. One that would destroy if fallen into the wrong hands.

"If I leave now, I could be back in a day." Ash's voice tugged me back to him.

"Wait... what?" I rubbed my brow. "You left it in your house?"

"It's well protected. It's not like I'd carry such a huge weight around where anyone could take it from me," Ash responded.

"Exactly. With the fae doors, bad roads, and gangs hunting the motorway..." Warwick shook his head. "It's too dangerous to do by yourself. You almost drove right into the fae door on the way here."

Before the Otherworld and Earth came together, fae doors had still been here in specific places. They were more easily accessible on days like Samhain, when the layers between worlds were thinnest. But when the two worlds merged, it caused thousands of slits in the atmosphere, creating doors everywhere. I had yet to see one, but we lost people to them all the time. They were invisible to human eyes and easy to step in by accident, the person never to be seen again, lost in the endless maze. They were said to be like black holes, and even fae vanished into them.

"Don't worry, Mom." Ash nudged Warwick's shoulder. "I'll be fine. Be a fast trip. And you know it's worth a shot." Ash lifted his shoulder. "Actually, be better without you. You're like a giant neon sign." We all knew Ash was full of shit. Though Warwick was a beast, he was fast, deadly, and was intimidating enough for gangs to question attacking him. "It's not like I haven't saved your ass a time or two."

Warwick tipped his head to the side.

"Come on, there had to be at least once." Ash huffed, already backing away from us. "Plus, man, you are kind of stuck here for the moment." He winked at us. "Maybe a good time to work your shit out."

"Ash..." Warwick warned, starting to step toward him, dragging me with him.

Ash grinned wider, giving us a salute before jogging up the dozen steps and out the church door, disappearing into the night.

"Ash!" Warwick bellowed, but only silence responded until we heard the firing of a motorcycle engine, the sound of it rumbling away. "Stupid asshole!"

He ran his free hand through his hair. It was down and hung loosely around his face. His aqua eyes rose until they met mine.

The air shifted in the room with the realization we were alone, with no buffer and no immediate threat to deal with.

Just us.

Every wall slammed up between us, pushing us the farthest we could be from each other and still be touching.

Resentment. Anger. Hatred. Desire.

And an unwanted connection.

I had so much to say, but nothing would leave my mouth. I would not ask for his help dealing with the ghosts. I wouldn't ask him for anything.

A growl reverberated from Warwick's throat. He pulled me in, his jaw clenching.

"What?" I snapped.

"You were supposed to stay in the *fucking* house with Ash." He gritted through his teeth. "Was that so *fucking* hard?"

"Excuse me?" My shoulders rose, moving away.

"You heard me." He took back the space between us, using his height to loom over me. "But even that you couldn't seem to do."

72

"Because I don't take orders from you." I sneered back. "Don't you dare treat me like I'm some helpless woman who will bend to your will, bat my lashes, and swoon. If that's what you want, you're looking at the wrong girl, you misogynistic asshole."

"Fucking hell, woman." He pinched his nose, a snarl rolling underneath. "This has nothing to do with the fact you are a woman. Fae don't think women are less; fae women are brutal warriors. We think of *humans* as less."

"Coming from a guy who's half human."

He grunted, annoyance rolling his head back. "I'd ask *anyone* who was being *hunted* by various groups to stay fucking indoors."

"Not sure why you give a shit." I hated how bitterness and jealousy sprouted in my tone. "You looked perfectly content. She's beautiful... and he looks just like you, by the way. Thought you were against marriage?"

"Who said I was married?"

"Ahhh... so she's a woman you got pregnant and abandoned, so you can be free to fuck everything else?"

Warwick's jaw rolled, anger rolling over him so intensely, then he stilled. Any normal person would be terrified, but I continued to needle him.

"Are they why you turned me over to Killian?" I tried to keep my voice steady. Unaffected. "For your child and... what would you call her?" I didn't know what she was to him, except she stared at him like he was her whole world.

He yanked me into him, our bodies fully lining up, the jolt of adrenaline zinging down my veins.

"You have no fucking clue what you're talking about," he growled, fury firing in his features. "So, for once, do what I say, and shut the hell up."

My lids lowered at his demand. A dark smile hinted on my lips as I went up on my toes, my lips brushing the shell of his ear. I could feel him inhale, his fingers pressing harder into my arm.

I nipped at his skin, my breath heavy in his ear. I felt his desire curling around me, making my lips twitch.

My breath raked down his neck. "No." I stepped back, my phantom self was punching a fist into his abdomen with all the force I could muster, using his as well.

His back curved, his lungs sucking in at the sudden assault, fingers dropping away from me.

Freeing me.

73

"Good night." The spirits came for me instantly, so I didn't hesitate. Turning around, my legs wobbled, my head pounding, but I shoved through, hurrying back down the stairs, slipping into the bunker and away from Warwick and the ghosts of the Bone Church.

I made it all the way back to my room. The giddiness of getting away from him tripped me through my door and into the tiny quiet room, and I locked the door behind me.

Opie and Bitzy were nowhere to be found, which worried me. I hoped they wouldn't get into mischief here; I was already walking a thin line.

For one moment, I believed I was safe.

Stupid.

The lock snapped like it was plastic, and the thin metal door swung open, slamming into the wall with a boom, my heart leaping into my lungs as I spun around. Warwick's corded physique barreled toward me; his rolled forward, fury bristling off him.

Shit! Standing my ground, I felt my own anger rise, my defenses stacking up my vertebrae.

"What the fuck, Kovacs?" He growled, not stopping, shoving me back into the wall.

"What?" I held my chin up, glaring back at him. "I said good night, didn't I?"

His jaw ground as he slammed his palm next to my head. "You can shove your good night up your ass."

"What the fuck is your problem?"

"You want to know what my problem is?" He growled, leaning into me. "You fuckin' disappear on me. Ash and I thought you were kidnapped... being tortured. You cut me off, Kovacs. I couldn't reach you," he spat. "And when I do, you are being attacked by a hundred soldiers with guns in a train station with your new boyfriend."

"He's cute, huh?" I sneered back. He didn't need to know Luk would rather sleep with him than me.

He snorted derisively, his other hand pinning me against the wall, locking me in.

"I couldn't give a shit who you fuck, princess." He leaned in until his mouth was barely an inch from mine. "How many times do I have to tell you? You do nothing for me."

"Really?" I lifted an eyebrow, my hands staying at my sides as my phantom ones glided down his chest under his clothes, tracing down his insanely ripped abs until I reached his deep V-line. His muscles flexed and tightened under my touch, his dick pushing against the fabric of his pants.

"Yeah, seems like I disgust you."

"Stop." He growled, anger bursting off him.

"Make me," I challenged, my imaginary thumb skimming over the head of his cock, able to feel the pre-cum, warm on my fingertips. I sucked in, feeling the heat throbbing from him, the softness of his skin. The pad of my finger traced up the pulsing vein along his cock, causing it to twitch and grow harder. Desire flooded through me, hitching my breath, the game flipping on me. I was supposed to be toying with him, but need hardened my nipples and strummed between my legs like a heartbeat.

He inhaled sharply. "Kovacs." He rumbled under his breath, full of warning, but he didn't make one move or block my touch. "I. Said. Stop."

"*And I* said *make me.*" Without moving, my invisible hands wrapped around him, a groan heaving from his chest. My mind kept reminding me he had a family, to do the right thing, but I couldn't seem to care.

My spine pinned to the wall, I stared defiantly at him while I reached through our link.

He jerked as my phantom tongue traced up his dick, following the vein, feeling it pulse. A low growl rose in his chest as I tasted the top of him, saltiness exploding on my actual tongue.

"Fuucck." His hands rolled into fists by my head, his voice gravelly.

"Why are you here? Why come all this way to find me?" I asked while the other me licked up the other side of his cock, playing with him. "Why bother? You feel nothing for me, right?"

He snarled, his shoulders rolling, his muscles trying to lock down and not respond to what I was doing.

Inside my head, I dug my nails into his ass, pulling him in, my lips sliding over him, taking him into my mouth.

"Fuuuuuuucck." A huff pulled from his nose, his chest heaving for air, his teeth grinding together. "Ko-vacs."

"I saw you with them." While I spoke, I could still feel him in my mouth, feel every pulse of his massive size. Wetness seeped from me, need crashing through every nerve, spinning my head. Which only pissed me off. I was supposed to be in control.

"You have a family—a son," I sneered, anger climbing into my bones. "So why do you care what happens to me or come all this way to find me? I don't take anyone's seconds."

"Coming from the girl whose mouth is wrapped around my cock right now." His hand dug into the back of my head, yanking it back roughly, spiking pain and pleasure, his other hand squeezing around my throat.

"I'm not doing a thing," I taunted, using the excuse he used on me while I sucked him harder, a guttural noise coming up his throat. "I'm just standing here."

"Really?" His fingers dug into my throat. He thrust his hips forward with a grunt, his ghost fingers pushing my head down crudely, forcing more of his massive size down my throat. Even in my mind, I could feel myself choke, my eyes watering, not able to take it all. I cut the link, fury wrinkling my nose.

A malicious smirk hinted on his mouth, knowing he won. "You can't have my dick down your throat and take the morally superior ground. It's not a good look for you. I know you, Kovacs, you are twisted and fucked up; stop pretending to be a good girl. We both know you're not."

"Fuck you," I growled, wiggling against his hold.

"You wouldn't recover from it."

"Get the hell off me." I shoved at his chest, not moving him an inch.

"Be honest. Me having a family wouldn't stop you from fucking me right now."

The admittance of who they were slashed across me like a knife.

*He has a child. A woman he loves? Gods, Brex, what are you doing?*

Recalling the fight at the train station, using his energy, I slammed my palms into his chest. With the sensation of him gliding through, licking at my nerves and pumping my muscles with adrenaline, I turned it back on him. His body stumbled back, colliding with a wall.

Not hesitating, I darted for the door, my hand touching the metal knob.

A strangled cry rose from my throat, his arms sweeping around my waist, my body flung back, crashing onto the mattress.

"Fucking hell!" Warwick climbed over me, pinning my arms to the bed, the small bed groaning under our weight. "You are the most infuriating person I've ever met."

"Back at you!" I thrashed against his hold as he was forced to put more of his weight on me. "Get off me!"

"Stop moving." He groaned, pressing me down harder. "Like I'm not already hard enough."

"Good! Hope it breaks off." I continued to squirm and fight him, the weight of him heaving my chest, his erection rubbing against me, driving my teeth into my bottom lip. "Probably the only thing your mate actually likes about you."

"You want to hear about how I make my *mate* scream?" He stressed the word, making me flinch as if I had been lashed. It was torture, pain, but I also couldn't hide the fact it seemed to turn me on. *What the hell is wrong with me?* "Want to know how hard and good I fuck her?" He ground into me, my lashes fluttering, my cheeks flushing with need. His hands were locked on my wrists, but I also could feel fingers trail down my throat, brushing over my nipples. Teeth nipped at my inner thigh, a tongue dragging up, stopping right at my folds.

A groan stuck in my throat, my hips widening without my permission.

Aching.

Desperate.

"How feral she gets when I lick her pussy?" The sensation of his tongue sliding through me rolled my eyes back, making me feel every bit the wild animal he was describing.

"How her pussy clenches around my dick, her body twitching, screaming like a banshee as she comes..."

Against my will, my mouth parted, my lungs dragging in air.

"You want that, Kovacs?"

Fuck yes.

"No." I snarled. "You might have no morals or care about your family, but I respect myself more than that."

"You're a fucking liar." He snorted, his hips moving as he dragged over me. It was as if I could feel him bare, his cock sliding through me. My back arched, responding with painful desire as I pushed up to meet him, showing what a pathetic hypocrite I was. "You don't give a shit about morals; you are as dark and depraved as me. You just haven't admitted it to yourself yet."

The feel of his tongue sliced deep inside me. Oh. Gods.

"Please..." I begged, not knowing which I was begging for—to stop or keep going.

He growled, rolling into me again, shredding a violent shiver down my spine.

Doing nothing more than pinning me to the bed and rolling his hips into me fully clothed, I felt consumed. Every nerve burned; every inch of my skin pulsed. He incinerated me inside and out. He was everywhere. Stealing my mind, body, and soul.

And I wanted nothing more than for him to finish me. Burn every last piece to the ground.

Our eyes locked.

I couldn't move or speak, his mouth barely a breath from mine.

His chest heaved in and out, his eyes tracking mine. Desire assaulted every molecule, licking and stroking the air with ruin.

Something deep inside me hummed with life. With death. The two sides circling and lashing out in an endless battle.

I wanted him to kiss me. To thrust inside me so deeply there would be no beginning or end.

His mouth lowered, the heat from his lips grazing mine.

I craved to take everything like I did the other day. Instead of my shadow touching his body, I dove underneath, grazing his mind, his soul, reaching for his truth.

I barely slipped under his skin when I felt energy slammed back into me, engulfing me.

Mind-blowing pain.

Blinding pleasure.

Intimate. Raw. It broke me down to a single shred of existence, like being hit by a strike of lightning. The power infused us, blinding, painful, but filled me so full only the deepest, rawest carnal passion thumped and ripped through me.

A howl echoed through the room at the same time a cry tore from my lips, the energy penetrating and winding around us, and I quickly retreated, the extreme emotions overwhelming every sense.

"Fuck!" he bellowed, scrambling off me with a snarl, his lids lowered on me like I was some demon. "What the fuck was that?"

My breath was ragged; I wondered the same thing. "I-I don't know."

He stared down at me, his chest heaving. "Don't ever fuckin' do it again," he rasped out, fury and disgust curling his lip.

"Don't worry." Sitting up, my lip rose. "I won't. I want nothing to do with you."

"Good," he snapped, his shoulders still surging. "Let's keep it that way."

He turned abruptly, slamming out of the door, leaving me gasping, horny, scared, and rejected.

Which assembled into one pissed-off bitch.

# Chapter 8

Sleep abandoned me, leaving me out in the cold, harsh land of my thoughts.

Tossing and turning, I searched for reprieve over and over, only to end up even more restless and cranky. My head filled with everything that had been going on, though one thing seemed to dominate it, one person, but I was trying really hard not to acknowledge the endless space he was taking up in my mind.

I gave up around three a.m. I turned on my lamp and sat up, hugging my arms around my legs. Warwick wasn't the only thing churning in my brain. I was also worried about Ash. Wondering if he was back in Budapest yet, if he was okay. Andris, Birdie, and especially Scorpion were constantly circling through my thoughts. Were they safe? Found a new base? Andris was probably freaking out, thinking something horrible happened to me.

The one person who would know I was at least alive was Scorpion.

Breathing out, I laid my head back against the wall, shutting my lids, trying to reach out to him. The link was still there, which told me he was alive, but I couldn't actually see him or project myself to where he was. Our connection wasn't strong.

Was it because I was buried underneath thousands of energy-sucking spirits? I couldn't link to Warwick when I was down here before either. Only when I was away at the train station was he able to find me.

Which landed on the big issue really bothering me: I attracted the dead. Had brought some back to life.

Who the fuck could do that? Not even fae could, except a high Druid/obscurer, and they could only bring back them half back. Where they were alive but living half-lives. Shells. Tortured souls who were neither alive nor dead. And the theory that necromancers brought people back from the dead was slightly misconstrued; they just reanimated skeletons. There was no soul or anything left.

Druid or necromancer, all their victims were zombie-esque.

Warwick and Scorpion were neither. And I wasn't a Druid or a necromancer.

So, what the hell was I?

Rubbing at my face, I felt the draw to head upstairs. Like the ghosts were calling me to come play. Ash *did* tell me I needed to challenge them. Take control. The curiosity of talking with them simmered under my skin. Would I be able to fully communicate with them? What if they could tell me what I was?

"Fuck it." I shoved back the covers, dressing quickly in a tank, cargo pants, and boots, tossing my hair into a ponytail before venturing out.

The halls were silent, most of the humans fast asleep, and many fae were probably out "hunting" for food, which usually meant humans in some form. Fae fed mainly off sex, emotions, or human sins for energy. The human/fae food pyramid was far from perfect, but I no longer looked at every fae as the devil now. They were only trying to survive like everyone else.

Going up the flights of stairs, the weight of each soul began to push down on me. This time I understood why I was so tired and nauseated when I got close to the surface. They could sense me and reached for me through the layer of soil between us.

Taking the last few steps, I crawled out of the crypt and into the Bone Church. The moment I did, the spirits came for me, rushing for me like a stampede. "No!" I ordered. "Stop."

They did not listen.

"No!" I shouted again. My muscles started to wobble, blackness seeping into my vision, my teeth clenching down. "Get back!"

More and more charged, the spirits brushing against my skin, their voices joining together like the hiss of static until it pounded in my head. A strangled cry broke from my lips.

"I said stop!" I screamed, my back curving over, vomit climbing up my throat. I fell to the ground, trying so hard to shield myself, but my energy continued to drain out quickly.

My gut knew they didn't mean to hurt me, but there were so many. They were ripping bits of my life away, sucking everything from me.

With utter clarity, I understood this was what I did to Warwick the other day, taking his energy. If the link hadn't been cut, would I have stopped? Would I have killed him? Because without a doubt, I felt in my soul this was what was happening now.

Leave it to me to die because I was too stubborn to ask for help.

My face hit the stone floor, my conscious thoughts slipping away.

*"No! Get the fuck up, princess."* A deep voice lifted my lids, and Warwick's shadow loomed over me. *"Get the hell up and fight!"*

*"I can't."* Every bone felt like jelly. I just wanted to sleep. Forever.

*"Fuck that,"* he growled. *"You had the capability and strength to tear through time and space to save me, and you're going to give up now?"* He squatted, his anger igniting his eyes. *"You have more power in you than you know. Use me! I will not lose you. Not to a bunch of ghosts,"* he bellowed. *"Now get the fuck up,* sotet démonom. *FIGHT!"*

He reached down and touched my face, and I felt his force filling me, giving me strength.

My lids burst open, a gasp tearing from my throat. Power snapped down my spine, and I sat up, energy exploding from me. The dark church burst with light, crackling like lightning, exposing the jumble of ghosts surrounding me in the shadows. No faces or even bodies, but their presence, their need for me, hazed the air.

"Get. Back!" The order boomed from my chest. It was like a bomb went off. The spirits flew back, the voices in my head going silent. Energy discharged from me, crackling the air, rumbling like thunder, as I rose to my feet, my shoulders rolling back. "Now!"

"You do not touch me or take my energy unless invited." The force of my voice made them slink back farther. "Do. You. Understand?"

I felt like they did. A connection with them settled deep in my bones. They knew who the alpha was.

It was like a switch, the strange light fading out. My body sagged over, taking in deep breaths, my hands going to my knees. *What the fuck just happened?*

A noise near the stairs twisted my head to the side. Aqua eyes burned into me through the dark. Warwick stood on the last step, watching me. Rage and another emotion I couldn't grasp vibrated off the beast like a drum. His gaze moved over my figure, making every place it touched shiver. Then his eyes landed back on mine.

Straightening up, my chin rose in a challenge. An unspoken threat. Daring him to test me. I would not let him hurt or take any more from me either.

"I didn't mean to take from you."

"You didn't," he rumbled, his chest moving up and down. "I tried to help you... but that was all you."

*All me?* How was that possible?

Swallowing down the fright, I lifted my head higher.

"You think I need you, but I don't, Farkas. I don't need anyone."

His eyes tapered, his shoulders rolled back, and a deep growl rumbled in his throat. That was the only warning I got. He barreled toward me like a train, fury streaking his face. As if I survived the ghosts only to become his victim.

His kill.

His name caught on my tongue as he crashed into me. His hands clutched my arms, my spine slamming against the wall, his body pressing into mine.

"You got it all wrong, Kovacs." Anger and desire stormed through his eyes as a deep growl shook the room, raking down every nerve and bone in my body. "It's *us* who needs *you.*"

His fingers curled around my ponytail, yanking my head back roughly. Ecstasy and pain sizzled down my vertebrae. His free hand slid up my jaw, cupping the back of my head.

"Warwick?" His name came out a question. A want. A plea.

"For once, princess, shut up." His hands clutched my ass, lifting me up, my legs wrapping around him.

"Make me."

His mouth crashed into me like an explosion.

Life. Death.

Love. Hate.

With just a kiss, everything ignited, making me realize we had not actually kissed before. The feel of his actual lips on mine was ruthless and vicious, snapping fire and electricity into my nerves.

Pure pleasure.

Pure pain.

Downright feral.

The barricade we tried to keep up between us splintered into pieces, dousing us in white-hot flames, making me more desperate. My nails raked through his hair as I pulled myself closer to him, demanding more.

"Fuck." His fingers dug into my head, his tongue slipped and curled with mine, creating a deep moan in my chest. "Why does kissing you feel this fucking good?" His hands wrapped around my neck, tipping my face to his, his eyes burning into mine.

Hungry.

They would devour and rip me into shreds.

I wanted every bit of my destruction. And I would be his.

Staring down at him, I dropped back to my feet. His thumb pushed harder into my throat, the pulse matching the need beating in my pussy. I unbuttoned his pants, shoving them down his thick, muscular thighs. My body responded with desperation as my hand took hold of his massive erection.

Fuck. He felt a hundred times larger, hotter, and thicker in my actual hands.

In my mind, my mouth covered him, sucking and licking as I stroked him. His lids fluttered as he leaned in closer to me. "Kovacs." His voice cracked as he greedily captured my mouth again while I felt his tongue also glide down my stomach to my core, licking through me. A gasp erupted from my lips.

Maybe we just needed to get this out of our system, then it would go away.

"Fuck me, Farkas. *Now.*"

My demand was a detonator. We went from needy to vicious and frenzied.

His fingers ripped my tank over my head. Our kisses were frantic, the kind that would devastate and destroy. He bit into my bottom lip, driving my desire for him into a fury.

He growled, his hands breaking the zipper of my pants as he ripped them down, stripping me until I was bare. His gaze glowed as his eyes and fingers traced over my small curves.

I understood. Screw foreplay.

The need was so feral it choked the air. Even the spirits stirred around us, their energy pumping, adding to the electricity in the room. Zapping and hissing.

Ripping off his shirt and getting rid of his shoes, he swept me up again, my legs circling him, his cock throbbing against me, making me more desperate. My head went back as he kissed down my neck, my nails clawing at his back.

His warm mouth covered my breast, arching me farther into the wall. The bones fashioned into the stone dug into my spine.

Life and death.

It branded us.

Owned us.

Created us.

This man would consume me. Devour and destroy me.

He'd burn me to the ground, but I would rise up from the ashes and demand more.

"Warwick..." I moaned as his tongue flicked my nipple, his lips sucking. Fuck, this man's mouth alone could obliterate me.

He was everywhere, imaginary and real, gliding inside and out, twisting me into nothing but desire. My mouth opened in a silent cry as his real fingers slipped inside and curled into me.

"Fuck, princess," he hissed, pumping harder into me.

"Gods..." My arms wrapped tighter around him, trying to end the ache in my pussy; the hunger was turning to pain. "Now."

"I'm not going to be gentle." He growled, pushing me back into the wall, our eyes meeting. His hand pressed against the wall, the tip of him hinting at my opening, making me try to climb higher, my emotions so tuned I felt like a cord about to snap. The need for him was something I had never experienced before, so intense I became savage.

"Don't you dare," I grumbled, scratching his skin until I drew blood. "I think you know I am far from fragile. Death doesn't even want to fuck with me." I glared into his eyes, challenging him. "Do you, *Wolf*?"

Like I summoned the beast, an animalistic snarl reverberated off the walls, his mouth taking mine, his imaginary tongue sliding down my body, sucking my clit, forcing my chest to heave.

With a growl, he thrust deep into me. I experienced every inch of his skin, his soul, his heat, as he slammed into me.

*Oh. Holy. Fuck.*

"Fuuuuuccck!" I heard him bellow while the same cry ripped from my lungs.

We both froze at the intensity. Blinding light and flashes of scenes went through my mind too fast to catch. My body was overwhelmed with so much pleasure and pain, tears pricked my eyes.

84

The ache of his size mixed with the unbelievable bliss. It was so much; every muscle started shaking. I could feel him inside, creating surges of electricity shattering through nerves, tearing oxygen from my lungs, like a thousand mini orgasms building together.

I had been with enough men to know this was not normal... not even in our abnormal situation.

A vein bulged from his neck, and I could feel the same blood pumping through the vein in his cock, turning me even more delirious. A deep sound hummed from his chest. His grip on my hips bruised my bones as he thrust in deeper. A roar boomed off the walls, his chest heaving like he was feeling everything I was.

"Kovacs." His hands went to the wall beside my head, and for a moment, his legs dipped. "What the fuck?" His voice was like gravel. "I can't hold back."

"Don't." I snarled, needing him to let go. "Give me everything."

He dove in so deeply a bellow broke from my lips. He grunted, taking my hands and pinning them above my head. I grabbed onto the bones decorating the wall behind me, holding on as his mouth sucked my bouncing tits as he sank in deeper. Fucking me so hard, moans I couldn't even control heaved from my lungs.

"Harder!" I demanded, though my body already felt like it was splitting in half in the most delicious, unbelievable way. He was everywhere. Inside and out. Completely consuming me, ripping me from reality. The feel of him skated over every inch of my body, his teeth biting, his tongue licking, his hands touching. And I gave it back with a vengeance.

The spirits zoomed around us, whipping up more electricity, rocking the skeleton chandelier. Frantic and devouring, the energy coming from us crackled in the air. It was like I had been electrocuted. Gasping, I bucked against him, meeting his passion with my own, his cock throbbing deep inside me. The sound of him fucking me, our ecstasy resonating off the stone, embedded into the bones.

The bones in the wall scraped and dug into my own, cutting into my flesh, my blood spreading over them, becoming part of me.

I felt my orgasm scratching and clawing its way through my body, shattering what was left of me. The tsunami, if I let myself fall, would obliterate me. I understood that, but I also couldn't stop it.

"No... not yet," he gritted through his teeth, pulling out of me, placing me back on my feet. Before I could object, he flipped me around, pressing my breasts into the wall of bones, plunging back into me so hard, a hoarse moan rasped up my throat.

His hand wrapped through my hair, pulling my head back, sending shivers down me as he drove in harder, my naked body rubbing and smearing against emblems of death.

It was morbid and perverse, which only made it more erotic.

There was such a thin line between life and death. Deceased and living. And Warwick and I trampled that line, suspended between both.

"You like that, princess?" He growled in my ear as he forced me firmer into the wall, rubbing my core against a bone. "You are so fucking twisted and dirty." He yanked my head to the side, his mouth consuming mine hungrily.

I felt his tongue everywhere, flicking my clit, while his mouth claimed mine, he nipped down.

"Oh gods!" A bellow coiled my spine as my pussy clamped around him, pulsing and taking.

"*Szent fasz!*" *Holy fuck!* He roared, going even deeper, spiraling me out into oblivion.

Like earlier, light burst through me, a crack of lightning. Electricity took over every molecule, rupturing every nerve, taking me away from this world.

Light. Darkness.

Life. Death.

Nothing. Everything.

Suddenly my brain flashed with an image of a screaming baby coated in afterbirth, the night sky igniting in vibrant colors above the infant, then it switched to a man lying motionless in blood-drenched grass. Warwick... his eyes closed, his form black and burned, his neck at an unnatural angle, the same night sky cracking and glowing over him.

His eyes burst open, and like in the book, he looked right at me.

"*Sötét demonom,*" he growled, his hand touching my face.

The moment he did, a booming howl came from behind me, bringing me back to myself. Warwick drove in so deeply I felt myself fall over again. A piercing cry broke free as I felt him release inside me, my fingers curling around the ribs bones to keep myself standing. Every pulse was hot and claiming, reaching far deeper than skin.

He invaded.

He invaded and consumed me, touching me far deeper than skin. Destroyed. Took, burned, and razed me to the ground.

Nothing would ever come close to the feel of him. My chest heaved with the utter destruction, the bliss shattering everything I knew or had understood.

"Fuck, princess," he growled in my ear. He swept my hair over my shoulder, his chest moving in and out against my spine, his breath skating down my neck over my sweaty skin. "What the fuck was that?"

Still deep inside me, he took in a stilted breath. It took me a moment to realize it wasn't just me shaking.

"I-I don't know." My voice was raw, my mind a jumbled mess of bliss and fear. What the hell *was* that?

He stepped back, pulling out of me, instantly making me want him back. A hollow feeling. Empty.

Twisting around, I watched his firm ass stroll toward his trousers, snatching them up. He paused, leaning over a stand holding skulls, the chandelier above his head still swinging. Taking a deep inhale, his back muscles flexed with every intake.

I sensed his confusion and the fear he was trying to hide and felt every wall he was trying to put up between us again.

"What the fuck are you?" he mumbled, more to himself than to me.

I couldn't talk, my mind and body still in pieces.

"You fucking lit up." He whirled back to me, his lids narrowed, almost accusatory.

"I what?"

"When you were fighting back the spirits..." His gaze traced over my naked form, the feel of his fingers brushing over my hips and breasts, forcing me to suck in. "I was like a fucking moth to a flame." He prowled toward me until his toes hit mine, his nose flaring. His chest pushed out with fury. "*I* couldn't stop." He snarled at me. "I'm a legend. A warrior. Death can't fuckin' touch me... but I *couldn't* fight you."

"Maybe *I'm* death," I snapped back.

"No." His hand clamped down on the back of my head, bringing our faces an inch apart. His chest brushed my nipples, hardening them. "You feel like fucking life. Like air in my lungs."

He yanked me into him, his mouth finding mine, savagely devouring me. Flames shot up my spine, melting me into him.

Warwick didn't kiss. He devoured. Conquered.

Owned.

And I knew I would never have enough. His lips parted mine; his tongue deepened our kiss. His hand twisted into my hair, digging into my scalp, yanking out my ponytail, letting my hair tumbling loosely down my back.

"I'm no better than them," he muttered against my mouth. "A fiend... the devil clamoring to drain everything from you. Destroying you." He tugged on my bottom lip. "*Never* having enough."

"Good." My nails dragged around to his ass, pulling him into me. "Because I'm not your angel of mercy, Farkas. I'm not good. Like you said, I'm dark and twisted. I don't care about morals or the fact you have a family. I'm your dark demon."

A growl vibrated off the walls as his mouth seized mine, kissing me so powerfully I could feel it through every inch of my bones. His fingers laced through my long strands, yanking my head to look up at him.

"My family," he grunted. "I would do anything for them. *Anything*. They are the last bit of me I have left in this world." His grip tightened as he felt me trying to pull back. "He's my nephew... that woman is my half-sister."

"What? Your half-sister?" I tried to jerk back, but he kept me close. "Why didn't you tell me? You—you let me believe she was your lover!"

"You were the one who ran with that idea, accusing me without even asking."

"Why wouldn't I?" I snapped. "The boy in your arms... he looked so much like you, and she was so beautiful and stared at you like you were her universe." Now that I recalled, she had the same dark features as the boy, as Warwick. My brain twisted it to see only one option. "You betrayed me. Gave me to Killian."

"I'd betray anyone for them." His fingers wrapped tighter in my hair. "Killian was using them as leverage." Warwick's lips rose in a snarl. "He hid them from me while I was in Halálház, making sure I behaved. Spied for him." He leaned closer into me. "If I traded you, he'd let them go, let me be free. Their location was in the envelope he gave me." He growled, his forehead hitting mine. "I would give anything up for them. I *still* would."

I actually understood. I would have probably done the same.

"I'd kill, betray, or destroy anyone who hurt them. I swore on my mother's death I would take care of Eliza. And now Simon. And yet I hesitated for three days—*three* fucking days. Every morning I would go to meet Killian, to make the arrangement... and stop. Find myself turning around..." His gaze burned into mine, his jaw straining. "Because of you."

My throat tightened, swallowing roughly at his admission, the mix of anger and passion swirling in his words and face.

I wanted to be mad. To hate him for what he did to me, but I couldn't. If anything, his loyalty to his family caused my heart to stumble over itself, which speared fear through my chest. To "get this out of our system" was one thing. Falling for the mythical Warwick Farkas was another.

Something I could never do.

I wasn't that stupid.

"Well." Clearing my throat, I glanced away. "You should have told me."

"Why?" He grinned roguishly. Taking my hand, he wrapped it around his growing erection, his hot skin pulsing in my palm. "I get fucking hard seeing you jealous," he rumbled in my ear, sending goosebumps down my flesh. Still glistening with me, his cock grew harder under my palm, desire clawing at me again. After the last orgasm, I didn't think there was any way in this century I could go this soon.

Warwick seemed to prove me wrong.

"I hate you." I glared at him, making him smirk.

"Take out all your hate on me then." He hitched me back up his body, my legs wrapping around him as he fell against a wall, sliding down until he was sitting, my body straddling his. "I want to feel your pussy greedily clamp down on my dick again, milking it fucking dry."

His blunt words heated my cheeks, stirring my body awake again.

Real and imaginary, we taunted each other. Hands touched, lips kissed, tongues licked, fingers stroked every patch of skin.

"Gods." He clenched his teeth as I kissed him while I also took his length into my mouth, sucking and humming. Deepening our kiss, I could feel his tongue between my legs, stealing my breath.

"Kovacs," he growled.

I lifted my hips, sliding slowly down him, his size filling me to the point of torture, jolting my nerves with desire. Both of us halted with a sharp inhale.

My head fell back, my lids fluttering. Nothing had ever felt so good, forcing me to walk the line of sanity.

His hips hitched up, hitting a different place inside me, forcing a hoarse gasp from my lungs.

*"Kibaszott pokolba!" Fucking hell!* His fingers gripped my hips as I rode him harder, hitting even deeper than we had before, the man's presence filling every inch of me. Haunting. Looming. I couldn't hide or run. He was everywhere and in everything.

Sparks danced around us, the bones clattering. Our vigor crashed into every surface, breaking like waves, drowning us.

My climax raced even faster to the edge than the first, knowing now how unbelievable it felt, though I never wanted to stop.

"I want to feel your fuckin' pussy clench around me, Kovacs." His fingers rubbed the bundle of nerves, lashing a scream from my lungs, blinding my vision.

Once again, scenes flashed behind my lids. A bawling newborn, the night sky exploding with magic over the fussing baby coated with afterbirth, the thick substance sliding into the dirt. Images jumped to Warwick dead in the field, the war bustling around him, me over him.

His eyes popped open, gasping with life. *"Sötét demonom."*

My vision snapped back. Aqua eyes stared back into mine, the same ones from that night. Our bodies were too close to bliss to stop, but I could see it in his eyes, the way he stared back at me with confusion and awe.

He had seen the same thing I did.

Again and again, he slammed into me. Sweat trickled between my breasts, his tongue catching the drops before he tossed me onto my back, pushing up my knees and fucking me with brutal ferocity. The skeletons jangled and clattered as our energy filled the small room.

My cries rose as I felt myself start to spin out of control.

"Now, my dark demon," he ordered. "Fucking come for me."

My body shattered on demand again, seizing around him intensely, and I burst into stardust. Bolts of lightning tingled my skin and twirled over my nerves. He exploded inside me, bellowing loudly, spurring another climax within me.

My mind blacked out, forgetting to breathe, nails digging and scratching into his back. I felt him pulse in me as my body continued to clench him like a vise. He fell on top of me with a groan.

We both stayed frozen as we came down, breaths heavy and panting.

"Holy shit," I whispered, dazed, no longer part of reality. Energy tingled and melted my muscles, my mind shattered. I could still feel him inside and around me.

"Yeah." Warwick blew out. Going up on his elbows on either side of my head, he lowered his head, kissing me. "I think I lost consciousness for a moment." He kissed me again before rolling off me, falling on his back with a huff, splaying out like he couldn't move. "Fuck, woman... I've been with human, fae, and mixed... sometimes six at a time—"

"Seriously?" I hit his chest, frowning.

He snorted, snatching my hand, his voice low and coarse. "Let's just say I've never blacked out. Not even close." He tugged me into his side.

"So that wasn't normal sex with a legend?" I arched one brow in a taunt.

"I didn't say that." He grinned cheekily. "But no one has ever been able to keep up or challenge me." His throat vibrated. "That's why I always needed so many."

"Are you saying little ol' me was enough to please the great Warwick Farkas?"

His body curled over mine, his lips claiming my own. "Whatever the fuck you are... you did more than that."

*Whatever the fuck you are.*

"What am I?" My teeth bit into my lip.

"I don't know." Tucking an arm under his head, he peered at me. "You aren't human."

Tears pricked my eyes. I had already known, but feeling the power inside me, the light...

"I know," I croaked.

"But you aren't fae."

Again, I somehow knew. But if I wasn't human or fae, what the hell could I be?

"Like me," he blew out, staring at the ceiling.

Another thing linking us. Were we the same nothing? No auras or species. Standing in a void of no man's land, between life and death.

The gray.

"Okay, I can't take any more of the postcoital crap." A man's voice snarled from the other side of the church. "I'm gonna vomit."

"Holy shit!" I yelped. Warwick and I scrambled to our feet.

Across the small church, a man lounged on a stone coffin, carving into an apple. His back leaned up against the wall, his ripped, dirty pant leg dangling on one side. He turned his head, tangled brown hair

91

hanging down his scruffy face, hazel eyes sliding to me. His gaze rolled down my naked figure, a smirk hitching the side of his mouth.

"Did I interrupt something?"

My mouth fell open, shocked to see the link to him so vivid and real.

"Scorpion?"

# Chapter 9

"Who the fuck are you?" Warwick shoved me behind him, trying to hide my naked figure, his words so heavy and rough they scraped the ground.

"Who the fuck are *you*?" Scorpion shot back.

"I won't ask again." Warwick's shoulders puffed, expanding his width and height, moving to Scorpion.

"Wait..." I blinked, stepping around Warwick, my attention snapping between the men. "You—you can see each other?"

"What do you mean?" Gesturing to him, Warwick's fury shot my way. "Of course I can see him."

"It means..." Scorpion jumped off the sarcophagus, strolling closer, chucking the apple. "I'm not really here." He dipped his head to me. "She brought me here. I was in the middle of a mission, and the next thing I know, I'm getting so fuckin' hard I was about to get myself off in front of everyone before I had to watch you two fuck like fiends."

Warwick's head shot to me, his jaw rolling. "You have a link to him?"

Right. I forgot to tell him about Scorpion.

"Um. Yes." I winced, wrapping my arms around my breasts. "But you aren't supposed to see him."

Warwick's lids narrowed, a hum quaking from his chest like a wild animal.

"That came out wrong." I held up my hand.

Warwick snarled, swiping up his T-shirt and tossing it to me while he stomped over to his pants, pulling them on, every muscle rippling with tension and anger.

Yanking his shirt over my head, it fell well past my thighs. I took in a deep breath, both men staring at me, waiting, their chests puffed, arms crossed, spraying their alpha scent at each other.

Both men were feral and rough with long hair and tattoos, but now seeing them together, it was clear one was king. Warwick dominated every space he was in, took over and governed every molecule of air. He wasn't fae or human, man or beast. He was something else entirely, and no one could even come close to him, though I had no doubt Scorpion would go down fighting to the death.

"So..." I rolled my lips together, wrapping my arms around myself as well. "It seems the night of the fae war, you weren't the only one I saved." I motioned at Scorpion.

"What?" Warwick's expression darkened. "You brought him back to life as well?"

Scorpion's head jerked to Farkas, his eyes widening. "Brought me back to life? What the fuck are you talking about?"

I gritted my teeth together. When I met Scorpion, I hadn't fully understood why we were linked.

"And you didn't tell me?" Warwick ignored Scorpion, his fury propelling toward me, stepping closer. "Who else did you bring back that night? Your harem is getting pretty full, princess."

"What do you mean *brought me back to life?*" Scorpion moved in with him.

"Whoa." I held up my hands in front of them, my shoulders back. "Both of you calm the hell down."

"Calm down?" Warwick growled. "How long have you known about him?"

"Since leaving Andris's base, but it wasn't until the book that I understood more about how."

"How what?" Scorpion exclaimed.

"The book?" Warwick barked an angry laugh. "The book showed you him too... and you just forgot to slip that in? You outright lied to me?"

"Lied?" I scoffed. "That's rich coming from you!"

"Damn, you work fast, Kovacs. What? You were at Sarkis's base a few hours at most?" Warwick ran his hand through his hair, starting to pace, sneering. "Surprised you haven't gathered more along the way. How long is the list of boyfriends you brought back to life now? You collecting us?"

"Fuck you." I pointed at him. "This isn't something I can control. And no, I didn't tell you about Scorpion, like you didn't tell me about your sister or Killian. Funny enough, I didn't think you'd handle it very well."

He was suddenly an inch from my face, oxygen thrashing through my lungs with a gasp. "And why do you think I give a shit about who else you're linked with?"

"You don't?" My brows arched up, mocking.

"No." He huffed, leaning back. "You could be linked to every fucking douchebag here. I couldn't give a fuck, Kovacs," he snarled, his shoulder brushing mine as he strode past me, stomping down the stairs and disappearing into the base.

My head dipped, trying to ignore the lash I felt across my heart.

Scorpion laughed, pulling my attention back to him. "Yeah..." He rubbed his chin, smirking. "*Sure,* he doesn't give a shit."

Tucking my hair behind my ear, I took in a deep breath. "Sorry if I brought you here. I've been trying to reach you and couldn't."

"Yeah." He dipped his head. "I was trying too. I could sense you were alive, but I couldn't get past that. Like you were too far or something."

"So why now?" I dropped my shoulders.

Scorpion scratched his pierced brow, a funny look on his face. "What?"

"I could feel you two." He folded his arms. "Fucking."

"I'm sorry?" I blinked, heat sprinting for my cheeks.

"I mean, I could feel it in my bones. Hear you... a streetlight flickered where I was standing, for fuck's sake. The link went from static to dropping me right here. I think it's you two. I couldn't reach you before. But now?" He threw his arms out, motioning around the room. "It's like I'm really here. And why couldn't I see him before and now I can? Who the fuck is he? Why do I feel like I know him?"

"Ask Birdie." I rubbed my head, feeling a headache coming on. Sex might have made the connection between Warwick and me more substantial and more complicated. We were so tangled already.

"Now tell me, what did he mean you brought me back to life?" Scorpion huffed.

95

Scrubbing roughly at my head, I sighed. "The night of the fae war... Maddox saw you get killed, right? You were hacked in half."

"How did you know that?" Scorpion's lids narrowed.

"Because..." I bit my lip. "Because I was there. I saw it happen too."

"I'm sorry?" He tilted his head. "What do you mean you were there? I thought you weren't even born yet."

"I was born that night, but... oh hell... there is no easy way to say this." I huffed. "I somehow went back as me currently and saved both you and Warwick in the past."

Scorpion blinked at me.

"Yes, I know it sounds crazy."

"No. It *is* crazy." He stepped back. "It's impossible."

"So should our connection be!" I gestured between us. "But right now, you are in Budapest *and* in a tiny church in Prague at the same time. Tell me that's not crazy and impossible."

"It is." He grunted.

"But yet, here you are." I fiddled with the hem of Warwick's T-shirt, his rich smell wrapping around me. "I know it sounds impossible, but I know I saved you that night. I watched you die, and then somehow magic from me went through you—" I stopped. Hearing it had me thinking I was crazy as well.

"Lightning," he muttered.

"What?" My head bounced up.

"I don't remember much about the night... but I dreamed about a white light... lightning going through me." He shook his head. "I never understood why before. So much is making more sense."

"Like what?"

"When I met you, it felt like I had before." He shifted on his feet, the conversation clearly making him uncomfortable. Vulnerable. "It felt the same as my dreams. A draw to you. A smell."

"Smell?" My throat croaked.

"Like life and death." He turned away from me. "It's hard to explain."

I chuckled darkly. "Like the moment between night and day breaking?" I repeated what Opie had articulated to me once.

Scorpion's jaw ticked. He didn't respond, but his head dipped, agreeing with my statement.

"Fuck," he eventually muttered, peering away from me. "I need to go."

96

"Wait." I took a step toward him. "How is everyone? Are you guys safe?"

"Yeah, we're still scattered, but Andris has a temporary place near the old Central Market." Scorpion frowned.

"What?"

"Just a lot of strange stuff happening."

"Like?"

"About a hundred fae and human bodies have been found floating in the Danube. The fae are drained of all bodily fluids." He clicked his teeth. "Some humans look like their brains melted out or something."

Dread plunged into my gut. Did I know one of those dead bodies?

"Birdie and I are on watch right now." He shrugged. "See you." Scorpion's words disappeared as fast as he did, the link cut off, leaving me alone with only the ghosts surrounding me.

A chill ran down my spine, and I wrapped my arms around my frame.

I knew exactly what happened to all those corpses in the river.

I just wasn't sure which side was dumping more of them.

Stepping out of the shower, I froze for a moment, seeing a familiar figure sitting on the sink counter, her fingers playing with the end of her blue braid.

"Oh, little lamb." A coy smile tugged at her lips, her dark blue eyes glinting. "Talk about the epitome of the lion eating the lamb... or, in this case, the wolf eating out the lamb."

"Kek." Wrapping the towel around me, I rolled my eyes, my shoulders dropping on a sigh. I strolled to the sink next to her, feeling like we stepped right back into Halálház. "It's not like that."

I had tried to reach out to Warwick, but he had firmed up his wall to keep me out. I knew I could push, force myself through, but stubborn or not, I didn't want to. I didn't do anything wrong.

"Please!" She laughed loudly. "You are a horrible liar. And too late. Everyone here not only felt it, but you guys had all the fire bulbs pulsing and climaxing with you guys."

"What?" It was the same thing Scorpion said happened where he was.

"Plus," she leaned back into the mirror, turning her head to look at me, her smirk growing. "I know what a Warwick-inspired orgasm feels like, remember?" Her eyes darkened, wagging her head. "Those nights when women were brought in for him. Fuck, he got all of us riled up. Like one big orgy."

Yeah, I remembered. And I recalled how, even when we didn't understand the link, he was coming to me then too. He was the one who had me screaming out, not the image of Caden.

"But this was a whole other level." She dramatically shook her shoulders in a shiver. "I haven't come that hard in years."

"Kek!" I palmed my face, my wet hair falling around my heated cheeks.

"What?" She laughed. "It's true. You guys were making the furniture hump each other!"

"Okay, wow... embarrassing."

"You shit in front of hundreds of people, were stripped, and watched people fuck in the showers next to you. This should be a prideful moment. I'd be ringing the bell of the church... oh wait... you guys did that too."

My mouth dropped.

She snorted. "You didn't hear it?"

"Noooo," I exclaimed, my face flaring red with the thoughts that not only everyone here heard and knew, but my uncle did too. It felt like my father had caught me.

"Don't be ashamed. If anything, you should have a badge of honor. To think, my little lamb did what three or four escorts couldn't." She flipped her braid over her shoulder, hopping off the counter. "Starting to think *you* are the wolf in sheep's clothing." She winked, turning for the door, motioning for me to follow. "Come on, I think you need a high-calorie breakfast. But I warn you, there might be a lot of people high-fiving you on the way."

"High-fiving me?" I scoffed, following her.

"You two had *everyone* over puberty age getting off at once." She flung open the door, grinning at me. "In a place where tension is constant, they might be feeling a little grateful."

"Yeah." I pinched my nose. "Not mortifying at all."

The gawks and attention I got on the walk to the canteen solidified what Kek had told me. There were a lot more smiles but also more wariness. Fear and unease toward me. They sensed something was off about me. Not normal.

Kek and I hit the second level, and instantly I felt him. His energy slammed into my chest, full of irritation and anger.

Shouts and cheering hit my ears from the workout room, dropping my stomach.

"Fight! Fight! Fight!"

Kek looked back at me, her eyebrows lifting.

"Oh shit," I muttered and darted for the room, coming to a stop at the entrance. The entire place was packed with people circling the mat, obstructing what was in the middle.

But I didn't need to see. I knew.

"Move!" I shoved between the throng of bodies, wiggling to the front, my mouth still dropping at what I saw in front of me.

Lukas danced at one end of the mat, his expression pinched and hard. Warwick stood on the other, his body language suggesting he was bored. I knew better. I could feel the fury swirling off him and see the tension in his jaw, the twitch in his hands.

"What the hell is going on?" I yelled, but my voice got lost in the crowd's enthusiasm. The man next to me answered.

"These two started to go at it in the canteen. Luk challenged him to a fight."

"Luk challenged him?" My voice rose. Was he nuts? Warwick would slaughter him.

My gaze darted between the two guys. I knew this was about me.

*"Warwick..."* Standing where I was, my presence was right in front of his face, looking directly into his eyes. This time it felt so strong. I was as real in front of him as I was still standing in the crowd. *"Don't touch him."*

Warwick's nose flared, his glare dropped to me briefly, his jaw rolling.

"He challenged *me*, princess," he muttered for only me to hear, his shoulders rolling back, trying to step around me, though I wasn't actually there. "Guess your boyfriend didn't like me fucking you."

*"Oh my gods..."* I jumped into his path again. *"Stop being an asshole."*

"Too late." He shoved through me, snapping our link, his massive physique progressing toward Luk.

Lukas pulled his arms up near his face, bouncing nearer to the massive legend. Warwick smirked, letting Luk get closer and get a swing in. Warwick's gaze darted to me with humored smugness. Lukas was no more than an irritating fly to him.

Glowering at Warwick, my lips rose.

*"If you hurt him..."* my ghost slunk behind Warwick, my lips brushing his ear. *"You deal with me."*

It was enough to distract him for a moment.

Luk's fist smashed into his face, splattering blood from his nose onto the mat. The crowd roared as Warwick wiped the blood from his face, a deadly grin curling his mouth.

Fuck.

An animalistic noise came up his throat before he lunged for Luk.

My mind didn't even contemplate what I was doing as I leaped. Using Warwick's strength and my own, I shoved Luk out of the way. His body flew, landing hard on the end of the mat, rolling off into the crowd. I didn't give him a second glance. I knew he was fine. If I hadn't jumped in, he wouldn't have been.

The group gasped in unison as I took Luk's spot, facing Warwick on the mat, the legend jerking to a halt at my sudden appearance, his nose flaring.

"X!" Luk scrambled up, trying to get back into the fight.

"No!" I held my hand up to Luk. "This has nothing to do with you."

"What the fuck are you doing, Kovacs?" Warwick snarled, both of us starting to circle each other.

"Finishing what we started in the Games." I snarled back. "You angry? Then fight me. It's what you want anyway."

He grunted, his head shaking. "You sure about that, princess?"

"Fuck yeah." I lowered myself into a defensive stance.

His eyes sparkled, his lips twisting with wickedness.

"You think I'll go easy on you like I did last time?"

"I hope you don't, because then I won't have to go easy on you."

He snorted like it was funny.

My blood burned through my veins; adrenaline and the need to fight clawed at my bones like a fiend. I needed it like air. Craved the high between life and death like a drug. I could taste it on my tongue, sense it calling to me, ready to pull me down into its dark depths.

Warwick's licked his lips, his eyes wild, as if he needed the same high. This was the place we both belonged. The space between... where the monsters lived. Every pulse of our blood, every twitch of muscle, we could feel each other.

On the outside, this fight might not look fair, but it was equal.

"Again, you gonna spend all night dancing with me?"

He chuckled darkly. "Remember, princess, the only thing I do all night is fuck."

"Typical man... exaggerate your prowess." I rolled my eyes. "You barely lasted an hour."

"Who said I was *anywhere* near done?" Warwick taunted, stepping closer.

We moved around each other like wisps of smoke, weaving and rolling, taking me back to our fight in the Games.

Faster than I was ready for, he lurched for me. Ducking too late, his elbow clocked me in the eye and nose, bursting light behind my lids, blood flying out of my nose as my face hit the mat with a smack.

Fire zoomed up my spine, energy arousing me.

I could feel him hesitate for a second.

Rule one with Bakos—never hesitate.

With a grunt, I shot my feet out with all the force I had, my heels slamming into the weak tendons in the knees, sending him tumbling to the ground. Instantly I sprang for him, my fist cracking along his jaw, cutting his lip. My other fist barreled down for his throat. In a blink, his palm wrapped around my wrists, halting my attack.

The air filled with shock as the audience watched us with anticipation.

Holding my hand away, he wiped at his mouth with his free hand, looking at the blood. Hunger, hate, and desire built behind his irises, a cruel smile hinting on his face.

The wolf was being released.

I tried to scramble up, but he flipped me onto my back, crawling on me, his hand pinning my arms to the mat.

"You actually make this fun, Kovacs." He leaned over, licking the side of my face where my blood leaked down. I sensed the eyes of the crowd on us, wondering what was going to happen next, but like when we fought before, all I felt was him. The heat of his heavy erection pressing into me, tipping my head back, spiraling all the logic from my head.

Lust.

Hate.

Want.

Anger.

"Fuck you." I thrashed against his hold.

"Finally, your mouth and body are agreeing." He nipped at my ear, rolling into me. "I can feel how much you want to fuck me, Kovacs. Violence and death turn you on. I'm happy to help you out since your other boyfriends don't seem to satisfy you."

I growled, hating how easy he could wrap around me, ensnare me in desire. I would not let him win.

With a move I used on Lukas, I shifted my weight dramatically to the side, tipping him off-center. Absorbing his energy, I mentally and physically shoved at his chest. Warwick toppled to the side, letting me slip away.

Getting to my feet, I felt a punch burrow into my side, his feet trying to knock me back down. Spinning, I kicked, the tip of my boot clipping his chin with a thwack. His head snapped back, red liquid dripping down from his jaw onto the mat.

There was a pause. He touched his chin and peered at the red liquid staining his fingers, bruises already darkening the skin. Slowly his head rose to look at me. Flames scorched his aqua eyes, his nose flaring as he leaped to his feet, his chest heaving. Threatening. Brutal. Vicious.

*Fuckfuckfuck.*

"Get out." He growled, his shoulders rolling forward. The horde of onlookers looked at each other, no one knowing who he was talking to.

"I. SAID. GET. THE. FUCK. OUT." Warwick's voice boomed, the order driving through the room like a scythe. People yelped and quickly started to dash for the exit. Luk tried to get to me, but I shook my head at him, halting his steps, his brows furrowing.

"Come on, pretty boy, buy me some coffee." Kek pulled Luk to the door.

She wiggled her eyebrows at me as she shut the doors, the room silent except for our breaths.

Warwick's eyes never left me, his physique primed to kill. My heart pounded in my chest, adrenaline scorching my skin with fear and energy, turning me just as feral.

"You upset because I actually hurt you, big man?" I mocked.

"Hurt me?" He sneered, his intense glare never leaving me as he prowled forward.

My feet stayed planted while he stalked up to me, his expression stone. He loomed over, his hands curling into claws, as if he could snap my neck in a moment.

"You think you hurt me?" He drew his fingers over his bloody chin again, coating his fingers. He reached out, painting his blood over my lips, pushing his thumb into my mouth. The metallic and rich earthiness burst on my tongue like whiskey. "*This* is just foreplay, princess."

Desire thrummed down my thighs at his intake of air when I sucked and nipped at his finger. He leaned into my ear, withdrawing his hand.

"I wasn't talking about physically." My gaze was full of meaning.

His eyes flashed, his voice low and cold. "Better run."

He gave me a beat to retreat before he charged for me again. I twisted around, looking like I was going to run, but instead swung back, slamming my fist into his temple. A snarl rose from his throat, fire igniting his eyes.

*"I don't run,"* my link whispered tauntingly in his ear while I took another swing for his throat.

He rotated, his arm deflecting my blow. He moved with unbelievable speed as his hands wrapped around my biceps. I was suddenly flying in the air over his head, landing on my back with a brutal thud, knocking the air from my lungs. Gasping for oxygen, I rolled just as his fist came for me, hitting the mat with a crunch. The buzz of adrenaline spiked a rush of blood through my veins. Lying on my side, I donkey kicked, connecting with the side of his head, dropping him to the ground with a roar.

He leaped for me, a yelp coming from my lungs as I tried to scramble away. His hands clutched my legs, dragging me back on my stomach, my nails scraping across the mat. Warwick yanked me underneath him, straddling me, holding me in place. A low steady rumble bled from him as I thrashed and fought to get away.

His hands curled at my waistband, wrenching my pants and knickers down over my ass. Instantly my nipples hardened, the cool air licking at my exposed skin, and energy pumped off me, pounding my pulse.

"What are you doing?" My voice came out hoarse, my back already arching in need as his fingers tore at his zipper.

"As you said earlier, finishing what we started in the Games." He wrapped his fingers in my hair, tugging my head back, curving my ass into him. Energy coursed through every muscle, quivering with the high of adrenaline and lust. The *fight* between us was our foreplay.

I needed him so badly it hurt.

He gave me no warning when he thrust into me. A half scream/half

103

moan choked my throat. His girth was tearing me in half and making me feel satisfaction beyond anything I could even imagine.

A long groan from his chest hummed along my spine. He plunged in deeper, his lungs stumbling as he quickened the pace. "You feel so fucking unbelievable... Fuck... this is..." His words trailed off, but I understood. There were no words for this.

Sex was good.

This was... legendary... mythical.

Lethal.

He pulled my damp locks harder, pushing me more into the mat, dragging me back and forth. The friction burrowed my fingers deeper into the fabric, leaving punctured crescent shapes. Deep moans huffed from my lips, and flames nipped up my vertebrae.

Sharp teeth dug into the curve of my shoulder, turning us both into feral beasts.

I slammed back into him, not caring if this whole place could hear or see us. The glass windows by the double doors completely exposed us if anyone walked by, only upping the force filling the room.

He sat back on his heels, grabbing my hips, dragging me up to my knees. My knuckles curled until they were white, screams and moans catching in my throat.

Violent. Brutal. The pain ignited unequivocal bliss. I wanted to drown, to never come back up for air.

"Oh gods... Warwick!" I cried, bucking back into him, not feeling close enough. Needing more, drowning in the sensations of us, the sounds of us fucking slapping off the walls.

"Pleasure" wasn't even a word for how this felt. The first time was not even in this realm, but this time was even more powerful. As if each time, the connection between us would continue to heighten. It was too much, but not enough. I was not just in my body, but his. Literally and figuratively, and feeling everything he did.

My climax came barreling for me. The fire bulbs flickered; the snap of electricity sang in my veins.

"Am I the only one you want to fuck, princess?"

"Yes... gods... never stop."

"This pussy is mine," he gritted into my ear, thrusting harder as I felt his tongue drag down my ass, sinking into me. A shriek, like a wild beast, rocketed from my throat, my limbs shaking so hard I could no longer hold myself up. He fell with me as I collapsed, sinking in deeper.

"Fuuuuccck... Brexley..."

Hearing him say my name, my climax hit like an avalanche, blinding my lids with white light.

*Vivid colors wavered in the sky. Death bleeding the field. Hands cupped a newborn baby, holding it off the dirt. The skin was coated with a sticky residue that dripped into the earth. A whoosh of magic ripped through the last layers of the Otherworld.*

*The wall falling.*

*The baby let out a wail.*

*Crack!*

*A lightning bolt struck the earth; ear-splitting shouts and yowls echoed in the night.*

*Warwick's eyes burst open, his lungs drawing in life.*

*"Sötét demonom."*

The lights in the workout room snapped on and off with fury as I felt him release inside of me, tearing another cry from my lips, bursting me into particles. I was caught in the bliss of the in-between, where I was everything and nothing.

Where life and death met.

Grappling for air, I slumped into the mat, his weight over me, his mouth grazing my ear, his breath sliding down my neck. "I think you might be the only one who could kill me."

"I don't have that kind of luck." I grinned over my shoulder.

He chuckled, nipping at my neck before pulling away from me and falling onto the mat next to me. Letting out a long gasp of air, his head fell onto the mat as he tucked himself back in his pants.

I hated how I instantly wanted him back, filling me with life and desire.

Hauling my pants back up, I flipped around on my back. "Well, that was..."

"Far from over." He got to his feet, pulling me up with him.

"What?"

"Like I said," he tucked a strand of hair behind my ear, "I can go all night."

"It's daytime."

"That too." He smirked. "We have to wait for Ash anyway. Should keep ourselves busy."

"Good point."

"I know." He grabbed my hand, leading us out of the exercise room, and we headed downstairs to my room, eyes from the canteen and everyone we passed on us with knowing smiles.

I didn't care.

Warwick ruined me. Broke and demolished what was left of me. Like a wave, all I could do was continue to smash myself against the rocks, battering and bruising, but never stopping.

# Chapter 10

"You sure?"

*Chirp!*

"Oh yeah, you're right. He totally likes it."

*Chirp!*

Voices stirred me from a deep, warm sleep.

"You can try... but she didn't seem keen before."

"I swear, if there are fingers anywhere near my nose..." I mumbled, my lids blinking open with a glower.

"Oh, don't worry, Master Fishy." Opie took over my eyeline, Bitzy on his back. "That's not where she was putting them."

Groaning, I dug my head into Warwick's arm I had been using as a pillow. Stretching, every bone and muscle ached and felt like melted butter.

The man was arrogant as hell, but my gods, did he have reason to be. The legend could not only fuck all night, but all day as well. What startled me was I was right there with him, tasting and exploring every inch of him, craving more each time. Our bodies finally gave out in the middle of the night, which I'm sure the base was thankful for. We were not quiet or restrained in our energy.

Rubbing my eyes, I took another peek at Opie, a snort tickling my nose. "What in the hell are you wearing today?"

"You like?" He twirled around in what had to be a doll's baby bonnet, likely taken from one of the kid's toys here. It was streaked with glitter. His chest was bare, and he wore a pink baby bib around his waist. Shoelaces were braided through his beard. Bitzy was wearing another bonnet, with earholes cut out and dazzled with glitter. "This place tested my creativity. Everything is so drab and boring. When can we go back to Ms. Kitty's? Her stuff was so fun. Bitzy misses her hat."

"I can think of other uses for Bitzy's hat," Warwick muttered sleepily, rolling over onto his side. He pulled me against his warm body, his hands gliding over my ass before he pressed his heavy length into my back.

"Did you just purr?" Opie blinked at me.

Fuck... did I?

Warwick hummed with pride, digging his head deeper into the back of my neck, pulling me firmer into him.

"And why the hell are you two on the floor?" He motioned to the single bedframe over his shoulder, which now was nothing more than scrap metal. "What the hell did you do to it? Origami?"

Warwick snorted.

It wasn't far off. I doubted a steel-enforced bed could survive Warwick. The tiny little cot didn't have a chance, not even making it through the first round. The entire middle caved in on itself until the footrail and headrail met.

"You can't see what it is?" Warwick chuckled into my neck. "It's a 'fuck off and leave us alone' sign."

*Chirp!*

Warwick didn't even look up, just stuck his middle finger over my shoulder at Bitzy, saluting her back.

*Chirp! Chirp! Chirp!* Fingers flew.

"Wow." I laughed, peering over my shoulder at him. "Better sleep with one eye open."

He grunted, his head still hiding in my hair.

"You destroyed this room." Opie wrung his hands together, peering around. Clothes were strewn everywhere, furniture broken, the lamp cracked. "I mean, not that I care... it's fine... I mean, if you like living in a war zone... sure... I mean, why would it bother me?"

"Especially because you hate to clean."

"Right!" He threw out his arms in agreement, but his expression was pinched, his attention still circling the mess. "I hate to clean, even when people live in pigsties." He inched closer to a pair of pants, pretending not to fold them. "Really, really hate cleaning..."

"I bet the showers don't need cleaning either." I lifted an eyebrow at him. "Good excuse for a new outfit."

Opie's eyes opened wider. "I think I saw an old loofa in there!"

"Ew... but okay, sounds fun."

"Come on, Bitzy, it's pool time!" He turned around, sauntering away.

Laughter burned up my nose, my hand clapping over my mouth. The bib only covered his front, leaving his entire backside open. And painted on his two tiny ass cheeks were Xs.

"The 'O' is hidden." He winked over his shoulder at me before he and Bitzy disappeared.

I groaned, uncontrollable giggles spewing from me, my eyes watering.

"Remember, those menaces are yours *forever* now." Warwick tipped up an eyebrow, rolling me onto my back, shifting his body over me. He clutched my thigh, fitting himself between my legs.

"I seem to like menaces." My voice came out breathy, his cock pressing into me, making me dizzy. I couldn't believe I could even go again. Chafed and sore, I still wanted more.

Continuously. Incessantly.

My hands dug into his hair by his temple, drawing his mouth to mine, kissing him so deeply, tingles erupted through me. He growled, hungrily claiming my mouth, wrapping himself around me, both physically and through our connection, which scared me.

We hadn't talked much last night, skirting around the elephant in the room—the link that joined us. He made it clear it was not what he wanted. And I didn't know if our feelings were real or only because we had this connection.

When he sank into me this time, he was slow and thorough, deep long strokes, taking me to more incredible highs. He watched me fall apart, spilling inside me right after.

Even after we came back down, he didn't move, his gaze intense. "Why can't I get enough?" He spoke low, his Adam's apple bobbing. "I never want to stop being inside you," he growled, and I could feel him start to grow hard inside me again, heaving my lungs. "What the fuck is this?"

My mouth opened to speak.

"It looks like you two worked your issues out." A voice twisted both our heads to my doorway.

Appearing exhausted and dirty, Ash leaned against the doorjamb, motioning around my room. "Looks like you took your issues out on this room. And from what I heard... on each other... and the workout room..." Ash tipped his head. "Oh, and the church."

"Get the fuck out." Warwick barked at his friend, waving at him to leave.

"Come on, I didn't drive twelve straight hours to wait for you two to fuck—from what everyone has told me, it's like the hundredth time in the last day." He patted the bag on his shoulder. "We got work to do." He adjusted himself. "Damn... the insane sexual aura coming off you two now."

"Ash," Warwick snarled.

"Ten minutes, not twenty." Ash pointed at us.

"Out!" Warwick chucked his boot at his friend. Ash dodged out of the way, laughing as he shut the door.

"We better go. I need to take a shower." I was covered in sweat, blood, and Warwick. "And I'm starving."

Warwick huffed, rolling off me. Getting up to his feet, he sauntered to the door. He flung it open, still naked, his firm ass flexing with every step. Peering over his shoulder, he eyed me hungrily. "I'm eating my breakfast in the shower." He lifted a brow. "You coming?"

Scrambling to my feet, I raced after him.

Hell yeah, I was...

And would be.

More than twenty minutes later, coffee in one hand, a pastry in the other, Ash, Warwick, and I sat on a step in the corner of the church away from everyone's view or possible foot traffic. Ash didn't want anyone to know he had a fae book. They were coveted since there were so few now and could be dangerous in the wrong hands—to both the book and the person.

"So... looks like it wasn't just this bastard you worked things out with." The smirk on Ash's face hadn't left since the moment we strolled in, freshly showered and momentarily satiated.

A grunt rolled from Warwick, making Ash grin wider.

"The spirits aren't attacking you." Ash yanked the old giant book from his bag, placing the fabric on the floor before gently laying the book on the bag.

They weren't bombarding me, but I could feel them hovering, getting close enough to buzz by, scraping at my energy. Warwick didn't have to touch me, but I noticed his knee pressed into my thigh as if he were making sure. "What did you do?"

"Uh..." I took another sip of coffee, trying to put into words what exactly happened. It was so hazy that I barely felt like it was me.

"Right." Ash chuckled. "Probably shouldn't ask tough questions... brain a bit fried there, sweetheart?"

"Shut up." I tried to glower at Ash, but it fell flat.

"Comes with the legendary status." Warwick leaned back against the wall, smugness curling his lips as he chomped down on his pastry, stuffing almost half of it into his mouth in one bite. I tried to be annoyed but found myself staring at his mouth, the way his muscles moved along his jaw and throat, remembering the way his lips felt on my skin. His heated gaze lifted to mine, his presence swirling around me, the feel of his mouth sliding down the back of my neck, giving me shivers.

"Enough eye-fucking and whatever else you're doing." Ash adjusted himself again. "I may not see it, but I can *feel* it. Just stop."

Warwick lifted a brow, drinking his coffee, while I still sensed his hands and mouth moving down to my thighs.

"Warwick," I chided. "Stop."

He grinned mischievously, going back to his pastry.

"Think I'm going to be wishing for the days you two still pretended to hate each other."

"Oh, we still do." Warwick's eyes caught mine through his lashes so intensely my lungs stumbled for air.

*"Hate fuck me later."* Warwick's link nipped my ear.

I slammed down the link between us, producing a chuckle from him.

"Hey." Ash waved his hand in front of my face, pointing to the book. "Focus."

Taking a deep breath, I shook off the lust still clinging to me, putting all my attention on the book.

The energy pulsed off it, zeroing on me immediately. I felt it yearn for my touch. My hand tentatively curled away from the power.

"I have you." Ash laced his fingers with mine, moving closer to the book. "A tether to reality if you need it. There is a wall behind you, so you can't fall this time."

111

Nodding, I tightened my fingers around his warm hand, feeling secure and safe.

"Do I just go in? Will it know what I want?"

"Yes, the book knows your desire, but it's always nice to ask for permission. They are of the old ways, where manners and etiquette go far. But be clear and concise... they are known to twist interpretation if it is not exact."

"What am I asking again? Where this nectar is?"

"Yes, what has happened to it." Ash squeezed my hand again, probably sensing my nerves. "You ready?"

"Yep." I nodded, my throat tightening. To others, the book showed them the past, but I became part of it and could be trapped in there forever.

"Close your eyes and clear your mind," Ash spoke softly, his sexy voice soothing and calming. He took our joined hand to the pages.

*"Brexley Kovacs,"* the inhuman raspy voice boomed into my head. *"The girl who challenges nature's laws wants more from me? Have I not shown you enough?"*

*"Yes."* I swallowed. *"You have been most kind and helpful. Thank you."*

*"But you want more?"*

*"I was hoping you would show me what happened to this substance called* nectar. *What happened to it after China? It was last with a Dr. Novikov."*

*"Interesting."*

*"What?"*

*"That you should be asking me."*

*"Why is that?"*

*"You only get one question,"* the book replied robotically. *"And you already asked it."*

*"No—wait! Let me ask again!"* I knew I hadn't been clear enough, my question way too general.

*"Too late, child of the gray."*

A blast tore through my body as images whirled in my mind—visions and scenes of the past, like I was scrolling through time. This time from past to present, moving through time so quickly, my stomach heaved with bile.

Coming to the final written page, everything stopped. The page I landed on was blank, and I could feel with every breath, ink was scrolling over the sheet, writing the moment in present time.

A cool, damp chill shivered over my skin as I took in the carved rock walls and low ceiling, man-made archways forking off into a labyrinth of passages. Only a few fire bulbs flickered on the walls, creating ghostly shadows. Nerves twisted in my gut, the familiar dank smell sparking a deep-rooted fear in my body. The taste of adrenaline on my tongue tripped me back to a time Killian's guards were hauling me through an underground tunnel to my doom.

Intuition told me this location didn't just remind me of the maze underneath Killian's palace. It *was* the same place.

A pull moved me toward a mostly empty vestibule. There was a lone table in the middle—an altar with items spread over it. I couldn't decipher what was on it from where I was, but I knew it was not of the old human religion which used to dominate this area. I noticed a discolored shape on the wall where a cross used to hang but was no longer.

Stepping closer to the altar, the sound of a dry hacking cough behind me spun me around, my heart thumping in my chest. A shadowy figure shuffled down a dark passage near me. I couldn't see any features, but it appeared feeble and old, each step slow and uneven.

Then it stopped. Awareness prickled at my spine.

"Hello? Is someone there?" The low, crackly voice clicked something in the back of my head, gnawing on my subconscious. "Show yourself! I can feel someone there."

Before I could figure out why it felt familiar, the book yanked me out.

*"No!"* I screamed, not ready to be taken away yet.

*Whoosh.*

Darkness shrouded me, everything spinning as the book hurled me out.

My head slammed back, my lids bursting open, but instead of hitting stone, a hand cushioned my skull. Warwick's large, warm palm cupped the nape of my neck, like he sensed my head was about to hit the wall before it happened.

"Brex?" Ash's worried green eyes were in my face, his brows furrowed. "You okay?"

"Yea-yeah." I licked my lips, my mind still swirling, my stomach rolling with nausea.

"It kicked you out really fast." Ash squatted down in front of me. "Did it show you anything?"

"I don't know." My forehead wrinkled with the flashes and images. Warwick's hand didn't move; his fingers threaded softly through my hair, easing down my shoulders. "It was strange. Doesn't make sense..."

113

"What?" Ash prodded.

"I think it took me to the tunnels underneath the palace."

"The tunnels?" Warwick dropped his hand away, tilting his head.

"Yeah, but they weren't the exact ones they took me down to get to Halálház. This felt like a different area." I rolled my lips together. "Someone was there, and... they sensed my presence."

"They sensed your presence?" Ash's eyes widened.

Nodding, I added more. "It was in real time... not the past. I was there right now."

Ash's brows shot up. "What? Right now, as in this moment?"

My head bobbed again, watching Ash pinch his nose, confusion and astonishment mixed on his face. Everything about my interaction with the book defied the rules.

"I could feel the book recording every step and movement," I stated. "Writing present history."

"Fucking hell." Ash scoured his face, muttering under his breath.

"Did you see them?" Warwick asked.

"No... they were in the shadows" I started to shake my head, though a prickle of something kept dragging across my gut. "It showed me what looked like some underground room... an altar, I think. I got the feeling it was once used for the old religious practices."

"An altar?" Ash's eyes widened as he stood up. "In a cave?"

"Yeah, why?"

*"Faszom,"* Ash muttered, tipping his head back.

"What?" Warwick rose warily.

"I know exactly where the book showed her... and neither of you is going to like it."

Warwick's chest expanded, his fists rolling into balls, waiting for Ash to continue.

"What?" I stood up, already knowing the answer, but hoping I was wrong.

"The old Gellert Hill Cave." Ash cringed. "The gutted church at the bottom of Lord Killian's palace."

"Killian?" Warwick barked. "He has it? He's the one who has the nectar?"

Ash rubbed his forehead, frowning deeply, his head wagging with puzzlement.

"That doesn't make sense. I don't think he does." My thoughts settled back on Killian, my time with him. If he knew about the nectar, had it the whole time, why would he have been so concerned about the pills?

"You are clouded by your feelings for him, princess." Warwick gritted his teeth, his gaze drilling into me. "Your *boyfriend* is not the nice guy you like to think he is."

"Think about it." I ignored Warwick's pointed tone. "If Killian had the nectar, he has the ultimate prize, especially for humans. I mean, game over. Killian wouldn't be concerned about the pills or what Istvan is doing. I get that you hate him, what he did, but I spent every day for a month with him. If it's there, he doesn't know about it, or he hasn't found it yet."

Ash's eyebrows curved up. "He literally could be sitting on a gold mine and doesn't know."

"Exactly." I smiled at Ash, his grin spreading, both of us turning to Warwick. "One we can take off his hands."

"How do you expect to get in?" Warwick's jaw rolled. "Knock on the door, bat your lashes, and ask nicely?"

"No." I put my hand on my hip, irritation tapering my lids. "Figured you would just blow it up."

"Funny." He scowled back. "That only works when you are *fleeing* an area, not trying to get in. Have any brighter ideas, *princess*?"

"Yeah, actually." I twisted, getting in his face. Warwick's chest hit mine, closing the distance, his nose flaring. "How about you shove—"

"Okay! Ease back, you two." Ash pulled us apart. "I thought you would have worked all this tension out by now. You didn't hate fuck enough?"

"Not even close." Warwick scoffed, still using his massive size to loom over me. I didn't flinch, daring him to test me.

Ash grasped my arm again, tugging me farther away.

"Man, you guys are killing me." He cupped his pants, his face pure agony. "I'm about to dry hump the skeleton over there if you don't take it down a notch or two."

A dry laugh rose from my throat, the visual making me cringe and laugh. I really hoped he was kidding.

"Warwick's right." Ash folded his arms, taking a deep breath, switching the subject back. "We need to find a way into the underground caves that won't be guarded by a dozen sentinels. If he knows about the nectar or not, he'd have every entrance around his palace highly secured."

A memory flashed from my time in the underground tunnels when Sloane, Conner, and Vale hauled me through, and especially my exit from them.

My eyes widened, my tongue sliding over my lip. "I think I might know."

"What?" Ash and Warwick replied in unison.

"It's a long shot..." I trailed off, my mind still rolling around the idea.

"Out with it." Ash gestured for me to keep talking.

"While getting me to Halálház, I was taken through the tunnels from the palace area to the old citadel before being escorted into the prison."

Warwick's head tipped back, understanding seeping in quickly. He knew the area, what I was saying.

"What?" Ash's regard bounced between us.

"There is a door by the old prison, which leads down into the tunnels. At one time, it was highly guarded because of the prison—"

"But the prison is no longer in use," Ash filled in, getting my meaning. "The area has been basically abandoned."

"Killian would still have a patrol, but..." Warwick scratched his beard.

"Nothing like what used to be there. I know he has a lot of his focus on rebuilding and watching the new prison," I finished.

A naughty grin tugged at the side of Warwick's cheek, his aqua eyes burning into mine.

*"Good plan, princess."*

*"Thank you."* I tipped my head to him, neither of us actually opening our mouths.

"You know it will be like stealing treasure from a dragon's lair." Ash rubbed his brow. "Very dangerous. We might not make it out."

A devious sneer hinted on Warwick's mouth. "Sounds exactly up our alley."

"Now tell me again how you know where it is?" Mykel paced behind his desk, a deep, furrowed line carving into his brow. "It just so happens fifteen years after its disappearance, you suddenly know where it is?"

"*Possibly* know where it is," I added. Technically I hadn't seen it, but I felt the book showed me the place for a reason. It would make sense to bury it in the forbidden tunnels, right under the most powerful fae in Hungary, to protect it. As Ash said, bury it under a dragon's lair, and your treasure will probably stay hidden.

"How we know isn't important. We just do." Warwick folded his arms, raising his height over my uncle, his deadly glare on him.

"Excuse me if I don't take your word for it. I didn't become leader by trusting everyone I encountered, no matter what you and my niece are doing." Mykel glowered at Warwick, tension flinging between them like mud. Chagrin crawled up my neck, knowing Mykel had probably heard and felt us. He wasn't my father, and I barely knew him, but it still felt like I had been caught by my parent like some young teenager.

Warwick stepped closer to the desk, the vibration off him punching the room with violence. "And *I* haven't gotten where I am by trusting every arrogant leader I encountered." He snarled at Mykel, both their chests growing with aggression.

"O-kay." My hand pushed at Warwick's chest, moving him back from the desk. "Let's calm down."

*"Warwick."* My link spoke into his ear, my hand wrapping around his arm while both of my real hands stayed on his chest. *"Please."*

His nose huffed, but he let me step him back, his angry glare still locked on my uncle.

Twisting back to face Mykel, I took a deep breath. "I understand you barely know me." I moved closer to the desk, looking in the same eyes as my dad. "You are my uncle. Father would want us to know each other. Be part of each other's life. Trust each other. Can you give me the benefit?"

Mykel's head dipped.

"We are heading back to Budapest tonight."

Mykel shifted on his feet.

"My team will go with you," Mykel stated.

"What?" Ash and Warwick pelted out.

Mykel regarded them directly. "I have not been searching for it over the last fifteen years for it to fall through my fingers now."

"I see your trust in family is conditional." A vein along Warwick's neck pulsed, his ire canvasing the air, his temper always on a thin line.

Mykel shot him another glare, his fingers rolling into balls. "It's not conditional unless you are planning to backstab me first. I protect my family. Which is this place. These people. Brexley is part of it if she wants to be, but she is not my only focus. I will always put my cause first. And I think she understands that." He motioned to me. "Tracker, Ava, and Luk will go with you. If you are heading into Killian's territory, it will be dangerous."

"Dangerous?" A woman's sultry voice swung our heads back to the door. A blue-haired demon leaned against the jamb, a coy smile on her lips. "Then you aren't leaving me behind, little lamb. Sounds like fun."

117

# Chapter 11

The roars of the motorcycles rumbled down the motorway through the night; their arrow formation directed for Budapest like a dart. Air whipped my ponytail against my face, snapping painfully at my frozen skin, the cold night air chilling my bones underneath the heavy coat. The warmth coming off Warwick's body was a furnace, and I huddled into him as the bike sped closer to our destination.

Curving my head over my shoulder, I saw Ash on his bike flanking our left, the bag on his back full of prized possessions: the book and my two little friends who had become my family. I had filled Ash's bag with as much material and stuff as I could find to occupy Opie for the road trip back. Luk and Kek were on our right, Tracker and Ava taking up the rear, watching our backs, which took some negotiation with Warwick in the lead.

He didn't trust them, but Mykel didn't trust them not being with us. I understood both sides, their distrust of each other, and I became the thin line of truce between.

"It's up to you, Brexley." Mykel came up to me right before we took off.

"What is?"

"Keeping the balance." He flicked his chin to Warwick and Tracker, the animosity between them stabbing like daggers.

"Kovacs," Warwick called to me to get on his bike.

I turned back to the uncle I had recently met.

"It has been..." Mykel cleared his throat, speaking first. "To finally meet you. I do not regret the choices in my life, but I do wish I had been there more when you were growing up—for you and your father. You remind me so much of him. He was a good man. I miss him."

"Me too," I agreed, shifting on my feet, having no idea what to do. He didn't seem like a hugger like my father was.

Mykel shook his head. "Your father was right."

"What do you mean?"

"After years of silence, he showed up here barely a month before he died. We got drunk, and he confessed to me you were different. Special. He told me to watch over you, protect you. Bring you here if things took a turn at HDF."

"Did he tell you anything more?" Andris told me my father knew something was odd about me, but to hear it from another constricted my chest, making it hard to breathe. "What he thought I was?"

"No." Mykel pinched his lips together. "He shut down when I tried to ask him more, saying he had already said enough to put me in danger."

My throat tightened. Did that mean my father knew more? Found out?

"I didn't really believe him, but I still did what he asked. It was strange that he came to me then... like he knew he was going to die," Mykel said. "I know it seems impossible, but he wasn't wrong about you. I feel it in my bones. You are special... critical. You were meant to come here. The rock that launched an avalanche."

*A single drop of water can be the one that breaks the dam.*

"I will see you again, Brexley." He dipped his head. For a moment, I saw a softness in his eyes, then it was gone. "Be safe." He turned, stiffly strolling back toward the base.

Now only minutes away from Budapest, Warwick raised his arm up, signaling for the others to follow his lead. He turned the bike off the motorway, taking a less used road back into the city. We went far enough south to cross over into the Buda side, out of Killian's domain, heading toward the Savage Lands.

It wasn't guarded by Killian's soldiers, and the streets were abysmal, no longer maintained, slowing our pace. It was easier to be picked off by thieves and gangs. It was a toss-up which way was worse:

get caught by Killian's trained fae army or be hunted down by thieves who would kill for a coin without thought.

Darkness clung to the deteriorating buildings, dawn still far off. The smell of the city hit me like a punch, the rotting decay of both human and animal. Animals were fenced in their own feces, homeless peeing and shitting in the street. The war-torn buildings were sagging and hollowed out, on the verge of collapse. Only a few lights from buildings gave a slight glow to the street, creating thick shadows, every outline playing with my vision.

"You sure this is the better way?" I murmured in Warwick's ear when he slowed down to steer around huge potholes and debris.

*"If Killian gets notice of our return... especially yours, our element of surprise is gone."* Warwick's hot breath tickled my neck. Instead of yelling over the engines and wind, we had communicated the whole trip through our link, which he kept brief, saying no more than necessary. I could feel tension in his muscles, his regard on every inch of the road, on the lookout for threats. Our little entourage was a neon sign for those wanting trouble.

*"Be ready, princess."* His voice was flat and void of emotion. *"Have your gun out."*

Snatching two handguns from the back of my pants, my gaze rolled over every dark corner and alley we passed. Fires in barrels burned dimly in occasional places, people's empty eyes looking at us while we rolled by. The heavy misery weighted the air, the desperation for a moment of reprieve, an opportunity to escape their life, made me feel like we were being hunted. Tracked. A shiver skated over my spine, like a warning.

"Warwick," I muttered, my knees clasping tighter on his thighs so I could look all the way around and up into windows. I couldn't shake the prickly sensation of being watched.

"Yeah," he rumbled, sensing the same alarm, his shoulders tensing. His fingers on his left hand, where Ash was, made a sign I didn't understand, but I saw Ash instantly react, his eyes moving up to the tops of the buildings and around, understanding their code. "Don't hesitate to shoot, Kovacs. Anything that moves in our direction."

"I won't." I kept my guns up, my fingers on the triggers, glaring at anyone who gave us a double look. The girl before Halálház would have hesitated. I had pretended to be fierce, but I had no clue what true fear or depravity was. To actually fight for your life. To kill.

Anyone coming now for those I cared about, I would shoot on sight.

We crept farther into the city, the destitution growing along with the stench burning my nostrils. People huddled near fires or tried to sleep under rags in the cold temperatures. It was past midnight, but time wasn't a factor here. They had no jobs to get up for, nothing to do except wonder how they would feed their kids or themselves. The crying babies, the low murmur of voices, and fire crackling were the only sounds.

Tension roped around my muscles, ready for something to come for us, but we continued on without incident. My anxiety heightened because I could feel the palpable prickle of eyes on me, pursuing us relentlessly through the city like a wild animal hunting its prey, staying far enough back in the dark to stay hidden.

Warwick stopped right at the green ironwork of the Liberty Bridge. The fae lord's palace glowed brightly on the hill, a god far above his disciples.

Across the water, I could almost feel Killian's presence there, on the balcony, looking out into the night, feeling I was somewhere out there as well. The connection to him wasn't like what I had with Warwick or even Scorpion, but I couldn't deny Killian had left a mark on me.

Ash's bike came to a stop next to Warwick, his feet hitting the pavement. "The main entrance has been boarded up, no longer used for the old human religion. It would be well guarded and locked up." Ash nodded at the structure built into the side of the mountain on the other side of the bridge.

The two neo-gothic turrets and pale stone church blended in with the terrain, appearing like part of the mountain. Unobtrusive. Hidden. And very much protected and restricted from the public. Any enemy descending on this city would probably miss it. Like Halálház, had the nectar been hidden in plain sight this whole time?

Luk, Kek, Tracker, and Ava stopped around us.

"We cause too much attention. You guys should stay here." Warwick snarled at our new companions.

"Fuck off," Tracker barked, his eyes flashing. "You are not leaving us out now. Kaptain wants us here the whole way until it is put in his hands."

"Who the fuck said he would be the one to get it?" I felt a muscle in Warwick's back flex, his jaw clenching. "You may do his bidding, but I certainly don't. It is not his to have."

121

"It's not yours either, Farkas." Tracker puffed up, fury straining his frame.

"You may be hot stuff at Povstat, human, but you're in the big boy's game now. You are going to get us caught." Warwick sneered. "Or killed."

Tracker started to climb off the bike, challenging Warwick. "Why don't you come over here and I can show—"

"Track! Stop it!" Ava grabbed for him.

"Come on, *legend*... you all talk? Nothing behind the name?"

"Shit," I hissed as Warwick started to get off his bike. I knew this would be bad. Tracker, an egotistical human, had no clue who he was challenging.

"Hey, hey!" I held my hands between them. "Everyone, calm down."

"Damn, this is so hot. You get in there, pretty boy." She poked at Luk. "You too." She flung her hand at Ash. "And all you start wrestling, and then it turns into hate-fucking each other." Kek grinned deviously, her demon eyes darkening, devouring the abhorrence and ego that was swimming between the two men, making Ash snort.

"Don't tell me you wouldn't want to see all this testosterone go at it?" Kek wiggled her blue eyebrows at Luk.

"Track." Luk pointed at his comrade, ignoring Kek. "Take a breath. This is their terrain. In ours, they'd follow our lead. Here, we follow them. We can't fight amongst ourselves and be able to battle our true enemies."

"Wow, someone actually using logic." Ash winked playfully at Luk.

For a moment, I swore I saw Luk's cheeks heat, but he quickly turned to Tracker.

"Get back on your bike."

Tracker's chest rose, his glower on Luk now. I didn't think many, besides my uncle, told Tracker what to do.

Just like someone else I knew.

"Too many alphas." I pressed my thumb into the bridge of my nose. "Not enough brain cells."

*"Your fault. You killed them all yesterday and this morning, princess."* Warwick's gravelly voice brushed up my neck, my eyes flicking up to the real man with a glare. His lips twisted in a smirk. *"Though I wouldn't mind your mouth wrapping around my cock right now."*

"You really are insufferable," I grumbled, the side of his mouth hitching higher.

"Tracker," Luk said his name like an order.

"Fine," Tracker growled. "You can lead, but we *all* go." Tracker plopped back down on the bike.

Warwick's shoulders flexed, and I knew he was about to toss Tracker into the river.

*"Warwick."* Invisible hands traced up his back and around his abs, my fingers following down his V-line, producing a slight rumble from his throat. *"Behave."*

*"You should know I don't behave."* His actual hand clutched the top on my thigh, yanking me closer into his body, his thumb rubbing along the seam of my crotch. *"If you want me to not kill this guy, you owe me. I've slaughtered men for less."*

*"I promise to destroy those few brain cells you have left if we get through this."*

*"Now I'll make sure we do."*

"Hey, fuckers!" Ash yelled at us, our heads snapping to him. "Stop mentally screwing each other. Focus!"

It was a switch. Warwick cut off the link, his attention going in front of us, the warrior mode on.

"Follow me," Warwick barked, revving the bike forward. The moment we crossed the invisible line on the bridge, we would enter the Buda side.

Killian's realm.

The princess was about to steal and betray the dragon guarding the most coveted treasure in the world.

If he caught me, he would burn me to ashes.

Rubble and fragments of the old citadel were scattered across the hill like headstones. A sinkhole buried what was hidden under the stone and earth, but I swore I still heard the phantom cries of agony and the stench of death bubbling up to the surface. Everything was left exactly how it was after the bombing. A time capsule.

My stomach twisted into knots, a chill shivering my frame when Warwick stopped the bike at our old "residence." The place still plagued my dreams, my soul forever stained with blood and trauma.

I climbed off, my feet taking me closer to the ruins, my chest tightening. I stopped at a chunk of stone. The notable statue, the woman holding the feather, used to look over the city and was a symbol in Budapest. Part of the woman's face stared blankly up at me. A corpse left on the battlefield. The haunting screams and terror still saturated the ground.

*This place can't hurt you anymore.* I inhaled deeply, trying to loosen the rope strangling my lungs. I didn't think being back here would affect me so much. When I was here, I hadn't been outside more than twice. Now, like vibrations from an earthquake, I could feel what was still underneath my feet, empty of life but filled with the ghosts who died, as if the Games and life in Halálház had never stopped. I had little doubt that below me were dead bodies of people I knew now were entombed forever.

Was Tad there? Did he make it out?

*"Hey."* Warwick's shadow pressed into my back, his warmth cutting out the cold wind gusting over the hill. *"This place might have hurt and changed you, but they didn't break you, Kovacs. You survived... came out stronger. Don't let it take anything more from you."*

My attention darted to the man who was busy hiding the bikes, acting like he wasn't also over with me, patching parts of my soul with his words. He could feel my weighted gaze on him, his eyes darting to me for a moment, connecting, before he looked away again. It would seem like nothing to the outside world, but to me, it felt like everything.

"Brex?" Ash waved me over, the rest of the group waiting for me. We might not have much time until another patrol came through here. We had seen one pass through the area right before us, not even stopping, just making sure everything looked undisturbed and quiet. This part was no longer of use or of importance.

Sneaking down by the bombed building, we came to the area where I remembered coming out. The almost seamless private door leading us straight into the heart of the fae city was hidden by foliage and large pieces of debris. The bomb had left this place in shambles.

The seven of us rolled the wreckage away from the door, then Ash stepped up to it first.

"Fuck," he hissed, and I quickly understood his reaction. The door had no knob, the entrance seamlessly part of the wall. I had only come out of here, not in. I had no idea there wasn't an actual door handle on the outside.

"Do you guys have a knife blade?" I peered around. "I can jimmy locks with a flat blade."

Warwick snorted, reaching for the one he kept in his boot.

"Doesn't matter." Ash shook his head, curving to us. "I can feel it. It's magic-locked. Goblin-made." Ash blew out a breath in irritation.

Goblin-made was pretty much impossible to break through. It was expensive, hard to get, and used very little here, but I was not surprised the lord of the fae would have access to it.

"Fuck," Warwick barked, running his hand through his hair, his feet moving. "Now what?"

"I don't know," Ash exclaimed, tensions rising. "There is no way we can get in... unless you have one of those fae lock picks handy."

I used to. In my thieving days, I learned quickly that "magic-locked" items were impossible to crack unless you had one of those black-market devices, and sometimes those didn't even work.

Knotting my hair in my fingers, I let out a frustrated growl, understanding none of us could break through the door.

"So that's it?" Tracker threw out his arms. "Your entire plan was based on whether we could get through this door." He scoffed. "And, Luk, you said to let them lead. Idiots."

Fury exploded through Warwick, his body curling, ready to lurch at Tracker.

"No!" I leaped in front of Warwick, his aqua eyes set on his target, his body pushing forward like I wasn't even there.

"All of you are idiots!" A gruff voice sighed, and a tiny body, not even reaching the top of their boots, strolled between the two guys about to tear each other apart, his outfit flapping around like he was on some runway. "Broomsticks... seven brains among you, and not one of you thought about us." Opie cocked his head over his shoulder to Bitsy on his back. "Why should we be surprised? No one thinks about us *measly* sub-fae."

*Chirp!* Her fingers flew up, scowling at us.

"Oh my gods." Ava jumped back, her eyes widening. "Is that—is that a brownie? And an imp?"

"Master Fishy, you hang out with such brainiacs." He rolled his eyes, folding his arms, crinkling his new creation.

"*A kutya fáját!*" *The dog's tree!* Ash hissed, pointing at Opie. "Where the hell did you get that from?"

Instead of all the drab fabric I could find at Povstat to give Opie for a project on the way back, he was dressed in a parchment gown, folded like a fan. A page circled his waist like a long skirt, another folded up in an off-the-shoulder origami top. Two fanned pages were attached to his back like wings and one on his head like a crown. Bitsy had a matching crown and wings on her back.

"Oh gods, Opie." I cringed. "Please don't tell me that's from the book in Ash's bag."

The fae book.

"Like I could put anything together with what you gave me," he huffed, stomping his feet, which were also covered with paper. "I'm brilliant, but that was even beyond *my* talents."

"You..." Ash heaved in and out. "You. Made. A. Dress. From. The. Book?"

"You act like it's a big deal." Opie waved him off.

"Big deal?" Ash's voice pitched. "A big deal? The book is thousands of years old! It contains more history and knowledge in the first sentence than you will in your entire life!"

"Ugh. You should thank me; it sounds positively dull. I made it exciting again, brought it to life. Took me the whole trip. Don't you like it?" He spun around, the paper flaring up like thick fabric. Honestly, if I didn't think Ash was about to pass out, I would have admitted it was very creative and stunning. "It's pretty... just admit it."

"Oh my gods!" Ash exclaimed. The string of swear words, both in Hungarian and English, even had Bitsy's eyes widening with awe. "You used an ancient, irreplaceable piece of history to make your dress?"

I covered my mouth, not sure if I wanted to laugh or cry, while Kek howled next to me.

"I think I found my soulmate." She wiped her eyes. "His outfit literally will go down in history."

"Wait." A thought clicked in my head. "How were you able to get into the book? I thought it only opened for those it chooses. And those with good intentions."

"Except sub-fae." Warwick dropped his head in a huff, his hand rubbing his face.

"What do you mean?" I didn't know a lot about sub-fae. It wasn't something Istvan even considered to be worthy of my time.

"Sub-fae, which include brownies and imps, were always considered beneath fae. They were pets, slaves, irritating creatures... like you'd think of bees or squirrels." Warwick shrugged one shoulder. "Part of our world but not worthy of much thought. Never considered a threat... so they don't have the same limitations we do."

"Arrogance and entitlement are always man's downfalls. Fae and human." Opie stopped near my boot, winking at me. "Don't underestimate and misjudge the underdog. Am I right, Fishy? We bite back."

A grin tugged my mouth, and I bobbed my head.

"Move out of my way, inferior creatures!" Opie waved off Ash, Kek, and Luk dramatically, heading for the door. Bitzy sat in her pack, wagging her middle finger around like she was the queen of Hungary passing her minions on the street. "Let the experts through."

*Chirp!*

"What is going on?" I glanced back at Warwick; his mouth was curved with humor.

"You'll see." He flicked his chin for me to follow my friends. I watched as Opie neared the door, his head tipping back at its colossal height.

"Some help, peasants?" He sighed like he was greatly put out, gesturing up the door. "Must I do everything myself? My gods, Bitz, you simply can't find good help these days."

*Chirp!* Bitzy rolled her large eyes in agreed dramatic annoyance.

"Just because you amuse me." Kek leaned over, picking him up and holding him near where the lock might be on the other side.

"Thank you, my sapphire servant." He nodded at Kek before turning to the door. Opie's hands flattened against it, his tongue sticking out as he put his ear up to the door. "Hmmm... this is a gooey one." His eyes twitched, his tongue changing sides. We stood there watching him for a full minute before he spoke again. "Alllllmost have it..." He grunted. Another thirty seconds passed. "Allllll moooooossstt thhheerree," he stressed, his nose wrinkling. "Ah-ha!"

*Clink!* The sound of the lock broke, the door cracking open.

"Ta-da!" He threw up his hands, waving to the door like it was a prize.

"Holy shit!" I exclaimed, my mouth dropping.

"Sub-fae," Warwick replied, his body heat pressing into me, herding me toward the entrance. "We might be a hundred times more powerful than them, but they slip under the radar of most magic, allowing them to do things we can't."

"Like opening magic locks and magic books."

"Like that." Warwick's hands clasped my hips, moving me forward.

My eyes widened, turning to Opie and Bitzy, my smile growing.

To a thief, this was like finding the master key that opened everything in the world. There was nothing I couldn't steal.

"You two... you are the best." I blew a kiss at them.

A deep blush colored Opie's cheeks, a bashful smile hinting on his mouth, while Bitzy just flipped me off.

I loved them.

Taking the pair from Kek, I placed Opie on my shoulder, the duo holding on to my ponytail as we entered the pitch-black entrance.

I took lead since I had been through here. My memories were sharp because of whatever the healer had injected me with; every step now was like a callous rubbing against my brain. The smell brought me right back to when Killian's guards had towed my maimed carcass up the spiral stairs toward my doom.

Now I was descending into it.

As silently as we could, the seven of us advanced down the tunnel. My anxiety corded in a tightrope around me, hoping I wasn't leading them wrong. The odor triggered memories I had locked away, pumping my lungs with dread.

*"You made it out, Kovacs. You survived. Don't let it win now."* Warwick's ghostly voice seeped into my ear.

Taking a deep breath, my shoulders eased down. The memories wouldn't go away. They probably never would but feeling him behind me, Ash on my other side, my boys flanking me, Opie and Bitzy on my shoulder, all centered my wild thoughts, letting me focus on the goal.

"Double broomsticks. You get out of this place, Fishy, and then you purposefully come back?" Opie gripped my hair tighter. "I'm having flashbacks to when Master Finn made me bait the feral rats down here."

"You had to put out the bait?"

"No, I *was* the bait." He shivered. "He said it built character. But all it did was make me lose my bowels."

*Chirp!*

"I didn't know you could stuff character up there."

*Chirp!*

"Hey, time to muzzle the pets," Warwick grumbled, his physique coiled and tensed, his head darting around, even wary of the group behind us.

Luk and Kek were in the middle, while once again Tracker and Ava were guarding the rear, which did not settle Warwick at all.

I placed Bitzy and Opie back into Ash's pack to be safe, with the rule that he couldn't design any more outfits from the book.

Gesturing, I headed us toward the main tunnel, my intuition leading the way. With every step, I was aware we could be caught by a soldier, by the ruler himself, or even worse, by Nyx. That bitch would slice me down without hesitation. And oddly enough, I wasn't sure I blamed her. I killed her lover, and Warwick almost killed her. She kind of had a reason to hate me.

My boots tapped lightly over the stone as we rounded a corner, air sticking in my throat when I saw the room with the altar at the end. My heartbeat doubled against my ribs while we crept closer. Everything was exactly like I saw it in the book, but now that we were here, I didn't know what to do. If Killian knew it was around here but hadn't found it, how would we? Even if Killian didn't know, it still wouldn't be out in the open.

Where did we even start?

My curiosity drew me up to the altar, the small table filled with peculiar objects. Feathers, bones, crystals, and herbs were all placed around a symbol, which looked like a star lightly carved into the table. Warwick and Ash came up beside me, peering down.

"Holy... shit," Ash muttered, his eyes widening at the articles on the table.

"What?" His tone spiked anxiety in my gut, intensifying the knot in my stomach I had since the book took me here.

"That altar is a—"

"A Druid altar." A crackly voice came from in front of us, yanking our heads up to an outline in the murky shadows. Warwick and Ash pointed their guns at the silhouette, but I didn't move. A realization hit my chest before it fully unspooled in my mind.

The figure shuffled out of the shadows, a fire bulb flickering across his weathered features and distorted frame.

A sharp gasp burned down my lungs, my eyes taking in what I already knew deep down.

"About time you arrived, my girl." His blue eyes found mine.

Wearing exactly the same dirty white outfit I saw him in last, his hair even greasier, was the Druid.

Tadhgan.

# Chapter 12

"Tad?" My voice squeaked, my brain tripping and rolling over itself, trying to make sense of his presence here.

A soft smile pulled at his mouth as he hobbled closer to us, ignoring the guns pointed at him.

"Looks like the gang is together again." He nodded at Warwick and Kek. "Should have known they would gravitate toward you like the sun."

"Hey, old man." Kek smirked, flicking her head at the Druid. "And I should have known someone as stubborn as you wouldn't die. Not that lucky, I guess."

He grinned back at her. "Death will come for me soon enough, but not today."

"Wait." I held up my hands. "Wha-what are you doing here?" My head shook, not all the pieces clicking.

"Doing here?" He scoffed, lifting one arm in a general motion. "I never left here."

I took in his ratty hair and the soiled white Halálház uniform he still wore, his trusty cane gone.

"This is where you've been hiding since Halálház was bombed?" My mouth parted. "That was, like, a month ago."

"Was it?" His white brows curved up. "Time means so little to me."

"How?" I shook my head. "Weren't the doors to the tunnels magic-locked?"

"Oh, my girl, fae magic means little to us Druids." He batted his hand, stopping on the other side of the altar from me.

"Why are you in Killian's territory? Practically in his house." Warwick growled, keeping his weapon on him. "Don't tell me he or his guards haven't noticed you've been squatting so close for a month?"

"Hardly anyone comes this way anymore. No need since the prison is out of use, but you should know a Druid can hide in plain sight."

I'd heard powerful demons and some Druids had the power to almost cloak themselves in their surroundings. Your eye passed over them, seeing nothing on the surface unless you reached out and touched them, destroying the illusion.

"No better place to be than right under his nose." His gaze darted to Warwick then Ash, ignoring the others in the room. "You don't need those weapons. This old, crooked body won't put up much of a fight against you."

"Tadhgan, the Druid of old. The oldest living Druid in the entire world." Ash kept his gun on him. "You think it's your physical body I'm afraid of?"

"Dear boy, if I wanted to hurt you, I would have already. But I am a white Druid. We do not harm; we heal and help. Plus, why would I when I've been waiting for you to arrive? Well, her most of all."

"Waiting for me?" I gestured to myself.

"I felt you visit me before. I knew you were coming." Tad's gaze landed back on me. His eyes were like oceans of knowledge and life. They slowly went from me to Warwick, his lips flattening together in slight confusion.

"You mean through the fae book yesterday?" Ash lowered his arms, peering over at me.

"Was that yesterday? Like I said, time is a funny thing to me now." His attention went back and forth between Warwick and me intently. "Incredible... I have never seen anything like this before. And I have lived for many, many centuries and seen the most unbelievable things."

"What?" The sensation of bugs crawled over my skin.

"Still no auras, but there is now an astonishingly bright glow between you two." The Druid's brows creased. "Life connects you, but death binds you."

As if Tad could peel back my skin and see everything inside, letting in the chill of truth, my limbs started to tremble.

"And your sexual glow... oh my..." His eyes widened.

"Yeah, we heard and felt it." Kek snorted. "Allllll night and morning nonstop. Do you want to know how many times I had to take matters into my own hands or out on the grumpy coffee guy? Like an *obscene* amount."

"Jan? Really?" Luk's mouth dropped in shock. "Wow, I guess he's cute in a gruff, cranky way." Luk tilted his head in thought.

"He's pretty decent in bed. Next time you should join us, pretty boy."

"Okay, enough," Warwick barked. "We are wasting time. We need to get back on mission."

"For the nectar," Tad said evenly, snapping every head to him.

"H-how did you know that?" My eyes widened; my muscles tightened defensively.

"Because I am old and wise." He winked. "And because there is no other reason to come straight into Killian's domain. Most people have forgotten the rumors, lost over the years into the void. As I keep saying, time is a funny thing to an ancient mind. What it remembers was yesterday and yesterday is what it forgets."

"You know about the nectar? What it is?" I licked my dry lips.

"The last object to hold pure fae magic? So strong it can survive being in Earth's polluted realm." His head dipped. "Yes, I am aware of it."

"Is it here?" I advanced to him. "Have you found it?"

"Would I be here if I found it? Still look like this?" He motioned to his bowed body, a flinch of pain straining his cheek. "No, if it is here, it is not showing itself to me. I have hunted it for years, and *even I* have not been able to locate it." Tad reached for my hand. "Help an old man sit down. I can't stand for long like I used to."

He grunted as I assisted him onto the floor, taking a seat in front of the small altar table. "I only know of a possible rumor stating it was last seen here." His eyes slid to Ash. "But possibly our old friend on your back might be able to help us."

Ash automatically touched the strap of his backpack.

"I can feel it," Tad said. "It calls to me. In the ancient days, Druids were the historians for the old high fae kings and queens. The original fae books are of our making."

Ash's unsure gaze went to me. I nodded, having no other ideas about how to find the nectar. He pursed his lips but walked over to us, shedding the bag off his shoulder, dropping it next to the table.

"Sit down, girl." Tad motioned for me to sit opposite him. I lowered on my knees as Ash dug the book out of his pack.

"Those little fuckers!" He growled. "They got into my mushrooms again!"

My attention shot down to the bag as he yanked the book out. Two passed-out figures snored and drooled on the cover, tiny crumbs of mushroom stuck to them. Bitzy was curled up, sucking on her middle finger, on top of her crumpled paper wings. Opie was spread eagle, his crown down over his eyes, his dress askew, showing off his naked bits.

My hand went to my mouth, trying not to laugh.

"Oh my." Tad fought a smile. "I wondered why the book was so vexed."

"I thought you sealed the mushrooms away from them," Warwick grumbled, stomping over to the brownie and imp, picking the pair up off the book more gently than I thought he would. Bitzy opened her eyes for a moment, reaching out to Warwick with a coo before passing out again. Warwick shook his head. "You know better."

"I did secure it!" Ash exclaimed.

Except locks didn't work on them.

"Never underestimate sub-fae. Especially when it comes to their mushrooms." I winked at Ash, making him grumble under his breath. He wiped the gummy remnants of the fungi off the book cover and placed it in front of Tad and me.

Instantly, the mood shifted.

Tad inhaled shakily, his hand hovering over the book, his chest heaving.

"Everything okay?"

"Yes." He nodded, swallowing. "Just been a long time since I've been in the company of such a powerful book. It's even older than I am. It holds so much knowledge." He tilted his head in wonder. "Except for a time in the 1400s, there seems to be a few pages of a war missing."

All eyes turned to the creatures in Warwick's arms, donned with the omitted pages.

Ash grunted and swore with fury.

"Oh well, they are being used for a much better purpose. War is always the same, no matter what time period. It was a horrendous, dark, and bloody time anyway. Not missing much." Tad winked at me, smiling. "I, for one, am glad to see it gone."

I grinned back at him. Out of the corner of my eye, I saw Ash still shifted with irritation.

"Good to see you, old friend." Tad reached down, palming the book. "Hmmm... that's interesting."

"What is?"

"This book seems very interested in you." Tad's piercing eyes met mine. "I was wrong when I said you were an ordinary human. You hid yourself well."

My throat dry, I tried to swallow. "What do you mean by that?"

He stared at me like I was a bug pinned to a board. Heat filled my face, a trickle of sweat sliding down my back.

"There is something about you." His brows furrowed together, his gaze intense. "Familiar... but not. I can't place it. I ignored it when we first met, but I can't now. There is something there I should know, but I can't grasp it. It's like a wisp of a cloud I'm trying to capture."

"I don't understand."

"Me neither, child."

"Please..." I begged. "I don't know what I am. Do you?"

Tad studied me for a moment, his brows furrowing.

"I don't." He looked astonished at his own claim. "Which is extremely perplexing. Everything is *something*... but you and him." He nodded to Warwick. "I can't fathom it. I used to think it was because you hid your auras from me. It was the only explanation. *Everyone* has an aura... like a fingerprint. I have been alive a very long time and have seen every possible species of human, fae, and animal. I don't understand, but you and Warwick aren't in any of them... you're somewhere..."

In between.

Gray.

I gritted my teeth, keeping back the flood of emotions. I kept hoping someone would come along and tell me all the theories had been wrong—I was a normal girl, or at least have an idea, a name. Tad of all people should see what others couldn't. He should be the one who would know. But even *he* couldn't see what I was.

*"And here I thought I was the only freak, princess."* Warwick pressed up behind me as the actual man stood feet away.

*"Cac!" Shit!* Tad's curved spine jerked, tipping him over on his side, his eyes wide and darting between Warwick and me. "How—how is it possible?"

The link snapped in a blink as Warwick jerked back.

"How were you here and—and there at the same time?" Tad stumbled over his words, the fear and confusion genuine.

"You could see me?" Warwick rumbled, a vein in his neck twitching. The entire room, except Ash, was completely confused.

"Y-yes." Tad pushed himself back up as much as he could, his expression twisting to wonder. "It was like when I saw her visit me yesterday. An impression. An apparition."

Ash's head bounced in agreement. "I can't see it, but I can feel it when they do the link thing."

Tad rubbed his head. "This makes so much more sense now."

"What does?" I asked.

"Back at Halálház, I would think I'd see a glimmer of Warwick near you—a few times when you were in the ring fighting in the Games—but when I looked again, he was gone. I thought my eyes were senile, and this old mind was starting to lose its last marbles."

I recalled those times, too, when this thing between us could still be explained away and denied.

"You two are becoming so interesting. I thought I had seen it all." Tad brushed a few strands of his knotted hair back.

"So, you've never run into anything like this before?" I hoped he had an explanation and examples of whatever this was between us.

"No." He continued to stare at us with utter shock. "Never in my years have I see anything close to this. It shouldn't be possible."

"Hey?" Tracker's voice boomed from a doorway he was guarding, Ava on the other entrance. "Sorry to rush the catching up and all, but can we get this moving? We are still in enemy territory."

Tracker was right. Finding the nectar and getting out of here was the most important. The rest could wait.

"Give me your hands." Tad reached over. "Don't let go, okay? I will be right with you."

I nodded, knowing what to do. I reached over, clasping onto Tad's bony fingers. I shut my lids and took a breath as our twined fingers touched the page. Electricity shot through me, the inhuman voice vibrating through my bones.

*"Tadhgan, the Druid. It has been a long time,"* the book spoke. *"And Brexley Kovacs, the girl who defies nature. Tell me what you seek. Do not waste my time."*

*"I apologize I wasn't clear enough last time. I would like to see where the nectar is hidden,"* I asked as concisely as I could.

*"Again, you requesting this information is interesting,"* the book replied. *"I can only show what is written."*

135

The moment the book uttered the last syllables, the sensation of falling and spinning rattled my head, bile coiling in my stomach as Tad and I fell into the archives of the past.

When I opened my eyes, the book had placed me in the same dark tunnel it had the other day.

Alone.

"Tad?" I whispered, peering around the cool, murky passageways, goosebumps breaking out over my arms. Looking for the Druid, he was nowhere in sight. "Tad, are you here?"

"This way," a deep voice muttered. The sound of multiple boots hitting the ground right around the corner flung me automatically into a dark crevice, my spine stinging as I slammed into the rock wall.

Two figures were about to pass me when another man stepped into the path, cutting them off.

"Once a thief, always a thief." A gasp shot up my throat as I took in a younger version of Killian. He was dressed in a nice but outdated suit, his hair a little longer, flipping around his ears. Less polished than the man I knew now.

"You would know." A tall, broad dark-haired man with a deep voice stepped up closer to Killian, coming into view. My chest sucked in at the man's rugged, sexual aura. He possessed a feral quality, like he could fuck you at the same time he sliced you in half with the long sword attached to his side without blinking an eye.

Standing about six feet, slender but ripped, with dark almond-shaped eyes, thick dark lashes, and long black hair, I had no doubt he was fae by his unbelievable beauty.

"Wow, look at you." The dark-haired man's eyes went over Killian with aversion. "All fancy now, aren't we?"

"Looks like nothing has changed with you. Still a second-rate thief..." Killian puffed his chest, glaring at him.

"Tradesman." The man stepped closer, challenging him. "And you think because you wear an expensive suit and have a title before your name, you are above the rest of us now?"

"I am the Lord of Budapest. I rule everyone here now. This is my king-dom." Killian's silky voice frayed at the end, his anger curling his hands.

"You don't rule me." The thief moved closer, threatening. "You forget, Killian, I know the *real* you. I was the one to put the brand on your chest. Know where you come from." I saw Killian's eye twitch at this claim. "If your minions only knew how you really got this role—

who you were before—would they still worship you?" The man flicked the pocket square at Killian's chest with a scoff. "Play dress up all you want. I know the real street rat underneath."

"Fuck you," Killian growled, lurching for the man, his pure fae magic crackling the air.

A petite dark-haired woman next to the man, who almost blended into the shadows, got between them. She put a blade at Killian's throat, halting him on his feet.

"Step back, Kil." Her long, shiny black ponytail whipped around. Her frame was so small you might mistake her for a young girl, but her face was so utterly breathtaking, you could see a sensual woman there.

Killian stared at her, shock and hurt on his face.

"Kitty-Kat." Killian's voice changed, going low. Pained.

"Don't call me that." Her face twisted, a flicker of agony dancing over her expression, pushing her blade deeper against his jugular.

"So, you're with him now?" Killian shook his head, sadness in his tone. His gaze moved over her with such deep longing, agony, and... *love.* "You hated him." He sneered. "Wanted to kill him. Guess we're all liars and thieves here."

"This has nothing to do with him," she spit out. "Let us leave, Killian, and no harm will come to you."

"Too late for that, Kitty-Kat." His tone suggested he meant something else entirely. A history between them I wasn't privy to.

Her lashes fluttered like she wanted to cry, but instead, she rolled her shoulders back, locking down her features. "I don't want to hurt you, but we're leaving with the nectar—*no matter what.*" Her head tilted slightly to the small messenger bag hanging off her hip.

It was like a punch to my gut. Without one inkling of doubt, I knew the nectar was in there. It was real. And a few feet away from me.

My eyes latched on to the satchel. I swore it felt my presence, coming alive with awareness. I could no longer hear them or even see past what I knew was inside. The pull coming from her bag pushed my back off the wall, and I took a step. It called to me and wanted me to take it. As if it had its own heartbeat, I heard it pulse with power, the beat in rhythm with my own heart. Energy hummed in my veins.

I took another stride, about to step from the shadows when a violent stir of activity snapped me out of my trance. A muscular blond guy came up behind Killian, a blonde girl with him, hitting Killian in the back of the head with the butt of his gun. Killian hit the ground with a thud.

"Thank me later, asshole! Come on!" Blondie waved them forward, running back down the tunnel with the blonde girl.

Both the dark-haired woman and man hesitated by Killian. The woman he called Kitty-Kat bent over, her fingers touching his pulse, letting out a heavy breath.

"He'll be fine." The guy yanked her up, pointing her for the exit. "You were meant to rule. You always were," The man muttered down at the form, a mix of resentment and fondness shading his tone. "Still think you're a huge douche, though."

The pair started to move, but she paused, her head twisted in my direction, her lids narrowing, almost catlike, as if she were trying to see through the darkness. See me.

"What's wrong?" he asked, his head snapping around with caution.

"Thought I saw... Nothing." She shook her head, heading down the passage, while he glanced around suspiciously.

I didn't move or breathe.

"Croygen, come on!"

He gave Killian one last look, turned around, and ran after her.

*The nectar.* I pushed forward. The need to follow it, to take it from her, moved my feet, but I was yanked back by the book, letting me go no farther.

"Noooo!" I screamed, fighting as it flung me back into darkness.

"Fuck!" A growl hit my ears, a hand clutching the back of my head, padding it before it slammed back onto the stone. Cracking my eyes open, aqua irises stared down into mine, long hair tickling my face, a slight smirk on Warwick's face. "I'm getting you a helmet."

Groaning, my lids fluttered for a moment, nausea making my stomach spin, the need to vomit coating my tongue.

"Sorry, Fishy, that one was a one point five at best." Opie marched up my arm beneath Warwick. "No dismount at all. We should try something higher."

"Why aren't you still passed out with your friend?" Warwick grumbled, brushing him off me.

"I have a fast metabolism. Mother always said it was how I stayed so trim." He waved at his body, a potbelly protruding from the space between his paper skirt and top.

Warwick scoffed, turning back to me. "You all right?" he muttered huskily, slowly sitting me up, his large warm palm brushing back the hair sticking to my face.

"Yeah." I leaned my head against him, still feeling queasy. He felt warm and safe, and I longed to curl up against him and nap.

With a burning gaze on me, I shifted my head to see Tad across from me. His jaw was set, his eyes a mix of perplexity and fear.

"What?" I croaked, pushing my weight off Warwick's corded arm. Dread slithered into my stomach.

"It didn't let me in," Tad replied, stunned. "It blocked me from following you."

My attention drifted to Ash, then back to Tad. "It didn't let him in either."

"But *I* am a Druid." Tad adjusted his bowed back, his head shaking. "We are its maker. My kinfolk created these books. *Our* magic. But this time, it tossed me back out, only wanting you..." Tad slanted his head, really peering at me. "Why?"

I had no answer.

"What did it show you?" he asked.

My mouth opened, then shut, the images of Killian, the things that were said, the hints about his past. He knew about the nectar. The whole scene created more questions than answers, and for some reason, I didn't feel like divulging all I saw to this entire room. There was just one question they wanted to know anyway.

"It's not here. Someone took it."

Ash groaned, his hand running through his hair. Warwick blew out a long breath, his head falling forward.

"Are you saying this was all for nothing?" Tracker moved away from the entrance he had been guarding, stomping up to us. "Are you fucking kidding me? You dragged us into enemy territory, and it's not here?"

Warwick rose to his feet, his chest expanding as he took one step to Tracker, his physique like a boulder. "Step back, asshole."

He would not tell him twice.

"Track." Ava rushed forward, pulling him back, a lot smarter than Tracker in understanding Warwick's dominance and threat level. She was fae and probably felt Warwick's power. "Calm down. It's not her fault."

"It's not?" He huffed. "How do we know she's even telling the truth? She could be saying that so we don't get our hands on it."

Warwick growled. Ava yanked Tracker back out of the legend's reach.

"Did it show you anything else?" Tad brought me back to the topic. "Did the book show you where it was taken?"

"No." I shook my head, my shoulders sagging.

"Not one clue where the pirate took it?"

My head jerked to Tad as if ice water poured down my back, scrambling me up to my feet. "I-I didn't say anything about a pirate." Fear clutching my lungs, I rose, stepping back, a warning bell twanging in my chest. "How did you know a pirate took it?"

Sadness furrowed his bushy eyebrows, his blue eyes finding mine with such devastation.

"How did you know that?" I gritted out, his silence storming fear and fury. "Tell me!"

"You remember when I said one day I might need kindness in return from you?" He swallowed, his head dipping. "I am so sorry, dear girl."

"For what?" Panic heaved my lungs.

"For the fact this was all a setup." The beautiful voice I had come to know poured over the room like dark chocolate—smoky, bitter, and smooth—spinning me around to one of the unguarded entrances. Our group was quick to react, guns drawing up, pointing at the lord of the fae. He merely smirked, looking as handsome as ever in his expensive suit, his hair cut short and styled perfectly.

Groomed and polished, he looked like a true king compared to the man I saw in the book.

His guards filed in behind him, covering all the exits, outnumbering us by triple. I saw a familiar pair of brown eyes among them. Zander kept his expression blank, but his eyes were intently on me. Right next to him, Nyx stared at me just as attentively, but with an opposite emotion.

"You betrayed *my* kindness, Ms. Kovacs. I house you, feed you, protect you. And this is how you repay me?" Killian's violet gaze latched on to me, adding more weight to my chest. "As you humans like to state... fair is fair."

"You don't play fair," I replied.

A slow smile spread over his face.

"You're right; I don't." His head tipped, indicating the Druid behind me. "But I wasn't the one who gave you up so easily."

# Chapter 13

Betrayal knifed through my gut, my gaze darting to Tad, his eyes sorrow-filled, which burned this deeper into my chest.

"Why?" My head wagged in disbelief. We had gone through so much. He had been one of the few friends I had at Halálház. "Was any of it real?"

"Yes." He nodded. "It was all real. I had no idea who you were until your human friend outed you. From the moment I met you, I felt drawn to you." *Drawn to you*. How many times had I heard that now? Was any relationship I had genuine or was it because they felt this 'draw?' "I'm sorry. I never wanted it to happen like this."

"Fuck you." I tried to keep my eyes from watering, shutting the walls around me. Nothing felt true anymore... even Warwick. His connection was even more forced. Not something he picked or chose for himself.

"I care about you, but you don't know the full truth," Tad said quietly.

"Care about me? You only care about yourself." I huffed, wagging my head, turning back to Killian, a sneer riding my lip. "You tricked us. Good job. Now what? Lock us all in cages? Force us to be your guinea pigs?"

Killian rubbed his chin with a cool detachment.

"You knew about the nectar this whole time," I whispered hoarsely.

141

Warwick's and Ash's heads jerked from me to Killian, taking in the information I hadn't shared with them yet.

Killian dipped his head in agreement, his hands sliding into his trouser pockets. It was what he did when he wanted to show he felt no threat. "I did." His gaze met mine, challenging, and I didn't relent.

"I saw you." My sentence was simple, but my sentiment was full of context. I wanted him to know I saw and heard more than he probably ever wanted anyone to know. Things he might kill to keep quiet.

A nerve along his cheek was the only thing I saw tic, his glare staying cold and elusive, but I knew he understood my meaning.

We stayed locked on each other for a few beats before he turned to my group.

"Lower your weapons."

"You first." Warwick vibrated with violence, barely holding back. No doubt he would try to tear through this room while the guards pumped his body with bullets, Ash right next to him.

The seven of us could make an impressive dent, but death would be absolute in the end. Even if it wasn't Warwick or me, it would be for the others.

I couldn't chance their lives.

*"Don't."* I spoke to Warwick through our link. *"Do what he asks."*

*"Not how I work, princess."*

*"Don't let your ego get the others killed."*

Warwick growled under his breath, his weight shifting. It took him a full minute before he very reluctantly dropped his gun, his jaw locked down and anger straining his muscles. Ash blinked at him in bewilderment, shocked the killer wolf was surrendering so easily, before he followed his lead.

One by one, the rest of our group followed suit. Several guards came up, taking our weapons away, more guards staying on Kek and Warwick, as they were the two more powerful ones in the room.

"Not at all surprised by these two..." Killian weaved through us, pointing at Warwick and me, landing in front of Ash. "But you." He slanted his head. "And here you told me you despised Warwick, that he betrayed you, and you'd kill him on sight."

Ash smirked at Killian smugly as if saying, "You were the fool to believe it."

When I first got to his cottage, Ash said he worked for Killian as a healer, but it was something I had forgotten along the way. Now I realized how much Ash had risked coming with us. His friendship with Warwick put his life on the line, but it would always come first.

Killian moved closer to Ash. "Little did I know we had a spy amongst us."

With all my willpower, I kept my attention from sliding to Zander. Ash was no spy, but Killian wasn't wrong—he had one among him.

"You know what I do to traitors? I cut out their tongues, scoop out their eyes, and display their heads on a spike along the wall," Killian declared evenly, like he was stating the weather. The guy I saw in the book, full of heartbreak and palpable anger, was no longer; he had chiseled himself into an aloof leader.

"And I'd still be prettier than you." Ash's chin went up, his nose flaring.

Killian's smile was full of dark humor, his face even with Ash, both not giving an inch.

Gradually, Killian stepped back, turning to me. Any amusement he found with Ash was gone, his eyes growing cold.

"I should kill you," Killian snarled, traveling to me.

Warwick made a move to me, the guards reacting to his shift with more weapons being stabbed into his skin and bullets ready to enter his temple.

"Both of you." Killian motioned to both of us. "Bombing my house, killing my soldiers... ." He flicked his head to Nyx. Her entire form vibrated with fury, barely checking herself. "I could so easily let her go... let her have her revenge."

Warwick scoffed, a mocking grin tugging his lips.

Intrigue danced in Killian's eyes, his head wagging. "I knew something about Brexley ensnared the infamous Wolf. But willing to give up our truce for her?" His eyebrows curved up. "Become her servant boy?"

Warwick lurched forward, his teeth bared.

*"No!"* My link stood between the men, my hand pressing into Warwick's heaving chest. *"He's trying to provoke you. Don't let him win."*

Warwick's lip hitched in a snarl at me. Tension and aggression rose in the space, but he eventually eased back.

"The thing is, this will work in my favor. You will protect her at all costs, and I need her alive." Killian's head swiveled to me. "For the time being, anyway."

Dread spread through my stomach like cement.

"I almost had it..." Killian's hand rolled into a ball like he could feel the object in his hand. "And it slipped through my fingers... disappearing for good." By a sexy ass pirate and a girl who I had no doubt broke Killian's heart in some way.

"And you are going to find it for me." Killian nodded at me.

My head shook. "Why would you think I could find it? How did you even know to set us up? That I had a connection to the book or the nectar?"

"Because I told him you could," Tad spoke up behind me, rising back up to his feet, his face pinched with pain.

"You?" Hurt flushed once again through me. "How would you even know?"

Tad put his hand on the wall, keeping his S-shaped back from causing him to topple over. He looked even worse than when I last saw him. "I can see Markos did you no favors in not teaching you the power of Druids."

He was right. Istvan pretty much brushed off us learning anything substantial besides the basics about Druids. There were hardly any in this part of the world, and he thought it was a waste of time, saying they were no more than glorified witches.

"Our magic is different from fae. I can do spells no fae can do. I tried to reveal the nectar's location... you know what it showed me time after time?" Tad licked at his cracked lips, his gaze twisting rot into my gut. "You."

"Me?" I jerked back. "Why me? I don't understand."

"I don't either. However, the one thing I've learned, we beings can be wrong on many things, influenced by feelings, circumstances, and outside forces. The one thing never wrong... is magic itself." A flinch of pain crossed Tad's face as he adjusted his stance. My heart longed to go over to him, to help ease his agony, but I also couldn't forget his betrayal. "As old as I am, I still do not know or understand everything. This world is full of mystery. I cannot answer your question as to why. I simply know it is. The spell showed me you. The book only allowed you in. You are the key, my girl. I just don't know to what yet."

"Wouldn't the book know where it is? Can't I go in and ask it?" I had, but it showed me the nectar leaving here, not where it went after.

"Unless it has been lost," Tad replied.

"I swear, if that brownie made thong underwear out of that

chapter..." Warwick mumbled under his breath, making me snort. Looking back at where Opie and Bitzy were supposed to be, I saw they had vanished, hiding from Killian, their old master's boss.

"So..." Hands on my hips, I blew out a breath, closing my lids briefly before lifting my head to Killian. "If I agree to look for the nectar, you will let us all go?"

"You think I would fall for that?" Killian's mouth curled, an eyebrow cocking up. "The devil is in the details." He clicked his tongue at me, strolling up until he was a breath away, his rich smell causing me to inhale sharply, not able to control my reaction to his nearness. "You *find* the nectar and bring it back to *me*." He leaned in, his mouth barely an inch away from mine. "And *only* me... Do you understand, Ms. Kovacs?" he said low, his lips almost brushing mine.

I nodded, my pulse fluttering against my neck. I couldn't deny there was an attraction between us. A bond.

"Do you *promise*?" His breath skated down my throat, his words sensual and coy. I understood they were anything but. A promise in the fae world was absolute. They couldn't break it, unlike humans, who broke them all the time.

"I can promise, but I'm not fae," I responded. "Means nothing to us humans."

"Oh, come now, *Brexley*." The sound of my name from his mouth pulsed through my body, shivering my bones. A growl hummed from Warwick, but Killian only moved in closer, whispering in my ear, my lashes lowering. "I think we all know you are not human either."

My eyes bolted open with a jerk. Hearing it from multiple people didn't make it any easier to accept.

"Need more incentive?" He stepped back, snapping his fingers. "Nyx?"

Nyx stepped into the tunnels returning with two figures. A dark-haired woman and a young boy. My eyes widened, recognizing them instantly.

Damn.

"Uncle Warwick?" The boy looked up at him with wide, scared eyes.

"Nooooooo!" Warwick roared, shoving through the guards like they were paper dolls, his legs coming to a sudden stop as Nyx held a gun to the woman's temple.

I'd seen them briefly through our link, but I had no doubt who she was. She was even more beautiful in person, and the little boy was a carbon copy of her and his uncle. Eliza Farkas stood firm, her arms protecting her son, her shoulders back, the same determined strength I saw in Warwick running through her veins.

"You fucking coward!" Warwick seethed at Killian, barely holding himself back. "This your only play? Holding them prisoner? Using an innocent child and woman as bait?"

"I didn't want to do anything." Killian pulled his hands away, advancing back toward Warwick. "You forced my hand. Betrayed me. Blew up my home and stole what was mine when I had graciously let you be free—let your family free. You are the one who put their lives back in danger." He tipped his head at Eliza, her chin notching up, her lids lowering in a glower at the Seelie lord. "And we both know she's not some damsel in distress. She's too much of a Farkas."

"Fuck you," she spat at him.

"See?" Killian motioned to her.

"Someday, Killian." Warwick bared his teeth, his tone low and threatening. "I'm going to kill you."

"I look forward to seeing you try," Killian replied, flicking his chin at me. "But until then, Wolf, you keep her alive, and I will keep your family unharmed and secure."

Both men peered at me. I felt the heaviness of the quest pressing down on me.

"Why me?" I indicated to myself. "I mean, you knew the people who took it from here. They were your friends, right?" I trailed off, seeing Killian's eyes darken with warning, his jaw clenching.

"They are not my friends." His silky voice had a jagged edge through it. "And I have already been down that road. It's a dead end. They no longer have it."

"What happened?"

"Someone got the better of them." A slight glint shone in his eyes, as if he loved the idea his old friends had been defeated too. "The only thing I know is it was lost here in Hungary. The thieves escaped with it by boat."

"It could be anywhere by now. How am I supposed to find it?"

"That is not my problem, Ms. Kovacs." His gaze zeroed in on me with intensity, the feel of his magic tingling my skin. "I'm letting all of you live, walk out of here unscathed, even though you've broken into *my* property, planning to rob *me*. Do you know what happens to people who do that?"

"I've already been through your house of horrors, *Killian*." I folded my arms, feeling the power of his name on my tongue grazing my thighs and forcing him to inhale sharply. I forgot how powerful names, especially his, could be. "And survived."

"You think you would survive again?" His teeth ground together. "There will be *no* escaping the new prison. I can guarantee that. You two made sure of that."

Fighting back the chill shaking my bones and the sickness knotting in my stomach, I knew there would be no way I'd endure another time in prison, not with my mind intact. Death sounded far more desirable than going back to the House of Death.

But I had no leads on where the nectar was taken after it left here fifteen years ago. If the pirate and his group lost it soon after, it could be anywhere, with anyone. It could be gone for good.

"You have one month, Ms. Kovacs." Killian moved in so close I could feel his body heat soaking through my clothes. Leaning in, he whispered in my ear. "And then I come to collect."

Escorted by a few guards, we were shoved roughly out the same door we came in, with fewer weapons than we started with. Killian's men took all but one from each of us, which he considered a "favor."

Nyx and Zander stayed with Killian when we left, both looking unhappy they didn't get the opportunity to chaperone me out, but for opposite reasons. I didn't even chance to look at Zander as I passed him, knowing Killian was watching me, but I could feel Zander's eyes on me. Burning with concerns and questions.

The tunnel door slammed shut, leaving the seven of us back on Gellert Hill. Dawn was over an hour away—the time when everything was at its darkest, when even night dwellers were thinning out and heading back home. The silence of the dead lands was unnerving and eerie.

The time when nothing good happened.

Blame, anger, aggression, and resentment fueled the spark in the air around us like gasoline. Tracker came after me, his fury bellowing from his mouth. "I knew not to trust you!" He stomped up to me. "I knew something was off about you! You are a fucking traitor!"

"How am I a traitor?" I didn't back down, instead getting right back in his face. I would gladly fight him. "Because of me, you are still alive."

"I'm only here because of *you*," he shouted, trying to loom over me. "It seems it was all bullshit. You're working with Lord Killian!"

"I didn't have a choice. You should be thanking me. You are still breathing."

"Thanking you?" He huffed. "I don't thank traitors. Kaptain thinks you're getting the nectar for him, to help our cause, to help us. However, it appears you are getting it for a fae lord... so which side are you on? You can only have one."

"Mine," I snapped. "I'm not working for anybody. And right now, no one gets it. I have to find it first."

"So what?" Tracker sneered, his eyes darting to Warwick. "He let us live, do his bidding like little bitches, because you are the fae lord's little whore *too*."

*Crack!*

A fist smashed into his face, snapping cartilage and bone. Blood spurted everywhere as Tracker crashed to the ground with a howl of agony.

Warwick moved over him. Leaning down, he fisted Tracker's jacket, yanking him until their faces were inches apart. I could already see the bruise pillowing the side of Tracker's face, his lip and nose cut and bleeding all over.

"I warned you," Warwick seethed, furiously spitting his words. "You speak to her again like you did, and I will have no problem cracking your human spine like a twig. Or I'll let her do it." He flicked his head to me. "Don't for one minute think she couldn't kill you and not even break a sweat. You are nothing but a puffed-up façade. You have no idea what true strength is." As Warwick brought him closer, Tracker's swollen and wounded face tried to glare back. "I know you've heard the tales about me. They are all true. Give me a reason to kill you... I'm *begging* you."

*"Warwick."* I felt his rage humming like a live wire, summoning up the darkness of death. He was close to slipping, to falling over. My invisible hand slid up his spine. His muscles locked at my touch, then relaxed, his shoulders lowering. He took a deep breath, growling at Tracker before shoving his head back into the cement and stepping back like he was a vile piece of shit.

"Next time you're dead," Warwick snarled at Track, pushing past me to where the motorcycles were hidden in the brush. It wasn't a threat; it was a promise. I remember him killing Rodriguez's buddy in prison without hesitation or conscience. Tracker was lucky to be getting more than one warning. And I knew it was only because of me.

Ava darted to Tracker the moment Warwick was no longer a threat, pulling him into her lap and inspecting the damage.

"Damn, that was so hot." Kek blew out, cutting through the thick silence. "Anyone else so fucking turned on right now they could dry hump a wall?" She peered around, and her hand raised. "Just me?"

"I'm a tree fairy... when am I not turned on?" Ash rubbed his head, hitching his bag with the book and my two friends higher on his shoulder. Taking a moment, he closed his lids briefly before he glanced up. "So, what now?"

"I have no idea." I shrugged. I felt so lost, like being told I had to find one single strand of hair in the entire world. "But I think we need to get far away from here, regroup, and talk then."

"We can't go to my house, too many people, and it's certainly being watched." Ash frowned.

*"Kitty's?"* I spoke to Warwick privately.

*"Fuck no. I don't trust anyone except you and Ash. I'm not putting her in more danger. It's enough when I do it."* He straddled the bike. *"But she's not the only place that takes in vagabonds and the depraved in the Savage Lands."*

*"So, we're going to your house then?"* I sneered.

Warwick's brow arched up at me, dripping with carnal wickedness, the feel of his mouth grazing my pussy. *"Don't have one... there's only one place I plan on burrowing into."*

He smirked as he watched my breath hitch, turning to the group.

"Follow me," he said, revving the engine and pulling the motorbike up to me. I hopped on behind him, feeling eased and turned on when I tucked myself behind him.

"What about Tracker?" Ava hissed, waving down at him.

"Figure it out." Warwick gave her no shred of concern. "Or leave him here. I don't care. We ride now."

Ava's face twisted with anxiety, probably knowing she would be left if she didn't act quickly.

"I'll take him." Luk rushed over to help her pick Tracker up and set him on Luk's bike. Tracker was conscious, but not alert enough to be the one driving. "You two ride together." Luk nodded at Ava and Kek, neither looking happy about the switch.

Without another word, Warwick tore down the road, away from the place where we used to be imprisoned. We had left this hell before on a bike, but this time we weren't shredding through wilderness, being shot at, with guards on our tail and an owl overhead tracking us.

Though I strangely felt we were still running for our lives.

*Chapter 14*

The others finally caught up with us at the bottom of the hill. Our group traveled over the Elisabeth Bridge this time, crossing the line between the fae kingdom and the human one, heading for the lawless land in between.

As soon as we got off the bridge, I felt a tingle at the base of my neck, a shiver of dread chafing my spine.

The awareness of being watched.

Preyed on.

It was the same feeling I had when we had entered the city hours earlier. The one I should have listened to.

Everything was too quiet. Too still.

"Warwick..." His name barely made it off my tongue.

*Bang! Bang! Bang!*

Shots inundated the night, fracturing the peace that once hung in the air. Bullets volleyed around us, kissing the space near my ears, blowing out our front tire. My forehead slammed into Warwick's back, the wheels rolling to a rough, bumpy stop, air wheezing out of the tire.

Everything turned to chaos as gunfire descended on our group.

"Go!" Warwick yelled, both of us clambering off the motorbike, darting for safety.

Peering over my shoulder, my eyes caught on shadowy figures moving up the road toward us in formation while we dove into the shadows.

It took me a moment to realize what I was seeing. The familiar uniforms and formation.

An army... once *my* army. One that was fully loaded and ready to put down an HDF traitor and anyone with her.

"Fuck!" Warwick grabbed my hand, yanking me from the defenseless shadows to what looked like the remains of a small burned-out car next to a crumbling church. Eroded and thin, the hunk of metal wouldn't stop the bullets for long.

They waited until we were in a place where we had nowhere to hide and could pick us off one by one.

Ash crawled in next to us while Kek, Ava, Luk, and Tracker scrambled to the other side of the road, hiding behind signs and cement road barriers.

"HDF, right? How did they know we were even here?" Ash hissed, pointing his gun over what was left of the scrap of metal.

"Why don't you go ask them?" Warwick replied dryly, his weapon turned toward the enemy.

The three of us fired at anything getting near us. But we all knew we had to be smart, not waste the ammunition we had.

Killian's men had stripped us of the majority of our weapons, and now we were faced with what looked like the entire HDF army. Far too many against seven. Istvan clearly didn't want to leave this to chance.

We were going to die here. No way my group, fae or not, could fight against all of HDF, and they were gaining ground. We needed help.

There was no conscious thought, only survival instinct that brought me to a small windowless room. Two sleeping forms filled the cots, and I felt the strings pulling me to one.

*"Scorpion!"* I bellowed.

His body wrenched, jumping awake. He sat up with a sharp inhale, startling the person in the cot on the other side of the room, but it was his hazel irises I concentrated on.

"What's wrong?" He scrambled out of the bed, sensing my terror.

A gunshot zinged by me, and we were back outside, Scorpion's eyes growing wide as he looked around, taking in our situation. *"Holy shit!"* he hissed through his teeth, standing in nothing but his briefs.

152

"*Fasz*," Warwick grumbled, reloading his gun with the last of his ammunition, his eyes flicking to Scorpion before pointing his weapon at the enemy. "I think I liked it better when I couldn't see your boyfriends, Kovacs."

"We need help—" A bullet from high above whizzed through Scorpion's phantom, cutting the link. My eyes darted up to where it came from, up high in the church tower window, the glass long gone.

A cry jerked my head back, seeing the bullet had found a target.

Luk's body spasmed, his hand going to his stomach before his body collapsed to the ground.

"Luk! No!" The shriek barely left my lips when another shot cracked through the air from the same direction, hitting the person next to Luk. With the precision of a marksman, the bullet went right between her eyes.

A scream howled in my lungs, never making it out as I watched Ava's body go still, her eyes wide open, her mind and body still not understanding... she was dead. The dark spot in the middle of her forehead barely bled, but it stained my memory as her figure tipped over, thumping to the ground. She stared lifelessly up at the stars, her eyes still wide and in shock.

"No!" Tracker bellowed. He crawled over to her, his pitch high and full of torment. "Ava!"

My head whipped up to where the shots were coming from, my lids narrowing, trying to find the culprit, but I couldn't make out anything in the window except a dark form. It was clear they had a sniper taking us down one by one. We were easy prey from above. A fishbowl.

"Wake up, Ava!" Tracker roared again, turning my head back to him. "No! Please... no." He leaned over her, shaking her, not wanting to believe what we all knew.

*Crack!*

Tracker's spine jolted. It was only a second, but time was suspended for a moment. Then he slumped over her body, joining her in permanent darkness.

*Crack!*

"Kek!" I screamed, watching my blue-haired friend go limp against the barrier she was hiding behind. The demon seemed invincible, the one girl who had befriended me in hell. She had stood up for me, had my back.

I didn't realize I was moving toward her. "Kovacs!" Warwick yanked me back into him. "You want to be shot down too?"

My eyes snapped back up to the tower. Something shifted in the dark shadows, stepping closer to the window.

As if a hand yanked out my lungs, a gasp tore through them, terror wrapping around my ribs, squeezing down. No. It wasn't possible. He was dead. I killed him. But death had spat him out too, disliking the foul taste of this man.

Kalaraja stood there brazenly, wanting me to see exactly who had killed my friends. His dark eyes burned into mine with sinister smugness, and I knew it was he who I felt watching when we entered Savage Lands hours earlier. How long had he been tracking me? Staying in the shadows, lying in wait?

He was purposefully killing my group off one by one, letting me watch. He would kill them all... except me. He wanted me. Or his master wanted me. The rest were in his way.

"Warwick! It's Kalaraja in the tower!"

Before he could even look up, more gunfire went off.

*Pop! Pop! Pop!*

I waited to feel the bullets sink into my flesh. Watch Ash and Warwick being executed right in front of my eyes, but then I saw some of the soldiers who were coming for us drop. Gunfire came from the side alleys.

In a blink, I was with Scorpion, Maddox, and Birdie, slinking through the alleys. I could see the HDF troops scrambling, trying to react to this new threat, coming at them from the side. More of Sarkis's army approached from all angles toward HDF, coming to help us.

Tears filled my eyes with gratitude.

*"Thank you,"* I muttered to Scorpion.

He walked right by my spirit with a wink, murmuring so only I could hear. "Had nothing better to do anyway."

"They're here." Back with Warwick and Ash, my chest heaved with relief. "Scorpion's here."

"Who the hell is Scorpion?" Ash questioned.

"Her other, *other* boyfriend," Warwick muttered, aiming at our enemy, waiting for one to get close enough. We were all running low on bullets. I was down to one; Ash also had just one round left.

"While they are distracted, you two run for the alley." Warwick's tone was an order.

"I'm not leaving you," I snarled, looking up at the tower. It appeared empty, though I knew he was somewhere in the shadows.

Waiting. "And what about them?" I motioned over to the rest of our group.

"It's too late for them," Warwick replied.

"You don't know that!" The thought of leaving Kek or Luk was painful. My brain couldn't even contemplate the fact she *could* die. Not like this.

"Ash," Warwick said his name poignantly.

Ash nodded like they could communicate with only a different tone of voice.

"What are you doing?" I looked between the two men, fear rushing in my veins, slamming my heart against my ribs.

Warwick pointed his gun at the troops moving closer. "Go!"

Ash's hand grabbed my arm, yanking me out from our hiding spot. Warwick covered us as we darted across the lanes. Blasts rang in my ears, skating over my skin, the iron discharge burning the inside of my nose, the fear of knowing any moment this might be my last.

A bullet hit Ash's shoulder as we dove behind the old crumbling church, the one Kalaraja was shooting from. He was close... hunting me in the dark.

"*Faszom!*" Pain seethed through Ash's teeth as we dove behind the wall. Sweat beaded his brow, his expression twisting in anguish. "Fuck, fae bullets hurt."

Before our time, I guess bullets were mainly made from lead, but since the fae had become known to live among us, humans switched to iron bullets. Iron was a poison to pure fairies like Killian, and to all other fae, iron still caused a severe amount of damage and pain.

He sucked in, cringing through the discomfort as he pointed his gun back toward the army, covering Warwick.

A noise came from down the alley, icing my veins. I twisted, not seeing anything through the murkiness. There might be a chance it was a rat or stray cat, but my gut screamed with warning.

Kalaraja.

Aiming my gun, a single bullet left in the chamber, my feet slowly inched down the path, worried about the murderer sneaking up behind. Kalaraja would kill everyone I cared about for the sole delight of hurting me. He was a fuckin' sociopath.

As Ash was distracted by the battle in the opposite direction, I crept away, my weapon aimed and ready to kill. A sound came from an adjacent path, twisting me down it. My pulse thumped in my ears, my boots padding silently, feeling like prey stepping into a trap. But I wasn't the fragile girl he thought I was. His ego was his weakness, thinking no one was better than he was.

Out of a doorway, a leg kicked out, a boot cracking at my arm. My gun flew from my grip, scattering across the cobble. The figure lurched for me.

There was a moment of shock, realizing the person wasn't the hired killer I had expected, but someone I used to call my friend. The slight hesitation allowed her a chance to slam her fist into my cheek, causing me to stumble away from her.

"Hanna," I breathed out her name.

"Don't say my name, traitor!" Blonde hair whipped around as she swung to me, her foot ramming into my stomach, doubling me over. "You are on their side now! How could you? You *fae lover*."

In our world, it was a slur, an insult worse than any other. Now I realized how brainwashed they had us. I would wear the title with honor now.

Ire shot up my back, spreading my shoulders. Snarling, I lurched for her, ramming into her like a train, causing her to slip. My knuckles slammed into her temple, almost dropping her to the stone. She regained her ground, her lip rising as she bounced back for me. My hand cracked across her cheek, pain zinging up my arm as it crushed over the bone.

She let out a wail, both of us falling back before we lunged for each other again.

As it had been with Aron, Hanna and I knew each other's moves. We were taught together, fought together, were pitted against each other.

She darted for me, and I jumped to the side, smashing my boot into her ribs. Tumbling to the ground, she rolled over and stood back up. Hanna had always been a good fighter. Quick. But I was faster. Before she could fully get to her feet, my fist connected with her throat, her head whipping back. Gagging and coughing, she collapsed into the wall, trying to recapture her breath.

"I don't want to hurt you." I put my hands up, my body still crouched, ready to defend myself if I needed to.

"Shut up," she croaked, her voice struggling to make it out of her throat. "Don't talk to me like we're friends."

"Hanna." She was the one person besides Caden I considered a true friend. "You don't know the full truth. Istvan is lying to you. What you think—"

"Caden was right. You have been brainwashed." She snarled, leaping for me. "You are nothing but a fae puppet!"

Moving faster than she could react, my arm struck out like a whip, dropping her. Her spine cracked against the cobble, knocking the wind out of her. She gulped for air as I pressed my boot on her chest, warning her to stay down.

"Like I said: I don't *want* to hurt you." I leaned over her. "But you know I *can*."

Her eyes went wide, sliding over my shoulder. I had been too focused on her to notice.

Rookie mistake.

My spine stiffened, feeling a presence when a muzzle of a gun pressed into the base of my neck.

"Release her now." A man's voice spoke into my ear, a hand latching on to my hip to keep me from spinning around.

It was instant. A reaction deep in my heart. My lids shut briefly, grief billowing in my soul like a storm, frozen in pain and sorrow. His voice was as familiar to me as my own. His smell, his touch, the feel of him near me.

"Caden." My voice came out soft, tainted with grief.

"I said *let her go*." He gripped me tighter, pressing the gun harder into my head as if my saying his name stirred hatred in him.

Dropping my boot from Hanna, she climbed up to her feet, hacking and spitting, her lids narrowed on me with disgust.

"Go tell Father we have her," Caden ordered her.

"Wow, Istvan is here? I feel special," I mocked.

Hanna glared at me.

"That's an order, private." Caden ignored me, speaking to Hanna. "Go!"

Hanna dipped her head, giving me one last scowl before darting down the passage.

"She's already in the field?" I watched her turn the corner. "My class wasn't graduating for another year."

"Yeah, well, we've had to accelerate the program. Everyone capable of fighting is now on the field," he hissed into my ear. *Capable* of fighting and *able* to fight fae were two different things. I knew Istvan didn't care if they weren't ready. He needed bodies, which was a sacrifice he was willing to make.

"She's not ready. None of you are," I said truthfully. They would all die. They weren't prepared for what really was out here.

"Father sees the threat is bigger than we first thought... because of *you*."

"Then maybe you should be thanking me? At least a round of drinks on the house?"

His fingers pinched into my hip harder; a small, frustrated groan bubbled in his throat. I knew that sound. It was when he was irritated with me, but at the same time, he wanted to laugh at my crazy shenanigans. The two sides of him at war.

"Brex," he muttered, torment in his voice. His head tipped into the back of mine, and he took a deep breath of my hair, sighing again. Drawing me into him, he pressed our bodies together. For one moment, it was like we were back in the place where it was just *us*. No fae side or human side. No right or wrong. Best friends. Two people secretly in love with each other. Everything about him was so familiar. He was like an old sweater I held on to because it was so comfortable, taking me back to a time I was innocent. Happy. A life when everything was simple, and we were each other's world. Children who couldn't imagine their bond would ever change or break.

"Don't do this, Caden," I whispered. "Please. You aren't like him. You aren't your father."

It was as if I electrocuted him. The boy I knew and loved dropped away; the man his father was trying to create stepped in. He jerked back, his form stiffening, the gun shoved roughly at my temple.

"Shut the fuck up, traitor." Caden's tone was icy and aloof. "You know nothing about me."

"I know you better than anyone."

"The girl I used to know knew everything about me. The one I trusted and loved," he seethed, emotion slipping through his teeth. Most might not catch it, but I knew all his tells. The way his cheek twitched when he was so pissed he couldn't speak. The way his voice sounded when he was happy, sad, annoyed, and turned on.

He cleared his throat. "But that girl is gone," he said coolly. "To me, she died the day she hopped on the back of the fae's bike. Became a traitor."

"It's not so simple," I replied. "You don't know the whole truth. Your dad—"

"I said *shut up*!" His finger pressed firmer on the trigger, making my body stiffen. He shoved me forward. "Move."

"No, I don't think she will." A voice spoke from the other end of the alley, the charm in his voice twining around us like vines, twitching my lips in a smile. "I'd let her go if I were you."

Caden wrenched both of us around to the intruder, keeping me locked in his hold, the gun to my temple.

"Two can play this game, right?" Ash's green eyes glinted, stepping from the shadows.

Caden's muscles tightened, but it wasn't the gorgeous tree fairy who made him react. It was the hostage Ash had at gunpoint in front of him, his hand over her mouth.

Hanna's eyes were wide with fear, her body trembling. HDF trainees were all ego and pompousness, bragging about how they'd kill fae like rabid animals. But if they were actually face to face with the fae, most would freeze up. We weren't trained to consider or fight fae glamour, probably because we had no defense for it. They used it as propaganda, turning the fae into even more soulless monsters and humans the helpless victims.

Ash took a step closer.

"Stay back, fae," Caden snarled, adjusting the gun at my head like he was ready to kill me.

"Please," Ash smirked. "We both know you are not going to shoot her."

"You don't know anything about me. Or what I will do." Caden's chest puffed up.

"I can feel the binds you have to her." Ash inched him and Hanna closer. "You love her. You won't shoot her." He moved even closer. "So how about this? We make a trade, like going to market. Your girl for my girl." Ash's eyes glinted, looking at me with a wink, knowing he was getting a rise out of me. "You know, you're probably getting the better deal." He flicked his chin at me. "That one is quite lippy and a real *pain in the ass*. Never listens... always getting into trouble and *wanders off* when she shouldn't..." He tipped his head, making the last point clear.

I glared at him but couldn't deny it. Yeah, I was all those things.

Ash moved him and Hanna closer still, a mischievous smirk twisting his lips. Hanna's eyes went wide, fear blasting through them like stars, her head shook, her screams muffled.

"I said *stay back*." Caden pressed me closer to him. I could feel him becoming rattled, not knowing how to get out of this without sacrificing Hanna or me. The need to please his father would override his decision. Between saving a soldier or losing me? Istvan would have made his choice clear on that. Hanna would be sacrificed. "And I don't make *deals* with *fae*." He spat the word like it was dirt on his tongue.

159

"That's a shame," a gravelly voice rumbled behind Caden. The gruff sound slithered over me, instantly igniting fire in my veins, rushing life through my body, coiling between my legs.

Fuck, that man...

The sound of metal cracking against flesh and bone echoed off the walls. Caden's frame dropped away from mine, plunging to the ground with a thud.

"Caden!" Whirling around, I dropped down next to my old friend, checking to see if he was still breathing after being pistol-whipped. His head gushed with blood; a large wound cut into his scalp. "*Basszus, Farkas!* You could have killed him!"

"But I didn't," Warwick grumbled, pulling my gaze to him. Aqua eyes scorched through my soul, his massive physique heaving with adrenaline and fury. Blood and cuts covered his face; his lip curled up in a snarl. "Yet."

I could feel his wrath, the line of death he still walked, his fury at me and at the boy who laid next to me. I could also feel his walls shutting down the link between us.

The pounding of footsteps hit the alley, whipping Warwick around, his gun pointed.

"No," I exclaimed, rising to my feet, already knowing who was running up.

Scorpion, Maddox, Birdie, and Wesley came around the corner. It was subtle, but I watched Scorpion's shoulders drop in relief the moment his eyes met mine.

"Oh good, more of your fan club," Warwick muttered, running his hand through his tangled hair, his eyes rolling back.

"X." Birdie was covered in wounds and blood, looking like a warrior princess with her long white-blonde hair and angel face. She flicked her head between Warwick and me. "Legend."

Warwick snorted, dipping his head in response to her.

Seeing Birdie, Scorpion, even Maddox and Wesley, I felt another puzzle piece click in. I didn't know how it all fit together; I just felt in my bones. These people were meant to be in my life. I had known them for barely a day before we had to part, but it was already there. Like they were an extension of Andris. My true family in this fucked-up world.

"HDF has retreated," Maddox told us, his glance dancing between the form on the ground and the terrified one in Ash's grip. "But you know it will only take them a moment before they regroup and return. Especially for him." Maddox pointed at Caden. "Kill them, because we need to go."

"Kill them? No!" Panic fizzed in my lungs like lava.

Maddox looked back at me like I was insane. "Yeah. We don't take prisoners out here, and we don't let people trying to slaughter us go free. They will turn around and kill us without blinking. This isn't training camp. This is real life. It's kill or be killed."

No one disputed his claims. Wesley cocked his gun, heading for the body lying on the ground next to me.

My best friend.

My first love.

The person who curled up next to me after my father died and held me at night when I cried. The one who would sneak into my room and share his dessert with me because Rebeka thought it would ruin my figure. The boy who had always been by my side through all my pranks and mischief.

"No." I moved defensively in front of Caden, blocking Wes, a snarl on my lips. "You will not kill him." I ground my teeth, ready to fight if I had to.

"X, get out of the way." Wes tried to move me.

"You will have to go through me first."

Wes stopped, glancing back at Maddox then me, wondering what to do.

"You willing to fight me?" A snarl snapped off my tongue, my body rolling in a threat. I would fight to the death for those I loved.

Wesley took another step.

In a blink, Warwick moved in next to me, a deep growl penetrating the walls. Low, but the threat was felt down to your toes.

"Your guard dog can muzzle it." Scorpion stepped forward. "We take them alive."

"But—" Maddox started, but with one look from Scorpion, he shut up.

"Let's move out." Scorpion motioned for us to exit the alley, signaling for Warwick to get Caden.

Warwick's nose wrinkled as if he were about to attack Scorpion.

"Either it takes three or four of us to carry him, or just you." Scorpion motioned down Warwick's frame.

Warwick inhaled deeply, his eyes darting to me before he huffed.

Walking over, he roughly grabbed Caden, throwing him over his shoulder like a sack, which was better than I was expecting. Ash hauled Hanna behind us.

We all traveled back to the main road, spotting more of Sarkis's army moving around, picking up dead soldiers' weapons and items that could be sold.

"Hey!" A man crouched over Luk. "I think he's still alive."

"What?" I sputtered. Taking off, I bolted toward where Luk lay, my knees scraping the pavement as I hit the ground.

"Luk?" I bent over him. "Oh gods... Luk..." Hope danced in my chest with the chance he might still be alive, ready to do anything.

*Bring him back to life?* A voice slithered into my head.

"Take her!" Ash shoved Hanna at Scorpion before elbowing me out of the way, his ear going to Luk's mouth, fingers at his pulse, trying to find a sign of life. "Shit! It's barely there, but he's still breathing." Ash sat up, ripping the backpack from his shoulders, tossing it onto my lap as he ripped off his sweater. Using it as a tourniquet, he wrapped it around Luk's torso, pressing down on the wound, trying to slow the bleeding. "I need to get him to a place I can clean this out and heal him."

Maddox whistled at two bulky guys pinching shiny objects nearby, waving them over. I stood, pulling Ash's discarded bag onto my shoulders, watching the guys run to us. They looked like they were half pig or something, with flat noses and no necks. They weren't ripped or tall, but you could tell they were strong.

"Take him to base. Hurry!" Maddox ordered the two. "Follow them!" He waved at Ash as the guys swept Luk up, hauling him off with an effortless speed I wasn't expecting from them. Ash tore off after them, having to sprint to keep up.

"Of course, the pretty boy gets all the attention." A deep woman's voice grunted from a few feet away, turning us all to the figure trying to sit up, her face scrunched in pain. "What does a girl have to do around here to get mouth to mouth?"

"Kek! Oh my gods!" I shoved people out of the way, trying to get to the blue-haired demon, my heart busting. I dropped next to her. "You're alive."

"Oh goody," she replied, expressionless. She held the side of her stomach. She also had a bullet wound in her leg.

Tears hinted behind my lids. "I thought I lost you."

"Can't lose me so easily, little lamb." She flinched, readjusting herself, leaning back on the barrier she had hidden behind. "Demons are like cockroaches. You think you got us, but we just keep coming back."

I let out a short laugh.

"Can you walk?" Warwick stood over her, forcing her head to tilt back.

"Seems you got your hands full there, big guy." She winked at him. "But if you're offering up your other shoulder, I'll let you know now, it's a yes on spankings."

She actually coaxed a smile from Warwick. "Say the word, demon, and I will happily dump Captain Douche here and take you." Warwick jostled Caden on his shoulder, causing me to glare daggers at him.

"Don't even think about it," I warned him, turning back to Kek. "Come on, I'll help you." I put her arm over my shoulder and helped lift her up. She grunted, sweat dripping down her face as she limped, our steps slow. Fae healed a lot quicker than humans, but it didn't mean it wasn't painful as hell.

"Joy killer." She hissed between her teeth with every step. "I could have gotten a free ride and spankings. The least you could do is offer up the same."

"Sorry, I'm not carrying your ass."

"Spankings?" Her brows went up in hope.

"Only if you're good."

"Dammit."

As dawn hinted on the horizon, my misfit group walked, limped, or were carried back to Sarkis's base.

Hostages, friends, and some barely allies.

At the center was me.

The glue or a bomb.

163

# Chapter 15

"Brexley!" Andris's arms wrapped around me the moment we entered the temporary underground base. His familiar cologne and voice hit me like a hammer, making me feel like a little girl again.

"*Nagybacsi.*" I hugged him back, his arms squeezing me so tightly I could feel every ounce of his fear and relief in the hug.

"I was so scared, *drágám.*" *My dear.* "The thought of anything happening to you... I just..." He tapered off.

"I'm okay." I squeezed him back.

"Thank the gods." His voice cracked in my ear. "I've been going crazy from the moment I said goodbye last time. We looked everywhere for you. I thought the worst, though Scorpion kept reassuring me you were okay. Then tonight..." He finally released me from the embrace, his Adam's apple bobbing as he looked me over. "I think I aged ten years in the last hour."

He did look tired, but still handsome in his stoic way. His hair was turning grayer, a few white specks in his dark brows, youth seeping slowly from him every day. This time I could see the human frailty in him, and the fact he would grow old and die. The vulnerability of humans compared to fae seemed so real suddenly. In that moment, I understood the desire to find the nectar or create the pills. I had lost so many people I loved, grew up without a mother, and now a father.

Andris was the closest I had to a father figure, and I didn't want to lose him.

"I know you must be tired, but there are things we need to discuss before you rest."

I nodded, finally looking around the dark and dingy space, taking in the commotion in the smaller headquarters. Dozens of people were moving down hallways and through the main room, buzzing like bees. Maddox and Scorpion took Kek, Caden, and Hanna away the moment we stepped in. Ash was already somewhere here working on Luk.

The transitory base was in the middle of a nondescript block of abandoned buildings near the old marketplace. The entrance was tucked in an alley and behind dumpsters and piles of rubbish. All the windows were boarded up, and the space underground was cramped and old. A rush of guilt clipped my chest, knowing I was the reason the last place was found. Why they were "homeless" right now.

"Don't fret, *drágám*." Andris patted my arm, seeing right through me. "We will find a new home."

"I know, but—"

"No buts. We would have been discovered eventually." He shook his head. "That is the life we chose. At any moment, this place could be compromised. Just how it is. Do not blame yourself."

We took all the precautions coming here, but I hoped it wasn't in vain. Kalaraja was a master at what he did, and he was set on finding me. He was the reason HDF knew precisely where to attack us tonight. How could he always discover my location without any other fae sensing him? The man was like a ghost.

"Lieutenant, we placed the girl prisoner in the empty storage closet." Maddox strolled up, reporting to his leader. "Scorpion is watching her."

"Her name is Hanna." I gritted my teeth.

"Hanna?" Andris's eyes went wide. "You mean little Hanna Molnár? Albert and Nora's girl?"

Five years ago, we were little and young to him. I was fifteen and Hanna had been fourteen when he left. And he had very little interaction with her or her parents, probably only remembering a scrawny blonde teen who sometimes hung out with Caden and me.

"We have her here?" His eyes widened, irritation furrowing his bushy brows at Maddox. "You know the rule. We don't take prisoners."

Maddox's nose flared, his jaw crunching. "I know."

"It's my fault." I stepped in. "She's my friend. I wasn't going to let them kill her."

"Even if they'd turn around and kill us?" Maddox asserted.

Andris palmed his head, rubbing feverishly, muttering under his breath.

"Tell him who we have taking up a cot in our healing ward." Maddox pursed his lips, his eyes on me.

Andris's head snapped up, his spine straightened. "Who?"

I cringed, already knowing how his name would be received.

"Who, Brexley?"

"Caden." I winced, watching the word hit Andris and soak in, a vein in his forehead bulging. Andris of course knew him well; Caden and I were inseparable. He treated Andris like a pseudo-uncle because I considered him so. Andris worked for his father before Caden was even born.

If possible, I think Andris aged another ten years in that single moment.

"What?" he exploded. "You are telling me we have the son of my enemy, the one who thinks I'm dead! In here? Right now?" He pointed off down a hallway.

Maddox arched an eyebrow at me in an "I told you so" expression.

"Yes." I nodded.

Andris's mouth opened, then clicked shut. He started to pace, his mouth opening again, then closing.

Uncle Andris didn't usually show emotion or get "mad." He kept his cool and worked things out, while my father popped off like fireworks. It was rare, but there had been times I had seen Uncle Andris upset, mad, and even furious. I had never seen him speechless.

A strangled noise clogged his throat, the vein on his forehead dancing. "You." He pointed at me. "Follow me now!" He marched off, anger riding his shoulders like a cowboy.

"*Someone's* in trouble," Maddox sang under his breath.

"Shut up," I snarled, feeling every bit the adolescent teen about to get grounded. I stomped after my uncle, Maddox snickering like an older brother getting his sibling in trouble.

Passing a makeshift war room, I spotted Ling at a computer, her fingers flying over the keyboards. She briefly looked up, her dark eyes meeting mine. She was good at keeping her emotions unreadable, but I swore I saw her sigh, like, "See. Once again, danger and violence follow you."

Yeah, it did.

I followed Andris into a small cement cubicle, which only held a desk and two chairs. The table was covered in folders, and a map of the city, circled with black marker and sticky notes, was flattened out in the middle.

The room made me feel trapped, like a weight was sitting on my chest. The need to run back up the stairs and breathe in fresh air pulsed in my muscles and ached my lungs. I would never like being underground, especially in confined quarters like this. The panic instantly bubbled, sweat dripping down my back.

"Sit," Andris ordered.

I perched on the edge, my leg bouncing.

"Brexley..." He leaned over his desk, taking calming breaths. "I know you are new to this world, but we have rules for a reason."

"You can't possibly be saying I should have let them be killed. Someone who has been my best friend most of my life, who was there for me when I lost my father... when I lost *you*. When you chose to *leave* me."

He flinched. "Brex—"

"No." I stood up, my body itching to move. "I fight for those I care about. I don't murder them in cold blood because suddenly we are on two different sides."

"You don't think they wouldn't have killed you?" His voice rose, letting emotion bleed through. I realized this reaction was more from his fear that he could have lost me to them tonight. "Don't be fooled, girl. Caden is a chip off the old block."

"No," I growled defensively, jerking Andris's head back. "He's not. Caden might believe he is or wants to be, but I know him. I know him better than I know myself. He wouldn't have hurt me."

"But he wouldn't have stopped Istvan from killing you, though," Andris replied honestly, point-blank, and I felt the arrow hit the target dead center.

"How do you know?"

"Because." His eyes and posture softened, sorrow in his stance. "That boy was never as strong as you. He wanted to please his father too much, even as a child. You were the one who always got him to do things outside the lines. He never would have. He followed you, Brexley... not the other way around. You were the force, the strength. So full of vigor and fire. He would have caved under Istvan a long time ago if it hadn't been for you. You gave him life. Courage."

"We gave it to each other."

Andris shook his head. "Name one thing *he* instigated when you were kids."

My mind tried to file through all the memories of the mischief we got up to, not able to recall one that wasn't my idea.

"He was a follower... you have always been the leader."

"Doesn't matter." I shook my head. "Caden is part of me; he's my heart. And if I have to fight you and everyone in here, I won't let you hurt him. Or Hanna."

Andris watched me for a while.

"I don't want to hurt him either, Brex. I remember sitting with both of you on either side of me, reading stories to you guys for hours. I care about Caden too, but he still is the enemy. Istvan's son. Do you know what Istvan will do to this city to get him back? To my people if he catches them? This is my family. People I love and promised to protect." He placed his palms on the desk, his head dropping. I could see the anguish and tough position I put him in. "I can't let him go free, but I won't kill him, because I know how much it would break you. I'd lose you too. And I won't lose you again." The cheap chair squealed as he flopped down in it. Exhaustion and torment lined his face.

"I'm sorry." I felt horrible for putting him in this spot, but there was no other choice for me. Caden was not a sacrifice I was willing to make. "Maybe if we tell them the truth... show them what's really going on. Fae aren't the enemy."

"Please." He pinched his nose. "Caden won't turn against his father. And I doubt the girl will either. They have been brainwashed since birth to despise fae."

"So was I." I tipped up my chin. "You and I both changed."

He dropped his hand, leaning his head back into the chair, staring at me.

"Just let me try."

He took a full minute, sixty seconds of silence, before his head dipped.

"Fine. You can try. But Brex... if it comes down to my people or them?"

"I know." I dipped my head. I knew it was only his love for me that swayed his decision. "Thank you."

His mouth quirked, but he didn't reply.

About to turn and leave, my eye caught pictures of grainy images sticking out from underneath the map, moving me closer to the desk. Dread sank in my belly, recognizing what I was seeing.

Dead bodies.

"What's this?" I tugged one out, my mouth coating in bile. Mostly decomposed, I saw a naked woman. The next one was a naked man, bloated with water, but his face was still recognizable. Fae. The next one was a young girl, the next a teen girl, the stack of photos showing various ages and gender types. Human and fae.

"What—what is this?" I asked again.

"Those are some of the bodies being found along the banks of the river in the last month."

My memory flickered to something Scorpion had told me back in Prague.

*"About a hundred fae and human bodies have been found floating in the Danube. The fae are drained of all bodily fluids. Some humans look like their brains melted out or something."*

"You have definitely found both fae and human?"

"Yes, but lately it's been mostly fae or half-breed. Ones who aren't noticed when they go missing."

"What do you mean?"

"The destitute, runaways, whores."

Dread collapsed my lungs, making me shudder for breath.

Whores like Rosie? Though I knew she was too high-scaled for what he was referring to; the majority of prostitutes, both men and women, were working the streets without the protection of a whorehouse. People with hopes and dreams of escaping the hard life, merely trying to survive.

"Who is doing this to them?"

"I don't know for certain, but I think we both can guess."

I struggled to swallow, my lids closing briefly. It was sad—I still held out hope that the man who raised me the last five years wasn't this monster. But fae essence was the main ingredient in Dr. Rapava's formula, and you couldn't take fae essence without killing them.

"Ever since you told me what he was up to, we've been scouting some of the factories he or a Leopold elite is linked to. There are so many, and we've only been able to cross off a few. Istvan is smart, and he will make sure it is hidden well." Andris sat up in his chair, tapping the map. A few circles had Xs crossing them out, spread over the city. "We've been scouting various places, but all the leads have turned up dead ends. The places are empty or regular factory plants."

169

A loud knock rattled the door, cutting off our conversation. Not waiting for a response, the door swung open.

"Lieutenant! Brexley has return—" Zander came to a stop, his huge brown eyes landing on me, his mouth dropping open in shock. "You're here!" His face brightened. He galloped to me, gathering me into a hug, a neighing sound humming in his throat. "I am so happy you are all right." He held me tight, his lips brushing my cheek and temple. I squeezed him back, glancing over his shoulder, the door still wide open.

Warwick leaned against the wall, one foot propped up, like he had been there for a while. Waiting. We watched each other, his expression unreadable, but I felt annoyance and anger ooze from him. Huffing through his nose, he wagged his head, pushing off the wall, and strolled down the passage. His barriers slammed up tight around him, cutting me off from even getting a sliver of his emotions.

"It killed me to stand there..." Zander brought my attention back to him. He leaned out to see me better, hands holding my arms, his deep brown eyes assessing me. "I can't tell you how worried I have been when Lieutenant told me you disappeared. To see you tonight... I almost blew my cover."

"I'm fine." I stepped back, tugging on the backpack straps, Ash's bag with the fae book still on my shoulders. "You guys all act like I'm a walking disaster."

They both stared at me.

"Yeah, okay."

"How did you know she was back?" Andris addressed Zander.

"Oh, I thought..." Zander's regard bounced between us. "You would have told him."

"Hadn't gotten to that part yet."

My uncle's lids closed briefly, sensing there was much more story to come. And he would be right. I had so much to tell Andris: my time in Prague; finding my Uncle Mykel; Povstat; the nectar; Killian; the deal. It had been two weeks since we fled the old base, and a great deal had happened.

"Get the largest bottle of your Unicum." I sighed, strolling back for the chair. "It's gonna be a long night."

"It's morning."

"Yeah, that too."

By the time I exited Andris's office a few hours later, my eyes were blurry. I was about to fall asleep on my feet, and my head pounded with fatigue.

Zander had made a quick exit, needing to get back to Killian. He had nothing new to report besides what I already knew, saying since my escape with Warwick weeks earlier, Killian had become obsessed with being down in the labs, which I figured meant he was testing the pills on more humans. He rarely checked on the opening of the new prison, and Zander backed up Killian's claim suggesting it was impossible to break out of. The magic and security were top-notch with Goblin surety. It was designed deeper underground, in what used to be the Buda Landscape Protection area.

Killian was a puzzle to me. A part of me believed he was a decent guy, but then another part wondered if he was killing these people. He took Warwick's sister and nephew prisoner, using them as leverage, but then I'd remember the look in his eyes the night on his balcony, the relaxed, kind side he showed me acting as my nurse, and I'd flip back to the idea he wouldn't hurt them. He was probably housing them in the luxurious room he set out for me.

As much as I couldn't deny I cared about him, he was someone I couldn't allow myself to trust. At the end of the day, he was still the fae leader and would choose power and his own kind over anything else.

Stumbling down the hallway, I longed for sleep, but needed to check on everyone. The place was not even half the size of the last base, and I easily found the "clinic." It was a windowless, dank, square room with a dozen foldout cots and minimal healing herbs. A healer moved through the room, checking on the handful of patients.

Near the back wall, Ash sat in a chair next to a cot, his clothes covered in blood, his wounded arm wrapped up and healing. His chin perched in his palm; lids lowered as if he were dozing off. Luk laid in the cot beside him, his skin gray and sweaty.

"How is he?"

Ash jolted at my voice, his lashes fluttering open. "Oh shit, did I fall asleep?"

"You need to rest." I touched his arm where he had been shot. "Are you okay?"

171

"I'm fine. Went right through." He rubbed at his face, both of us peering down at Luk. His chest quivered with labored breath. "I don't want to leave until I know he can get through the next twelve hours without assistance. We thought we lost him twice already." Ash flicked his chin at the other healer. "She's too busy to watch him properly."

Tears burned the back of my lids. I threaded my fingers through Ash's. "Thank you." I couldn't find the words for his kindness. He didn't even know Luk, but he was a healer, and helping others was who Ash was.

He squeezed my hand, giving me a slight nod.

"At least pull up one of the extra cots and rest. Won't be any use if you are collapsing too."

"I will." He rose, letting my hand go. He reached up, sliding the backpack from my shoulders, dropping it to my feet. My instant reaction was to take it back, like the book was mine, it wanted me, but I shook my head, pushing the feeling away. No one owned fae books.

"Caden and Kek okay?" I took a deep breath, distracting myself from this sensation.

"Yeah." He nodded. "A good night's sleep and Kek will pretty much be back to normal. We'll have to watch Caden for a concussion, but otherwise, I think he's fine." He nodded to where my friend slept.

My shoulders sagged when I looked at Caden. He was handcuffed, a guard sitting in a chair next to him, watching over the hostage.

"I heard they have Hanna in a storage closet." I turned back.

"Yeah," Ash scoffed. "Scorpion is on watch. Guess she has given him hell."

I grinned. "That's Hanna."

"Sounds like you."

"Girls don't make it in training at HDF unless they're tough, and I don't mean just physically. Hanna and I were the only two girls in my class. There's a reason she lasted." I massaged my burning eyes.

"Looks like you need some sleep too."

"Have you seen Warwick?" His retreat earlier in the hallway still bothered me.

"No, sorry, I haven't left this room or looked up since we got here."

"Okay, I'm gonna go look for him. See if I can find you some tea and something to eat if you're determined to stay here." He nodded, lowering himself back down, tucking his bag between his feet.

I swore I felt the book calling me, yanking at my brain to come closer. To fall into its pages.

Trying to ignore the feeling, I moved toward the exit, my mind already weak and pliant with fatigue.

Sleep. I needed sleep.

*"Brexley Kovacs."* A deep inhuman voice scratched through my mind, spinning my head, my body stumbling, colliding into cots and chairs. *"The girl who challenges nature's laws will defy me? You cannot fight me."*

"Whoa." The woman healer grabbed for me. "I think you need to lie down, honey."

I couldn't seem to speak or fight as she lowered me onto an empty bed next to Kek. Dizzy and nauseated, my eyes closed.

"Sleep," she ordered, my body already curling like a cat, drifting off, feeling like I was spinning and falling into the pages.

The book was across the room from me, yet it grabbed hold, drawing me into its familiar darkness, flipping through the pages of time long since passed.

# Chapter 16

"Bitzy, get your finger out of there." A voice slunk into my dreams, tugging me from the depths of my mind. "You don't know where that one has been. It might be rabid."

*Chirp.*

"Yes, I can see she likes it... *a lot.*"

*Chirp.*

"I do not! Total misunderstanding." He huffed. "Now get away from the cerulean hellion."

My lids cracked open, taking in Opie's figure standing on my pillow, a groan leaking from my lips.

"It's alive!" He deepened his voice, his arms going up. "It's alive!"

*Chirp!* Bitzy's tweet came from the bed next to mine, her tiny form leaping over to us, scrambling up my pillow. Her fingers waved in a morning salute.

"Good morning to you too," I muttered, the heels of my palms digging into my eyes.

The dream from the night before stuck to me like syrup. Gooey and thick, muddling to just flashes and a deep feeling of something important.

Was it only a dream? The book couldn't pull me in if I wasn't touching it, right? I couldn't explain the visions. They were blurry and distant, but I recalled a small cottage I had never seen before, though something about it felt like home. I had seen a secret hiding space and a notebook of some sort in it. My dad was there. I didn't see him; it was more that I felt him. His presence whispered in my ear like he was trying to tell me something.

"We've been waiting forever for you to wake up, Master Fishy." Opie swung his arms dramatically, spinning his layered skirt up. Today, he wore white bandage strips constructed into a long skirt and a bra made out of cotton balls. His hair was in a Mohawk, a cotton ball speared through each spike like marshmallows. Bitzy had the same layered skirt, but pulled up to her chest, and had two cotton balls on the end of her ears. All stuff you'd find in a small clinic.

"Like for-ev-er," he emphasized. "We got bored."

Sitting up, I wagged my head to shake myself awake. Something in my hair knocked against my shoulders. Reaching down, I found over a dozen tight braids with white cloth plaited through one side of my head above my ear.

"Told you we got bored." Opie's smile was full of chagrin. "And your hair was lacking oomph."

Sticky, sweaty, bloody, and dirty, I lacked more than oomph.

"Is this..." I picked up, examining the material. "Sheets from a bed?" I peered down at my shredded top sheet. "My bed?"

"Did you a favor... you looked hot." He shrugged, batting his eyes, trying to look innocent. "Like I said, we were really, really bored." He grabbed his strands of the striped sheet and twirled, the fabric floating around him like kite tails in the wind. His Mohawk was the perfect juxtaposition. "It was worth it, right? Though the fabric is dull. I mean, I had very little to work with here. I still think I added a certain flair to it."

"Flair is certainly one way of describing it." Blowing out a chuckle, I knew I could never stay mad at him.

Rubbing my temple, I tried to reach out for Warwick, feeling nothing but a wall. Was he blocking me? He looked irritated outside Andris's office before, and I had no idea why. I passed out before I had a chance to see or talk to him.

Peering over where Kek still slept, I noticed strands of her blue hair were re-braided with white cotton, the brownie clearly finding her hair in need of a little more panache also. The color was back in her cheeks, and she looked mostly healed.

My eyes twisted over to Caden's sleeping form. Wes was guarding him now, trying not to doze. My heart wrenched seeing Caden chained to the bed. His expression was already strained as if he subconsciously knew he couldn't relax. A captive in enemy territory. I didn't even want to contemplate how Caden would react once he woke. It was going to be bad. But what choice did I have? No matter what happened, I would do everything to protect him, even if he didn't think I was.

Luk still lay in the same position, ashen and sweaty. Ash was in a seat next to him, bent over the bed, fast asleep next to Luk's legs.

"How long was I asleep?"

"For-ev-er," Opie moaned.

*Chhhiiirrp.* Bitzy flipped me off like it was all my fault.

"Okay, let's try this. What time is it now?"

"I don't know. Do I look like a time fairy?" Opie motioned to himself.

"I'm starting to see Master Finn's side," I grumbled, rising from the bed.

Opie's eyes widened to saucers. "You want to spank me with rubber gloves and a dustpan too?"

"What?" I blinked.

"What?" he squeaked back.

*Chirp?*

"Did you say *dustpan*?"

"No." Opie's eyes moved around the room. "I didn't say *spatula* either."

"You didn't say *spatula*."

"I know; I told you I didn't." He busied himself, fiddling with the layers of his skirt. "You must be hearing things, Fishy."

*Chirp!*

"I did not," Opie hmphed.

*Chirp.*

"Oh, don't bring it up again. He wanted to know how the vacuum got stuck."

*Chirp.*

"I did not show him five times."

"O-kay." I held up my hands. "I'm gonna stop you two right there while I still have an appetite."

"Oh, I'm not sure you want one." Opie wrinkled his nose. "We already sampled the breakfast, the after-breakfast, snack, lunch, afternoon snack, and dinner. All blah..."

"Dinner?" My eyes widened. I had gone to sleep just when the sun rose. Had I slept all day? It felt like I was scarcely out for a moment. Parts of the dream were still vivid in my mind, rubbing at the back of my head like I could step right back into it.

With no windows or way of telling what time it was, I had no idea how long I had been out. My stomach grumbled, telling me it had been far too long since I last ate.

"Yeah, dinner... it's eight-thirty."

"Eight-thirty." I lifted an eyebrow. "You know what time it is?"

"Yeah, why wouldn't I?"

My lids shut, fists rolling up, breathing in and out of my nose.

I had slept more than twelve hours.

"Have you seen Warwick?" Trying to reach out to him through our link, I still found it barred, which shifted me onto my feet with irritation. Why was he blocking me?

"You mean that *big,* bad, sexy wolfy?" Opie fanned himself.

My cheek flinched. "I'm thinking we're talking about the same person."

"Like you don't know, Fishy," Opie scoffed, Bitzy copying his response. "Weren't you the one screaming out, "'Oooooohhh, Wolfy, what a colossal dick you have—'"

"Stop. Now." I cut him off. "And I did not call him *Wolfy.*" Folding my arms, I lowered my lids. "I probably called him *a* dick."

Opie winked at me. "That too."

*Chirp!* Which sounded something like, *"You're an idiot and a liar."*

"Before this train went off the rail, I asked if you had seen him?"

"We were on a train?" Opie tilted his head, peering at Bitzy. "Do you remember being on a train? I thought we were on those zoomy-zoomy things."

*Chirp!* Which I was sure was, *"You are all idiots."*

A groan climbed up my throat. "You know what? I'm gonna go find something to eat." I motioned over my shoulder.

"Good luck, Fishy!" Opie waved at me. "Wear protection!"

*Chirp!* Middle fingers stabbed the air in response.

I didn't even want to know.

Leaving them, my legs carried me out of the room. Loud chants down the hall took me to one of the largest areas in the condensed compound, discovering where most of the inhabitants were located.

177

They were circling two fighters in the middle of what had to be their training workout room.

A tiny blonde warrior against a man who had to be at least eight feet tall, his body built like boulders.

Birdie scaled up his back, leaping on his shoulders, her legs wrapping around his throat.

*"Bir-die! Bir-die!"* Her name was chanted as the huge man flailed about, trying to get her off his back, swinging her around to me.

"X," she called out my name, her eyes glinting with fire. Like me, she came alive when she was fighting. Some might find it sick, but walking the line between life and death sparked my blood with vigor. "You're awake."

"Yeah, I was gonna go get some dinner."

"Oh, I'm starving." She talked to me like she wasn't in the middle of battling this half-giant man. His face had turned a deep red, his fists trying to punch her as he slammed her back into walls, trying to dislodge the bird perched on his back. Her legs only tightened down on his esophagus, forcing him to gasp for any air. People bellowed around them, money in their hands waving in the air with enthusiasm. "Hold on a moment."

I laughed as her face went serious, done playing around. Her bitchy, bored expression covered her features as she used both of her arms and legs to constrict his airway.

The man clawed and struck her, but the girl held on like an octopus. He stumbled, his skin shading into purples, blood vessels in his eyes popping before he fell, hitting the ground with a thump, tapping his arm to say he was out.

Birdie unlatched herself, standing up and brushing back the loose hair from her ponytail. "That was fun. Maybe we'll do this again tomorrow." She patted the guy on the shoulder before turning to me. She strolled over, one eye bruising with a shiner, but otherwise, her heavily lined eyes were perfect, not a scratch on her.

"Think tonight is *krumplileves* again." She rolled her eyes, sauntering right by me while yelling and money changing hands continued behind her.

Snorting, I trailed after the petite girl dressed in all black. The miniscule canteen was a few rooms down, a rectangular room filled with folding chairs and wood slabs propped on cement blocks for tables. Against one wall, food, drinks, and snacks were spread out. Nothing like the setup they used to have, and not even close to Povstat's situation.

Birdie stopped in front of a crockpot, her nose wrinkling as she scooped out the traditional Hungarian potato soup.

"Oh goody, seven days in a row." She grabbed a roll, biting into it as I got my soup and roll and followed her to a table. The area was mostly quiet, with only a few groups sprinkled through the room, drinking tea or eating supper.

"So..." She plunked down on a chair across from me, shoveling in some soup. "One legend wasn't enough for you?" She arched a brow at me.

"What do you mean?"

"Come on, there's no way you're not screwing Farkas, and if you aren't, then you're an idiot, and I volunteer," she said evenly. Her tone always held a hint of boredom. "But I heard rumors of you and the seriously sexy fae lord, Killian, and now the son of the HDF leader? I was there, girl. I could see something between you two. Caden Markos is like another make-believe character I've heard about for years. The human prince. But I guess at one time you were too."

"He's my best friend." I inhaled, staring down at my soup, drowning a chunk of potato in the broth. "Or he used to be. We grew up together."

"You crushed on him, didn't you?"

My brows creased, not sure how to respond.

"Please. You totally did. Do you still love him?" She scooped up another spoonful, sucking it down. "Seems a bit pampered for you."

"Pampered?"

"He's a total pretty boy." She shoved a piece of roll into her mouth, barely swallowing. "I'm mean *really* pretty. More muscles than I thought he would have, but probably not much upstairs or down, though he is easy on the eyes. Not that I like guys like that."

My head tilted.

"I don't! Far too prim for me." She shook her head, eyes darting to the side. "I'm just saying he seems like the typical spoiled human boy. Entitled. All ego and a very tiny dick."

We may never have had sex, but I had slept next to him and touched him enough to know. Caden certainly wasn't small by most standards. Far from it. But after Warwick, it was hard to compare anyone to a normal measurement.

Gods... that man.

179

"Wait." Her eyes widened at my heating cheeks. "Is his dick actually big? A secret freak in bed?" She barely took a breath. "He looks vanilla, but sometimes those guys can shock you."

"You and Kek would really get along," I muttered, kneading my head.

"Okay, tell me about Killian then."

"Nothing to tell."

She pursed her lips, not believing me. "Well, it *also* seems Scorpion has a bit of a thing for you. Anytime your name is mentioned, he perks up." A slight annoyance flickered over her bruised eye.

"It's not like that." How could I explain to anyone what my connection was to Scorpion or Warwick? *Yeah, so, I went back in time through a fae book and saved their lives, even though technically I had just been born, and now we were linked in this strange way that shouldn't exist. As in, we can see, touch, and feel each other no matter where our physical bodies are.*

My mind flickered to Warwick, wondering where he was, but I felt nothing in our link except that he was alive. He was still shutting me out.

"Oh shit." Birdie's spoon fell noisily into her empty soup bowl. "Speaking of, I have to relieve pretty boy's watch. Wes needs a few hours of sleep before heading out tonight."

"What's tonight?"

"A few are staking out some factories tied to Markos and the elite in Leopold. We're looking for the location where they're harboring fae." Andris assumed one or more of the factories were operating more as a fae murder plant than an actual factory. It was a great cover, but there was a possibility they were looking in the wrong places. "The moment your pretty boy is awake, I will get it out of him." She stood up, lifting her pierced brow.

"Caden doesn't know anything."

She huffed derisively. "Please, he's the son of a powerful general and is being groomed to take over."

"I know him. He doesn't know."

"How do you *really* know anyone?" She shook her head at me like I was naïve. "Everyone keeps secrets. Even from those they love."

Her statement felt full of meaning, but it scraped at the doubt building in my gut. Since I left HDF this last time, turning my back on everything I knew, even the boy I loved, so much could have changed. Istvan would certainly use Caden's anger to turn him even more on me. Maybe Caden couldn't kill me, but he'd be fine with testing and killing fae.

My stomach twisted, not sure how to handle the fact that Caden was here as a prisoner. A situation I forced on him, but the other way was not an option for me, though he might disagree. I had to try and show both Hanna and Caden the truth—everything we were taught was wrong.

"I want to come tonight," I stated. "Who knows, I might have insight I don't know about."

"That's up to the lieutenant." She started to turn. "Though if you do, I'd bring the legend. He seems good when you need a distraction." She winked at me.

"Have you seen him?"

"I saw him storm out of here this morning. Haven't seen him since. And he's not someone you can miss down here." She twisted, glancing over her shoulder. "Or anywhere."

Birdie dashed out of the room, her long white-blonde hair swishing down her back. She was like being around a hummingbird. A murderous one. She fluttered in and out of your life at transient speed, but you couldn't help feeling awed and a little fortunate you got that time.

And lived.

Following the connection I had to Scorpion, I found my other ex-friend being held in an old furnace room. Two fire bulbs flickered above the mainly empty concrete, windowless space.

Scorpion sat in a chair near the door, his legs stretched out and crossed at the ankle, a gun on his lap. Across from him, handcuffed to a pipe on the cold ground, was Hanna. Leaning against her arms, she tried to turn as much as she could away from him, her lids closed, but I knew she wasn't fully asleep.

My entrance startled Hanna, her body flinching, going on defense. Seeing me enter didn't ease her; it only made her grit her teeth more, her eyes sparking with fury and disgust.

"I thought *you* were difficult, but your friend here is a grade-A pain in the ass," Scorpion grumbled under his breath. He hadn't even looked up at me, probably sensing my presence before I even entered.

"Same to you, *fairy*," she shot back.

"I told you. I'm not a *fucking* fairy." He pulled his legs in, leaning closer, snarling at her, both glaring at each other. "My family roots are *Aos sí*. Unseelie."

"What's the difference?" She rolled her eyes.

To them, there was a huge difference. It was like saying Hungarians were the same as Australians. It was who they were, their race, beliefs, and where their powers stemmed from. Humans tend to think Seelie, meaning light, were good, and Unseelie, dark, were bad. But that wasn't true at all. Queen Aneira was a good example of that. Just one used to live more in the light, and the other prefers to slink through the dark.

"What's. The. Difference?" Rage boiled under Scorpion's skin, his hands flexing with aggravation. "Fuck, this one has a mouth on her. One that won't do her any favors."

"Certainly not for you, *fairy*," she spat.

Scorpion stood up, and I darted between them. "Okay... calm down." I pushed at his chest, his shoulders rising, his lip curling, his eyes set on the figure behind me. "Scorp, take a breath." He didn't respond; his ire was still directed over my shoulder. I took in how tired he looked and realized he was the one who had been guarding her since we first arrived, which was more than fourteen hours ago. "Have you been here the whole time?"

His lips curled, but one shoulder shrugged.

"You haven't left this room since this morning?" Again, he didn't respond, but with us, he didn't need to. I pointed at the door. "Take a break. Get a drink and something to eat. Has she eaten?"

"She threw it in my face," he grunted, his attention flickering down to the stain on the ground. It was an oil splotch from the potato soup. "Next time, I'll force it down her throat."

"I dare you, fairy-boy," she seethed, the cuffs scraping against the metal.

"Don't tempt me, blondie." He stepped forward, bumping into me.

"Go!" I pointed to the door. "Take a walk. I got it." Scorpion's eyes dropped to me, and, again, without saying a word, I felt his concern. "Believe me, I'll be fine. She's latched to a pipe, but also, I always kicked her ass in training."

She snorted with a derisive breath.

His gaze went to her, taking in a breath, contemplating before his head dipped. "I'll be back in ten minutes." He pointed at her. "You do one thing, you even blink at her wrong, and I will use your bones to pick food out of my teeth."

Her scowl followed him as he stomped out of the room, the door slamming, echoing the quiet, awkward silence inside.

Her hatred turned on me, her jaw locking down.

Blowing out, I grabbed the chair, pulling it closer.

"And here I didn't think Scorpion liked anyone." I sat down.

"And as usual, every man is bending over and pining for you, fae or human doesn't seem to matter." A pointed, spiteful tone curled around her words.

"What does that mean?"

"Please." She glowered at me. "Like you didn't notice. Actually, knowing you, you didn't." She shook her head. "Every guy you got near was drawn to you like they were in a trance."

The term stabbed into the back of my neck like a needle. *Drawn.* It was the word they all used, like they had no choice.

"Every guy in our training group had a crush on you. You know Aron was secretly in love with you, right? Bakos adored you. Caden worshipped you. Princes, lords, nobles. Fae don't seem immune to you either... even Istvan let you get away with almost anything."

"Istvan?" A bubbled laugh came up from my throat. "He wants me dead."

"Gods, you really didn't see it." She stared at me with bewilderment. "What makes me mad is it would be so easy to hate you, but I can't. I considered you a friend. Someone I trusted."

"I am your friend."

"No," she replied, emotionless, shifting her back flat against the wall. "You're not. You *chose* them. You chose fae over *us*!" Her voice rose, grief watering her eyes. "Your friends, family. *Caden.* You turned on us that night. You killed Elek!"

"I-I didn't." I didn't actually kill him, but I was the cause of his death in the alley.

"You let them brainwash you. Erase everything you used to stand for and believe." Her head shook. "I-I don't understand."

"No, you don't." I rubbed my face, frustration pinching my nerves. "It wasn't until I was outside the walls of HDF, fighting for my life in Halálház, that I realized HDF is the one brainwashing. The world is so different outside those gates, and we aren't truly trained for any of it. Fae are not what you think."

"Wow, you really drank the Kool-Aid, didn't you?" Disgust curled her lip. "I thought you were stronger than that."

183

Whatever I said would sound like some excuse, a scripted line. The more you denied something, the more it rang true. "I won't convince you with words." I stood back up. "I can only hope time will show you the truth and change your opinion."

"You might as well kill me now, because no matter what, I will never choose the fae over my kind. Never!"

"I hope you're wrong about that, Hanna." My lips pinched together as I moved for the door. "I really hope you're wrong." *Your life depends on it.*

Stepping out the door and moving a few steps down the passage, I suddenly was no longer just in the underground base. I also was in a room. A space I knew well... the smell of sex and body odor filled my nose. Low flickering fire bulbs disguised the wear of the run-down bedroom of the whorehouse.

Warwick stood by the window, his back to me.

"You are playing with fire. Nothing good will come of this." Kitty's voice jerked my head to her, near the door. She was reserved and elegant, wearing a gold dress with a slit up to her hip, matching heels, her hair curled, and her lips painted bright red.

"You don't think I fucking know that?" He growled, his hands gripping the sill until I heard wood crack.

"We have lived many lifetimes, brother... I've never seen you like this. She has changed you."

Fury flexed his back muscles; a strangled snarl hummed from his throat.

"Why are you even here then?" Kitty shook her head with frustration. "Go back."

Warwick stiffened, and I knew he sensed me, his head whipping around, his piercing eyes landing on me.

Fury twitched his eye, his head wagging slightly, speaking out loud to me. "I should have known you'd still find me no matter how much I blocked you."

Kitty peered around, her brows furrowing, not understanding the sentiment was meant for me.

I didn't speak, feeling his resentment and anger searing into me, but something else was there he wouldn't let me reach.

His eyes slid to Kitty. "You know what? I changed my mind. Ask Nerissa to come with friends... have her bring the English girl."

"Rosie?" Kitty asked.

"Yes." His eyes met mine.

Like he knifed my chest and placed a bomb between my ribs, pain exploded through me, freezing me in place as parts of me splattered in pieces.

"Warwick..." Kitty's tone held warning.

"I'm a paying customer, aren't I?" he growled.

"You are a *fool*." She lashed at him, slamming the door after her.

He didn't respond, only stared at me, his jaw set.

*"Fuck you."* I could barely get the words out. *"Don't bother coming back."*

Cutting off the link, I shoved up my walls, blocking him from reaching me.

My chest heaving, I leaned against a cold cement wall, feeling like my lungs were caving in on themselves. Fighting the urge to cry, I bit down on my lip until I tasted blood.

Knowing he was with Nerissa and others was bad, but him purposefully adding Rosie sliced to the bone. She was my friend. He wanted to hurt me on purpose. To make it clear to me on what we were to each other. We fucked, and that was it. Don't get attached.

Leaning over my legs, I inhaled ragged breaths, trying not to collapse under the sensation of betrayal... again.

*What did you expect, Brex? The legendary Wolf would be yours? He was a good guy? That he cared about you? Then you are the one who is a fool.*

One night of hate sex didn't mean we were together. We weren't anything besides connected by this stupid bond. Our feelings were probably not even real. As Hanna mentioned, men were "drawn" to me, not able to fight it.

Not their choice.

It wasn't *me* they wanted; it was whatever I was.

Clamping down any feelings I had for him, I shoved all the pain away. It was how they trained us for the field, to compartmentalize and continue on with our mission. It was how I dealt with losing my father.

I had one mission now: finding the nectar. The clock was ticking, and I had no real leads. The only option was going back into the book.

Something in my gut warned me the book was no different. It was drawn to me too.

And some day, it might not let me out, locking my mind in there forever.

# Chapter 17

"You look like shit." I strolled up to Ash, forcing a smile on my face. My attention darted briefly over to where Birdie was now watching Caden. He shifted in his sleep, telling me he was slowly stirring from unconsciousness. It was a relief that he was rousing, but at the same time, I was scared for him to wake. To face my best friend as a prisoner.

"Thanks." Ash yawned, sitting back in the chair, scouring his face. Exhaustion left darker rings under his eyes. His hair was knotted, covered in grime and blood, and he could still do a photo shoot. It wasn't fair how gorgeous these guys were.

"How's he doing?" I leaned over Luk, brushing his blond hair off his forehead, his skin hot and sticky.

"Better. I think he made it through the worst of it, but he'll still need more time to heal. There were some close calls. He's a tough kid." Ash looked down at Luk before his gaze went to me. "How are you?"

"Fine." My response sounded honest, but his lids narrowed, his head slanting.

"What's wrong?"

"Nothing." My pitch went higher than I wanted.

"Fuck." Ash tipped his head back. "What did he do?"

"Who?" I deflected.

His eyes leveled with mine. "You can't lie to a tree fairy. We sense and feel everything. And you forget I *know* Warwick."

"It's nothing." I kept trying to dig in, more for me than Ash. I needed to stay focused.

"Where is he?"

My mouth opened about to say I didn't know, but I let out a breath. "Kitty's."

His brows went up. "Why is he there?"

I shrugged, staring at the floor.

"Brex?"

"He's at Kitty's." Swallowing, I kept my voice steady. "As a 'paying customer,'" I quoted with my fingers, repeating Warwick's pointed statement.

"*Faszszopó!*" *Dickhead.* Ash hit his leg, bolting up, anger clenching his jaw. "He is such an idiot."

"He can do what he wants."

Ash gave me the same leveled look again. "Don't give me that... you two... everyone alive, hell even the dead, can feel it. You guys are—"

"We have a link," I inserted. "Doesn't mean we have to be together. We don't even really like each other."

"Please." He let out a laugh, cutting sharply in the quiet room, his head shaking. "What bullshit. Warwick knows it too—that's why he's being an asshole. He doesn't handle emotions well. I mean, at all. Believe me, I've known him a long time. How he is with you—"

"It doesn't matter," I cut him off again, the feelings I was trying to stifle fizzing back up. "I'm not here to talk about him." I tugged at the ends of Opie's handiwork, brushing the braids over my shoulder. "I need to go into the book again."

Ash folded his arms, his shoulders moving with a heavy exhale. "You sure?"

"Yeah, why wouldn't I be?"

"I don't know. The book is different with you. It worries me."

"You never had a problem or concern with it before."

"I didn't really pay attention until the last time with Tad. It didn't let *him in*, Brex. I thought it was strange when it kept me out, but he is one of, if not the most, powerful Druid alive. If anything, the book should be bowing to him. It is made by his kin." His forehead wrinkled. "But it's like it's obsessed with you... drawn to you."

"If I hear that fucking word again." My lids shut briefly, growling under my breath. "I don't have another option." A flare of anger prickled at my spine. "I have no leads on the nectar, except for some pirate stealing it, which Killian says is a dead end. I need to see for myself what the book knows. It has to be in there, right?"

"Not necessarily. The books will show you what truly happened, not someone's version of it, which doesn't mean every single moment was recorded if there was no contact with it."

"What do you mean?"

"Just like your history, ours is recorded through people. They don't follow inanimate objects if they aren't in contact with people."

"Someone had to take it. Worth a try. I only have a month and nothing to go on." I licked my lips. "I have to try... for Eliza and Simon."

Ash's head bobbed, lips pinched together, a sadness flickering his expression. "Yeah," he replied with a heavy sigh, reaching over, picking up the bag on the floor next to him. "Lead the way."

It was hard to locate a room that was free of people or not jammed with weapons and supplies, which is why Ash and I found ourselves sitting on the floor in one of the only private rooms available, crammed with potatoes, wilting vegetables, stale bread, and canned items. Pulling out the book, Ash set it between us. I instantly felt the vibrations buzz at my skin, the magic curling around me. It felt as if the book and I had known each other far longer than I had even existed.

Ash watched me closely.

"Stop looking at me like that." I sensed a seesaw teetering in my stomach, the balance of magic tipping toward me.

Lines dented into his forehead. "I've never seen a book act this way toward a person before. It's like you are its master or something."

"I thought these books weren't owned by anyone."

"No." He wavered. "Books are available to anyone if they deem you worthy. But at one time, centuries ago, the first ones, the original fae books, were gifted to a fae king from his Druid servant. Other fae kings heard about it, and all wanted one. There were originally ten, which were technically owned by each noble family. The book was crafted for the family, to be passed down through the generations, staying in the magic line."

"Magic line?"

"Each family, no matter how many generations, has a signature magic characteristic to them."

"You think this is one of those books?" I motioned to the ancient volume.

"I doubt it." He scratched his head. "Those volumes are said to have been destroyed or lost a long time ago. This book is one of the oldest I've come across, but I couldn't imagine it being an original. If it survived, it would stay within the family." Ash's mossy green eyes met mine, his sexual aura always humming at the edges. "It seems to be draw—"

"Don't you dare say it." I held up my hand. "I will hurt you if I hear that word again."

His lip curled up on the side of his mouth. "Don't tell me you are upset people are draw—*attracted* to you."

"But it's not me." I folded my legs in front of me. "It's not real. It's not who I am; it's because of *whatever* I am..." My voice cut out, coming back soft and wobbly. "What am I, Ash?"

"I don't know." His tone was quiet, matching mine. "But I swore to you I'd help you figure it out, and I meant it. I'm not going anywhere until we do." His sentiment caused my eyes to sting with tears. He cupped my hands in his. "And Brex..." He squeezed my fingers, lifting my focus back to the sincerity in his eyes. "It's not because of what you are... it's *all* because of *who* you are. You can't be one without the other."

A small smile pinched my lips, my chest lowering with Ash's support and love. It would be so easy to fall for him. Not just gorgeous and intelligent, he was a good man.

Except I didn't seem to like nice men.

I liked assholes.

Before Warwick could take any residence in my brain, I blocked all thoughts of him, turning back to the book. "Okay, let's do this." I breathed out, my hands still in Ash's.

"Probably won't let me go with you, so remember to ask precisely for what you want." He lowered our arms to the cover, the tingle of magic rubbing against my palms like a cat. Blowing out tension, Ash placed our hands on the book.

The familiar burst of magic whipped through my body, twirling my mind into a vortex. Electricity pumped inside my veins, crackling at my skin.

*"Brexley Kovacs,"* the raspy inhuman voice greeted me. *"The girl who defies nature... the one who should not have survived or even exist."* It had called me that from the beginning, but I never really questioned why.

"What do you mean?"

*"Is that your question?"* the book replied.

There were far too many other things that came first over his cryptic greeting. Various inquiries rolled around my head, but the most direct came off my tongue.

"Where is the nectar now?"

*"Not all questions have a clear answer."* Before I could even reply, images flipped through my mind. Nausea thickened in the back of my throat.

Images flickered quickly through the scene in the tunnels with Killian and the pirate. Them running out with the box. I followed them for a while, everything on fast forward. They headed toward the river to a ship. My skin prickled as dark figures shifted in the shadows, moving toward them, expanding across my vision like fog.

Then it went dark, stepping into a black void almost like the pages were cut out or history just stopped.

"Wait?" I spun around. "What happened? Why did it stop?"

Instead of answering, I felt myself tumble, scenes flipping again, like pages being thumbed through in a picture book.

Now I stood in a small cottage-style house. There was a bed in the corner, a sofa and chair in front of the crackling fireplace, a table and two chairs by the tiny kitchen. Simple, clean, and cozy.

I had been here before. In my dream. This was the same house.

My gaze caught on a coat hanging from the coat rack by the door. Grief punched a hole through my lungs, a soft sob hiccupping in my throat, my eyes burning. The coat was my father's. I'd know his officer's coat anywhere. Long, gray with red trim, a patch on one elbow, the recognizable metals and insignias on the breast and arm. One I knew he got in a battle a year before his death.

Like a magnet, I ventured to it, the floor squeaking under my feet as my hand reached out slowly. A gasp hitched my throat when the wool material brushed my fingertips, the rough fabric of the military bands sewn onto his sleeve. How many times as a child had I traced them? Felt the scratchy material on my arms and legs when he picked me up?

Gritting my teeth, I leaned over, inhaling the familiar scent. Tears choked my throat as the comforting smell of my father, his cologne, pounded into me in brutal waves. Joy and sorrow so deep my legs dipped. The few things I did have of his, which were still back at HDF, had lost his smell years ago. Now I had nothing. I wanted to wrap myself in it, pretend for a moment he was alive, that we still had time together. Imagine it was his love surrounding me again. Hugging me and telling me it was all going to be okay.

A pop from the fire twisted me back to the room. Nothing really stood out about the place. There were no pictures or personal touches, but I sensed something homey about it. Made me feel protected and safe.

Why was I here? Why was my father? And why was the book showing me the same house from my dream?

An object on the small table caught my attention, pulling me closer. A journal lay open, and a picture was stuffed behind one of the pages. My heart thumped against my ribs as I pulled it out, seeing a beautiful, dark-haired woman laughing, her hand on her growing belly.

My hands shook as I plucked up the picture, another violent wave of emotion smashing down on me as I stared into the stunning face of my mother. The only picture I ever saw of her was a blurry, faraway one. People told me I looked like my father, but I could see I had her smile and onyx eyes.

Tears slid down my face as I took her in. Her hand lovingly rubbed her belly.

Me.

Little did she know, I would take away her smile, the love of her life, my father's heart. The night I came into this world, I destroyed both parents, even if I only killed one.

My fingers brushed her face. "I'm so sorry, Mom." It was a sentiment I said countless times, but now it felt more real, seeing her, young and beautiful, full of joy and possibilities. I took it all away from her.

A tear slid down my face, landing on the journal with a splat, blurring the ink. My focus dropped down to the journal itself, scrolling over my father's handwriting.

*I understand now...*

The sentence popped off the page as I felt the book grip me, the picture in my hand fluttering to the floor.

"Nooooo!" I screamed, thrashing against it, but the scene flickered in front of me like it was set on fast forward again, jumpy, choppy, and unclear. Like the dream, I watched my father grab something, his face set with grim fear, shoving the object underneath a stone near the fireplace before I was yanked back, a cry tearing from my lungs, the book spinning me through the darkness and out.

My body flung back into a bag of potatoes, the spuds digging into

191

my spine as the ceiling spun overhead. Shutting my eyes, I took a deep breath.

"Are you okay?" Ash shuffled over to me, his hands touching my face softly.

"Yeah." I inhaled again, trying to center the rocky waves in my stomach.

"At least this time, you had something to land on," he scoffed. "Guess we're having mashed potatoes tomorrow."

I opened my lids, scowling.

"What? That was funny." His breathtaking smile was directed at me, his sexual energy throbbing down my legs.

"Ash..." I groaned, feeling the weight of his charm.

"Sorry." He helped me sit up. "I'm usually pretty good at reining it in... not always easy with you."

I rubbed my head where a potato had dug into my scalp.

"So what happened?" he asked.

My mouth opened, then shut, my expression twisting into confusion. "I don't know; this one was bizarre." I brushed back my hair. I so needed a shower. "I asked where the nectar was now, and I went back to the tunnels. Those pirates were running to the river where there was a boat... and then everything went black. Nothing."

"What?" Ash tilted his head. "What do you mean *nothing*? They still had it, right?"

"Yeah." I rubbed my brow. "I think so."

"That makes no sense."

"I did feel something lurking in the shadows, waiting for them." Killian had said it was taken from them soon after. But something about whatever was waiting in the shadows made me shiver.

"It still would have been recorded in the book if it was with someone." Ash's confusion only added to the unsettled feeling I got. "It shouldn't go blank like that. Not if they still had it."

"Maybe it was one of those pages Opie used as a dress." I shrugged one shoulder, not understanding either.

A nerve twitched in Ash's cheek. "Was that all you saw?"

"Nooo..." I let the syllable drag out. "There was more, but it makes even less sense."

"*Szerelmem*, that is becoming the norm with you."

I scowled at him, but I couldn't refute the claim.

"It took me to this cottage. It was the same place I dreamed about last night."

"Wait." Ash held up his hands. "You dreamed about a place the book took you just now?"

"Yeah." I shifted back onto my knees. "Why?"

His mouth twisted, shaking his head. "Go on."

"I've never seen it, but I knew my father was staying there. His coat was there, and this journal, with my mom's picture in it." My lashes fluttered at the memory. "I've never really seen a good picture of her... she was so beautiful. In the picture, she was pregnant with me." I wiped at my eyes, clearing my voice.

"I'm sorry, Brex."

"Just strange looking at her, so full of joy, not having a clue what tragedy lay ahead."

"You know it's not your fault, right?"

"You know, people have told me that all my life." I rubbed absently at my chest. "It doesn't change how I feel. If it wasn't for me..."

"Brex."

"They could have had another child, many of me... but for my father, there was only one woman he ever loved. And he lost her."

"Listen to me." Ash pulled in his hands, clasping my jaw, turning my head to him. "There's just *one* you. You realize how many lives you have already changed? Without you, the man I consider my brother wouldn't be alive. I've known you for a short time, and I already can't imagine my life with you not in it. And I can guarantee your parents would do it all over again, even for the briefest moment your mother had with you."

Ash wiped at the tears now flowing down my cheeks; I swallowed the sobs to keep them inside. Seeing my mother opened all my old wounds. Guilt, anger, sorrow. I was pissed I never had even a single moment with her.

Ash's thumbs stroked my cheeks, his touch calming me down. It was intimate and charged, his eyes locked on mine softly, his sexual energy coiling around me, our eyes connecting.

Not thinking, I tipped forward, my lips finding his. He responded, his mouth soft, warm, and... wrong.

I couldn't deny a slight spark, but it felt empty.

Ash sensed it, too, his lips twisting playfully as he pulled back, not a shred of rejection or embarrassment.

"You can be mad at him right now, but it's there. So deeply rooted, it vibrates and weaves through time and space." His hands cupped my jaw harder. "You can't run from it."

"From what?"

He gave me a look. "I knew from the first night he brought you to me. I felt it deep in my bones. You two go beyond mated."

My lids blinked, my mouth not able to answer, the truth of his words settling into my bones. I tried to jerk back, but Ash held onto my face.

"The link you two have... there's no breaking it."

"There has to be. It's not fair to him... he doesn't want it." He was making the point clear right now. The thought of him and Rosie crunched my teeth together, acid rotting in my stomach.

"There is a lot Warwick says he doesn't want... doesn't make it true."

"*I* don't want it." I tried to fight back, but nothing was behind it.

"Believe me." He placed his forehead against mine, a smile curving his lips. "If there wasn't a Warwick or a bond between you two, I'd be all over this. Nothing would stop me." He chuckled, his lips pressing into my skin between my brows. "And if you ever get sick of his cranky ass, I'm your guy, okay?"

I snorted, my head bouncing. Ash had a way to completely put me at ease.

"Anything else the book showed you?" He sat back on his heels, seamlessly turning us back to the issue. "I'm still confused why the book even showed you your father. I'm not getting the connection."

"Something was written in his journal I saw on the table." I bit into my bottom lip. "It said 'I understand now.'"

Ash stilled. "Understand? What?"

"Didn't say, but then I got another vision of my dad hiding something next to the fireplace."

Ash's eyes widened.

"You have no clue where this place is?"

"No." My brain clicked with an idea as I jumped to my feet, already heading for the door. "But I know someone who might."

Uncle Andris was in his office. Ling was next to him, both huddled close at his desk, going over documents together. I paused to watch the intimate moment between them.

Ling looked to be explaining something to him, pointing to the paper. His gaze drifted to her. Reaching up, he softly brushed her hair off her face, tucking it behind her ear, completely absorbed with her. A small smile flickered her lips at his touch, but her finger stabbed down at the paper, pulling his attention back to the document.

It was subtle, but knowing Andris the way I did, I could see the complete adoration in his eyes, the deep love he felt for her. Profound and irrevocable. Something I realized even as a kid, I never saw between him and Rita.

Ling noticed me first, her dark eyes peering at me impassively.

"Brexley." Andris sat straighter in his chair, the sweet moment between him and his love dissolving as he turned back to the stoic man I knew. "Come in." He motioned for me to enter.

I cleared my throat. "Sorry to interrupt."

"No, no, please... I was going to check on you soon."

I stepped into the office, Ash staying slightly behind me.

"What can I do for you?" Andris gestured to the chair, but I stayed standing, my nerves not able to settle.

"This might be peculiar."

"You are peculiar." Ling's emotionless to-the-point tone made Ash snort behind me.

Again, I couldn't disagree.

"What is it, *Drágám?" My dear.* Andris encouraged me.

"Did Father have a house away from HDF?"

Andris blinked like that was the last question he expected from me. "Your father and I had numerous safe houses over the country. And through the East."

"Right." I dipped my head, hope deflating from my lungs. The place could be anywhere, a straw in a haystack.

"What brought this up?" Andris sat back in his chair.

"I had a dream... and then the fae book showed me the same place." When I arrived here, I caught Andris up on everything, including the fae book. He was one of the few I trusted to tell everything to. "It was a small cottage. Father's jacket was there." I swallowed. The memory of his smell, the memory of the coat, prickled at my eyes. "A journal was on the dining table."

"Journal?" Andris's spine went straight, the chair squeaking as he sat up hastily.

"Yes." My heart started to pound at his reaction. "I saw a picture of—"

"Your mother." He stood up.

"How did you know?" My mouth dried.

"Your father was always careful, but before his death, his paranoia had grown extreme. He never carried the journal on him in the event he was ever captured... he kept her picture there." Andris's dark eyebrows crowded together. "I can think of one place it would be—a place only I knew about, in case something happened."

"Where?" I breathed.

"A cottage where your father and mother secretly lived together before her death. Where I had met her once. I didn't realize he kept it. He never told me..." A sadness gripped Andris, his thoughts taking him away.

"Location?" Ash stepped up with me, jerking Andris back to attention.

"*Gödöllő*. Not far from the old human Royal Palace."

My mouth parted.

It was only thirty minutes from here.

# Chapter 18

Far past working streetlights from before the fae war, the onetime bustling hamlet was now quiet. There were people here trying to make a living, a few inns for the weary traveler, a few farms, but life was even harder out here. Protecting what livelihood you could scrape out was a challenge under the constant fear of bandits and thieves. It was why most moved closer to the city, letting nature encroach on the territory they once inhabited.

Working from a map where Andris scribbled out the coordinates, Ash ventured the motorcycle to a forested area not too far from Gödöllő Palace, the rumbling of Maddox's bike behind us.

Andris wanted me to have more protection, but the more we had, the more we gained attention. My uncle wasn't happy Warwick was not one of them. Even if he didn't care for him, he knew Warwick was the best security and weapon to have. Most would run at the sight of him.

Following my instructions, we turned off on an unmarked dirt road. The forest quickly filled in around us, absorbing the motorcycles' dim headlights. The eerie stillness of the night, the feeling of the things hiding in the dark, had me on edge. After a few more turns down even smaller lanes, which could no longer be counted as roads, we came to a dead end.

"Did we take a wrong turn?" Ash stopped the bike, peering around.

"We lost?" Maddox came beside us.

"No." Tugging at the bag on my back I borrowed from Ash, I climbed off the bike. I yanked the gun from my belt, strolling to the edge of the lane. "It's got to be here." Glock in one hand, a light in the other, I found an almost undistinguishable footpath heading into the woods.

Following my gut, I stepped slowly down the trail, my boots crunching over the foliage. It wasn't long before I spotted a structure, almost hidden by overgrowth. I inhaled sharply seeing the tiny cottage, emotion fluttering my lungs.

This was where my parents lived together. Loved. Shared their hopes and dreams... little did they know their love would be tragic and short.

The cottage was like a time bubble of the life my mother and father had before me. It sat here waiting for the owners to return.

They never would. But their daughter had.

The boys stepped in beside me, flashlights in hand. Maddox checked around the house for any alarms or traps.

"All clear," he pronounced, but I didn't move.

"You all right, Brex?" Ash bumped my shoulder.

"Yeah." I nodded. "It's just... this is the closest I've ever been to anything of my mother's. Things she touched..." What if it still smelled like her? What if something of hers was here? "The last place I have that is my father's." All small objects I had of my dad were left back in HDF, sacrificed to escape safely. "This is where they were happy. Together," I croaked.

Ash took my fingers in his, leading me closer to the front door, where Maddox picked the lock. Ash and I had our weapons primed for any kind of an attack, inside and out.

"*Bassza meg!*" *Fuck me!* Maddox hissed under his breath. "This has, like, five deadbolts and a trick lock. Your father wanted to make sure it wasn't easy to get in." He stood up. "And we lost our fae lock pick when our last base was attacked." His dark eyes darted to me with a frown.

My fault.

I was good at picking locks, but I doubted I could crack all five and a trick lock. Those were highly intricate and difficult. Nearly impossible.

"The windows are barred too." Ash motioned to the one near the kitchen area. The cabin was small, but my dad had made sure it was bunker safe.

"This is when a brownie and an imp would be handy," I mumbled.

"You called, Master Fishy?" A voice popped up by my ear.

"Holy shit!" I jumped, my hand going to my chest as Opie climbed out of my backpack up to my shoulder, Bitzy in her bag on his back. They still wore the same outfit I saw them in earlier, but Opie had doubled up on the cotton balls speared through his Mohawk, and now he had a cape made from a sock. "Were you guys there the whole time?" I gaped at him and back to my sack.

"Of course, Fishy." Opie patted my cheek. "You couldn't last a day without me."

*Chirp!* Bitzy's middle fingers went up.

"And, of course, Bitzy too."

*Chirp!*

"Don't put this on me!" Opie peered back at Bitzy. "You were the one who wanted to nap in there because it still smelled like mushrooms!"

*Chirp! Chirp!*

"I licked it once! Just seeing if there were still some crumbs left over... for *your* safety."

*Chirp!*

"I was not! You were the one suckling it like a newborn."

*Chirp! Chirp! Chirp!*

My eyes widened.

"Someone is awfully cranky," Opie huffed.

*Chir—*

"Okay, I'm gonna stop whatever is happening here." Ash motioned over the pair. "And get back to our task. Can you open the locks?"

"Please." Opie snorted, his eyes rolling. "Peasants..." He strolled down my arm, hopping down onto the ground. "Move, underlings, your miracle is here." He motioned for Maddox and Ash to get out of the way of the king, Bitzy flipping them off as they passed. Opie stopped as he reached the door, his head tilting back, his brows pinching.

My lips rolled together, trying not to laugh. "Does the *miracle* need a little assistance reaching the door?"

"My greatness is in a tiny package."

*Chirp!*

"Not that package!" he retorted. "I'll have you know I've been told by many it's above normal for my size."

199

*Chirp.*

"Okay, maybe not many, but plenty."

*Chirp.*

"Okay, not plenty, but some."

"My gods..." Ash rubbed his head. "If I was told I'd be listening to a brownie argue with an imp about his dick size on a mission for some fable nectar in the middle of the night, I would have thought it was me eating mushrooms."

*Chirp?* Bitzy's eyes turned to Ash, her ears going down as she blinked up at him with hope.

"No. I don't have mushrooms. You ate them all," Ash said back, then stopped. "Holy shit, I answered her, didn't I?" He looked startled. "I'm talking to an imp."

"Welcome to the club." I chuckled. Leaning down, I lifted Opie up to the lock.

"I say you are all fucking crazy." Maddox shook his head with annoyance.

Opie's hands went over the lock, his tongue sticking out of the side of his mouth. For several minutes he worked, his tongue switching sides. "Oh, this is a tough one." He moved his hands around, his thick brows coming together. "I'm getting closer... broomsticks... I think I almost got it." He closed his lids, face straining. "Wow... sticky one..."

Bitzy sighed, her long prong-like fingers reaching over his shoulder, slipping into the lock.

*Clank. Clank. Clank. Clank. Clank.*

Each one rang in the air, the door squealing as it swung open to a dark room. I stepped back, a wave of stale air blowing out.

"Well..." Opie bristled at Bitzy. "*I* loosened them for you."

I sat them back on my shoulder as Ash and Maddox moved into the small cabin.

"Clear." Ash checked the bathroom.

Maddox tugged open a closet door. "Clear here."

The place was small, no other places to hide, but it was exactly like I saw it in the book. Like the very last time my father was here was that night.

Stepping in, I felt like an intruder to their sanctuary. The musty air was the most prominent, but under, I swore I could smell my father's cologne. My hand brushed the wood chair at the table, and I imagined him sitting there, writing in his journal. I still struggled to really picture

200

my mother, though I was sure I could feel her presence touching the room. She was a stranger, but familiar at the same time.

Opie and Bitzy jumped off my shoulder onto the counter while I took in the little things like the sugar and black tea, which I knew my dad loved. In a small bottle was cinnamon. My father never used cinnamon. Was this my mother's? Did she like it on her toast like I did?

"Brex?" Ash yanked my attention to him. "Where are we looking?"

Moving to him, I went to where I saw *apa* stuff something into a hiding place, my hand going to the stone, running over it. "Somewhere here—" I felt the rock wiggle under my palm. Energy burst up my nerves, knowing I found it. What would be inside? Would it be the journal, or was it the nectar?

My nails dug into the crevice, pulling at the stone. My breath hitched as I lifted it away, adrenaline pumping down my arms as I shone the flashlight into the hiding spot.

"Oh gods..." I croaked, my heart beating against my ribs. Jammed into a hole laid a leather-bound book.

My father's journal.

It was here. I found it.

My hand shaking, I reached inside, like I found a piece of my father I had never known about. A hidden gem, more precious to me than any real treasure. Blowing off the dusty cover, I coughed, billows of dirt filling my nose.

"That's it? We came here for a notebook?" Maddox frowned.

I brushed at the cover with care. "It's what's inside the note—"

*Bang!*

A bullet sparked off the stone right above my head, coming through the door. My body jolted, a cry breaking from my lips as arms wrapped around me. Ash hauled us to the ground with a thud. Glass shattered through the kitchen window with another round of shells.

"Opie?" My gaze darted to where I had left Opie and Bitzy. The counter was empty.

"Here. Fishy!" His figure darted from under the sofa, carrying Bitzy, diving into the bag, where I stuffed in the journal.

More bullets shot through the open door and window.

"Fuck!" Maddox yelled, diving next to the table below the window. "Who the hell is attacking us? Who knows we're here?"

"I don't know," Ash gritted while we both scrambled up, tipping the sofa back. Using it as a barrier, we pointed our weapons, ready to shoot out into the pitch-black night.

We couldn't see anything in the thick woods beyond the door.

"We're sitting ducks here," Maddox hissed as another round of fire burst into the room, tearing into the couch. "What the fuck is our plan?"

We may have cover now, but the endgame didn't look good for us. We could close the door, but then we locked ourselves in a box for them. Had a shoot-out ever gone well for the people inside? I had one time seen it play out in real life when I was a kid to a wealthy elite not conforming to the new life after the worlds meshed. He went crazy, holding his wife and son hostage, spouting conspiracy theories. Istvan had him shot in the head by a sniper by the third hour.

Whoever was outside could have a sniper trained on us too, ready to wait us out or even try to burn us out. No matter what, they had the upper hand.

"Girl, I'm starting to think you have a tracker device installed in your ass!" Maddox pulled out a second gun, leaping up and firing out the broken kitchen window at the mystery assailants.

A moment of panic scorched my skin, wondering if Istvan had done something like that to me. I never would have believed it before, but now I wasn't sure.

"If we get out of this, I will personally inspect your ass myself." Ash grinned, though I felt his tension growing, his focus still out the door.

More shots shredded the couch, instantly upping the urgency in the room.

"We can't stay here." Maddox snapped at us, his gun blasting off. I heard a cry from right outside the house, sounding like he hit someone.

They were closing in on us.

"Why don't you go ask them to kindly stop?" Ash volleyed.

A figure darted by the door, and my finger pulled the trigger multiple times. The person cried out, hitting the ground right outside the door, but it was too late. A device rolled over the threshold, smoke hissing out of it, spinning my head and making my throat spasm.

"Fuck!" Ash yanked up his shirt over his mouth, trying to reach for it and toss it back out, but gunfire forced him back behind the sofa.

I covered my mouth with my sweater, my eyes watering painfully, and my mind went sleepy.

These devices that dispersed gas were rare, but I knew it was something Istvan was firm on having in his arsenal, even if it meant cutting costs elsewhere. Fae had a bad response to the synthetic chemical, and though their bodies might get it out faster than humans, it still leveled them as quickly. Gave humans a chance to have the upper hand.

The device came from Ukraine and had a unique design, exactly like the one poisoning us now. I had no doubt who was outside the doors along with HDF soldiers. The only one who could have tracked me down again.

The man of death.

Kalaraja.

"Brex! Stay awake!" Ash shook me, my body slumping over. Maddox coughed and hacked, trying to drag himself closer to the chemical weapon, probably wanting to chuck it back outside, but with every move, his body slowed.

Fuck. Fuck. Fuck.

Kalaraja might take me, but he would kill Ash and Maddox. Two fewer fae in Istvan's eyes.

"Ash..." I croaked, taking his hand.

Panic pumped the toxin faster through my bloodstream, my eyes meeting Ash's. I could see in his eyes he had come up with the same ending. Whether we ran outside or stayed, the end result was the same.

Darkness inched into my vision. Every breath felt like daggers through my throat, and my mind was getting cloudier, detaching from reality.

*"Don't you dare close your eyes,"* a fierce voice snarled, fluttering my lids to a huge outline standing over me. A dream and a nightmare. Warwick... larger than life, sexy as fuck... and pissed.

*"Stay the fuck awake, princess,"* he growled. *"Be ready to move!"*

"Wha—?"

*BOOOOOOM!*

Flames ignited the night, crackling and billowing up, filling the dark sky. Shouts rang through the air, the flames outlining the bodies in the woods, moving toward the explosion. Shouts turned into squeals, like people were being gutted.

With all the energy I could muster, I shoved at Ash. "Go!" My muscles were slow, like I was swimming in tar, while I pushed myself up using all the strength I had left.

Ash grabbed Maddox, helping him to his feet. We were all struggling to function, stumbling out of the cottage. The bite of fresh air hit my lungs and ripped through my throat, causing me to wheeze, my head throbbing with discomfort.

Gunfire popped off, but it was no longer directed at us, the figures scurrying between the trees away from us. They were dressed in dark fatigues with an emblem I recognized on the arm. An outfit you were issued at HDF for night missions.

Ash practically dragged Maddox toward where we left the bikes, but my feet came to a stuttering stop as my vision cleared.

Like the devil rose straight from the ground, destruction and darkness surrounded him. Warwick whirled, swinging a weapon with dual blades on the end like a crab claw, blocking bullets and hacking through the attackers without pause. I had thought I had seen him fight before—ruthless, clean, and fast. This was far more brutal with his precision.

Callous fury thrummed off him like music, his massive size dwarfing the puny humans as he wielded his weapon. The killer who thrived off death. The legend come to life with the wrath and destruction of a fae god. He was graceful in its violence, a deadly dance, soaking the forest floor with blood.

Some retreated. However, there were those last naïve HDF soldiers who still believed they could challenge the legend. Their heads tumbled off into the dirt.

I probably knew every dead body there, though I couldn't seem to look at any of the corpses to identify them. My interest was locked on the lethal lore.

Covered with blood, Warwick lowered his cleaver, heaving out his breath. His eyes slowly lifted to mine through his lashes, shredding through me like another victim, gutting me until I was nothing but slices of a corpse lying on the ground with the rest. His fury seared and split me in half, his dark clothes glistening with the blood of his victims.

His nose flared, his shoulders rising up and down. The energy between us crackled louder than the fire consuming the branches from the explosion, scorching with vehemence, devouring me in the firestorm of his rage.

With his arm, he wiped the blood from his eyes, smearing streaks over his face. He strode for me like a bull, his energy ramming into me, stumbling me back into the wall of the cottage. His boots hit mine, and he towered over me, his body engulfing mine like it was his meal to devour. He stared down at me, his jaw twitching. Each breath skated down my neck, sparking desire, fury, and fear into my system.

I watched him back, my chin up in silent defiance.

He lifted his hand, his fingers dragging down my face, painting the blood of my fellow HDF soldiers on my cheek like a brand. Energy clamped through my muscles, shooting through my veins. Bristling and twitching with violence, he pressed me roughly into the wall, his mouth hovering over mine. I could taste his strength like a storm about to rain down on me.

"Warwick!" I heard Ash bellow through the burning trees. "You fucking asshole!"

Slowly, a smirk bent Warwick's mouth, his gaze still claiming me. His nose flared before he dropped his hand and pushed away. Turning, he strolled toward his friend, disappearing through the trees.

My body slumped into the wall, exhausted and dizzy, though I felt far better than I should and had everything to do with the man who just walked away. He took away my pain, balancing me from the inside out, clearing my mind, and firing energy into my veins.

I hated that the moment he was near me, nothing in the world existed. Now the ire and hurt from what he had been doing before he arrived here bolted my spine straight, casting back up my armor.

Stepping from the path to where the road was, I found the reason for Ash's anger.

"You blew up my fucking bike!" Ash motioned to the machine, shattered in charred pieces, flames catching the tree limbs around.

"I needed a distraction." Warwick shrugged, swinging his leg over his own motorcycle. His weapon was already attached to the back, like a flag waving in warning.

"You couldn't have blown up his?" Ash gestured to Maddox, who was curled over his legs, hacking and spitting, looking like he wanted to vomit.

"No." Warwick's motorcycle roared to life, his eyes sliding from Ash to me poignantly, as if he knew we had kissed earlier.

He spun the bike around, stopping next to me. "Get on," he barked.

I wanted to say no, to punch him in the face, but we were down a bike, and I knew there was no point.

"Wait." Ash's arms swung as I climbed behind Warwick. "How do I get back?"

"Snuggle in close." Warwick's eyebrows lifted, nodding to Maddox. "I suggest you drive. He looks like he's ready to puke."

"You are a real bastard," Ash scoffed, his head wagging.

"I *really* am." Warwick winked sardonically, the bike peeling off down the road.

And he meant it. Figuratively and literally.

As we tore off down the dirt road, the unmistakable sensation of eyes on me climbed up my spine, jerking my head to the side. I could feel him, his dark beady eyes hunting me from deep in the forest where he hid. He was smart enough to know when he was outnumbered. He would wait to strike. But it was like I could feel Kalaraja's sentiment crawl over me.

*I will come for you again... I always get my mark.*

Our motorcycle traveled through the night like a black steed, our dark hair whipping into the air like manes. Dipping temperatures flattened my body closer to Warwick's. My thighs clutched against his. My breasts pressed into his back, seeking the warmth, and I had to fight the urge to curl into him like a cat. My chest cracked every time I took in a whiff of his rich woodsy scent. I couldn't describe it, but it was all Warwick, and it felt like home.

I hated him.

No, I *wanted* to hate him. So much. But even without us reaching out, strumming the cord between us, I felt him buzzing inside and outside of me, pulsing at the edges.

I didn't ask him how he knew I needed help or how he found us. I already knew. And deep down, without even reaching out, if he were in trouble, I would feel it, and nothing on this planet would stop me from finding him.

With Ash and Maddox behind us, the two motorcycles entered the city, the smell of the impoverished filling my nose. It had grown familiar, a scent that told a thousand words of the harsh life in Savage Lands. The smoke from the factories still clung to the air like heavy fog. The decaying buildings covered with graffiti rose high on either side of us.

My gun was ready to put a bullet into any threat. The city was full of depravity, looking for trouble in the witching hours before dawn. And Warwick and I attracted it like bees to honey.

Tonight was no different.

*Pop!*

Hoots and hollers rang out, and I whipped my head around to see men on horses ride out from a side street. With hats on their heads and bandanas over their faces, they had guns aimed at us, like a cowboy posse.

*Fuck.* My gut sank with terror, recognizing the group, though there were more of them today. The memory of our run-in with them last time slammed back into my mind.

The horsemen of the apocalypse. The Hounds. A gang of thieves who would slice anyone's throat for a coin. They had no conscience or any hesitation about who they attacked. Anyone passing by was fair game, and they would collect payment from you—through your pocket or life.

"*Kurva anyád!*" Warwick spat, punching the gas, his gaze snapping to Ash.

A bullet pinged off the building right by my head, spewing debris into the air. Shooting back, I watched the horses galloping toward us, gaining on us far faster than I liked.

Warwick snapped the handlebars, squealing the bike down another road, Ash right behind us. Maddox fired back at them.

*Bang! Bang! Bang!*

The sound of gunfire shrilled the night air, bouncing off the buildings, exploding in my eardrums. With every breath, I tensed, ready to feel a bullet sink into my skin.

Warwick made a gesture with his hand, his head darting back to Ash. The friends understood each other with looks and simple gestures after so long fighting together.

Warwick gave Ash a nod when his bike came even with us. Ash responded in kind before peeling off down a side alley while we spun the opposite way, hoping to split or falter the gang.

I twisted, firing back at the four horsemen who came after us, the other three going after Ash. My legs clung to Warwick for life, dread shimmering under my skin, terrified this would be the night our number was up.

Bullets pinged off our bike, scraping close to my body, the heat of the slug sizzling my clothes. Warwick's muscles tensed. I sensed his need to pull me in front of him, shield me like he was also afraid the next shot would embed itself into my brain.

The clops of hooves on the concrete vibrated my spine, the hollers growing louder, icing my veins with panic.

"*Hold on tight,*" his voice hissed into my ear, my arms constricting around him right as he snapped the bike to the left, the wheels slipping on the damp cement. His foot struck the ground to keep us upright as he spun us down another street, the engine revving as he tore down the road. Just a few yards later, three men on horses tore from an alley right as we passed, shooting at us.

I yelped in shock, realizing they were the ones I thought went after Ash and Maddox. Instead, they had gone around, coming at us from another angle, boxing in their prey. It was smart. Cunning. Like they knew we were important targets, coming for us as if we really did call out to danger like a siren song.

The horses galloped up next to us, one of them getting right next to the bike. A Hound reached out for me, his fingers wrapping around the strap of my backpack, yanking on it. With a cry, I struggled to keep my balance on the seat, almost falling off. To thieves, the bag *might* hold something of value—money, drugs, items to sell or trade, but it held nothing of worth in the conventional sense. But to me, it possessed *everything*: Opie and Bitzy and the last thing I had of my father's. His words, his thoughts, his writing, and possible knowledge of what I was.

There was no way I would let it go.

Twisting to my assailant, I pulled the trigger right as he wrenched the pack from my shoulders. *Bang!* The bullet hit its mark, sinking into his side. His body jerked. A grunt huffed from his chest, his frame sliding off the horse.

Slamming into me.

A scream caught in my throat as his weight knocked me off the bike, plunging us to the ground. Bones crunched, smacking the stone. The bike was shoved over by the force of our weight. All of us skidded across the pavement like scattered cargo. The shrill sound of metal scraping over stone pierced my ears. My head spun as I tumbled, not even comprehending any pain yet. The clip of hooves on the road echoed in my head like an alarm, telling me to get up. Run.

*"Kovacs!"* I felt Warwick's call in my soul more than I heard it. My lids fluttered, and I turned my head to the gang. Their horses pranced and huffed as they took in the body of their fallen comrade a few yards from me. Then one of them leaned over, swiped up my bag, and without a second glance, steered their horses around and rode off.

"N-n-no..." I cried out, struggling to sit up. The need to run after them had me on my feet, picking up a gun and opening fire.

The shots ricocheted off the stone walls, mocking me with their empty threats as the gang continued to ride away.

"Nooooo!" I tried to run after them, limping, my arm twinging in agony as I continued to shoot, panic blanketing me with the need to not let them out of my sight.

"Kovacs!" Warwick wrapped his arms around me, yanking me back, ripping the gun from my hands. "Stop!"

"No!" I tried to wiggle from his embrace. "Let go! We have to go after them!" He didn't relent. "Do something!" I thrashed harder. "Or get the fuck out of my way!"

"No." He grunted when my elbow dug into his gut.

"They have Opie and Bitzy. They have the journal," I heaved, knowing they were too far to catch by now anyway, but logic didn't matter. Tears prickled at my eyes. "Let me go! You fuckin' pussy!"

He didn't surrender his hold or move, but I could feel him explode around me, his anger and violence scraping and scratching against my skin, pushing in deeper, halting the air in my lungs. It only pissed me off.

"Get off me!" I kicked my heel into him.

I heard a soft groan and, at first, I thought it was Warwick, until the noise came again.

A louder grunt came from the man lying on the ground. Warwick's arms dropped, clicking the gun he took from me, strolling over to the man and raising the weapon to his head.

I reacted on instinct.

"No. Stop." I moved quickly to him, ignoring the pain streaking down my muscles. I pressed my palm on the weapon, forcing him to lower it. Warwick's brows furrowed in question. I peered down at the gang member, still barely holding on to life, then back to Warwick. "He could be useful."

"Don't think for a moment they care about this asshole enough to trade him." Warwick snorted. "That's not how they work. He's better dead."

"No." My voice was firm, my gaze telling Warwick this was not a question, but an order. "He can lead us to their hideout."

"He'd kill himself before he'd tell." Warwick shook his head, annoyance flickering on his features.

"It's worth a shot." I gritted my teeth. "I am not stopping until I get my bag back." I didn't fear for Opie and Bitzy, as I knew they would get away. They could vanish in front of my eyes, but my father's journal was worth everything to me. To find it, I would flip over this city if I had to.

Warwick watched me for a while, probably seeing the

determination on my features. He sucked in a deep breath, irritation twitching his eye.

An eerie growl-like howl cried out into the night, followed by another, his head jerking up.

"*Faszom...*" Warwick tensed, his head moving, trying to pinpoint the location of the noise.

"What?"

"Hyenas."

"What?" I sputtered, whirling toward the icy shrieks, my mouth parting.

"They're coming." He twisted to run. "We've got to go."

"Like real ones?"

"Shifters, and even more dangerous. They sniff out blood and come running to pick off the corpses left in the street, taking whatever scraps remain. They're scavengers... deadly ones."

"Then we can't leave him here!" I motioned to the dying man, his breathing getting worse.

"Are you kidding me? I'm not in the mood to fight a clan." Warwick glowered down at me. "Hyena clans have no problem picking off the living as well, especially those weakened by a fight."

"We are not leaving him," I snarled back. Not a question, not an option.

His jaw clamped, a nerve thrumming along it.

"*Bassza meg!*" Warwick spat, slapping the Glock into my palm as he stomped over toward the thief. He leaned over, lifting the bleeding man over his shoulder. "Once again, I'm picking up your rescues."

More eerie howls, sounding just a block away, scoured over my body, shivering my bones.

"Let's go." Warwick spun around.

"How far are we from the base?" I was good with directions, but I hadn't spent enough time in Savage Lands to really gauge where I was.

"Too far on foot." He looked over at the bike. Fuel leaked onto the road, and the back tire was popped. He set the dying man down, grabbing the terrifying weapon from the back, blood crusted into the claw blades and attached it to his back.

"What is that?"

"A wolf blade."

"Wolf blade?" I snorted, though I could see, with its many claws, how it could resemble a wolf's talons.

"Had it designed specifically for me." He tossed the man on his other shoulder. "Come on." He veered around and strolled off, the man limply hanging off his shoulder.

"Where?"

"To the only place we can go."

# Chapter 19

Flames danced over my head from the hoop swing as the beautiful girl, whose features split down the middle like she was two people sewn seamlessly into one, did her party tricks with fire. A few feet away from her, hanging above in a hammock, was a naked human woman moaning loudly, her head flung back as she rode one man while a fae man entered her from behind. Her cries were so full of erotic bliss, my body heated with raw need, forcing my teeth to crunch together.

Music and the hum of talking, gambling, and fighting filled the tight passage. Nearly naked bodies pushed past me, their calls to enter their establishments directed to anyone who walked by. It was deep into the night, and Carnal Row was at the peak of its business—when indulgence was disguised by drink, and the misery of the day was buried in the depravities and sin of the night.

Not one person gave the bleeding man over Warwick's shoulder notice, though Warwick couldn't walk through without countless heads turning his way. Lust choked the air, widening the legs of those hungry to taste him. So many lifeless, empty eyes ignited when he passed, their bodies jolting with hunger. His aura was so virile, he brought the dead back to life.

*Like you do.* I shook my head, shoving the thought away as we pushed through the crowd, heading to the iniquitous dwelling on the corner, which at one point had begun to feel like a second home to me, with people I *had* considered friends.

Almost all the others I could have brushed away, but Rosie's betrayal hurt too deeply, no matter if I had a right to be or not. What did I expect? From either of them? This was the Savage Lands. I also knew better when it came to the notorious legend, who had multiple women brought to him in prison. And Rosie was doing her job. I doubted anyone in the world would turn Warwick down, but knowing she was with him... logic wasn't there.

In one strategic move, Warwick made sure he ended anything with me and also took away my one friend here.

"War-wick..." His name sang from the windows of Kitty's brothel, women and men calling out to him. Only a few were left trying to wrangle in their last customer at this late hour. I heard loud grunts and moaning from open windows and down the side alleyways.

"Bring me something tasty?" Peering up, I saw the snake-shifter sitting in the window, the one he had been with before.

"If you like them bleeding and half dead." Warwick started up the steps.

"I do, but I wasn't talking about him." She flicked her tongue out at him suggestively, and I hated that I knew where it had been. "I'm especially hungry tonight... want me to join you? She can watch. We can pick up from last night?"

Anger surged up my spine, my cheek twitching, a low growl emanating from my throat. Her word confirming my fears, eliminating any tiny doubt I clung to.

"Not tonight," Warwick replied, grabbing my arm and yanking me into the brothel, firing more fury through my muscles.

*Not tonight? As in, maybe tomorrow?*

Fuck her and *fuck* him.

"Let go." Ripping my arm away from him, I stumbled inside, straight into the Madam herself.

Her head was high, her hair in a long bob style. She wore skintight leather pants, a backless, almost sheer, red silky tank, and stiletto boots. Her arms were folded, her expression hard.

"No." Her jaw tightened.

"Kitty..." Warwick started.

"No." She lifted a perfectly manicured finger, pointing back at the door. "Return the way you came with that... thing." Her nose wrinkled, taking in the man over his shoulder.

"Kit—"

"Warwick, you are dancing on my last nerve. It is one thing to harbor you and even *her*." She eyed me. "But I'm not a halfway house or an infirmary. I have two soldiers upstairs. I will be jailed if they find you, and you will be quartered and hung on sight."

"Don't worry, Killian doesn't want my head on a plate right now." A cheeky smile curled up the side of his mouth.

"I didn't say the soldiers were fae." She curved a perfect eyebrow up. "And you think that makes this better?" She motioned to the limp man. I could see he was barely breathing. Time was running out. "He's certainly a criminal, and you both still have bounties on your head from HDF and who knows where else."

"Kitty—"

"I know you, Warwick, don't give me that tone. Do not make me a promise you have no intention of keeping." She held up her hand, gesturing toward the door as a wheeze came from the man. "Now get him out of here."

"Please." I grabbed her hands, her thin figure jolting at my touch, and I quickly let go. "This man is the only hope I have of finding where his gang is hiding. They took something important of mine. Something that could be vital." *To me and to this country.* "I wouldn't ask you if it wasn't exceptionally important."

Her dark brown eyes watched mine, no emotion flickering through them, like she was seeking out the truth in my claim. After a few moments, she exhaled, her glittery lids shutting briefly. "In the back bedroom behind the kitchen." She glanced up at the ceiling like she couldn't believe she was doing this. "I will send for the doctor. Now go before I change my mind."

Warwick bowed his head, moving around her, obviously knowing the exact location she was referring to.

"Thank you." I folded my hands together in gratitude.

"You two are like battling a tsunami. Pointless and exhausting." She shook her head, looking over my wounds and down my torn and bloody clothes with another sigh. "Suppose you will need *more* clothes also. I'll send them up to your room with a first aid kit and some food and drink." She huffed, looking past me, waving me off. "Go, before anyone sees you."

What I owed this woman seemed beyond a thank you. She continued to take me in, feed, and clothe me every time Warwick and I got into a life-and-death situation, which was *every* time.

214

I dipped my head in utter appreciation before slipping by her and following Warwick to the back room. It was small with no windows, barely room for a twin bed, a nightstand with a lamp, and a single wooden chair.

Warwick flipped the man onto the bed, the springs squealing under the impact. The thief's wound still oozed with blood, his clothes soaked, his chest struggling to rise with each breath. The guy was human, average height, weight, and looks, if not slightly baby-faced under the scraggly beard. Dirty blond hair stuck to his sweaty forehead, the round-brimmed hat he had been wearing long gone. His torn, bloody clothes were what I'd picture a gunslinger wearing, with a bandolier of bullets and guns strapped across his torso and around his hips. He appeared to be around his mid-thirties, but living the way he did had marked him with deep scars that hadn't healed right, making his age hard to pin down.

Warwick was stripping him of all weapons and ammunition when another man entered the room. He was at least half human—gray-haired, slight, short, and fragile-looking, glasses perched on his nose. He wore dark clothing and held a black doctor's bag. But something ethereal in his eyes and face structure suggested he might not be pure human.

His eyes widened at seeing Warwick, his Adam's apple bobbing nervously. "Warwick, I didn't expect you here. It's been a long time."

"Doctor Laski." Warwick nodded at him, moving out of his way so he could reach the patient. "This time, the call isn't for me."

The moment the doctor's eyes landed on the man in the bed, his demeanor changed. Locked on the patient, he scuttled to his side, tossing the bag on the bed. He ripped the man's shirt open, inspecting the wound, scowling.

"Unless you are here to assist, I need you to leave." Dr. Laski yanked off his jacket, rolling up his sleeves before diving into his bag and retrieving a syringe. Jabbing the needle into a small bottle, he flicked his finger at the syringe, filling it.

"Will he survive?" Warwick's tone was neutral, not caring either way.

"Doesn't look good. He's lost a lot of blood, and the bullet might have hit a vital organ," the doctor stated, jabbing the thief with the needle.

Warwick grabbed my arm, pulling me toward the door.

"I need him to live." A harsh demand broke from my mouth.

215

"I treat every patient I have with the same hope." The doctor didn't even spare me a glance, his focus entirely on his patient.

"Let the man work." Warwick dragged me from the room. "If anyone can save him, it's him."

"Have experience?" I clipped as Warwick shut the door behind me, yanking me toward the stairs.

He snorted. "More than once, princess."

"Is he human?" It was more out of curiosity, my mind still getting used to all the various people in Savage Lands. I grew up with one kind: human. They were all I knew or understood, never realizing the one who might be different in HDF was me.

"He has fae blood in his family line, but he's more human than fae. Still, it's there, and he can heal patients quicker and better than any human doctor. His own friends and colleagues turned on him when they saw how good he was, also realizing they were aging faster when he wasn't. It became a witch hunt, and he had to go into hiding, leaving his practice, his home, and wife of thirty years and disappear in the Savage Lands to survive during the years of persecution."

As a child, I learned about the dark years after the fae war when the East broke free from the Unified Nations and fought for power amongst itself. The persecution of half-breeds was at a fever pitch. Anyone even suspected of having a drop of fae blood was rounded up and sent away. I had never thought much of what happened to them. I was so young, but now I realized they weren't "sent away." They were hunted down and slaughtered. Most probably smuggled themselves into the Unified Nations or hid underground in the seedy world of the Savage Lands. They were no longer blatantly hunted like they once were, but the stigma hadn't gone away.

His plight invoked more anger in me—at myself, HDF, and the world. Why did people have to make life so much harder when it was already hard enough? All this death, pain, and agony were completely man-made. Why couldn't we all stop trying to put our own fears and beliefs on everyone else and just live our lives? Who are you to say this man, who had no control over the fae blood running in his veins, was less than you? Worthy of being murdered because he was different?

Living in this mixed pot of people, you saw every single being had a life, feelings, family, friends, hopes, and dreams. We weren't different at all; circumstances made our goals on how to achieve those things different. The anger toward each other, the drive to eradicate someone else hoping it would ease your life and burdens... .it was disgusting and totally wrong. It only made life that much tougher for all. Heavy, insufferable, and dark.

Warwick went up the stairs and I followed, my feet coming to a stop right at the top, my stomach twisting at the figure standing in front of our door.

"Luv." Rosie's red lips pulled in a smile. Her arms were filled with clothes, bathroom essentials, and a paper bag smelling of Thai noodles. "I was hoping it would be you."

I didn't move or speak. I was emotionless—gutted. I stared at her like a stranger. She was now. Right or wrong, I couldn't pretend the knife in my back wasn't from her. True, Warwick and I weren't together, and she was a prostitute, but that didn't mean I could be friendly toward her now. She was another harlot in the den of iniquity.

"I can sleep in another room if you were planning to be a *'paying customer'* again tonight. I don't want to get in the way of anyone making money by spreading their legs." I glared at Warwick, but my cold tone jerked Rosie back as if I slapped her. She blinked. Then her weight shifted between her feet, eyes drifting to the ground. Guilt. Shame.

Warwick's lids narrowed on me, rage bristling from him, getting my insinuation. "*Excuse* her." He growled at me, grabbing the items from Rosie's arms, then with his free hand, yanked me roughly in the room. "Thank you, Rosie." He slammed the door to the room we always stayed in, but this time when I stepped in, it felt different.

Tainted.

There wasn't an inch of this room not covered in what some considered sin. The walls retained moans and screams, the furniture was saturated with the smell of sex, the bed sagged with punishing use. I hadn't cared much before, but it was different now. Even when I had seen him with the four women in this room, it didn't tarnish the comfort and safety this space provided. They had felt distant and detached.

But now, all I could see was Rosie straddling him, her tits bouncing as she rode him, his hips plowing into her, their faces scrunching with pleasure on this very bed. Her lips on him, his hands fondling her.

I stood stiffly in the middle of the room. The thought of touching anything in here made me want to vomit. Fury bubbled in my stomach.

Tonight I had gained and lost so much. Although I was afraid for

Opie and Bitzy, I believed they could get away easily. It was my father who sat heavily on my heart.

I was an orphan. I never knew my mother and had nothing of my father's to hold on to. Finding his journal meant more to me than anyone could know. For a brief moment, I had a piece of him again, his inner thoughts, his findings about me, what he learned and saw. How he felt.

I held his heart and soul in my hands.

I wasn't even sure I cared so much about what he learned about me; it was more about having something of my dad's. He was my world, my everything. He was my mother, father, best friend, and protector. I missed him so much it tore me into pieces, pain so deep it engraved scars across my soul. Before I even opened the pages of his journal, it was taken from me, like both he and my mother had been.

I was heartbroken... and *furious*.

Now I was stuck in a small room with a man who traded me to the Seelie lord, who tried to kill me, who fucked me relentlessly, then screwed my one friend here just to prove a point. I had been gassed, shot at by my ex-best friends, punched, attacked, and robbed.

I was fucking done.

Angry.

Volatile.

Warwick strolled to the dresser, dumping the container of food and clothes on it. Grabbing a label-less bottle from the bag, he took a chug of the liquor. The cheap, acidic, grainy smell of whiskey tingled my nostrils. He slammed it back down, wiping his mouth and leaning over the bureau, his muscles tensing, flexing under his skin.

He didn't look at me, but I knew he was aware of every inch of space between us as I was. My gaze drilled into the back of him, the tension growing thicker with each beat of silence, weaving the room in snares.

So much had happened since he turned me over to Killian. Even if I understood the reason for his actions, the betrayal still sat in my gut, darkening with revenge the longer I pushed it away. I had never really let it out, our lives taking such sharp turns and becoming so hectic, it seemed like a frivolous thought to keep harping on.

But what he did then was only one layer.

He didn't even try to go after the journal. He could have. They were human. He was supposed to be a god on Earth. The book meant nothing to him, so why would he care? I was the fool. Pampered and protected. This world was not meant for trust or emotions. It was brutal. Cruel. Pitiless.

I thought I learned my lesson in Halálház, not to trust, to become just as feral as them, but I hadn't even come close. I let them all in. Believed. Rage filled me, shutting off anything resembling sentiment.

"Want to say something, princess?" Warwick snarled, his fingers drumming the table. "Just fucking say it."

No words slid off my tongue, my lungs sucking in more fury.

A low growl came from his chest before he slowly turned around to face me, pulling himself up to his full height. The notion he thought he could possibly intimidate me sparked my muscles, my own hands curling.

He could have said a million cruel things, and I might not have broken. It was the slight smirk on his lips that did it, the smugness, belittling my anger as if it were "cute."

A cry belted from my lungs, my body moving in a blink. I slammed into the wall of muscle, my fist cracking against his chin, slicing over his mouth.

My hand pulsed with agony at the impact, the pain making me even more enraged. A guttural noise thundered from my gut as I struck again, the sound of bone hitting bone cracking in my ears. He stumbled back into the dresser.

His smirk deepened, and his tongue swiped over his broken lip, tasting the blood. "Feel better?" he snarled, his eyes flaring.

"Not even a little."

"Good." His shoulders rolled, lurching for me. He was faster. His body slammed into mine, tossing us both to the floor with a painful blow. Instinctively, my knee drove up, ramming into his crotch.

"*Bazmeg*," he groaned, tipping to the side, his hand clutching his balls. Scrambling out from under him, he grabbed my leg, trying to yank me down.

Kicking, I wiggled the boot off my foot, freeing me from his grasp. Tossing my shoe, he jumped up, barreling for me. I didn't even try to shift out of his way. Fury galloped on my shoulders, needing to be released.

I wanted this fight.

Adrenaline and wrath pumped in my veins. My punch dug into his throat. Warwick's mouth curled up into a malicious grin, his hands wrapping around my arms, slamming me back into the door. My head

219

whacked into the wood, spurring flames up my spine. His body pressed into mine, forcing my hips to widen, to feel him. Hard and hot, his cock throbbed against my abdomen, heating my bones with violent ire and desperate need.

"I can feel you, Kovacs." He pressed into me harder, blood dripping down his chin from his lip. I ignored the urge to lick it, turning my head away. "Fighting the need to either fuck me or kill me." He rolled into me, my pussy pulsing, *begging* to feel him.

And he knew it.

My rage escalated.

"I choose the latter," I hissed, my head swinging forward, cracking into his nose.

Stumbling back with a grunt, his hands going to his face, noticing the fresh blood pouring from it. He looked at me, his eyes darkening, his chest heaving before he came back for me.

This time, I ducked, darting out of his reach.

The ghost of his touch circled around me, grazing my skin, pushing in toward my soul. My feet faltered, and my lids fluttered with the most intense ecstasy. The most unbelievable agony.

I couldn't find the difference between them, mixing and blending into the same intensity.

It was like setting the rawest nerve on fire.

Vicious.

Intimate.

Invasive.

There was nowhere I could hide. He touched every cell, consumed every part of me. The sensation was so deep and acute I no longer felt attached to my body. Just one second and a groan already burst from my lips, my body heaving and pulsing with an impending orgasm. But I knew it would be nothing like a normal orgasm. Nothing was ever normal when it came to us.

This would claim every molecule, own me, drown me. Keep me prisoner.

*Fuck no.*

Blinding rage burned through me. The monster unleashed. "Get the fuck out!" I snarled and spit.

*"Can give it, but can't take it, princess?"* He stood opposite of me, but his presence scraped up my neck. Reminding me when I had done it to him.

I snarled and barreled for him. He tried to grab for me, but my hands flayed, smacking him hard in the chest. "Asshole!" I sneered. "You betraying, narcissistic, vindictive bastard!"

"I'm all of those things and then some." He swung back, clipping my chin as I twisted out of his reach. I tasted blood, felt the bruise ballooning on my jaw. Energy sang in my veins, turning me more animalistic. Keeping low, I kicked my one booted foot into the side of his knee. He caught it as it landed, ripping that one off too, tossing it to the floor.

Whirling, my leg struck his hip, knocking him into the nightstand, the lamp crashing to the floor, shattering into pieces.

"You're spineless!"

"Spineless?" He snorted, standing up, his chest puffed, his teeth showing.

"You let those men ride away," I jeered, brushing my hair out of my face. "The notorious *Wolf*, the *legend*, is nothing but a coward!"

"You really want to call me that?"

"Oh, I'm sorry, am I not bowing at your feet like all the whores here?" I spat, my fury riding over everything I felt and said. "Maybe you should get Rosie back in here; I'm sure she'll suck on your massive ego." I nodded to his cock.

"Jealous, Kovacs?"

"Why would I be?" I taunted. "I have a whole fan club to pick from, remember? You weren't the only one enjoying someone else's company earlier."

His aqua eyes went almost black, his shoulders expanding, something snapping in him. The deadly warrior vaulted to the surface. He prowled toward me with lethal precision. My body filled with adrenaline, heating my skin and tightening my nipples.

Yanking out the knife in my belt harness, I craved the moment he was close enough for me to strike. I needed his pain... his blood. He twisted away from the knife while his hand tried to knock it out of my grip. Twirling, I pounced back for him, the tip of the blade cutting his side, ripping his shirt open, and slicing through to his flesh. His nose flared as blood soaked into the fabric, glistening off the dim light from the above.

"Think I won't actually kill you?" A growl emanated from him.

"You had your shot." I countered his step to me. "I told you. Don't ever threaten me again unless you're looking to be gutted."

"Just try, princess."

"You think I can't?" My lip curled. "I may be the *only one* who can. You are standing here now because of *me.*"

Fury rose off his features, the truth of my statement smacking him in the face.

He bared his teeth, which was the only warning I got. My legs started to move. He jumped for me too fast to get out of his way in the small room. His massive form collided with mine. Thrashing, I slipped enough from his grip, angling for the door.

His fingers wrapped through my long hair, yanking me forcibly back into him. A cry cracked at my throat, heat spreading through me, pulsing my thighs.

I slammed my elbow into his stomach, his grip loosening. I didn't hesitate. Pulling free, I twisted back to him, my knife slashing across his chest.

As if the blood and pain brought him even further to life, he filled the chamber with his roar. Fury and strength exploded in the space.

Clutching my arms, he flung me back onto the dresser. My shoulder hit the mirror, knocking it to the ground with a shatter. Everything on the table followed behind, tumbling across the wooden floor with a crash.

A large hand seized my throat, jamming me back into the wood. His frame pushed between my legs, capturing the hand with the blade against the wall. I couldn't move.

"You know what I think?" His face got within an inch from mine. "This has nothing to do with the journal or me trading you to Killian."

Glowering at him, my chest radiated with hate, my legs and arms trying to pry away from his hold.

"You would have traded me without thought to Killian to save those you love." He squeezed my throat harder. "You know what you're really mad about?" Pinching the nerve in my wrist, he forced me to loosen my hold on the dagger, retrieving it the moment it slipped free. Red liquid painted the tip of it as he brought it up, just below his other hand at my throat.

"What really angers you is the thought of my dick being anywhere else but in you." Warwick dragged the blade down my neck, nicking my skin. His mouth was a breath from mine, a snarl on his lips.

My chest heaved, wetness seeping from me as the pain from the blade cut through my flesh, our blood mixing on the edge.

"Admit it, Kovacs. The idea of any other person fucking me... my dick so deep inside them... coated in them..."

I tried not to react, but my breath hitched at his claim.

"Fucking their pussy so hard." His thumb pushed into my throat, and a buzz of adrenaline went through my bones. The knife cut through my shirt, nicking my sternum. My breasts heaved as the fabric parted away, the coolness of the room soaking into my bare skin. Blood trailed down, catching on the thin sports bra, which covered nothing. He trailed the flat of the blade over my peaked nipples, making them harder.

*"Not so sweet are you, princess? I know how rough you like it. How wet this makes you,"* his voice whispered into my ear without a word said out loud.

Wrath.

Lust.

Hatred.

Passion.

Every emotion consumed me, my spine arching into his touch, my brain shutting down to logic. It only desired. Craved.

He regripped my throat, yanking me forward, his teeth baring. "I *warned* you who I was. I'm not the dog you can put a leash on. I *fuck* who I want, whenever I want."

The knife cutting through my skin was nothing.

His words cleared my head. Brought the pain and loathing to the surface with sharp clarity. Without thinking, I pulled the strength from him, my hand shoving powerfully against his chest, as my leg came up, slamming into his torso.

Warwick sailed back, thudding loudly to the floor, the blade tumbling from his fingers. Jumping down, I scrambled for it. Just inches away from retrieving it, fingers clutched onto the hem of my pants, yanking them so hard, they slipped off my narrow hips, tangling up my legs. Tripping, I slammed against the floorboards, my nose smacking into the wood. He pulled me back farther, climbing past me, going for the dagger.

A growl came from me. Rage and adrenaline cutting the pain and dictating my movements. Kicking out of my pants, I clambered up, running into him at full speed as he leaned over to reclaim the weapon.

He stumbled, colliding into the wall, shaking the house. A framed picture crashed down, adding to the debris on the floor. He righted himself, his arm whirling back for me so fast I had no time to respond. Stars burst behind my lids at the impact, which flung me back onto the bed.

His body moved over mine, blood dripping from his nose, lip, and torso. A snarl curled his mouth as he straddled me, the blade in his hand.

"Get the hell off of me." I scowled, wiggling under his hold, his clothes rubbing my bare skin. "Don't you have a group of whores to go fuck?"

"You want to watch?"

"Fuck off!" Again, I pushed past his layers, siphoning his strength, trying to use it against him.

"Stop!" He barked, his expression twisting with wild rage. Seizing my arms, he yanked me up to standing, our feet on the bed, before he twisted, slamming me into the wall over the headboard. Fervor shot up my veins, soaking my knickers.

Feral, his form enveloped me, our bloody chests heaving together as he shoved me harder into the wall. His hips pinned me, again letting me feel his heavy erection through his pants. Fury billowed off him, his glare pointed at me.

"I cautioned you about who I was," he snarled, my bones groaning under his hold. "But maybe you should have been the one to warn *me*." He vibrated with anger, his aqua eyes glowing. Accusing. Blaming. "That once I met you," he sliced the blade through my sports bra, my tits spilling free, a gasp coming from me as the cool air slithered around them. "Knew what it felt like to be inside you." He ripped what was left of the shirt and bra from my body. "To be fucking near you... I'd become worse than a leashed dog." He regripped the dagger, pushing the tip into the soft spot at the base of my neck, a trail of blood sliding down between my breasts.

He throbbed harder against me, scorching every nerve into a painful desire.

"A leashed dog doesn't have a *choice* but to follow and obey."

"So, you *fuck* my one friend here to hurt me? Put me in my place? Get me to hate you?" I hissed through my teeth, abhorrence rattling my frame, wanting nothing more than to sink the knife into his heart. "You won. I do."

"I fucking hate you too." He huffed through his nose, his lips twisting barely a hair from mine. "Because you have me trained and salivating. You have possessed me. My cock suddenly craves just your pussy... only wants *you*." He rammed his hips into me. This wasn't some sweet declaration of his feelings. This was resentment and anger. "I didn't touch anyone last night. I *couldn't*. I kicked them out almost the moment they entered. You have fucked with my head."

His admission punched through my lungs, halting my breath. He didn't sleep with Rosie... or any of them?

Relief fluttered at my heart. Shame filled me over how I acted to Rosie. Then it flipped to rage. He let me believe he slept with them. He wanted to hurt me. Wanted me to turn away to make it easier for him.

"You bastard." I tried to shove him away.

"I am." He grinned callously, holding me easily in place. "And I would have slaughtered the Hounds in a blink if I thought I could do it without one of them shooting you." He ground into me harder, my spine grating into the wall, the burn sparking need through me. I could feel the bed next door knocking against me with a steady rhythm, their groans soaking into the air, twisting the tension higher. "If you think I wouldn't choose your life over a fucking diary..." The blade dropped from his hand to the bed. He seized my thighs, lifting me off my feet, curling my legs around his waist. "Then you're not fuckin' getting it, princess. This world would be in shreds if anything happened to you."

Heat, rage, and violence throbbed between us.

There would be carnage.

# Chapter 20

It was a single beat.

A suspended moment, dripping with violence and savagery.

Then it broke.

With clashing teeth and lips, our mouths crashed together. Biting. Sucking. Nipping. The kiss was brutal and ruthless. It consumed and devoured without thought or care. His fingers dug into my hair, pulling and yanking, taking control as his mouth claimed mine with fury.

Aggression speared the air. The room was thick with the desire to destroy. To hurt.

Punish.

With a deep growl, he cupped my wrists with one hand, pushing them onto the wall above my head, aligning our bodies, pushing out my breasts. The heat of his mouth wrapped around one, sucking until he had my core pulsing like a heartbeat.

His eyes on me, his tongue trailed up my sternum, licking up the trail of blood he had spilled.

It was primal. Raw.

Yanking my arms from his hold, my fingers went to his shirt, ripping what was left of it like it was made of paper. My nails scratched at his chest, leaving more dots of blood and torn skin behind. A deep hum vibrated from his body. While I ripped the cloth off him, his muscles flexed under his tattooed skin, his lip rising in a ferocious snarl.

He pushed me back into the wall, his mouth taking mine. He incinerated me from the inside out, burning all thoughts away, leaving me a feral animal. Needing to rip into my prey.

We both attacked. Shoving, clawing, scratching.

Invisible hands, teeth, tongues, and lips attacked with vicious passion. There would be no hostages, only decimation until just bits of us were left.

The false cry of satisfaction from next door shifted to groans of pure ecstasy, the bed hitting harder.

Like riling up animals locked in a cage, Warwick and I were set free.

I ripped at his pants, shoving them down, taking his massive girth in my hand and smearing the pre-cum over the tip, making me pulsate so hard for him it hurt.

"Fuck." He gritted his teeth, his palm skimming down my stomach, his fingers sliding through my pussy unforgivingly, producing a loud, unhinged moan from my lips.

A woman screamed from the room over, followed by several groans from others in the same room. I heard people in the hallway moaning with gratification.

The pleasure they derived from us only racked my body with more desire.

Our real hands explored, gripping and tearing at each other to get closer, wanting to carve through each other, marking and breaking everything in our path.

"Warwick." Desperation and fury coated my tone.

Consume me.

Devour.

Destroy.

I didn't care. I wanted to be left in cinders.

Hitching me higher up the wall, he teased my entrance with his tip, producing a whimper from me.

"You want me inside you? My cock deep in your pussy?"

"Yes." I breathed, too far gone not to plead.

He gave me no other warning before he thrust into me, my mouth tearing open in a silent scream. Electricity burned through my nerves, torching everything, ripping the oxygen from my lungs as he filled me.

227

Brutal and vicious.

Ultimate pleasure.

Extreme pain.

This was even more intense than before, like he had crawled inside me, striking everything on fire.

A roar clapped off the walls, the sensation shredding through him as well, doubling the feelings crackling through my system. I felt both our desires, making me choke for oxygen.

He pulled back and drove in with vehement rage.

I cried out, adjusting to his size, drowning in the overwhelming ecstasy as he pumped in again.

"Oh. Gods." I felt the ghost of his tongue trail down my back, nipping and licking over my ass. His fingers nowhere near my breasts flicked at my nipples, making my spine curve. I attacked back with as much vigor.

He wrenched my hair, yanking my head back as he drove in even deeper, his harsh grip making me pulse around him.

"*Pokol!*" *Hell*. His shoulders tightened as the phantom me licked up his thigh, taking his balls into my mouth and sucking. "Fuuuuccck." A deep groan belted from his chest, a wild spark flickering in his eyes.

He pulled out of me, dropping me to my feet. Before I could utter my grievance, he threw me down onto the mattress on my stomach. He shucked off the pants and briefs around his ankles, displaying his magnificent naked physique. He snarled and growled like a beast as he climbed down. He was no longer the man, but the myth.

*The Wolf.*

Yanking my hips back, Warwick drove in so deep, hitting every nerve making me howl like a savage myself.

I didn't care if the entire world heard. There was no etiquette left. No consideration.

We were monsters and beasts. Untamed and feral.

The bed creaked and screeched under his punishing assault.

"This fuckin' pussy is mine," he rumbled. Brutally he drove into me like he had no restraint, impelling loud cries from my mouth. "Say it."

I pinned my lips together, not wanting to answer. It was my way of punishing him in return. It only escalated his vigor.

"Say it, princess," he gritted, his fingers digging into my hips, the sound of his skin slapping mine.

Owned with need, my core pulsed, hungry for release but endlessly thirsty for more. I never wanted to stop. Bucking against him, I met his passion with my own. The building reverberated with the echoes of him fucking me viciously and relentlessly, our ferocity making everyone outside this room sounding frantic and crazed, adding to our sadistic demand.

Darkness bled into the edges of my vision, my head spiraling out of control. Sweat coated my skin as my climax stampeded up my spine, destroying everything in its wake. I couldn't stop it, but I also knew I would not be coming out of this.

Not the same anyway.

The bed scraped harshly across the floor, digging crevices into the wood, before I felt the frame give out. We crashed down with a loud bang, the impact pushing him in with force. He hit so deep inside a guttural scream exploded from my gut. The feel of him rubbing along my chest, my mind, locked me up with merciless carnality. My core squeezed around him. Unforgiving and punishing.

He let out a cursed bellow, barreling through any walls I had left up, scaping through my insides, and breaching my soul.

I thought I had felt pleasure before, had experienced agony.

This eclipsed and crushed it all.

It was like I had been electrocuted from the inside. The instant orgasm he caused earlier by invading my walls was *nothing* compared to this. The impact of sensation ripped me clean from my body, torn away from earth.

I became particles. Specks of the past and present collided together.

I felt Warwick inside me at the same time I leaned over his corpse during the fae war, almost twenty years ago. The sensation of magic punched through every molecule of our bodies, threading us together through time and space. I could feel no difference between then and now.

A loud cry of a baby in the distance, the engulfing power of magic singing through my bones. I could smell the thick, acidic odor of blood and dirt under me, feel magic sizzle at my skin, taste it on my tongue. I heard the crackling of lightning, the shots of guns, the screams of death.

Bringing him back to life while I could feel our climax burning through my muscles made me everything and nothing at the same time.

Life and death.

He penetrated every inch of me inside and out.

He possessed. Pillaged. Burned. Took. And shredded.

Anyone else would have been a husk. Remnants of his massacre.

But I was not anyone. I was his dark demon. A thief. A fighter. An executioner.

His savior.

I raided his flesh, stole his mind, and seized his soul. Pilfering everything I could as we climaxed together. Sizzling the air as if lightning would strike us here. Energy swirled in the room, swinging the dim chandelier above as if ghosts had been summoned from nearby, responding to our call, stirring up both the living and dead for miles. I felt their force, the crazed energy churning around us, adding to the fevered atmosphere.

A roar punctured the room, rattling the windows as he impaled himself further, filling me, marking and claiming my pussy as his. Sharp ecstasy wound through me, melting my muscles.

His body fell on mine as we collapsed onto the mattress, the bed in pieces around us. His cock still pulsated inside me, not done releasing, filling me more, burning me up, like he was making sure he engraved his very being into me.

There was no gentle fluttering down from the high, the release making you sweetly sleepy and sedated. This felt like war. Like I had crawled out of the trenches, bruised and beat up but thrumming with life. Blazing with fire. Energy knocked around inside me, injecting every molecule in my body with power. It was an elation nothing else could reach.

Pleasure didn't stop rolling through me. My frame shook violently; our energy tangled and fought together, like locked horns, unwilling to unwind from each other. Banging and knocking at each other till a bloody death, neither of us relenting.

*"Sotet démonom." My dark demon.* A deep growl sank in my ear, his hips rocking in one last time. As if he hadn't obliterated me enough, the power of that name crushed the last bit of my defense into dust.

I came again with a severe spasm, a noise crying from my gut, my body seizing.

My eyesight went dark.

"Fucking hell, princess," his husky voice rumbled, stirring me back to consciousness. I had no idea how long I passed out. It could have been seconds or minutes. Time didn't seem to matter or really make sense anymore.

His mouth skated up the back of my neck. I loved the weight of him on me, our skin sticky with blood, sweat, cuts, and bruises.

It felt like heaven.

I twisted my neck to peer back at him. His regard hadn't relinquished any of the hunger. If anything, I saw more eagerness in his eyes. Grabbing my chin, he kissed me deeply.

Warwick was never sweet or gentle, but this felt different from all the others, no question in it. No wondering what was between us. The link joining us had fully weaved and tangled together. There would be no untying it, no breaking it.

Not that we had a clue what it meant or what I was, but for the moment... I was home.

Breaking the kiss, he moved off me. I grumbled at the loss, the emptiness I felt when he slid out of me, climbing to his feet.

Grabbing the dresser, he pulled himself out of the wreckage. His fingers gripped the wood, his legs dipping underneath him, not quite ready to stand.

Warwick huffed out a dark chuckle. "Like a fucking newborn." His hand shook, swiping up the intact liquor bottle from the floor and dropping into the wingback chair. He was naked, beat up, dirty, dangerous, enigmatic, and sexy as hell—he took my breath away.

Downing a huge swallow, he let out a raspy sound before holding it out for me.

I twisted onto my side, tucking a sheet around me as I grabbed the bottle from his hand. Every muscle ached, every bone throbbed; my brain and body were melted butter. At the same time, I never felt more alive or powerful. Like liquid steel filled my veins.

Gulping back a swig, the burn lit a match to my already scorched insides. I jiggled my head, choking down the harsh liquid. Handing it back to him, I watched him take another drink.

The connection joining us had deepened. I could feel the strands moving and coiling between us, like live wire. As if it was another sense I procured, along with sight, smell, taste, touch, and sound. It had always been there, but it was no longer in the background. It was present and alive.

I felt with clarity the wall he was trying to put up to distance himself from the consuming sensation. This was even more

concentrated than our first time in Prague. I understood why he wanted
to. I desired to do the same. Not just because it was intense, but because
it was overwhelmingly *normal*.

To people like us, especially him, something so intimate was not
ordinary or even wanted.

"We really made a mess." I licked my lips, tasting the remnants of
whiskey and him, my eyes moving around. The bedframe was in pieces.
A mirror, water bowl, and picture were shattered. A lamp lay broken,
clothes scattered. This room was a debris field. We obliterated it.

"Kitty is going to be so pissed at you."

He didn't respond, swallowing down more liquor, his gaze on the
wall.

More seconds passed.

"She might actually kick you out this time."

"Stop the small talk, princess," he grumbled, taking another shot,
holding it out to me. "What the fuck was that?"

I hesitated with my response, only coming up with one. "Us." I
shrugged, snatching the bottle from him and taking a drink. I could
think of no other answer to what kept binding us tighter together. The
visions, the spirits congregating near us, the fact we could slip into each
other and visit the past.

"Us," he huffed out his nose, not really a question. His head tipped
back into the chair, lost in thought.

We had this connection binding us, but I realized how little I really
knew about him. I knew how he died, about his sister and nephew, that
his mother had been a prostitute, and he had grown up in a whorehouse.
Oh shit. Shame colored my cheeks. My harsh attitude to Rosie was also
an insult to his mother.

My fingers plucked at a hole in the threadbare sheet.

"What I said earlier... I didn't mean it." I cleared my throat. "I was
angry. Hurt. I was wrong."

"Brexley Kovacs admitting to being wrong?" He swigged the
brown liquor.

My lips lifted. "To you? No, you deserve my wrath, asshole." He
snorted at my reply. "But to her... yes."

"Someone like you, calling them out on what they deep down
believe about themselves already?" His head turned to the window. "It
cements their worth in this world; how they are looked at and treated.
No one cares to find the murderer of a whore. She deserved it, right?

She put herself in that position... When those in power are the ones who forced them into this life. They take away everything; the only choice they have is to sell their bodies to feed their children. And getting a so-called respectable job in a factory? You work nine times more, killing yourself every day for less than half the pay. This world is so upside down and fucked."

He kept his voice even, but I heard the emotion under his words, the anger and frustration.

"You told me you were born in a brothel, and she died when you were ten, right?"

He grunted in agreement.

"What happened after that? Ten is so young to be alone. You were a kid."

He stayed quiet so long I thought he was going to avoid my question, but he took another drink, a deep exhale rolling from him.

"I was never a kid. I never got the luxury. I took care of other women's bastard children in the brothel. By six, I was hustling and stealing food, medicine, and money to keep us all afloat. More pressure was put on my shoulders when my half-sister came along. When Mom died, my sister was a baby. A woman took her in to raise, but I wasn't wanted. Too wild and old." He exhaled, sipping down more. I didn't want to make a peep. The booze was loosening his tongue, which was beyond rare.

"Because I was so quick and scrappy, I thrived on the streets, building a gang of other orphaned and unwanted misfits. That's where I met Ash and Janos—Kitty. We were inseparable, each of our talents building us stronger. By the time we were in our late teens, we were running the streets, controlling our area of the city. By our twenties, we had control over the whole city. But with power comes enemies and people who will do anything to take it from you. The assassination attempts were constant, and with times changing and this country becoming seized by human dictators, we left. Moved around the world, fought in wars, stood by each other through thick and thin. And when we returned, old and new enemies wanted to make sure we didn't find a place in it or wanted to use us to get their own foot in the door."

Drinking another third, he handed the bottle back to me.

"Killian was one of those moving up. He secretly hired me to take out a few men he knew were traitors and spies in his own faction. It was really good money, so I did."

"That's when the others came after you."

He nodded.

And during the fae battle, Warwick was murdered by those men. I had seen with my own eyes what they had done to him. And after he came back to life, he tracked each one down and slaughtered them until he was caught and thrown into Halálház... Killian's prison.

"And Killian puts you in jail for something he hired you to do." My throat burned from the cheap alcohol while my body heated and warmed.

"Politicians for you." He smirked disdainfully. "Most wanted my head, so he thought putting me in prison, making me spy for him while giving me perks and more freedoms than others, was a very considerate trade-off."

Snorting, I scrubbed my temple. It perfectly fit the man I got to know in the palace. Shrewd, calculating, and oddly fair within the parameters of his goal. Killian didn't kill to kill or do something that didn't benefit him. He was reasonable, even kind, but if you betrayed him, he went for your Achilles heel, the very thing you would turn the world over for.

Like a sister and nephew.

"You think the journal will tell us anything about the nectar?" Warwick stared off, his obvious switch of topics not lost on me.

"I hope... or maybe something about me. What I am."

His head turned in my direction. "What you are... *is mine... Sotet démonom.*" His turquoise eyes flamed with a possessiveness.

No matter how many times he called me his dark demon, it affected my body with urgent desire.

His shadow flicked at my breasts with his tongue, fingers tracing down my stomach to my pussy, melting my brain to slush. I needed him now.

Setting the bottle down, I stood, the sheet falling to the mattress. My attention locked on him, I strolled confidently to where he sat.

"Is that so?"

I could distinguish the heat rising in him, his eyes tracking my naked body, his lust rubbing against my skin. His eyes shifted down me, his desire hardening him instantly, making me smirk.

"And here I thought I wasn't your type, Farkas. Too skinny and bony."

A wicked grin tipped the side of his mouth. "Guess that changed." He grabbed my thighs, pulling me between his legs.

"Or you lied."

"That too." A roguish grin glinted his eyes. "I seem to have no off switch now."

Absently, his fingers trailed over my hips and ass, his brows gathering in thought. "This time, it felt very real." He wagged his head, tipping it back into the chair. "I was back on the field, could smell the magic, feel dirt and blood. I was fucking you on the field and in here too. *Baszni...* I felt myself *coming* back to life at the same moment I was actually *coming* inside you."

My cheeks heated as my head bounced in agreement. Reaching out, I traced over his jaw, his thick scruff tickling my skin.

"How could I feel the dead here in this room?" His lids narrowed. "Feel them in the past... there was no difference. How is this possible?"

I exhaled with a shrug, having no clue.

"This is not natural, even to the fae world." His calloused palm continued to explore my skin, arousal tingling through me again. "Even with the rarest of magic, this shouldn't be possible."

I inhaled sharply as his touch glided down, rubbing through my folds, his erection responding to my arousal.

"*You* aren't normal," he breathed out in a horse whisper, cascading desire down on me like rain.

"You aren't either."

He grinned, his palms gripping my hips, leaning in. His mouth joined his fingers, tearing a gasp from my lungs. Tugging one of my legs onto the chair, spreading me open, his tongue parted me, his other arm pulling me in firmer to him.

"Oh... gods..." My head fell back, my lungs clenching.

"Guess we're both freaks," he muttered against me before he devoured me with fierce aptitude.

The screams and noises coming from me didn't sound human. My body trembled and convulsed. I could no longer breathe, blackness dotting my vision. My ache for release made me frantic and crazed. Right as I felt myself near it, he seized my waist, yanking me over his lap, and slamming me down on him.

"FUCK!" A deep bellow rang in the air, and I had no idea if it was from him or me.

Everything went dark as I exploded into fragments.

# Chapter 21

"You two get up!" A crisp voice jolted me from a deep sleep, my body feeling like it was wrapped in the most delicious cocoon.

My eyes fluttered open; early morning light bathed the room. Aches and pains wracked across my muscles the instant I stirred. Lying on my stomach, a massive body half covered mine, our legs and arms tangled. His cock was hard against my ass, our naked skin brushing against each other, his intoxicating smell wrapping over me. I never wanted to move.

"Now!"

Blinking, I lifted my head to see Kitty standing in the doorway, her expression tight with displeasure. She was regal in her annoyance.

I followed her gaze as it slinked around the room, landing on every item now destroyed, her nose flaring.

*When did we break the chair?* My mind tried to recall, but I remembered nothing after Warwick thrust into me. When did he bring me back to bed? What was left of it, anyway?

Warwick moaned into my neck, his body stretching over mine, his cock burrowing in deeper into my ass, forcing me to bite down on my lip.

"Kitty..." he murmured, his eyes opening, his tone full of the charm he used on her.

*"Ne szarozz velem,* Warwick." *Don't mess with me.* Her voice was low and controlled. "The only reason I'm not kicking you out of here for good is because as a result of..." Her manicured hand motioned to us. "Of *whatever* you two generated, which I really don't want to know about," she shook her head, her hand up like a barrier, "patrons paid triple the normal amount last night."

"See?" Warwick rubbed his face, rolling onto his back. "You should be thanking us."

"Thanking you?" Kitty's voice tightened, her shoulders rising. "You demolished this room. Again!"

"I never destroyed *this* room before."

She sucked in sharply. Warwick's mischievous smile grew; he enjoyed getting a rise out of her.

Her lids closed briefly, and she took a slow, deep breath. "Thanks to Dr. Laski, the bandit is still alive. Barely." Her heels clicked as she turned, her hand on the doorknob. "You better hurry while he is still awake and breathing."

The door slammed.

I sat up, cringing from the bruises and soreness. We didn't just fuck hard; we kicked the shit out of each other.

"Looks like you were nailed in a fight, Kovacs." Warwick smirked, motioning to the bruises on my face, moving the sheet away from my figure, tapping at the clear fingerprints marking my hips. "Or just nailed."

Amused, I peered down at the blood still dried around his nose, his swollen lip, and healing cuts covering him. We loved it. It was foreplay to us. Pushing the barriers. Walking the line of sensuality and torture.

"Looks like you got your ass kicked by a girl, Farkas."

"And, fuck, it was fun." He shoved his arms behind his head, his gaze intently on me. Invisible fingers rubbed over my core, teeth biting at my neck.

My legs instantly opened, a guttural pant escaping from me.

"Stop." I ground my teeth, glaring at him. "We have to go."

His brows lifted.

"I have to talk to this guy. He might not stay conscious long."

Warwick sighed, relenting with a nod, rubbing at his face. The moment he did, my body wanted to punch me in the face for impeding what could have been another mythical orgasm. I was a fucking idiot.

Grumbling to myself, I reached for an item of clothing lying on the ground, hoping it was something I could wear. I needed a shower more than anything, my skin sticky with dirt, sweat, sex, and blood, but the hostage was the priority. Everything might rest on getting back the journal.

Swiping up a pair of knickers, two huge dark eyes peered up at me.

"Holy shit!" I jumped, my hand clamping over my mouth as recognition hit me. "Oh gods, Bitzy!"

*Chiiiiirp.* A dark blue bandana knotted around her neck, covering her like a muumuu. She munched on something, her huge ears lowered, her head rolling as if she were swaying to music.

"I'm so glad you are okay." My arm dropped, relief spilling out of me. "Where's Opie?" I glanced around for him.

She cocked her head, a cooing sound escaping her.

No middle finger, no chirping profanity at me.

"Aw, fuck... you're high again."

*Chirrrrrp.* She continued to chew on something.

"What's in your mouth?" My hands went to my hips. "Spit it out."

She shook her head.

"Spit it out." I lowered in a squat to hold out my hand, but she already opened her mouth, letting the black substance splat onto the floor.

That wasn't mushrooms.

"What the hell is that?"

"Looks like someone found a box of snuff." Warwick snorted, pulling on a pair of pants he had in the dresser.

"Bit-zy." I pinched my nose. Snuff was straight tobacco, launching a straight shot of nicotine through your veins. A nice buzz, dimming the sharpness of reality a little. For the rich and poor, it had returned to fashion in the last ten-plus years. It was a cheap, easy high. And for something as tiny as her? The high must have been triple.

She plunked down on her butt, starting to pick the snuff back up again.

"Eww. No." I wiggled my finger at her.

Her forehead wrinkled. Ignoring me, she shoved it back in her mouth again.

"Gross." I sighed. "Where's Opie?"

She blinked at me a few times before her arm raised, pointing over my shoulder. Twisting, I glanced back at the nightstand.

Standing, I moved over to it, pulling out the drawer.

Choked laughter sputtered from my mouth.

Passed out, lying on his back, Opie wore a small blue bandana around his neck like Bitzy. He was bare-chested, and he wore a cut-up piece of leather out of which he made chaps that, thankfully, covered his front area. Penned dog tattoos were on his arm and chest.

Snoring, he absently munched on something in his sleep, no doubt snuff.

"By their outfits, it looks like your pets have been initiated into the Hounds." Warwick chuckled next to me, tugging on a T-shirt.

My body breathed with relief. At least they were okay. Buzzed out of their minds, but all right.

"Come on, we need to get downstairs." Warwick went back to the dresser, tossing me one of his extra shirts, heading for the door.

Hurriedly, I got dressed, following him out.

"No more snuff, Bitz," I ordered her as I closed the door.

*Chiirrp!* Fingers flew in the air.

I was pretty sure it wasn't an "Of course! Have a nice morning" chirp, which made me smile.

There was my girl.

The bandit sat high on the pillow, staring blankly at the ceiling, his skin grayish and sweaty. If it wasn't for the fact his chest was moving up and down, I would have thought he was a corpse.

Dr. Laski stood the moment we entered. "He survived the night, which was a shock." The doctor eyed his patient. "Tougher than he looks." He turned back to us. "He's lucid... though I can't say for how long or that he will be very forthcoming. He hasn't uttered a word to me or answered any of my questions."

"I'll handle it from here." Warwick's deep voice rumbled low. The bandit's eyes darted from the ceiling to Warwick for a beat, his throat bobbing.

Yeah, he knew exactly who Warwick was.

"His dressings need to be changed soon."

"Let Kitty know. She'll get someone to do it. You need to rest." Warwick patted the doctor's arm.

Laski dipped his head, slipping out of the room, leaving us alone with the thief.

He didn't look at us, but he was aware of every move we made, his muscles tightening as Warwick got closer, casually sitting on the chair like he was visiting a friend. I felt Warwick strategically let the silence fill the room, building it until it was palpable. A threat in the air. A warning his casualness was as deadly as the legend.

*"Go ahead, princess. This is your thing. I'm just the sexy arm candy here."* Warwick's shadow stood next to me, flicking his chin toward the man.

"Let's not play games. I'm way too tired for bullshit, and I haven't had my coffee yet." My boots scuffed the floor, stepping forward. The man's glance darted to me then back up, a flutter of annoyance in his eyes, as if I was nothing to waste his time on. I had little doubt all he saw was a human woman. Two things in this society people didn't seem to put a lot of worth on. Little did he know, I was like water hemlock—I appeared fragile and beautiful but was violently lethal.

"Your friends stole something from me. Something I need back." I folded my arms, looming over him. "Tell me where your hideout is or where to find your gang."

No response.

"I don't give a shit about you or the Hounds. I need my bag back. It has no value to you."

Still nothing, not that I expected him to talk so easily.

Lurching forward with a snarl, I reached for his injury, pushing down on the bloody bandage in his stomach, digging into the bullet wound.

A guttural noise grunted from him, his jaw slamming together, his nose huffing with agony.

"Tell me!" I got right in his face.

Spitting and snorting, his eyes watering, sweat coating his skin, he slammed his teeth together harder in defiance.

I prodded more, fresh blood soaking his badges. He looked ready to pass out from the pain.

"Fuck. You. *Bitch*," he seethed, saliva spewing down his chin. I heard a very slight accent in his voice but couldn't place it.

Warwick moved, cutting in front of me, his hand choking the man, yanking him to his face.

"She is the *only* reason you are alive. I wanted to watch the hyenas tear into you—strip the flesh from your bones while you were still breathing." His teeth bared, the man of death came alive. "You are going to tell her whatever she needs to know, or I will be using your veins to floss your teeth. You know who I am, and the rumors... they're all true."

A flicker of fear danced in his eyes before he hid it, his own lip curling. "I'm not telling you shit, asshole. Kill me."

Fury pumped through Warwick, his shoulders swelling. He would.

My mouth opened to stop him as the door swung open. Rosie stepped in with a bowl of water and bandages.

"Kitty asked me to rebandage—" She stopped dead in her tracks, her eyes landing on the man in the bed. The bowl in her hands crashed to the floor, splintering in pieces, her alabaster skin blanching. Her face was a mask of terror and shock, her blue eyes swimming with fear.

My stomach sank, my gaze going back to him. His attention was no longer on Warwick, but entirely on her, disbelief widening looking as if he'd seen a ghost.

"Vincent..." she whispered so quietly I almost missed it.

"Ni-Nina?" His voice stumbled and croaked.

As if the name had slapped her across the face, she jerked back, her chest heaving, her head shaking.

"Nina, what are you doing here? I-I can't believe this... They told me you were dead." His arm lifted, reaching out for her.

His gaze was full of adoration and confusion.

Hers was full of fear and hate.

"Rosie?" I touched her arm, jolting her focus to me. "What's going on?"

She took in a staggering breath, her shoulders rolling back, her eyes meeting mine.

"This man..." She swallowed, her mouth pressing together. "Is my husband."

# Chapter 22

"What?" I gaped, my memory reeling back to when she told me about him.

*"He saw me in a play, came to the back door every night for a week with flowers and promises. He was charming, and I was young. Thought it was love. I was looking for an escape from that penniless life and thought he was it. He was the opposite."*

*"I'm so sorry."*

*"No worries, luv. He's long gone, and I couldn't be happier."*

*"He's dead?"*

*"One can hope. He disappeared years ago after one of his business deals went bad. He was into a lot of shady shit, always trying to find the quick, easy way to make money, which usually went the opposite way. Had a lot of enemies. Left me with a lot of debt from really bad men."*

The same man who forced her into a life of prostitution to pay off his debt was a gunman in the most feared gang in the Savage Lands.

"Nina?" His voice cracked as he still reached for her.

The shock and terror were gone; the strong woman I knew lifted her head.

"Nina is dead. I never want to hear that name on your lips. Ever again." Cold and firm, her expression locked up with bubbling fury.

"I don't understand... What are you doing here? This is a whorehouse."

"Yes, it is. And *you* are the reason I'm here," she snarled. "But it was the best thing to happen to me. My life before was the real enslavement—forced to cook, clean, be the perfect demure wife, dress right, talk right. Be your punching bag when you were drunk, and spread my legs for a *lousy* lay." Fire spurted through each word, her figure moving closer to the bed. "Now I get paid to *fuck* an endless stream of men... all night long. Every delicious orgasm I used to have to fake with you? They pour money in my hand for them. I'm finally who I want to be. I'm free of you." She flipped around, marching out of the room.

"Wait. Nina—" He tried to sit up, falling back down, coughing, weak from his injury and blood loss.

Warwick peered at me, a question in his eyes.

Well... fuck.

My goal still hadn't changed: I needed my father's journal. But turning back to Vincent, rage at what he had done to my friend set my blood on fire. I wanted to rip him apart for the pain and agony he caused her, for forcing her into this life.

A noise twisted in my throat, my temper taking over. I sprang for him, my hands already swinging, ready to break every bone in his body.

"Whoaaaa..." Warwick grabbed me by the waist in a blink, pulling me back. "Easy there."

"Let me go." I wiggled forward, landing one hard punch to Vincent's face before Warwick lifted me off my feet, dragging me to the corner.

"Calm down." He placed me down, standing in front of me, blocking my way. His hands cupped my face, his body immersing us in our own little world. "You won't get any information out of a dead man."

"I can try."

He grinned, enjoying my fire. "Stop making my dick hard, Kovacs."

I rolled my eyes with a huff, my shoulders easing.

"I'm not telling you anything." Vincent wheezed behind us, turning us to him, his face drenched in sweat. "I will only talk to my wife."

"Not a chance, *faszszopó*." *Dick sucker*, I spat, Warwick gripping my arms to keep me in place. "I won't let you near her again."

"Then you get nothing." His chest spasmed, blood hacking out of his mouth. "And you will never find them. I promise you that." He took an agonizing breath. "I want to see my wife."

*"We don't have much of a choice,"* Warwick said through the link, keeping the conversation private.

*"He used to beat her! No... .no way."* My head shook.

*"What is our other option? These guys are notorious for a reason. No one has been able to find their hideout. How bad do you want the journal back?"*

Fuck. My lids shut, knowing the answer to that.

I hated what I was going to ask her to do. Negotiate with her abuser.

Seething, I stomped out of the room, slamming the door. I quickly found Rosie in the main living space, staring out the window. Morning was breaking over the buildings; the sun's rays streamed in dully, the early light nibbling away at the chilly shadows. The house was silent and still. Customers were long gone, the workers fast asleep.

Quietly, I walked over to her, the wood floors creaking underneath me. Her lips pursed, but she didn't turn to me.

"Rosie?" My voice sounded timid and raw in the vacant room. When she didn't reply, I repeated her name. "Rosie..."

She let out a dry huff, her head lowering. "Did you know Rosie was the name of a character I played? It was my greatest performance." She sniffed, brushing at her cheek. "It was right when I met Vincent. I was the toast of the theater circle. The darling ingenue." She wiped her other cheek. "Everyone told me I was destined for fame. I truly believed I would be some famous actress in London or on Broadway in America." A choked cry parted her lips.

Not someone good with comforting people, I stayed quiet, listening to her story.

"Now look at me." She motioned down at herself, still in a lace bustier and silk robe. "The only part I'm playing is the English rose— the whore."

"You are not a whore." I shook my head.

"That's *all* I am." She faced me, tears streaking down her face. "Think that's all I've ever been in one way or another." She glanced back out the window again. "You can't stand there and tell me it's not true; even you believe it." A slice of anger and resentment tacked on to the end of her words.

"That's not true." I folded my arms, leaning against the windowpane. "What I said last night... I was wrong. Very wrong. I assumed something, which wasn't true, and attacked you for it. I didn't really mean the cruel things I said. I'm so deeply sorry."

"What did you assume?" She peered at me.

I bit my lip. "I, ummm... I thought... you and Warwick had been together." I cringed at the statement. "That you fucked him."

Her eyes bugged out, her jaw opening; a howling laugh cackled from her. She covered her mouth, bending over.

"Hey, it's not that funny." It could totally happen. I mean, the girl was stunning and magnetic. You could see why she was so adored on the stage and so desired here.

"Yes, it is!" She fanned at her eyes. Another round of laughter fluttered out before she calmed down. "Oh, luv, what made you ever think that?" *Because he made me believe it.* The idea he purposely led me to that conclusion still fueled me. He would pay for it. "First, I would never do that to you, no matter how bloody hot he is. And second—if you had any clue how he looks at you. Acts around you. It is so evident how he feels about you. We all see it... fuck's sake, we *felt* it. I think people even in America felt it last night." She gestured out. "Thank you, by the way. My client gave me diamond earrings and three times my asking fee... and I had the most earth-shattering orgasm of my life."

I shifted on my feet, uncomfortable *everyone* could feel us when we were together. Experience it with us.

"Don't be embarrassed." She lifted her eyebrow coyly. "I don't want to know how it's possible for you guys to create that, but luv, if fucking that man is half of what we experienced out here, you should be singing in the clouds someplace. I know I would. I'm impressed you're walking this morning."

I snorted, my palm brushing back my hair, knowing I was still covered in him, inside and out. "Again, I'm sorry. What I said was cruel. And it's not how I look at you. Maybe before I came here, my mind was limited to what I thought right and wrong were, but you actually changed me. Getting to know you... you opened my eyes, became one of my dearest friends. And to me, that means everything."

Her lashes fluttered with emotion. "Me too." She hugged me, trying not to cry again, but failed. She pulled back, dabbing at her tears again. "I can't believe he's here. Part of me hoped he really was dead."

"He's part of the gang, the Hounds."

"The Hounds?" she sputtered, her reaction telling me she knew exactly who they were. Not many wouldn't in Savage Lands. They had become infamous, even in Léopold. "Vincent is part of that ruthless, murdering gang? Are you taking the piss?"

"Unfortunately not." I wiggled my jaw, still feeling the bruise there. "And last night, Warwick and I were attacked by them. Vincent was wounded, but the rest of them got away. They took something of mine. Something very important to me that I need back."

A weariness slanted her lids, understanding there was more to it.

"I would never ask this of you... ever... but this is extremely vital." I pressed my hands together, already begging. "He said he will only talk to you."

"No." She shook her head, stepping back. "No... I won't be anywhere near him."

"Rosie..."

"No!" she exclaimed. "Just being this close is twisting me into knots. I don't want anything to do with him."

My head dropped, bobbing in understanding. I couldn't make her do it. She spent many years tormented by him; I couldn't throw her back in it again.

"I understand."

She folded her arms across her torso. "He hurt me so much. I had nightmares for years of him finding me again. I can't let him do it to me again."

"I can't force you. I'm sorry I asked it of you." I squeezed her arm, shifting back for the room. "But if you think he's not still controlling you?" I motioned to her. "He probably always will. You are letting him still have too much power over you."

My feet strummed over the floor, my back to her, almost across the living room.

"Wait." She exhaled deeply, curving my head over my shoulder. "You're right." She nibbled on her bottom lip. "I will do whatever you need me to. For you."

"If you are going to do this, Rosie, do it for yourself, not me. Don't let him own any more of you."

"Nin-a," he whispered, a smile curving his face the moment we both re-entered the room. Warwick was against the wall, there to guard us but wanting to stay out of our way.

Rosie stiffened at the name. Inhaling, she rolled her shoulders back. "I told you, Nina is dead."

"No, don't say that, *mon chéri.*" Now I realized what his almost negligible accent was. French. "I've missed you so much. I can't believe the gods have brought you back into my life."

"No, the devils brought you back into mine."

"Nina, my love—"

"You wanted me here. I'm here. Now tell them where the location of your gang is." She folded her arms.

"Explain to me why you are here first." He bristled. "How you could open your legs for other men, become a common whore?"

"Shut the fuck up," she spat. His eyes went huge at her response, probably not used to her fighting back. "Do not call me that *ever* again. If you do, I will walk out of here and never look back. Let them do whatever they want to you." She stood over him, her voice cold and direct.

"You left me in squalor with your debts and crimes to pay off like the coward you are. I was beaten, tortured, and raped by the men you owed before Madam saved me. Here I am safe, fed, and protected from assholes like you. I have friends and independence. I choose who I want to sleep with, have my own money, and do what I want. I have finally paid off *your* debts, and I continue to stay because this is my home. My family. I have more here than I ever had with you." She sneered at him, the years of anger flooding out. "So, you don't get to judge me. You don't get to say a fucking word to me unless it's the whereabouts of your hideout. Do you understand me?"

He blinked, too stunned to move. The notorious, feared bandit was nothing more than a bully getting schooled. As if he were really seeing her, noticing the wife he knew, Nina, was nowhere to be seen now.

The English rose, the fiery bombshell, took the shambles he left her in and thrived. Grew thorns, becoming the strong woman she was today.

"I shouldn't be surprised you became part of a gang who murders people for trinkets."

"We are just trying to survive." He justified himself.

"So are the people you attack," she retaliated. "You are still a tyrant."

"I'm not like that anymore. I've changed." He tried to touch her again but drew back when she moved away from him. "I know it's hard to believe, and I know the things I've done. For years, all I wanted was to see you again, to make it right. I thought I would never have the chance."

"And you still won't. You can never make it right." Rosie sneered. "You don't get to ease *your* conscience. Though, I don't hate you. Hate means I feel something about you. I won't give you power anymore. You are *nothing* to me."

I saw pain and anger in his eyes. It was in that moment I knew. She was his Achilles heel, his weakness. He thrived off controlling her, manipulating her. He could kill, rob, and terrorize others and come home and say he was doing it all for her. That when he beat her, it was because she made him do it.

He needed his drug.

She did not need him. And it angered him.

His cheeks reddened, his expression locking down.

"You fucking ungrateful bitch," he lashed out. "I gave you everything. A home, nice clothes, an allowance, flowers every day."

"Except the most important thing—love." She tucked her red hair behind her ear, looking powerful. As if she just discovered the monster in her closet was nothing more than a stuffed animal. "Where is your hideout, Vincent?"

"I'm not telling you shit. Fucking *kurva*." *Whore. Slut.*

I felt Warwick move, but he was too late. The knife I shoved back in my boot was already pinned to Vincent's throat.

"You utter one more insult at her, and I will cut off your dick and force you to eat it." I pushed down on his wound again.

An anguished cry tore from him.

"Talk," I ordered.

Spitting and snarling, he tried to breathe through the agony, his jaw grinding together. Perspiration ran down his face.

The blade cut deeper into his throat, my knuckle burrowing and twisting into the gunshot. Blood poured out of it, driving another scream from him.

"Fine," he bellowed. "Stop!"

I stepped back, withdrawing my knife.

*"Makin' me hard again, Kovacs."* Warwick's shadow rubbed up the back of me, his voice deep and gravelly. I sucked in sharply, feeling

his erection pressing into me. For a second, the idea of him fucking me through the link, right here, heated my skin with a thrill.

*No, Brex... bad, bad idea.*

It took Vincent a few moments to control the loud grunting and breathing. "I'm bleeding out here."

"We'll get the doctor back in the moment you tell us something worth your life." Warwick crossed his arms, leaning farther back on the wall.

"I won't rat them out," he wheezed. "I won't tell you the hideout location... *but...*" he added in quickly, seeing my knife rise. "I'll give you the location of where you can get a message to them. Trade me for the bag."

"You think your buddies will really care enough about you?" Warwick snickered. "They left you there to die."

"That is our decree. We understand the risks out there. And there are a lot more of us than you think. We split into small groups so it looks like a bunch of gangs in the street, none worth coming after because of their insignificance. In reality, we are a huge organization... even expanding into Prague."

"Prague?" I blinked as a memory bubbled up. Mykel telling me about a gang terrorizing the streets there, reminding me very much of the Hounds. "Are you talking about the Mongrels?"

Vincent didn't respond, but the tic in his jaw, the change in his breath, suggested I hit the mark. The gangs were connected? How many more cities and countries did they reach?

Clearing his throat, he added, "They will want to know I'm still alive."

"Still don't see why they'd care about a foot soldier." Warwick shrugged.

"Because I'm not. I am the leader of the whole operation."

Warwick summoned Dr. Laski when we exited the room, an encrypted note folded in his palm from the commander of the Hounds. Rosie had instantly disappeared upstairs, needing to be by herself.

"Stay here. I'll go drop it at the location and come right back." Warwick tucked it in his back pocket.

"How do we know this isn't some setup?" I stepped in front of him, blocking his way to the door, worry etching my forehead. "That he's telling them where we are and to come attack us?"

Vincent told us his men would only take a secret coded message as legitimate. Of course, not letting us in on the cipher, he shakily wrote it himself. The problem was, we had no idea what he was really telling them.

"We don't." Warwick tipped his chin down, our bodies close, his gaze heavy, his physique immersing mine. The craving to touch him, to never stop touching him or kissing him, had my lungs compressing with anxiety. I never felt possessed like this before. And I needed to own him as much as he seemed to dominate me. "But I have a feeling he really doesn't want to start a war with me." He leaned down, his lips brushing mine. "One he knows he won't win. I am *the* legend, Warwick Farkas, after all."

"Having some trouble fitting that ego in this universe?"

"No, but I am having trouble fitting my dick in these pants right now." His mouth claimed mine with force, his fingers threading through my hair, devouring me with need. "I'll be back soon," he muttered, breaking away from me sooner than I wanted. His mouth remained an inch away, his forehead leaning into mine. Not moving.

"I'll be here. Probably in the bath."

"Make sure you are."

"*Te geci!*" *Son of a bitch!* A man's voice shouted behind me, spinning us to the doorway, instinctively tugging out our weapons and pointing them at the intruder. "You two are assholes!"

"*Faszszopó.*" *Cocksucker*, Warwick hissed, lowering his gun. "I almost fuckin' shot you."

Ash stood at the entrance, wearing the same clothes he had on yesterday. He was dirty, with scratches on his neck and face, his hair tangled, appearing exhausted.

"I was scared out of my mind, thinking you were dead, searching the streets and alleys for your bodies. And here you are... *csókolózás!*" *Kissing*. His arms flung out, relief turning to anger.

"You didn't think to check here first?" Warwick lifted one brow.

Ash's mouth opened and closed, as if he were now wondering the same, then his lids narrowed.

"No, I was too busy following tracks from where I found your bullet-ridden bike and pools of blood!"

"Ash." I walked over to him, hugging him. "Sorry we worried you."

It took him a while before he exhaled, his arms wrapping around me.

"When you guys didn't return to the base, I got so concerned," he muttered, squeezing me before he leaned back. "Though I should have known you two were not only all right but fucking each other's brains out. I mean, out of nowhere, I got fucking horny as hell, felt it in the air, the earth. I should have figured it was you guys."

"Yeah, and probably in the middle of searching for us, you took a pit stop at Kara's." Warwick snorted.

Ash's eye twitched, his head turning to the side.

"Holy shit, you did!" Warwick pointed at the marks on his neck. Now I could make out they were fingernail scratches.

"You know how tree fairies get when we're horny! I had to take the edge off."

Deep laughter roared from Warwick, his head tipping back, eyes squeezing shut, hands clapping together.

The sound penetrated through my skin, hitting every fiber of my being. It stroked a fire through me, warming every inch and spreading an instant smile over my face. His laughter was the sexiest thing I had ever heard.

"What?" Ash peered between us. "It's not like I could help it. I blame you guys."

I shook my head, chuckling as he tried to defend himself.

"Well, thank you for looking for us between your sexual romps." I patted his arm, making him huff and try to explain. "But you could have asked Scorpion. He'd know we were okay."

Realization dawned on his face, probably forgetting the link between Scorpion and me. "He's been a bit busy playing warden to your friend."

"Hanna? Is she okay? Is Caden? Lukas?"

Ash nodded. "They're fine. Lukas and Caden are both awake now."

The urgent need to get back to base to check in on them, talk to them, unsettled me, knowing it had to wait.

"Actually, glad you showed up." Warwick patted his shoulder with a smirk. "You can come with me. Also, *procure* another bike for me."

"This the eighth one this month!" Ash snorted, both men about to step to the door.

"What can I say?" He winked back at me. "I ride hard."

"Warwick, can I speak to—" Kitty came striding into the room, coming to a halt, her mouth still open, but no other words followed. Her gaze locked on the new arrival.

And he stared right back.

Tingles brushed over my skin, the tension robbing the room of the easy humor it just contained.

"Jan—Kitty," Ash corrected himself, his voice low and cracked.

"Ash." She replied with almost no emotion, but her throat bobbed, her hand fluttering slightly. "It's been... a long time."

"It has."

Awkward silence pounded in my ears. I knew there was a history between these two. Feelings, unrequited or possibly requited, but whatever happened separated the lifelong friends.

"You look well." Ash motioned down her. Tall in her heels and formfitting black knee-length dress, she reminded me of a fashion model, not the madam of a brothel.

"As do you," she replied.

Silence.

"Fuck, if we have to wait for you two to get through a full sentence, we're going to be here forever." Warwick gestured between them, irritation furrowing his brows. "You both are sorry—apologize and move on. You two have avoided each other over hurt feelings for years. We are a family. The only one I ever really had. No matter if things got messed up for a bit. Don't fuckin' let go of what we've been through. What you are to each other. I've had it with you guys and being in the middle of this stupid grudge."

Ash scowled, glancing away, Kitty doing the same.

"So... figure it out! Before I decide to kill you both for my peace of mind," he grumbled, stepping for the door. "But not right this second. Ash, come with me." He banged through the front door, his massive frame clomping angrily down the path.

Ash hesitated for a moment, glancing at Kitty before he followed Warwick out the door.

Kitty spun around and marched out of the room, a door down the hall slamming.

I stood there alone in the room, feeling the years of pain, anger, and embarrassment they stubbornly built between their friendship.

In a short time, they had become like family to me too. And I hoped they could work it out. In this world, family, trust, and love were scarce. You held on to these and fought like hell to keep them.

*A család nem egy fontos dolog. A család a legfontosabb.* That was a phrase my dad said a lot.

"Family is not an important thing. It's everything."

252

# *Chapter 23*

The rumble of motorcycles echoed in the cold night air. The waxing gibbous moon was a deep orange, lighting the dark streets.

Tomorrow, the harvest moon would be full.

Tomorrow, it would be my twentieth birthday.

The day of Samhain. The anniversary of the fae war.

The day my mother died.

And the time I brought Warwick back to life.

Tucking into Ash's back to block the cold, I pulled my hands into my sleeves, pushing the anxiety I always felt when the day of my birth was near. Something nipped inside, scratching at my intuition, warning me. I had no clue what, but I felt something was imminent—peril looming over me.

Warwick signaled in front of us to turn. The wounded captive was tied, gagged, and slightly sedated behind him. Warwick wanted Vincent with him, not trusting the man or the situation we were riding into.

Earlier, Warwick and Ash had placed the note in a location. Circling around later, they found a response waiting. We were to meet at the Fiumei Road Graveyard. Midnight.

Bandaged and with a shot of morphine, Vincent didn't put up a single fight when we tied him to Warwick's bike. I tried to ignore the deep feeling in my bones he was close to death, battling and fighting against the line, trying to stop it from taking him. Like a skipping record, it scratched at the back of my neck, stirring up something in me.

Something unsettling.

Warwick slowed, pulling up to the graveyard, the only light coming from the dull bike headlights and the moon. Ash parked next to him, the guys getting the hostage off the bike as I yanked the gun from my waistband, unlatching the safety.

Nerves scaled up my esophagus, and my eyes danced around the open space, the creepy headstones casting shadows that seemed to move. On high alert, I trained my senses to take in every little thing, my gun up and ready to protect us.

*"Sense anything?"* Warwick's link stood next to me while he was still busy getting Vincent off the bike and standing on his feet.

*"No."* But it was a lie. I could feel energy crawl over me like bugs, but that wasn't what he was asking about. He meant living people.

I felt the dead.

Reminding me of the Bone Church, currents tapped at my skin, their curiosity mounting, raising the hair on my arms, affecting my equilibrium. Ghosts swarmed and circled around. Steadying myself, I tried to block it, my teeth grinding together, fighting back the nausea. They sucked at my energy, brushing past me.

*"Back off!"* I commanded, my body blistering with authority. It took a couple more times for them to retreat .

A neigh of a horse jerked my head toward it, my finger tight on the trigger. Silhouettes of six horses trotted across the graveyard, five of them carrying men, pointing guns at us, the sixth horse for their leader.

Ash and Warwick yanked out their weapons, creating a standoff.

"This can go really easy. Him for the bag." Warwick gnashed his teeth.

"Let him go," one demanded.

"You drop the bag first," Warwick said back, tension already skating through the night, riling the spirits with more energy.

Fuck, why did they have to pick a cemetery?

"Show me," I replied. "I want to see everything is still in it."

The one who spoke before slid off his mount, holstering his gun and tugging something from his arm, holding it up. The headlights from the motorcycles lit up the gray canvas bag. He opened it up, showing me the inside. I could make out a black leather-covered notebook inside.

My dad's journal.

"We don't give a shit about some diary full of cryptic nonsense. But if you want it back, we think there should be a reward for it."

"One of your men isn't enough?" I scoffed, motioning to a dazed Vincent, who was so drugged out, he stumbled around on his feet.

"Money is always first in the creed of thieves." The man, who had taken lead, pulled something out of his pocket, making both Ash and Warwick step forward, ready to discharge.

A flame ignited the darkness. I flinched, and lead dropped into my stomach. The man held a burning torch near the bag. A spark. One flame and everything my father wrote would be in embers. The last bit I had of him would be gone.

He touched the flame to the bag. "Better decide if it's worth it now."

"No!" I jolted, rage surging through me. Bile coated my stomach, fear surging my adrenaline, sending shock waves out into the atmosphere like a boom. Electricity zapped in the air, crackling and hissing. The healed earth over the graves fractured and splintered, the ground rumbling.

The horses bucked, whinnying and thrashing, feeling the spirits probably as much as I did.

"What the fuck?" I heard a Hound yell, but everything felt far away as more spirits rushed for me, while my focus was on the one about to scorch my last bit of hope into cinders.

*"Get them."* The order spilled from me without a thought, surging over the spirits.

They reacted to my order. Some rushed for the man starting to burn my pack while dozens of others moved to the other men, scratching and clawing at their bodies, frightening the hell out of the horses.

The men let out terrified screams, batting at their arms and legs, feeling the assault but not able to see what it was.

"What the fuck? What is on me? Get it off!" The alternate leader yelled, the bag dropping from his grip, the torch hitting the damp grass with a hiss as it sputtered out. He clamored for his horse, getting on, his heels kicking into the animal. It galloped off, tearing across the dirt. The other men followed, racing back through the graveyard, their screams and howls trailing after them. The horse they brought for Vincent took off with its buddies, neighing and flicking its head.

I wanted to see the men burn.

"Kovacs." I heard Warwick say my name, but my attention was still following the group through the cemetery.

*"Brexley."* His shadow muttered deeply in my ear, my name feeling like the richest whiskey pouring over me. Arms wrapped around me, drawing me into his body though he wasn't there. *"Breathe, sotet démonom."* He snapped me out of my trance, breaking the connection with the ghosts. My lungs heaved for oxygen, my bones trembling with fatigue. I bent over my legs, sucking in gulps of air.

What the hell just happened?

My muscles twitched and tingled with adrenaline, recognizing a crash would be hitting me soon. Crickets buzzed in the air, echoing the silence around us.

"Brex?" Ash said my name quiet and low.

Slowly, I straightened, peering at them.

"What the fuck was that?" Ash stared at me with awe. Warwick was emotionless but for tightness in his shoulders and neck.

My mouth wouldn't move, my body shaking.

"Whatever that was... it came from you." Ash shook his head. "I felt it."

A horse neighing in the night snapped our heads to the sound.

"We have to move." Warwick shoved Vincent to the ground. The prisoner groaned, not trying to get up. Warwick strode over to the backpack, grabbing it, then made his way to me, slipping it on my shoulders, his knuckles brushing my cheek. *"You all right?"* he asked privately.

Nodding, I felt a sudden ease, like my energy was restoring. *Wait.* I blinked, my eyes darting up to his smirk, realizing that was exactly what he was doing. Intentionally.

Sharing energy wasn't something new, but this felt different. Easy. Instinctual. So many other times, we stumbled into it or awkwardly used it against each other. This was like breathing air. The innate response to protect ourselves as well as each other. The link no longer saw a difference.

"Hey, guys?" Ash whistled. "Let's go."

"Better?" Warwick rumbled.

"Yes." My breath hitched at the intensity and intimacy of the moment. Then it was gone. Warwick stomped over to his motorcycle, climbing on. Ash hopped on his.

"We're gonna leave him here?" I motioned to Vincent on the ground.

"Not our problem anymore." Warwick shrugged as the engine roared to life. "Get on, princess." He jerked his chin to the space behind him. "They find him, or they don't. Either way, I don't give a fuck."

My arms and thighs clasped Warwick as we tore off into the night, the bag with my father's journal tucked safely between us.

Turning back to the graveyard. I could no longer see or feel the ghosts, like I depleted *their* energy this time... used it as my own.

And created my own army.

"*Drágám!*" Uncle Andris's arms wrapped around me, pulling me into a hug. "I've been so worried about you." Andris was there the moment we came down into the base, probably watching our entry on the cameras.

"I'm okay, *nagybacsi.*" I hugged him back, again surprised Scorpion hadn't reached out in our link.

Andris released me, his dark eyes taking me in. "Now that I have you back, I sit with dread daily, fearing I will lose you again."

"I'm stronger than I look." I grinned at him.

Warwick snorted behind me, his fingers absently touching his side, where I stabbed him.

"I don't doubt that." Andris rubbed my arm. "Did you find it?"

"Yes." I clenched the book against my chest.

Andris reached out for it, and oddly, I stepped back, tucking it in tighter.

"I won't take it from you, my dear."

"I know. I just want to look at it first." I eased my shoulders down. "Before everyone."

"I understand." He nodded. "I'd like to see you as soon as you are ready. I might be able to understand things you do not."

"Of course." I wanted to be alone for a moment with my father's journal. To at least flip through the pages, see what his last words were before it was taken away from me to analyze and debate. To them, it was possible evidence; to me, it was my dad's soul.

"Okay, my dear, let me know. I will be in my office. There is a lot to take care of for tomorrow. It is crazy here on Samhain." I had heard Samhain had become a mix of celebration for fae and remembrance of those they lost twenty years ago on the same night. In the last ten or more years, it had also become a time to protest for those suffering in Savage Lands as well, to let the governments know the people would not be ignored by bombing the gates of HDF and the fae palace.

Léopold went on total lockdown this night while we heard fireworks, celebrations, and protest outside the walls.

"Your birthday, it's a big one this year," Andris said.

"I don't celebrate my birthday." I shut him down. The instinct to reject the day was ingrained in my bones. Not only for the tragedy, but because growing up in a human world, anything rejoicing fae and their culture was deemed almost treasonous in Leopold. "Too much blood and death."

*"But also life, Kovacs. Yours and mine,"* Warwick's shadow muttered.

Andris's head bowed in empathy, squeezing my arm before he walked away.

All I wanted was to head to an empty room and read, but I knew I had to check on everyone first.

When we entered the clinic room, Kek and Caden were gone. Only Lukas was there, but he was sitting up, a nurse rewrapping his wound, a flinch of pain over his face. Being a half-breed, you healed fast, but not as quickly as pure fae.

"Lukas!" I bumped the healer out of the way, hugging him. He still looked exhausted, but the color was back in his cheeks.

"Ow!" He laughed with a sharp inhale.

"Oh, sorry." I cringed.

"Don't be. I'll live." His smile dropped, a sadness flickering his eyes, realizing the choice of his words. His Adam's apple bobbed. "Ash told me Tracker and Ava didn't make it."

"I'm so sorry." Compassion filled me. It was easy to forget that they had been Lukas's team at Povstat, his family for a long time. Their deaths had to cut him deep.

His throat bobbed again, jaw clenching, and he looked away, dipping his head. He cleared his throat when Warwick and Ash strolled up.

"Thank you for saving me."

"It's really Ash you need to thank." I nodded at the tree fairy. "He healed you and stayed, making sure you made it through." Lukas's head jerked to Ash. "He's your knight in shining armor."

"No big deal." Ash shifted uncomfortably on his feet, embarrassed by the praise. "Just did what's in my nature."

"Well, thank you." Luk's voice went deadly serious, his gaze fixed on Ash. "I am in your debt."

"No need... like I said, part of being a healer."

"I don't know, Ash, *I* wouldn't turn down a hot man at my beck and call."

*"Is that what you want?"* Warwick growled in my ear huskily. His imaginary hands gripped my waist, his physique pushing into me. *"A*

*man at your beck and call?"* He nipped my ear. *"Or one who challenges you and fucks you relentlessly?"*

My lids shut, my teeth diving into my bottom lip, my body sweltering.

"What I thought," Warwick said out loud, a smug smile on his face. He turned, walking away, not even looking back. "Do your thing, Kovacs, then find me later."

"That guy is intense." Lukas shook his head, readjusting on the pillow.

"Yeah, tell me about it," I mumbled.

"No, tell *me* about it! I have to hear and feel you two." Ash swept by me, peering down at Luk's wound. "Looks really good." He brushed his fingers over the healing skin.

Lukas's muscles flexed under his touch, his jaw twitching.

"I'm glad you're doing better." Ash pulled his hand away. "Probably should let you rest."

"Yeah. Thanks," Lukas replied.

"Before we go." I motioned over my shoulder. "Do you know where Caden and Kek are?"

"Knowing Kek, she's either near the food or annoying someone." Lukas grinned. "And I don't know about your friend. When I woke up the last time, he was gone."

My stomach twisted. "Okay, thanks."

I leaned over, kissing Lukas's cheek and squeezing Ash's arm. "I'm gonna go look for Caden and check in with Hanna. You should finish wrapping that." I pointed to Lukas's bandages before heading out of the room in search of my ex-best friends, going to Hanna first.

Scorpion sat in the chair, as if he hadn't moved once since the last time. Hanna was curled up in a ball, a mat now under her to sleep on. She was still shackled to a pipe, her back to us.

"Has she been chained the whole time?" I blanched, snapping my head to Scorpion.

He huffed, rubbing his wrist. "The girl is rabid."

I noticed teeth marks on his wrist and fingernail scratches on his face. A laugh bubbled out of me.

"Did she do that?" I gestured to his wounds. He glared at me, then huffed again, making me laugh louder. "Good for her."

"You're for the human?" he snapped, sitting up in the seat.

"Not because she is human, but because she is my friend. And I love that she takes no shit... even if we're on opposite sides now."

Scorpion's eye twitched, but he didn't respond.

"Hanna has been my friend and the only other girl in the HDF training with me. You don't understand the brainwashing we experience at such a young age, the cult thinking they corral us into, giving us no other side. No other way." My throat stuck with patches of dryness, my heart aching seeing her as a prisoner. "I'm on this side of the handcuffs because I was forced to learn, to see. Being in Halálház opens your eyes to reality fast. To the truth. I just hope she will someday see it too. Because if she doesn't?" I knew too well she would not be freed or handed back to HDF.

Scorpion grunted under his breath, his teeth gritting, turning my focus to him, noticing how exhausted he looked.

"Have you been here the whole time?"

He shrugged like it wasn't a big deal.

"I'll get you something to eat."

"I'm fine."

"Then you should get some sleep."

"Last time I dozed, the little evil viper bit me."

A genuine smile tugged at my mouth, causing Scorpion to grumble at me as I went back out the door, genuinely pleased with my ex-comrade. Human women were always underestimated, and I loved that Hanna could hold her own with Scorpion.

Crossing the hall, I found where they were keeping Caden. If I thought seeing him would give me any relief, I was wrong.

"Get the fuck away from me!" He tried to sit up the moment I entered the room. Metal rattled against the pipe he was cuffed to, his head bandaged, his eyes blazing with hate. "I don't ever want to see your fuckin' face again!"

"Simmer down, pretty boy." Birdie nibbled on an apple from her position by the door. It was pretty much the same setup as Hanna. "You're gonna pop that vein in your forehead."

He snarled at her but stopped lashing out for me, his nose flaring.

The deep hate in his eyes as he looked at me was something I could never have imagined. No matter what little tiffs we got in, we loved each other so much, they never lasted long. But now all I saw was abhorrence.

"I said *leave*!" He yelled so fiercely I jerked back with a gasp.

It was like hands were wrapped around my neck. Tears burned behind my lids, emotion thickening my throat.

"And I said *simmer down*." Birdie tossed her apple in a bin, getting up and strolling over to him. Grabbing his hair, she yanked his head to look at her. "Or I will use my fae magic on you."

He tried to hide it, his expression hard and threatening, but I saw the recoil in his throat—the deep-seated fear HDF instilled in us about their ability to glamour. That all of them could use it on us, and we would become their puppets, doing and saying things against our will. Trapped in hell.

Not to say something wasn't behind it, but in my case, it had been a complete lie. But I wasn't normal.

"Birdie..." I shook my head.

"You think I was gonna glamour you into being my slave?" Her eyebrow popped up. "Not a bad idea. How about my sex slave?"

"Fuck you." His Adam's apple bobbed.

"That's the whole point."

"Birdie," I warned again.

She let out a laugh, her head going back, clapping her hands together. "Oh, pretty boy, you are dumber than I thought. Your brain would be so easy to control."

"She can't control your mind." I shook my head, waving Birdie away. Snickering, she leaned against the wall, folding her arms. What I felt with Killian wasn't mind control, but more an influence over my emotions—and he held power most other fae didn't. "She's messing with you."

"Is there a difference to his precious tiny mind?" She popped her foot up on the wall.

Glaring at her, I turned back to my friend.

"Caden—"

"Brexley." He cut me off, his voice low, curling his finger for me to lean in. I did. "I'm not asking you again. Get. The. Fuck. Away. From. Me!" he bellowed at me with deep animosity.

I couldn't help the hiccup of emotions stuck in my throat, the tears threatening to escape.

"NOW!" He thrashed and screamed at me.

"Go." Birdie motioned for me to leave. "I think it's best right now."

Nodding, I yanked open the door, peering over my shoulder at him.

The boy I loved most of my life, my best friend in the whole world, stared at me as if I were nothing more than a stranger.

Worse, a fae sympathizer.

I was dead to him.

# Chapter 24

Sitting back on a cot, already filled with emotion, I pulled the journal from the bag, my hands quaking. After Hanna and Caden, I had to retreat to a quiet room by myself. I hoped someday they would see and understand. But what if they didn't? What would happen to them?

I couldn't think of that possibility. One thing at a time.

Leaning against the wall, I pulled my legs up, placing the book on my thighs. Nerves attacked my lungs as I slowly opened it, something slipping out and landing on my stomach. The picture I saw in the book, the one of my mom pregnant with me. A sob hitched my throat, my hand covering my mouth, tears pushing through and spilling over.

Until this moment, I had never really seen a close up shot of my mother. In my actual hands. She was laughing, her hand rubbing her belly. So happy, beautiful and young. In my head, she was always my mother, forgetting she was not much older than I was now. She was a three-dimensional person with hopes and dreams, opinions and beliefs.

I traced over her face, taking in every detail I could. She had long, dark hair and pale skin like mine, but she was much softer and sweeter looking, with bright green eyes, round cheeks, and a heart-shaped face. I took more after my father's Russian heritage.

My finger trailed down to her stomach. I was in there, and with me, her life would end. Why did I have to come that night? If she weren't giving birth to me, would she have lived? Tears burned my eyes. I placed the image to the side, no longer able to look at her. So much was there, so much grief and guilt.

Peeling open the first page, my heart thumped again at seeing my father's familiar handwriting. The first dozen pages were nothing but simple updates about me or his job.

*Brexley took her first step today. I wish Eabha was here to see how smart and strong she is.*

*Istvan has us building up our troops. Tensions are rising; another war is brewing with the fae.*

About a third of the way in, things started to shift, and he was no longer using my name.

*Something odd happened today. Age 4.*

*She fell over two stories onto a marble floor... very lucky. She should be dead. Age 5.*

*I'm noticing more and more as she grows. A sick feeling in my gut. Age 5 ½.*

*Fear. I feel it more each day. To even utter the word, even think what I am thinking, would be blasphemy. Age 6.*

*We are leaving today for the East. I can no longer ignore my gut. Andris agrees with me after what we've seen. How can this be possible? I must find out why. I tried to find Eabha's family—it has only led to dead ends. Age 8*

I knew very little about my mother's side. Other than they were refugees from Ireland, her family coming over here when the old Seelie Queen Aneira was still in power.

It was also understood Mom was human...

But what if she wasn't?

*Istvan is sending us east again in search of a substance, a nectar. Following the ideals of a quack scientist, it is said this substance gives humans fae qualities. Strength, infinite life. His need for power has become a sickness, eating away the man I used to know.*

*I feel dread today as I leave her again. I fear he will discover her. I fear he senses something. I'm afraid when he does realize, he will take her from me or kill her if I don't follow exactly what he wants. I have no choice. She is my soul. My world. We must be careful, spies are everywhere, but I use these trips to find more about her. So far, her abilities connect with nothing human or fae. Age 10*

My mouth pinched together. Neither human nor fae. Not fitting anywhere.

Gray.

*I have found leads. But eyes are watching me. Always watching.*

I flipped to the next page.

*I understand now...*

After that, every post became more paranoid, speaking in strange riddles. Then about a month before his death, he started writing in secret code.

All encrypted. The final page, dated the day he died, was filled with nonsense words and strings of letters, but a single row toward the end was different from all the rest. They looked like a dove, rose, forget-me-nots, violets, and a boat.

"Fuck!" I slammed the book closed, rolling off the bed, tucking the picture of my mom in my back pocket. "Dammit, Dad! What do you mean you understand now?"

I only knew of one person who knew my father's mind, one who could possibly understand his puzzle. My feet ran down the hall, bursting into my uncle's office, his head snapping up the moment I entered.

"Brex?"

"Can you read this?" I slapped down the book in front of him to one of the encrypted pages.

Andris put on his glasses, moving the journal closer to him, his brows scrunching while he scanned the page.

"It's not any of the ones we used to communicate with each other." His finger skimmed over the symbols, flipping through more pages.

Disappointment stampeded on my lungs, deflating them.

"Really? Nothing in there? Even the bottom there? Why is it different?" I motioned to the page again, desperation etching my voice. He was the one I thought would know. "Do you know what he meant?"

"No, I don't." Andris's expression flattened, appearing as deflated as me. "I told you he got extremely paranoid by the end. Stopped talking to me, afraid if I knew too much, it would be dangerous."

A strangled cry rolled around in my throat, my hand hitting the desk. It was always a step forward and a dozen back.

He held up his finger, grabbing his walkie-talkie off his belt. "Ling, can you come to my office?" He spoke into it, then glanced at me. "She does more magic hacking, but she still is well versed in breaking codes. She's our best bet to possibly breaking his cipher."

A pump of hope went back into my lungs. Ling—Ling-ks. A Kitsune fox, she had the magical power to deceive and trick magic spells that she used to hack computers and systems.

Barely thirty seconds later, Ling was next to me, making me jump at her sudden appearance.

"Can you look at this?" Andris turned the book to her. She stepped up to the desk, her dark eyes skimming over the pages. "I know it's not your forte, but I'm hoping you could try to decipher it."

Her body was still, only her eyes moving over the page, as if her brain was computing each letter and symbol, running through a database in her mind. The room was silent for a few moments before she spoke.

"No." She stood.

"What?" I rushed to the desk, shoving the journal back toward her. "Look again, there has to be a way. You can hack the most magical spells in the world." My voice rose, anxiety nipping at my nerves.

"Exactly," she responded, unemotional. "Magic spells and computer encryptions. This," she pointed at the book, "is none of those."

"Ling..." Andris went up on his feet. "Please, this is very important."

"I will need more time with it and put it into the database."

"Yes." I nodded. "Do it."

"Do what you can, my love." Andris picked up the journal, handing it to her.

She grabbed it with a nod, slipping out of the room as quiet and fast as she arrived.

Biting my lip, I fought the urge to run after her and tail her every move as if she had the most precious item in the world. To me, she did. I still hadn't had time to really pore over his words and thoughts, skipping to the end to see if he had any answers.

"She will do everything she can, Brex." My uncle's voice drew me back to him. "We will figure it out. No matter how long it takes. Okay?"

I nodded. The sensation that time was running out pumped panic into me. I had no idea why I felt the clock ticking, but it was like a bomb in my gut.

He peered down at his watch. "It's late; you should get some rest." He scoured his head, sitting back down in his chair, eyes bloodshot.

"What about you?"

"I will when our enemy is defeated."

"Do we even know who that is anymore?"
His mouth pursed, a huff coming from his nose.
"It's getting harder to tell every day."

I banged back into the vacant room with the single cot, my brain whirling with the strange symbols and phrases.

If the man who was like a brother to my father, who knew how he thought better than anyone, couldn't even figure it out, how would I or anyone else? My dad could use any cipher in the world. Something he made up and was so obscure only he would ever know.

Though something tugged at my gut as if my father were reaching through the pages, circling my mind with every possible idea.

My legs and brain wouldn't stop moving, anxious while time ticked into the first hours of October 31—Halloween to the western world, who dressed up and spent the day in fun celebration. To HDF, it was the exact opposite. We barricaded the windows and added more guards to the gates, preparing for the moment Halloween night and Samhain convened. The fae took over the city, howling through the streets like wild animals, taking the "tricks" part of the night to an extreme level.

Pulling out the picture of my mother, I stared at her joyous face. I wanted to jump into the photo, drink up every moment. Hear the sound of her voice, feel her touch, see her eyes really look at me. Smile. I knew nothing about her, but I felt this connection to her in my gut, something more profound than this physical life.

Pacing the room, restless and tense, I couldn't lose my foreboding feeling about the coming night. A heaviness I couldn't shake.

Prickles danced down my vertebrae, slinking through my skin, brushing at a deep intimacy, notifying me of his arrival. I twisted to the door. Warwick leaned against the doorjamb, watching me. He had the deadly talent of slipping up on someone silently and undetected. But not me. Our connection was too intense, the link throbbing like a violin string plucked between us.

No words were spoken as we stared at each other. He could feel my anxiety, grief, and fears. His calmness wrapped around me like a hug, easing my vexation, relaxing my shoulders.

He sauntered over, taking the picture from me, his gaze rolling over the image of my mother, searching.

"What?"

"Nothing." He shook his head, handing it back to me. "You can see a little of you in her. She's beautiful."

My tear-filled lashes lifted to him; I had no energy to put up any defenses. I was exposed, open.

"My father's journal was coded at the end," I whispered. "What if we can't crack it? Never find out what I am? What he knew? What if I can't find the nectar? What about your Eliza and Simon?"

His thumb slid over my jaw, tracing my cheeks and lips. "Then we figure out another way." His gravelly voice skated and scraped through my core.

"How? There are no leads. Not even in the fae book."

"There is always another way." His hands captured my face, bringing me closer. Nothing he did was ever soft or tender, but his fierce determination eased my fears. "We don't play by the normal rules, Kovacs. You and I make our own." His aqua eyes burned into mine. "I *saw* the ghosts at the cemetery earlier, felt them respond to you, bow to you like a queen... ." His fingers gripped my jaw firmer, his nose brushing mine. "And I'm on my knees with them."

His mouth claimed mine, hungry and possessive. Seizing my soul. Demanding every part of me, razing me to the ground, forcing me to claw my way back up and fight like hell.

His hands gripped my waist, lifting me up, my legs circling his hips as he carried me over to the cot. He dropped me down on it, climbing between my legs. Fingers tearing at my clothes, he stripped me as his invisible ones trailed over my figure. He kissed me while I could also feel him nip at my thigh, his tongue licking through me.

My spine arched with a gasp, spearing desperate desire into my chest. I ripped his shirt over his head, his mouth back on mine with a ferocity the moment nothing separated us. I unbuttoned his pants, yanking them down his hips, my palm grasping him, before the shadow of my mouth wrapped around him, taking him deep, humming.

He grunted, enticing me to go farther, generating a deep growl from him. "Fuck, princess."

I felt powerful, making him lose control, his hips pushing into the mouth that wasn't actually there. To us, we felt no difference.

A cry bucked from my mouth as the feel of his tongue drove in deeper, his lips sucking at my clit, hitting every erogenous spot inside, tearing the breath from my lungs.

Every inch of my skin felt him, inside and out, and I knew he could feel me the same way. We experienced each other's pleasure along with our own, lifting us away from the world around us. There was just us, his calloused hands running over my body, his teeth dragging between my breasts, sucking on my nipple, his tongue and lips devouring my pussy.

Ecstasy. Rapture. My bones burned with pleasure, my climax heaving my chest.

"Warwick..." His name came off my lips as a plea and a promise.

He lifted off me, his gaze heavy and penetrating as he stood over me, his attention gliding over my body. He yanked off his boots and pants before climbing back over me.

Our eyes were locked on each other as he pulled my knee up to his hip, plunging inside me.

Moaning, I almost came undone, wanting to break under the waves of pleasure. I relished the slight pain from his size as he filled me with deep, long strokes.

"Fuck," he rumbled, a vein straining along his law. "Gods, you fuckin' feel unbelievable." He grunted, driving in deeper. "This pussy is *mine*."

I didn't have to answer. He knew without a word he might not own the rest of me, but that part he conquered and possessed. The energy between us layered our connection with intensity and power.

He sat back, pulling me up with him, our bodies moving together. Fucking me so deep, my vision blurred, my head tipping back as his teeth nipped down on my neck.

My nails raked down his back, causing him to growl, thrusting harder into me. The flood of emotions, of extreme bliss and desire, twisted the pain and pleasure, life and death, into a single line.

Last night we went to war against each other. This time our battle was against the world, our connection weaving us together, where I could feel no difference between his satisfaction and mine. The forces outside shattered against our power, stretching farther than the walls of this building, spilling out into the atmosphere, where no rules existed.

Where we created our own.

I clutched his chin with bruising force, our eyes connected before my mouth captured his, my teeth biting down onto his lip until I tasted blood. A deep noise vibrated his throat. Desperation and desire were the same.

Flinging me back down on the cot, his face set like a warrior, about to obliterate. Kill and destroy.

No survivors.

"Oh gods!" I cried out, not able to control anything. I let go. Fire burned up the back of my legs and up my vertebrae, singeing my vision.

My legs wrapped around him, my spine arching, my tits bouncing, sweat dripping down my skin.

Again, flashes of our past took over my sight, mixing in with the present.

Our naked bodies rocked together while battle and death raged on the field around us. I could feel the blood-soaked ground damp against my spine, soaking into my hair. We were surrounded by screams and bellows, the clanking of metal. The magic of the fae wall crumbling danced on my skin. At the same time, we were in the bunker, me leaning over his dead body.

"*Pokol!*" *Hell.* Warwick seethed as I pulled him deeper with my legs, bucking against him ruthlessly.

"Brexley..."

"*Sötét démonom.*"

Two voices, two different time periods, but only one man called me.

I understood the power of a name now. The intimacy of him saying them. I could feel it in every molecule, pulsing my pussy around him as vibrant colors danced overhead, a bolt of lightning cracking in the sky, striking me.

My orgasm slammed into me, tearing and drowning me. And I would gladly let it take me.

I heard a scream, knowing it was me, but it sounded feral and inhuman.

"Fuuuuck," he bellowed.

My vision blackened at the edges, and my body felt electrocuted with pleasure as he emptied himself inside me. My climax collided into my bones like an avalanche, demolishing and obliterating everything in its path.

This time I could really feel the nonentity of death and the moment I yanked him back to the present. A torrent of magic burst through his veins, slamming into his heart, tearing him from death's grasp into the hands of a thief. Death didn't like being robbed of his prey, so it marked Warwick as one of its eternal soldiers.

My body and mind, unable to handle the flood of life and death battling out together, shut down, sinking into the thick blackness of the in-between.

*"Brexley Kovacs."* The unearthly voice gripped my mind through the darkness, the power pulling me toward it. *"The girl who defies nature. Who should not exist."* The fae book spoke as if it was my title. A badge worn on my chest. *"Should not have survived."*

*"What do you mean I shouldn't have survived?"* I peered around. There was nothing, but I could feel the book's force surround me, spark at my muscles. *"How are you here?"*

I understood I was dreaming the book, and somehow, like before, it found me without me touching it, just being near it.

*"Your very being is threaded in magic. You can never hide from me."*

*"What does it mean? Tell me!"*

*"That is not the question you seek."*

Without any other warning, I felt myself being sucked through the book, even without it physically being there.

Then I was suddenly in a room I knew so thoroughly. My childhood bedroom in the lower levels of HDF, the apartment with my father. A fire crackled in my bedroom hearth, giving off the only light. I heard the sound of a little girl crying. My father, dressed in his uniform, sat on my bed, brushing his fingers softly through the little girl's hair, wiping her tears away.

I sucked in, the memory of this moment barely a haze in my mind. I had no actual memories of it now, but my father told me I had incessant nightmares until I turned about four. I'd wake up screaming in pain, muttering things about lightning and my mother. They were never clear, a swirl of colors and impressions.

*"Shhh, Kicsim."* His voice was soft and low. *"It was just a bad dream."*

*"I'm so sorry, Daddy."* My muffled voice could barely be heard as my younger self tucked her head into the pillow.

*"Whatever for, lelkem?"* My soul.

*"I killed Mommy..."* A gut-wrenching sob hiccupped from her.

*"No, no... it's not your fault. Mommy wanted to save you for me, Kicsim. She knew I could not live without you."* He tried to soothe my sobs, a low hum coming from his throat, murmuring a folk song my mother used to sing while pregnant with me. He calmed me so many nights, singing me to sleep.

*"I'd like to cross the Tisza by boat*
*By boat, only by boat.*
*My dove lives there, lives there,*
*My dove lives there.*
*She lives in the town,*
*Red roses, blue forget-me-nots, violets*
*Are growing in her window."*


In a blink, I was ripped from the room and dropped into another. The secret cottage my parents stayed in. My body stilled as I saw my father hunched over the table, penning in the journal. Gray hair hinting at his temples told me it was years later, though the same song hummed in his throat.

My skin tingled as I stepped up to him, my gaze going over his shoulder to what he was writing. Nonsensical letters scrolled over the page as he frantically wrote, his head occasionally darting up to the window with a look of paranoia as if he expected someone to be there.

To find him.

My breath hitched as he muttered the words of the song, copying from a keycode next to him. He started to sketch out the last symbol in that peculiar line in the journal. The dove, rose, forget-me-nots, violets, and a boat.

My heart thumped in my chest. All the things he was drawing were from the song. The song he told me my mother sang to me.

The book shifted something in my sight, and suddenly I could read the line. It wasn't words, but numbers.

Coordinates.

*47°46'25. 18°59'06.*

He scribbled out a few more coded lines before his head darted up, tipping to the side as if he heard a noise. His body went rigid, icing my skin. He hissed under his breath, slamming the journal closed. Dashing over to the fireplace, he tossed the keycode into the flames. He wiggled the stone from the side of the hearth before shoving it in the exact place I had found it.

I sensed his fear, his anxiety, as he pulled on his coat, grabbing for his gun. I had an urge to follow to see what was out there... *who* was out there? Why he was so scared? But the book grabbed me. *"No! Please!"* I tried to push through, overpower its hold on me. The book easily flicked me out, tumbling me back into oblivion, not letting me see what was coming for my father.

It had given me what I went in there for—no more, no less.
How to break my father's messages.

I bolted awake, sitting up with a gasp, untangling the arms and legs
wrapped around me on the small, demolished cot. Warwick jerked up
with me, his body tense and ready to attack.

"Ahhh," a voice cried, and I felt something tumble into my lap. I
yanked at the sheet, covering myself. My lids blinked, seeing Opie
scrambling to stand up. "Dammit, Fishy! Warn a brownie before you do
that. I almost left fudge stains!" He was in a leather-and-lace bodice and
thong, with bright red lips, his hair still in Mohawk, and gold glitter all
over. A product of Kitty's.

*Chirp.*

I twisted my head to see Bitzy on the pillow between Warwick and
me, flipping me off. The butt plug strapped onto her head wobbled
around with her indignation. Her face had streaks of glitter, her lower
half in a leather diaper.

Right then, I couldn't even focus on their outfits.

I scrambled out of bed, grabbing for my clothes.

"What's wrong?" Warwick asked.

"I know..."

"Know what?" He rose, leaning on his forearm, watching me get
dressed, his free hand rubbing his nose. "Why do I smell lube?"

*Chirrrp?* Bitzy peered around innocently, her ears going down,
eyes wide, motioning to Opie.

"That was all her!" Opie pointed back at her, his head waggling. "I
just used it to warm my toes."

*Chirp! Chirp! Chirp!* She flung her fingers at Opie.

"I did not stick my toes in Fishy's ears!"

"What?" My hands went up, rubbing them.

"She's kidding." Opie swished his hand.

Bitzy looked at me deadpan, her head shaking in "no, I'm not."

"Seriously, gross." I used my shoulders to rub my ears as I yanked
on my boots.

"I swear, imp..." Warwick growled. "If those bony fingers get
anywhere near me again... I'm biting them off, using them as toothpicks,
and then showing you where the thing on your head is really meant to go."

"Warwick!" I stood back up, dressed, yanking his attention back to me. "I know how to break my father's code." I tossed his pants to him. "Get up."

He shoved the blankets away, jumping out of bed.

Even in this moment, I couldn't help but gape at his unbelievable physique, his muscles flexing and moving under his inked skin. The memory of how it felt over me... inside me.

*Chhhiiiiiiirrrpppp.* Bitzy let out almost a breathy whistle.

"Yeah..." Opie sighed. "That is the largest and thickest vacuum hose I've *ever* seen."

Warwick snorted, his heavy gaze on me while he yanked up his trousers.

"Keep looking at me like that, Kovacs, and the only thing we're gonna do is break the bed into more pieces." He strolled up to me, tucking strands of tangled hair behind my ear, his heat and lust encompassing me.

He laughed at my hesitation, kissing me quickly, and twisted me around, pushing me for the door. "Later, I'm fucking you in the shower."

My chest expanded, my thighs tightening at the idea, but I had to shake it off. This was far more important right now.

The clock on the wall read 9 a.m. The hallways were sprinkled with people moving around, the workout room and dining area buzzing with life as we moved to the operations room.

Ling sat at one of the stations, the journal in front of her, scribbling something on a piece of paper next to it. Her head rose when we neared.

"I have not solved it," she replied. "I have been through every type of encryption out there."

"I might know. At least one line." I swallowed nervously. Was I right? What if it came to nothing? Just a strange dream. "Can I?"

She shrugged, shoving it to me.

I looked over the markings on the page, my heart thumping in my chest. The song echoing in my brain. The symbols were the only thing on the page that didn't correspond to a letter—they were numbers. It might take longer to figure out the rest of the encryption if he used another code, but at least I was certain I had one part of it.

Perspiration licked at my lower back, my hands shaking as I wrote down the memory still strong in my mind. The dove, rose, forget-me-nots, violets, and a boat.

*Dove=47°, rose=46'25, forget-me-nots=18°, violets=59'06.*

*But what did the boat mean?*

Ling's head snapped up as her dark eyes filled with guarded curiosity.

"The code is based off a folksong he used to sing to me." I tapped the page. "But I'm not sure why the boat is there?" It didn't fit. Was it to throw people off? Was I wrong?

Ling moved, tapping the numbers into the keyboard, her body stilling, her mouth parting.

"What?" Dread slithered down my throat, wrapping around my stomach.

She twisted the screen to us, a place on the map highlighted.

"Shit." Warwick breathed out, his head tipping back, his palm rubbing his scruff.

"What?" I looked at him then the screen, not understanding both of their dreaded reactions.

"High Castle." He wagged his head. "Visegrád." He said the name of the area as if it was a feared nemesis. I had heard of the site a few times from teachers. It was an area not too far northwest of here, following the Danube. We didn't give it much interest as it was known to be hallowed ground to the fae.

"It's sacred land to you guys, right?"

He licked his lips, taking in my puzzled expression.

"Sacred is one way of calling it. But I'd say it is more cursed. Haunted and feared. No living fae enters that area anymore. *Ever.*"

"Why?"

"You don't know?"

"Should I?"

Warwick huffed, his arms crossing.

"Visegrád is where we fought the fae war twenty years ago."

# Chapter 25

"The High Castle in Visegrád?" Andris's mouth opened, his eyes rising up to Warwick and me in disbelief. "You think the nectar is hiding there?"

"I don't know what's there." I stepped up to his desk with the journal, coming straight over here from the operations room. Ling took a photocopy, working from that. "Ling is trying to figure out the rest based on the song, but he could have used another keycode. All I know is there's a reason my father wrote down those coordinates. Something is there he wanted to protect. And his statement about 'I understand now'..." I stared at the man who knew him best, who understood my father more than even I did. "I have to go and see."

Andris's shoulders lowered, peering back down at the markings, his fingers trailing over the pages. "I wish he'd talked to me." He tapped at the book sadly, then put his focus back on me. "Do I want to know how you figured it out?"

"It's... *complicated*."

"With you, my dear," Andris chuckled lightly, "I have no doubt."

Warwick snorted at Andris's response, causing me to shoot a glare at him.

"The one thing that doesn't make sense is the boat." I went back to the journal, pointing at the symbol. "It has no reason to be there. It doesn't seem to represent anything."

"Actually, it does." Andris pinched his brow, glancing at Warwick.

I twisted to Warwick, his fingers tugging at his lip, his head bobbing.

"The night of the war, all roads there were pretty much destroyed by the surge of magic, the castle on the hill left in ruins. Afterward, no one wanted to rebuild or be anywhere near that area. The land was avoided; people went around, found other ways. There were whisperings about it being haunted by the fallen. Cursed." Warwick flicked his chin back at the journal. "The lone way in and out... is by boat."

*"I'd like to cross the Tisza by boat. By boat, only by boat."*

In this case, it was the Danube.

"We need a boat to get there?" Their heads affirmed my question. "I'm certain I can steal one of those." I picked up the journal, pressing it to my chest. "Can't be much different from a train."

"You are going there *tonight*?" Andris's eyebrow curved up.

"Yes." I nodded. "Every second is crucial."

"Let me remind you that you are going to the very location the fae war took place, twenty years to the night?"

"Don't tell me you're superstitious?" I slanted my head, my tangled hair falling down my arm.

"This world has taught me not to be so skeptical."

"I'm going, *nagybacsi*." *Uncle*.

"Impulsive and stubborn, like your father." He clicked his tongue, but humor glinted in his eyes.

"Thank you." I grinned back.

"I don't have a lot of extra fighters to join you tonight, as they are needed for our own Samhain missions, but please get who you can. I don't like you being out there tonight."

"I'll be fine." I took a step back to the door. "What is your mission anyway?"

Andris sat down in his chair, a coy smile on his lips. "Let's say we like to make both sides aware we are still here, and we're getting stronger."

Snorting, my head waggled. "All those years, we had to guard the gates and barricade the windows at HDF thinking it was a fae mob... and it was you."

One of his rare grins crinkled up his features. "I thought leaving a 'fuck you, I'm still alive' card for Istvan from me was a little too on point."

I snickered, almost out the door, Warwick behind me.

"Check in before you leave tonight," Andris added. "Oh, and Brexley..."

I paused, turning to him.

"Happy birthday."

"You think you could go without me—"

*Chirp!*

"Us!" Opie went from gesturing to himself and Bitzy. "I meant *us*."

*Chirp! Chirp!*

"I did too!" Opie huffed, putting his hands on his hips. "You'd think with those large ears, you'd be able to hear me clear enough."

*Chirpchirpchirpchirp!*

Opie's mouth fell in shock before he shook his head. "That's not even possible..." He peered down at himself, moving in odd angles. "Nope, it can't reach."

*Chirp!*

"It's not tiny," he exclaimed. "I've been told by many... like many, many people."

"I thought it was only a few?" I teased.

"That's many!" He tossed out his arms.

"Do I even want to know?" Warwick strolled into the room, tying up his wet hair hanging around his face, a slice of his ripped torso on display. My chest pounded with desire, warmth filling my veins, making my cheeks heat, a smile twitching my lips.

After seeing my uncle, we got food, had sex, did some training on the mat, which led to more sex, a nap, and more food, then fucked like nymphos in the shower, where I broke the showerhead.

This man had turned me into a fiend, shattering me over and over today, and I seemed to just crave more. I knew he was trying to keep my mind off tonight. Not merely what was ahead, but what this night meant.

To both of us.

The constant twist in my gut grew as the day matured, something I couldn't shake no matter how hard he made me orgasm.

"No." I snorted, pulling my own damp hair up into a ponytail. Turning to face him, I went on my toes, kissing him. Both of us were dressed in dark clothes and boots and were draped with weapons. "And I'd rather block it from my mind too."

"But back to the point, Fishy. I couldn't let you go without me—*us*. I mean the messes I'v—*we've* already had to help you out of." He motioned to him and Bitzy. "I wouldn't be a good brownie if I wasn't helpful."

"Helpful?" Warwick muttered, kissing me again before moving around me, grabbing a handgun off the table, and stuffing it in his holster. "Not the exact word I'd use."

"Shush, long hose." He batted his hand at Warwick. "Fishy?" Opie whined, putting his hands together. "Please? Look, we've even dressed the part." He motioned to him and Bitzy, now dressed in an old black cut-up glove, using two of the fingers for his pants, then braiding and twisting the rest of the parts into a halter top. He had a cut-out mask around his eyes. Bitzy wore a onesie and black eye mask.

Pinning my lips together, I tried not to smile at their adorable burglar outfits.

"Okay, fine." I held up my hand. "But if anything happens, you guys get out, okay?"

"Yay!" Opie clapped his hands.

*Chirp! Chirp!* Bitzy twirled her middle fingers around in excitement, forcing a full laugh from me.

A knock on the door broke my attention away from them as I opened it.

"You guys done fucking for five minutes so we can go?" Ash sauntered in, his hair pulled back, showing off the beautiful structure of his face. Kek was behind him, their outfits similar to ours, guns and knives hanging from their belts and gun halters.

"Seriously, you sure you two aren't part demon?" Her blue eyes twinkled with humor. "You'd think how many times I got myself off today, I'd be in a coma."

Ash chuckled his head, dipping in accord.

My cheeks burned deep crimson. I knew we affected others around us, but it was still disconcerting for everyone to be so aware of what we were doing. Not that we would have stopped even if we could. Warwick was beyond a drug. The high of touching life and death at the same time was beyond a simple addiction.

"Well, let me know, tree-humper... if you ever need to let some energy out." Kek pulled her blue braid over her shoulder, her lashes lowered on Ash as she tugged on her ends.

For a moment, I saw Ash look over at her, his face staying blank, but I definitely saw a flick of something before another voice broke into the room, jolting Ash.

"I'm going too." Lukas ambled into the space, his expression set in stone, his skin still pale.

"No." Ash shook his head. "Absolutely not."

"I'm sorry... are you my mother?" Luk snapped back. "I don't remember you having any authority over me."

Ash's eyes narrowed. "No, but I'm your healer, who knows you aren't healthy enough to get out of bed yet."

"I'm fine." Luk brushed him off, pulling his frame up higher, trying to prove he was strong and whole.

"How did you even know?" I blinked at him. The last time I checked on him, he was taking a nap.

"I told him." Ash frowned, folding his arms. "But I didn't mean it as an invitation."

Luk shrugged. "I can't lie around while everyone else is going on missions, has a purpose, has something. My teammates are dead, and if I'm alone any longer with my thoughts, I will go insane. I'm healed enough. Tonight of *all* nights, I have to do something."

From what I noticed within the base today from the fae and half-breeds, there was a noticeable edginess. No wall existed between our worlds now, but magic still hummed louder once the sun lowered. Energy ballooned thicker in the air, stirring the fae. Samhain was a living, breathing entity. Even humans could feel it rolling over their skin, pulsing through their bones.

And certainly, whatever the hell I was could.

Taking Luk in, I noticed the determination set in his eyes. If he were healed or not, I couldn't take this away from him. Tonight was like every human holiday rolled into one for fae. Plus, he had to feel the pain of losing Ava and Tracker and being separated from his own faction because of me.

"You can come." I nodded at Luk, his chest easing down.

"What?" Ash gaped at me. I shot him a look.

"He's going, Ash." Conversation over.

Warwick snickered, his head shaking as he tucked another blade into his boot, then tugging on his jacket. "Let's go."

Opie and Bitzy leaped into the small bag on my back carrying extra ammunition, rope, flashlight, and duct tape. Some would call it a thief kit, though Warwick suggested it could be used later when we got back.

The five of us strode down the hallway, the place swarming with movement and energy. You could taste it on your tongue—the adrenaline and magic. Everyone was dressed like us, preparing for tonight's assignments.

Not much consideration was given to Istvan or HDF, though I felt a slight tug of guilt thinking about this group attacking Killian's palace. Not that he couldn't handle it. I knew Sarkis's army was only sending a warning. My feelings for Killian wouldn't allow me to put him in a box like my uncle or Warwick did. I spent time with him, saw the real man. He wasn't bad or good... He was a leader with flaws, but also greatness.

"X!" Birdie's voice called out, her white-blonde hair hidden by a black knit hat, her tiny figure almost outweighed by the massive blade attached to her back. Maddox, Wesley, Zuz, and Scorpion stood next to her.

"Too bad you aren't going with us. I'll pop in and say hi to your old comrades at HDF." She grinned at me.

"Yeah, send my love," I replied dryly.

"We are... it's called *distraction*." She winked at Warwick as the group headed for the exit.

Scorpion paused in front of me. "Be careful."

"You too," I replied.

"If you need me..." He tapered off, growing a smile on my face.

"I know where to find you."

His head bobbed, his gaze going over my shoulder, down the hallway toward the temporary holding cells.

I knew what was down there. *Who* was down there.

My thoughts went to Caden and Hanna. "Who's watching them?"

"Some trainee who has no idea what he's up against," he scoffed.

"Surprised you're letting someone else take watch." I lifted my brows.

He scowled, appearing like he didn't understand my meaning. "She's just a fucking human." Scorpion walked away without another word, jogging up the stairs and out of the base.

"Brexley." Andris moved to me, his expression tense with worry. "Be careful tonight."

"We will." I swallowed, taking in my uncle's face. He felt like home to me. So much more than my real uncle.

Pulling me into a hug, he kissed my temple. "I love you, *Drágám.* You are everything to me. Happy birthday."

Then he was gone, giving orders and moving around the room.

My throat thickened, tears burning the back of my lids as I watched him disappear down the hallway. My gut twisted with a deep fear, fluttering panic around my stomach as if devastation was swinging down on us like the scythe of death.

Energy danced on my skin, wrapping around my bones, the smooth laps of the water contradicting the anxiety moving around me.

The stolen boat glided down the inky Danube. The night was crystal clear, seeing in the darkness my billowing breaths and prickling my nose and cheeks.

Sailing through the city, tension knotted my muscles. The air was crammed with tension. We were on the cusp, the moment before the storm, where all was still quiet, but it pulsed with anticipation and power. Killian's palace bloomed with light, and I swear I could feel him, standing on his terrace, his eyes finding me through the dark.

*"Relax, princess,"* Warwick growled into the back of my neck, his heat around me, while he stood at the back end of the boat, steering.

Blowing out, I trained my gaze back on the river, trying to calm the thumping in my chest. The farther away we drifted, the darker it became, emphasizing the enormous golden moon in the sky, glimmering off the water.

Twenty years ago, I was born under the same moon. The same moon when the two realms became one on this night, fae were discovered to live among humans, and the world flipped over.

It was strange to think I was being born somewhere in Budapest, maybe even in the cottage, and at the same time, I was there in the war too—felt the blood ooze between my toes, smelled the dirt and sweet acidic fragrance of the magic dissolving and burning, and saw the bodies and experienced death.

"You smell it, Fishy?" Opie looked back at me from his perch on boat rail, Bitzy next to him. Neither had been on a boat before and were awed by this new experience.

"I smell the Danube."

"No, adventure, Fishy." His eyes sparkled. "And possibly dead bodies, but mostly adventure!"

I scoffed, my gaze dipping to the water. From the pictures Andris showed me, there were many bodies hidden underneath the dark inky waters of the Danube.

The boat curved around a bend in the river.

"There." Ash pointed.

Following his hand, I spotted a crumbling old stone castle on the hill like a headstone, marking the graves of so many lives lost in the soil around it.

Warwick steered the boat toward the shore, beaching it on the embarkment. Opie and Bitzy jumped in my pack. My lungs struggled to keep even while we disembarked, the knot in my stomach coiling tighter. My boots landed on the shore, and prickles skated up my spine, coating my skin in goosebumps.

Death.

Dead didn't mean nothing or emptiness. It hummed at the edges, desperate to feed, thirsty to taste. Life was death's drug, its addiction, its craving to feel again. And I could feel them coming to me as if I was the gateway. Nausea swept over me, my lids closing, trying to swallow down the bile.

"Brex." Warwick grabbed my arm. The moment he touched me, the sickness dissipated, allowing me to take a full breath.

"Shield yourself." Ash was on my other side.

Nodding, I pushed back at the dead, the ghosts drenching this land, coming to me. A light in the dark. A beacon. The source of its need.

"There's so many," I whispered. "Too many."

"You do not bow to them, Kovacs," Warwick rumbled in a mandate, his hand squeezing mine before he let go. "Make them bow to you."

They crashed into me the moment he let go, waiting at the barrier like hungry savages.

Gritting my teeth, I slammed down my walls. *"No!"* I screamed in my head. They pushed forward, my form bowing over. *"Get back!"* There were so many; they just kept coming. I felt myself throw up, my body swaying.

"You are their commander. They bow to you!" Warwick demanded of me.

With a bellowing cry, I dug deep and shoved back at them, power thundering off me. *"You do not touch me!"*

I thought I heard thunder crack in the clear sky, a flash of light.

The ghosts tumbled away, an unseen barrier going up around me, protecting me. It was something I understood I couldn't lower for a moment here. The dead possessed this area, claimed almost every inch.

Spitting out the vile taste in my mouth, I took a staggering breath, pulling myself up.

"Holy fuck." Ash blinked at me in awe.

"What?" I peered at Kek, Ash, and Lukas.

"You fucking lit up, little lamb." Kek huffed through her nose, her eyes wider than normal. "Like a bolt of lightning."

My gaze met Warwick's. He told me the same thing when I faced off with the ghost in the Bone Church.

Ash noticed our look between each other.

"That happened before?"

"Yeah." Warwick nodded. "At the Bone Church."

Ash's head bobbed. "O-kay, we're gonna come back around to that at a later time." He blew out in bewilderment. "Are you all right?"

"Yeah." I wiped the sweat beading my brow. "We better get moving."

"Get this done, so we can get out of here." Kek shivered. "This place is even too horrible for me, and I'm a demon. I like horrible."

"Fuck, I second that." Ash breathed out. "I never thought I'd come back here."

"Lead the way, princess." Warwick motioned for me to go. "This is your show."

Nipping my lip, I started the climb up the hill. I had no real plan. I was just following my father's message and my gut instinct. The fact that he used that song as his code made me feel he was speaking to me, leaving it for me to figure out. As if he knew someday, my choices would lead me here.

"Okay, Dad, show me..." I muttered to myself.

Scaling the hill, the stone steps eroded, we hiked our way up to the castle. Luk struggled the most, but he didn't complain, while Kek made up for it.

"Dammit, little lamb, if I'd known there'd be exercise involved, I would have stayed in the boat," she grumbled. "Not my preferred workout choice."

"Have no stamina, demon?" Ash jabbed back.

"Want to test my stamina, fairy?" she coyly countered. I heard Luk growl, but it could have been from the pain.

Ignoring their conversation, my feet moved faster until I reached the base of the High Castle, standing at the arched gate. My stomach rolled with something I couldn't explain, electricity zinging my skin, tingles at the back of my neck.

This place felt so familiar to me, though I knew I had never been here exactly. The battle took place in an open field behind the castle grounds. I hadn't even known a castle existed here, except, oddly, I did. I couldn't explain it, but the utter realization this place was known to me, as if I belonged here, thumped fear into my heart.

My pulse grew louder in my ears as my feet instinctively moved through the dilapidated ruins. The shell of the fortress remained, but most of the roof was now gone, allowing the moonlight to break through some of the darkness.

The pounding in my ears echoed my heartbeat, almost sounding like it was calling my name. I felt it everywhere. Death.

But these were not the same as spirits I encountered earlier. Oddly, I didn't feel any ghost within the castle. There was an emptiness. Void of that energy that comes from a soul.

I zigzagged and moved through the castle's pathways. The sense that things were watching us from the shadows raked across every vertebra. Just out of my peripheral, but when I looked, nothing was there, urging me to move quicker.

"Kovacs." I heard Warwick call my name, but I no longer felt I was in control of my body. I started to run, curving through an archway until I hit a small courtyard overlooking the Danube.

My feet came to a shuddering stop. A scream cracked across my ribs, dying on my tongue, terror trapping it in my throat.

"Holy fuck." Ash stopped next to me.

Warwick halted on my other side, Kek and Luk flanking them.

In the middle of the courtyard was an old water well, but it was what surrounded it which drove terror into me, pinning my legs to the ground. Seven hooded figures stood around the well. All lean and various heights, their faces were hidden under their hoods and shadowed by the night. Their bony hands held various weapons, like a bardiche, lucerne hammer, and a war scythe. Sharp edges gleamed in the moonlight.

I had seen their likeness before in picture books where humans got the inspiration for the image of death.

The seven stood there, but I could make out more boney figures deep in the shadows, waiting for a command.

I knew in my gut what they were.

"Oh, may a wheelbarrow of small monkeys fuck it." My voice barely hit above a whisper.

Necromancers.

# Chapter 26

Air hiccupped in my lungs, fear plugging up my veins, my gaze rolling over the figures. Warwick was right in saying no living person lived on this land, but not everything here was dead.

Necromancers lived in the in-between.

The gray.

*The gray... just like you.*

They were stuck between life and death, feeding on what was left of a person's essence. Necromancers lived off the souls of the deceased, then used their skeletons to do their bidding. There was no emotion or conscience in them anymore, only bones.

That was what I saw in the shadows. An army of bones ready to fight and protect their masters.

My gut knotted with a realization my mind was not willing to hear yet. Dread knocked around inside my body, making my head swim, like I wasn't fully attached to myself. This was all secondary to the magnetic pull I felt, a power inside the well, inside me, that I could not fight.

It called to me as if it was part of me. Singing the song of a siren.

Absently, my feet stepped toward the source.

Almost all the necromancers moved in a blink, their menacing weapons primed to gut me, triggering the group around me to respond in kind.

I could feel Warwick's presence expand, the wolf and the legend dousing the space with power, the promise of death.

The problem was, this group didn't fear death.

They fed off of it.

A smaller figure stood in front of the group, with long, stringy dark hair falling out of the hood. I was pretty sure it was a woman. She held up her slim hand, the gray skin so paper-thin it was almost translucent. The necromancers around her eased back. I had no doubt she was their leader.

She didn't speak or offer any encouragement, but for some reason, I took it as such, stepping forward again.

"Kovacs..." Warwick's voice skirted up the back of my neck, his gun still cocked and pointed at them. "What are you doing?"

I had no fucking idea.

Reaching the well, the pull became agonizing, a cry bounding up my throat, desperate to retrieve whatever it was.

Tugging on the rope, I yanked the bucket up. The necromancers shifted. The sense that they wanted to cut me down, keep me away from it, crawled over me like ants. Their leader put up her hand again, halting them.

An old wooden bucket broke through the impregnable blackness at the bottom of the well, revealing a metal box sitting inside the pail. Reaching for it, I sensed potent magic rattling against the container—a caged animal desperate to get out. Through its confines, power oozed out, stabbing at my skin like a thousand needles.

A crack of lightning danced across the cloudless night sky, the air rolling thick with magic.

*"Kovacs..."* Warwick's shadow growled in my ear. He could feel it too. The weight in my stomach warning me all day was screaming now, but stopping was no longer an option. My fate was set; the events leading me here were already in motion.

My hands wrapped around the box, letting the bucket rope go. Energy zapped through the night and down my muscles. Emotion I couldn't explain wheezed in my chest.

Shaking, I pried open the lid. Inside, all I could see was a substance almost like solidified honey.

A bell in the distance rang out, the first stroke of the midnight hour right as my fingers brushed at the substance.

It glowed, humming with not just a deep familiarity...

It. Was. *Me.*

*Crack!*

Whether the sound was inside me or outside, it made no difference.

My senses were ripped from me. A cry shredded up my throat, blackness engulfing me as magic exploded inside my body, taking me away from the present, dropping me instantly in the past.

Exactly twenty years ago.

Like with the fae book, I stood in the battlefield of the fae war, the sounds of metal clanging, of death screams rattling, of magic popping and crackling as what was left of the barrier between the worlds splintered and dissolved. I was in a different place, closer to the Seelie Queen's castle, figures running by me, dead bodies littering the ground.

"Eabha?" The sound of my mother's name whipped my head to the side, confusion clouding my mind. Was it a coincidence? Another woman named that? My mom was supposed to be giving birth to me right now.

"Eabha," the woman's voice called again, zeroing me in on her. Her light brown hair in a braid; dressed in black, she darted to another figure.

Everything in me froze, my eyes absorbing, while my brain stumbled over the scene.

My mother, her picture still in my pocket, was there. Not in the cottage giving birth to me, but here in the middle of the battle. She hissed, one hand grabbing the woman's arm, her other pressing against her pregnant belly, bending over with a groan.

"You shouldn't be here!" The other woman's voice shook with fear, her head darting around, searching for attackers. "The baby is coming."

My mother grunted, sweat dripping down her face. "It's too early."

"Clearly not! My niece is coming, Eab."

Niece? I blinked at the woman, now seeing how closely some of her features resembled my mother's, though her hair was more reddish-brown. I never knew I had an aunt or any family on my mother's side.

"You need to go. It's too dangerous. Think of your baby."

"I am," my mother seethed, anger pushing through her pain. "This is all *for her.*" She grunted through another contraction, crying out in pain. "I am the leader of this family now. If I don't fight, we have no hope, Morgan."

Morgan dipped her head, bowing. "What if he sees you?"

287

"He won't."

"How can you love him and keep the truth of who you are from him?"

"It's *because* I love him," my mother spat, her head shaking in sorrow. "If he knew..."

"You mean if he knew, not only what you are, but the fact we are fighting for the opposite side as him..."

I sucked in, stepping back.

Opposite side?

My father fought against the cruel Seelie Queen. That meant she was fighting *for* Aneira—in support of tyranny, of humans being nothing more than slaves—not against.

Why?

Betrayal knifed into my chest.

"We don't have a choice, Morgan!" Grief filled my mother's eyes. "She cursed us! If she dies..."

"So do we," my aunt croaked.

"No, little sister. Death would be a blessing." My mother jolted at seeing a group of Unseelie fae leap toward them. Instead of pulling out a weapon, my mother held up her hands. Hissed words chanted from her mouth.

The man's body went up into the air, his neck snapping with a chilling pop before plummeting to the ground in a heap.

*What the fuck?* A squeaked cry came up my throat, shock and terror stumbling me back even more.

Was my mother a Druid? A witch?

Morgan stayed next to her, and between them, they slaughtered the group of fae. Ones fighting for the king.

A pained howl burst from my mom, her hand grappling for her sister again, her legs bending until she hit the ground.

"Eabha!" Panic filled Morgan's voice, dropping to the ground next to my mom, her hand rubbing her arm.

"She's coming—oh gods no—the baby is coming now." Tears poured down my mother's face, her hands clawing at her sister in terror.

"I need to get the rest of our group. Maybe Finn will know what to do!" Morgan started to rise.

"Yes, go get them." A man's voice came from the side, jerking my head to him as he sauntered up. "Then I can destroy your perfidious clan all at once."

"Oh gods." My mouth parted, taking in the old man I had grown to love at one time. Strength and power curled off him. Carrying a staff, he looked pretty much the same except his back was straight, his frame less feeble and worn.

"Tadhgan..." Morgan sucked in sharply, stepping back, fear in her eyes.

"Finally tracked you down. Not a surprise you are fighting for *her*." He slammed his staff into the dirt, power vibrating through the ground.

My mother groaned, hissing out short breaths, her face creased with pain.

"You touch her and I will kill you, old man." Morgan stepped in front of my mom, guarding her.

"You really think you can take me? I was there the day you were born. You are a child, Morgan. It's heartbreaking to know your father destroyed all hope for you. You and Eabha could have been magnificent."

"My father was a great man," she bellowed.

"Your father was a traitor," he shot back.

A scream came from my mom, her legs parting as she huffed and grunted. Magic snapped and sizzled, raining down as a deep, long cry shredded my mother's throat, howling into the night.

Suddenly I was no longer in the field, but inside the castle, I could see the battle going on outside the window. But in this room, a man lay dead on the floor as two dark-haired girls stood over a woman in a breathtaking gown, a crown on her head. Aneira.

One girl who looked very much like a younger version of the Unified Nations' current ruler, Queen Kennedy, grabbed a sword off the ground. The moment she touched it, magic burst the blade with light. With a cry, she swung the blade down, driving it through Aneira's neck, her head rolling off with a whoosh of magic.

I felt the magic hit me. The wave of unbelievable power.

In a blink, I was back outside with my mother. The baby was crowning, my mother crying and screaming, not in happiness, but in terror, pain, and sorrow.

She pushed again, the baby slipping all the way out.

Thunder rolled and cracked.

The wall was falling with the Seelie Queen's death, spreading out in a ripple effect like a bomb. Waves of her magic hit the land like a tsunami, tearing the last bit of wall down and slamming directly into my mother and the newborn still covered in afterbirth.

My mother's head fell back as the baby wailed with life, the cry spiking through the air, magic enveloping the child.

*Crack!*

More magic splintered across the sky, colors flashing, billowing out from the baby with an electrical charge.

My head followed the streak of lightning, knowing somewhere across this field, another me was hearing the baby cry while bringing someone else back to life.

The baby I had heard wailing while I saved Warwick, saved Scorpion, was me. Deep down, I always knew.

Another thing I instinctively understood—the nectar so many were searching for? Killing for...

It was me.

My afterbirth. Magic soaked through the placenta, which absorbed it like a sponge.

I turned back and saw life was not only given to me, but life was also taken away.

Both my mother and my aunt were dead.

Now a cry bellowed from my lungs. I jerked out of the nectar's hold, the images of the past breaking as I yanked and tore my hand away, gasping for air. I collapsed on my ass, staring up at the bright stars overhead.

The cool night brushed at my skin, the remains of the high castle around me. Warwick was next to me on the ground, his hand on my lower back, keeping me steady.

"What happened?" he asked, his eyes still jumping to the necromancers, keeping his guard up.

I huffed, no words finding their way out of my mouth. I had learned so much but had even more questions than before.

*BOOM!*

Before I could even center any of my thoughts, I was ripped away again. This time it wasn't the nectar or book that took me.

It was Scorpion.

Debris from a building billowed in the air, huge chunks of stone, plaster, and wood crushing everything around us. Shouts of panic and terror clogged the thick air.

"Scorpion!" I yelled at him, but he didn't stop, running toward the devastation, not away.

It took me a moment to realize where we were through the cloudy smoke.

Vomit pooled in my stomach.

The explosion was Sarkis's base.

"No!" I screamed, my legs tearing after Scorpion, our link keeping us close. Birdie, Wesley, Zuz, and Maddox were right on his heels.

"Fuck! Fuck!" He searched for any way to get inside, heading for the secret entrance.

The one under the rubble.

"Andris!" I screamed, though I knew he couldn't hear me. Oh gods, what if he were dead? Caden? Hanna? Ling? They were all down there.

Tears rolled down my face as I watched as Maddox, Wesley, and Scorpion dug, pushed, and rolled large pieces out of the way until they made a hole, Birdie slipping through first, Scorpion after.

I was next to him, horror filling me, the dust crawling into my lungs as if I was actually there. Most of the top floor had caved in, blocking some areas. Debris and dead bodies were everywhere.

"Scorpion," a man yelled, turning our heads. He was cut up and caked in dust. I'd seen him in passing but didn't know him.

A relieved cry broke from my gut when I saw Hanna and Caden were behind him. Bleeding and wounded, but alive.

Scorpion darted to them, his eyes rolling over Hanna. "You all right?"

"Yeah," the man answered, though I was pretty sure Scorpion was talking to her. "Busted up a little, but fine."

I wanted so badly to hug my friends; they looked shaken and dazed, not able to bounce back as fast as fae.

"Get them out of here. Tell Zuz to help you watch them. There might be people trying to rescue these two."

The man nodded, moving Hanna and Caden toward the exit.

"This wasn't for a rescue." I shook my head. Scorpion was the only one who could hear me. "This was meant to destroy."

"Yeah." He nodded. "And kill."

"Scorpion!" Birdie's voice screamed. Her tone made my stomach burn.

We both took off, heading toward the direction of my uncle's office, a sob nesting between my ribs.

Crawling over rubble, I spotted Birdie's blonde hair... .and the figures she was leaning over.

"No!" I screeched, seeing Ling and my uncle covered in the wreckage as Wesley and Maddox tore through the rubble, uncovering their bloody, broken bodies.

Birdie felt Ling's pulse. "Ling is still alive." Her eyes filled up with tears. "But..."

I knew.

My uncle was dead.

His human body couldn't withstand the explosion.

Every memory of him flashed in my head, the little things he would do, like the treats he would sneak me with a conspiratorial wink. The stories he read Caden and me. The stuffed animal, Sarkis, he gave me so I'd feel protected and safe when they were gone. The love he and Rita always gave me. Even though Mykel was my real uncle, Andris was my family. He was all I had left in this world.

I lost my mother, father, friends, and home. Finding Andris again was like finding a piece of my father. My heart.

The thought of losing him...

No.

Fuck. No.

Anger, grief, and fierce love built in my chest. I could hear my heavy breathing. I could feel myself sitting both next to my uncle's body underneath the rubble and also far away in the cold night at the High Castle.

*"Kovacs?"* Warwick called me through the link, but my determination was drilled on one thing.

My uncle.

"We should get his body out of here." Wesley's throat bobbed with grief, all of them nodding with him.

They laid a hand on his corpse.

"Nooooooo!" Fire roared from me. My hand slammed down on his chest at the same time it grabbed for the nectar back at the castle.

I heard the last bell of the midnight hour strike in the distance.

An explosion popped behind my lids, funneling from the nectar, tangling with the thick magic still in the air. Electricity scorched up my throat and down my veins, burning everything in its wake. Energy surged my spine, the nectar's force powering through me.

Then I knew what I was.

I was nothing and everything.

The bridge between life and death.

The in-between.
I was *The Grey*.

**Bad Lands #4 Available Now!**

*Thank you to all my readers. Your opinion really matters to me and helps others decide if they want to purchase my book. If you enjoyed this book, please consider leaving a review on the site where you purchased it. It would mean a lot. Thank you.*

# About the Author

*USA Today* Best-Selling Author Stacey Marie Brown is a lover of hot fictional bad boys and sarcastic heroines who kick butt. She also enjoys books, travel, TV shows, hiking, writing, design, and archery. Stacey is lucky enough to live and travel all over the world.

She grew up in Northern California, where she ran around on her family's farm, raising animals, riding horses, playing flashlight tag, and turning hay bales into cool forts.

When she's not writing, she's out hiking, spending time with friends, and traveling. She also volunteers helping animals and is eco-friendly. She feels all animals, people, and the environment should be treated kindly.

## To earn more about Stacey or her books, visit her at:

**Author website & Newsletter**: www.staceymariebrown.com

**Facebook group:** www.facebook.com/groups/1648368945376239/

**TikTok:** @authorstaceymariebrown

**Instagram:** www.instagram.com/staceymariebrown/

**Facebook Author page**: www.facebook.com/SMBauthorpage

**Sex, Lies, & Blank Pages Podcast:**
https://linktr.ee/sexliesandblankpages

**Goodreads:**
www.goodreads.com/author/show/6938728.StaceyMarie_Brown

**Pinterest:** www.pinterest.com/s.mariebrown

**Bookbub:** www.bookbub.com/authors/stacey-marie-brown

# Acknowledgements

I hope you guys have fallen in love with this world as much as I have. It's always hard starting a new series, even though its set in the same world. I thank you for giving *Savage Lands* a chance and loving it so much you have been hounding me for *Wild Lands* release! Best thing an author can hear! The others I'd like to thank for getting this book out:

**Kiki & Colleen at Next Step P.R**. - Thank you for all your hard work! I love you ladies so much.

**Jordan Rosenfeld at Write Livelihood** - Every book is better because of you. I have your voice constantly in my head as I write.

**Mo at Siren's Call Author Services** - You have been my savior! Thank you!

**Hollie "the editor"**- Always wonderful, supportive, and a dream to work with.

**Jay Ahee**r- So much beauty. I am in love with your work!

**Judi Fennell at www.formatting4U.com**- Always fast and always spot on!

**To all the readers who have supported me**: My gratitude is for all you do and how much you help indie authors out of the pure love of reading.

**To all the indie/hybrid authors out there** who inspire, challenge, support, and push me to be better: I love you!

**And to anyone who has picked up an indie book and given an unknown author a chance**.

**THANK YOU!**

Made in the USA
Monee, IL
20 September 2023

2ffb5a5b-38cf-4143-b096-3ec0314e25a7R01